PENGUIN ENGLISH LIBRARY

JOHN FORD: THREE PLAYS

Keith Sturgess was a lecturer in English at the
University of Lancaster from 1966 to 1968. At
present he is working in the department of English at the University of Khartoum. He has also
edited *Three Elizabethan Domestic Tragedies* for
the Penguin English Library.

JOHN FORD · THREE PLAYS

'TIS PITY SHE'S A WHORE

THE BROKEN HEART

PERKIN WARBECK

*

EDITED WITH AN INTRODUCTION
AND COMMENTARY BY
KEITH STURGESS

PENGUIN BOOKS

Penguin Books Ltd, Harmondsworth, Middlesex, England
Penguin Books Inc., 7110 Ambassador Road, Baltimore, Maryland 21207, U.S.A.
Penguin Books Australia Ltd, Ringwood, Victoria, Australia

—

This collection published in Penguin Books 1970

—

Introduction and notes copyright © Keith Sturgess, 1970

—

Made and printed in Great Britain
by Hazell Watson & Viney Ltd,
Aylesbury, Bucks
Set in Monotype Bembo

To Fiona

CONTENTS

INTRODUCTION

LIFE

LIKE that of many Elizabethan and Jacobean playwrights, John Ford's biography is scant of detail and full of 'maybes'. He came of an old Devonshire family and was probably the second son of Thomas and Elizabeth Ford of Islington, Devonshire. His birth date is unknown, but he was baptized on 17 April 1568. He may have been the 'John Ford Devon gen.' who matriculated at Exeter College, Oxford, on 26 March 1601, but the next certain reference to him is the record of his entry to the Middle Temple, 16 November 1602. Like the other Inns of Court, the Middle Temple offered a general and cultivated education to the Elizabethan gentleman as well as legal training. In the Hilary term of 1605–6 Ford was expelled for not paying his buttery bill but he was reinstated on 10 June 1608. Thomas Ford, his father, died in 1610, leaving his son a small legacy, and in 1616 his elder brother also died and made him a beneficiary. In 1617 there was more trouble with the Middle Temple authorities when Ford joined a 'conspiracy' against the wearing of caps at specific times. It is not known when Ford left the Middle Temple, nor is it known if he subsequently practised law. He may have left London in 1639 and perhaps spent his last years in Devonshire, but all again becomes mere conjecture. One inevitably fills out this meagre picture of the man with William Hemminge's vivid sketch in *An Elegy on Randolph's Finger*:

> Deep in a dump Jack Ford alone was got
> With folded arms and melancholy hat.

WORKS

Ford's literary career dates from 1606 when he published two works. *Fame's Memorial* is a lengthy elegy on the death of the Earl of Devonshire, dedicated to the Countess of Devonshire, the former Penelope Rich. *Honour Triumphant* is a prose pamphlet on the subject of love and beauty, dedicated to the Countesses of Pembroke and Montgomery. Neither has great literary merit. 1613 saw the publication of a religious poem, *Christ's Bloody Sweat*, signed 'I.F.' and generally attributed to Ford; and in the same year appeared an anonymous prose pamphlet, *The Golden Mean*, which on strong internal grounds is regarded as Ford's work. Interesting in connexion with themes of the plays, *The Golden Mean* formulates laws for the conduct of the virtuous man. In 1615 *Sir Thomas Overbury's Ghost* by John Ford was licensed, but no copy is extant and it may never have been printed. The non-dramatic works are completed by *A Line of Life* (1620), like *The Golden Mean* a didactic prose pamphlet.

It seems probable, then, that two long poems, three pamphlets and the Overbury book served as apprentice work for the career of playwright which Ford began fairly late. And it is as collaborator that he first appears. Between 1621 and 1625 he is known to have shared the writing of at least five plays, two of which – *The Witch of Edmonton* and *The Sun's Darling* – survive. His main partner in these ventures was the prolific professional Dekker, and the usual subjects seem to be drawn from domestic life and to have a tragic colouring.

Seven independent plays, published by Ford in his lifetime, survive; and the anonymous play *The Queen*, printed in 1653, is thought to be his on internal grounds. Of these eight extant plays, three are tragedies – *The Broken Heart*, *'Tis Pity She's a Whore* and *Love's Sacrifice*, all published in 1633; four are tragi-comedies – *The Lover's Melancholy* and *The Fancies Chaste and Noble*, published 1633, *The Lady's Trial*, published 1639, and *The Queen*; and one is a history or chronicle play, *Perkin Warbeck*, published 1633.

Dating the plays has proved perilous and inconclusive. An argument based on where the plays were performed suggests that *The Broken Heart* and *The Lover's Melancholy* precede the other surviving plays; the inevitable disagreements have arisen when using 'evidence' from apparent artistic development (often based on the fallacy that a playwright improves as he tries again); and metrical counts have failed to produce significant results. The dedication of *'Tis Pity She's a Whore* appears to suggest that that is Ford's first play, though it may not mean that at all; and a couplet in Crashaw might indicate that *Love's Sacrifice* was a deliberate copy of *The Broken Heart*.

The independent work dates from the early years of Charles I's reign (which began in 1625), and it is worth noting how late Ford appears on the scene of the greatest period of dramatic activity in the country's history. By 1625 Marlowe had been dead for twenty-two years, Kyd for twenty-one, and Shakespeare and Beaumont for eleven; Fletcher died in 1625 itself, Tourneur in 1626, and Middleton in 1627. 1633, the great year of publication for Ford, also saw the appearance in print of Donne's *Poems*, and in the next year *Comus* was published. In *Perkin Warbeck* especially, one can see Ford's awareness of a period of dramatic excellence which time had carried almost out of reach. In reviving the long unfashionable history play, the Caroline playwright was paying homage to a golden age.

CRITICAL REPUTATION

Half-a-dozen full-length studies in the last few years show Ford to be well worthy of serious critical treatment, but his plays still arouse judgements ranging from outrageous praise to wholesale dismissal: he is considered the last major tragic writer of the period and a true successor to Shakespeare; or the real villain of the piece in Jacobean tragedy and an irresponsible decadent.

He was played on the Restoration stage on occasion. Pepys saw, without enthusiasm, *'Tis Pity She's a Whore* and *The Lady's Trial. The Lover's Melancholy* and *Perkin Warbeck* were revived in the eighteenth century, the history play to serve as a warning at the time of the 1745 Jacobite rebellion. But a real, critical appreciation begins for Ford, as it does for many other dramatists of his period, with Lamb's *Specimens of the English Dramatic Poets*, 1808. Ford suffers more than most from Lamb's anthologizing, but passages were printed from what are now the five best-known of the plays (the three here plus *The Lady's Trial* and *Love's Sacrifice*). In his appended notes, Lamb pays credit to the chaste techniques of Ford's verse, to the profundity of his insight into mind and emotions, and to the splendour of his characters:

Ford was of the first order of poets. He sought for sublimity, not by parcels in metaphors or visible images, but directly where she has her full residence in the heart of man; in the actions and sufferings of the greatest minds. There is a grandeur of the soul above mountains, seas and the elements. Even in the poor perverted reason of Giovanni and Annabella we discern traces of that fiery particle, which in the irregular starting from out of the road of beaten action, discovers something of a right line even in obliquity, and shows hints of an improveable greatness in the lowest descents and degradations of our nature.

Interest whetted by Lamb's book was served by two complete editions of the plays in 1811 and 1827, the former inspiring spirited attacks on Ford by Francis Jeffrey in the *Edinburgh Review*, 1811 and 1812. The most penetrating answer to Lamb's praise, however, came from Hazlitt who, in his lecture on the Jacobean playwrights, called *The Broken Heart* 'extravagant' and the other plays

merely exercises of style and effusions of wire-drawn sentiments. Where they have not the sting of illicit passion, they are quite pointless, and seem painted on gauze, or spun out of cobwebs. An artificial elaborateness is the general characteristic of Ford's style.

In addition, Hazlitt found little character ('I do not remember without considerable effort the plot or persons of most of his plays'), little imagery or fancy, and no action. The charges of immorality, artificiality and pointlessness reappear in modern criticism, and Hazlitt can be regarded as the initiator of a powerful line of attack.

Swinburne, on the other hand, echoed Lamb's praise and drew particular attention to

the passionless reason and equable tone of style with which in his greatest works he treats of the deepest and most fiery passions, the quiet eye with which he searches out the darkest issues of emotion, the quiet hand with which he notes them down.

He also noted a certain rigidity of method and characterization, and criticized a lack of imagination, of 'absolute poetry' and 'rapture'. But in a sonnet on Ford he grew raptuous himself, carving a memorial for a man, who, he said, 'With high funeral art Carved night and chiselled shadow'.

Havelock Ellis's introduction to the Mermaid edition of Ford (five plays, 1888) extends Lamb's and Swinburne's praise and takes a new departure. Ford, Ellis considered, is 'the most modern of the tribe to whom he belonged' because he was an observer and analyst, particularly of women, one who looked within, feeling for his characters 'with instinctive sympathy the fibres of their hearts'. And this, for Ellis, strained the limits of Ford's art and foreboded new ways of literary expression.

In the twentieth century there have been few productions of Ford's plays, less, one would guess, than of Webster and Middleton. Criticism has for the most part elaborated the main lines of discussion laid down in the nineteenth century. The attack on Ford's moral position – the moral position of a man whose most famous play treats incest sympathetically – has become part of a larger dismissal: of 'the Decadence' of the last years of the dramatic period. Here, Ford is associated with Beaumont and Fletcher and accused of a calculated attempt to arouse a sophisticated and blasé audience by recourse to sensational incidents and prurient suggestion. Further, it is a cliché of historical criticism that the late Jacobean and Caroline age had lost its moral bearings and Ford suffers from the general *malaise*.

On the aesthetic side, it is argued, Ford's decadence is seen in the 'thinness' of his verse and the verbal exhaustion of his characters. The vitality of an earlier age, with its colourful language and moral clear-sightedness, has suffered attrition and attenuation. In Ford, the dramatic period closes with a whimper.

Detractors often charge Ford also with imitation. There is a bookish quality about his plays, especially in their characterization. Shakespeare has been much echoed in plot, character and verse; and motifs from most of the important Jacobean playwrights can be spotted in Ford's work. Ford borrowed outside the drama also, extensively from that medical treatise of a divine, Burton's *Anatomy of Melancholy*. That much of Ford's psychological insight comes not from life but from Burton has been long recognized, and in the original quarto of *The Lover's Melancholy* Ford himself drew attention to specific borrowings in that play.

Answers to the charge of immorality have headed in entirely different directions. The romantic view – in part Lamb's – is to see Ford as the great rebel, deliberately turning upside down a traditional moral order which has been emptied of relevance. In this view, Ford appears a sort of 'modern', a 'prophetic' writer like Lawrence, and an arguer for the rights of the individual who alone must be allowed to direct his ethical response to the universe.

On the other hand – and this seems to be a trend of recent criticism – there is the view that Ford is essentially a traditionalist, supporting a recognized scheme of moral values, and exposing the rebel as a man courting destruction through his egotism. So Penthea of *The Broken Heart* chooses to die because of a rigid application of the existing rules concerning betrothals and marriage and not from an exaggerated, personal interpretation of her situation. The real rebels, like Giovanni, are exposed and even satirized. And support for Ford's traditionalism is derived from the prose treatises, especially *The Golden Mean*.

So much is ground for debate, but certain features of Ford's work are generally agreed upon, and from them may arise the critical problems that Ford poses. To begin with, Ford's themes and interests are of a limited sort. (Here, a comparison with Shakespeare is especially damaging.) He returns to certain situations and human problems with great frequency. There is a central interest in idealized, romantic love, and Ford had been associated with the

Platonic love cult inaugurated at the English court in the late 1620s by Charles I's French wife, Henrietta Maria. In particular, Ford explores with obsessive interest the love situation where a natural, spontaneous expression of that love is forbidden by society or convention. And so in several plays he deals with enforced marriage; and incest, which breaks the strongest of sexual taboos, is central to *'Tis Pity She's a Whore* and lurks beneath the surface of a number of other plays.

Hand in hand with the theme of obstructed love goes a pervasive interest in sexual jealousy. Studies in the jealous lover include Giovanni and Soranzo in *'Tis Pity She's a Whore*, Bassanes and Orgilus in *The Broken Heart*, the Duke in *Love's Sacrifice*, Auria in *The Lady's Trial* and Alphonso in *The Queen*. Exploring a small number of related themes in this way encouraged Ford to repeat characters and situations, and Crashaw's couplet complains about just that:

> Thou cheat'st us, Ford: mak'st one seem two by art;
> What is *Love's Sacrifice* but *The Broken Heart*?

Ford explores the emotions connected with obstructed love and jealousy by a psychological analysis of personality, the theory for which derives in part from Burton. And in Burton, Ford found something that evidently keyed in with his own temperament: a sympathetic treatment of contemporary melancholia in its many manifestations. Ford's plays are melancholy in a modern and a seventeenth-century sense. The typical Ford character finds his way blocked to the goal of happiness which he has set for himself. He must choose between compromising with his wishes (which is the solution of the comic world) or defending his notion of personal integrity in the teeth of a usually implacable fate (in *The Lover's Melancholy* fate is subverted by pro-

vidence, but things are rarely so sanguine). In Ford's tragic
vision, a defence of integrity is the only possible choice.

Rarely are Ford's heroes confronted with human evil in
a tangible or simple-minded form; the Jacobean villain is
unimportant in Ford's scheme of things. And so the intrigue
formula characteristic of Elizabethan and Jacobean tragedy
is really outside Ford's thematic requirements though he
finds it necessary, sometimes, for purely dramaturgical
reasons. Because the hero is not committed to action against
human evil, and because Ford supports the aristocratic code
of stoicism in the face of suffering, dramatic action is
difficult to motivate, and a tragic climax awkward to
manufacture: the deaths bring special problems and except
in certain circumstances (like Penthea's and Orgilus')
suicide would be cheating for Ford because cowardly for
the characters.

Stoical fortitude, besides committing the tragic protago-
nists to inaction in a world governed by fate, demands from
them an emotional restraint in which silence becomes the
best eloquence. Ford's most characteristic work is quiet, the
poetry simple and largely abstract, the rhythm a consistent
dying fall. When violence and noise occurs it is the more
obscene: Bassanes bursting in on Ithocles and Penthea in
The Broken Heart, III, ii; Soranzo hauling in Annabella by
her hair in *'Tis Pity She's a Whore*, IV, iii. There has often
been felt a note of strain behind the more histrionic
moments; and certainly, the comic interludes have been
properly deplored (though a case can be made for the
effectiveness of Bergetto in *'Tis Pity She's a Whore*; and
Perkin's counsellors in *Perkin Warbeck* have their admirers).

With the stillness of the verse there goes a taste for
stylized action and a striking use of the emblematic tableau.
Elaborate scene-headings, clearly the playwright's, usually

betoken a piece of ritual behaviour instinctively created by a character or characters. The effect is to inject meaning and dignity into moments – usually tragic ones – where fate has introduced random elements to complicate or utterly destroy the pursuit of happiness. And it is this that imparts an unreal atmosphere to the plays. Out of pain and suffering the characters create something which is more like art than life, and they seem to 'rejoice, having to construct something Upon which to rejoice'. Giving aesthetic form to the moment becomes a sort of religion, and the critic may properly recognize a certain emotional preciosity in this.

Finally, although Ford's skill in construction has rarely been admired, it is worth pointing out the experimentation apparent from play to play (even where their order is obscure). Narrow in theme and range as he is, Ford managed in the three plays printed here to achieve strikingly dissimilar effects. Perhaps *Perkin Warbeck* is the most evenly successful of the three; *'Tis Pity She's a Whore* is the most famous; and *The Broken Heart* is the most perfectly Fordian in flavour.

BIBLIOGRAPHY

M. J. SARGEAUNT, *John Ford*, 1935.

S. B. EWING, *Burtonian Melancholy in the Plays of John Ford*, Princeton, 1940.

G. F. SENSABAUGH, *The Tragic Muse of John Ford*, Palo Alto, 1944.

H. J. OLIVER, *The Problem of John Ford*, 1955.

R. DAVRIL, *Le Drame de John Ford*, Paris, 1954.

C. LEECH, *John Ford and the Drama of His Time*, 1957.

M. STAVIG, *John Ford and the Traditional Moral Order*, 1968.

F. E. SCHELLING, *Elizabethan Drama: 1558–1642*, 1908, pp. 327–36.

M. C. BRADBROOK, *Themes and Conventions of Elizabethan Tragedy*, 2nd. ed., 1952, chapter 10.

R. ORNSTEIN, *The Moral Vision of Jacobean Tragedy*, 1960, chapter 8.

I. RIBNER, *Jacobean Tragedy: The Quest for Moral Order*, 1962, chapter 7.

T. B. TOMLINSON, *A Study of Elizabethan and Jacobean Tragedy*, 1964, chapter 12.

P. URE, ed., *The Chronicle History of Perkin Warbeck*, 1968, Introduction.

S. P. SHERMAN, 'Stella and the *Broken Heart*', *Publications of the Modern Language Association*, xxiv, 1909, pp. 274–85.

P. URE, 'Marriage and the Domestic Drama in Heywood and Ford', *English Studies*, xxxii, 1951, pp. 200–216.

G. H. BLAYNEY, 'Convention, Plot and Structure in *The Broken Heart*', *Modern Philology*, lvi, 1958, pp. 1–9.

C. HOY, ' "Ignorance in Knowledge": Marlowe's Faustus and Ford's Giovanni', *Modern Philology*, lvii, 1960, pp. 145–54.

R. J. KAUFMANN, 'Ford's Tragic Perspective', *Texas Studies in Literature*, i, 1960, pp. 522–37.

D. K. ANDERSON, 'Richard II and Perkin Warbeck,' *Shakespeare Quarterly*, xiii, 1962, pp. 260–3.

D. K. ANDERSON, 'The Heart and the Banquet: Imagery in Ford's *'Tis Pity* and *The Broken Heart*', *Studies in English Literature*, ii, 1962, pp. 209–17.

TEXTS

Each play reprinted here was published just once in the seventeenth century. The dedicatory epistles in all three show that they were printed with the active agreement, if not supervision, of the author. The descriptive stage directions and a special and heavy use of italics make it likely that author's manuscript served as copy-text for all three. The plays were well printed and present no special problems to the editor. The original quartos have served as copy-texts for the present edition.

I have modernized spelling and punctuation, retaining '–'d' in preterites and past participles in the verse, and have regularized stage-directions (additions being in square brackets). Short, lexical notes are at the foot of the page, commentary, critical notes and selected textual notes at the end of the book, prefaced by a short account of sources and influences.

I have consulted Dyce's revision of Gifford's *The Works of John Ford*, 1869, together with the following editions: *'Tis Pity She's a Whore*: ed. N. W. Bawcutt, Regents Renaissance Drama Series, 1966; ed. B. Morris, The New Mermaids, 1968; ed. M. Stavig, Crofts Classics, New York, 1966. *The Broken Heart*: ed. W. A. Neilson, *The Chief Elizabethan Dramatists*, 1911; ed. D. K. Anderson, Regents Renaissance Drama Series, 1968; ed. B. Morris, The New Mermaids, 1965. *Perkin Warbeck*: ed. D. K. Anderson, Regents Renaissance Drama Series, 1966; ed. P. Ure, The Revels Plays, 1968.

I have not recorded in the commentary emendations which are of long-standing or self-evident correctness.

TIS
Pitty Shee's a Whore

Acted by the *Queenes* Maiesties Seruants, at *The Phænix in
Drury-Lane.*

LONDON,
Printed by *Nicholas Okes* for *Richard
Collins,* and are to be fold at his fhop
in *Pauls* Church-yard, at the figne
of the three Kings. 1633.

[DEDICATORY EPISTLE]

To the truly noble John,
Earl of Peterborough, Lord Mordaunt,
Baron of Turvey.

My Lord,

Where a truth of merit hath a general warrant, there love is but a debt, acknowledgement a justice. Greatness cannot often claim virtue by inheritance; yet in this, yours appears most eminent, for that you are not more rightly heir to your fortunes than glory shall be to your memory. Sweetness of disposition ennobles a   5
freedom of birth; in both, your lawful interest adds honour to your own name, and mercy to my presumption. Your noble allowance of these first fruits of my leisure in the action emboldens my confidence of your as noble construction in this presentment; especially since my service must ever owe particular duty to your   10
favours by a particular engagement. The gravity of the subject may easily excuse the lightness of the title, otherwise I had been a severe judge against mine own guilt. Princes have vouchsafed grace to trifles offered from a purity of devotion; your lordship may likewise please to admit into your good opinion, with these   15
weak endeavours, the constancy of affection from the sincere lover of your deserts in honour,

JOHN FORD

7. *allowance*: approval.
8. *in the action*: when acted.
9. *construction*: interpretation.

THE ACTORS' NAMES

BONAVENTURA, *a friar*
A CARDINAL, *nuncio to the Pope*
SORANZO, *a nobleman*
FLORIO, *a citizen of Parma*
DONADO, *another citizen*
GRIMALDI, *a Roman gentleman*
GIOVANNI, *son to Florio*
BERGETTO, *nephew to Donado*
RICHARDETTO, *a supposed physician*
VASQUES, *servant to Soranzo*
POGGIO, *servant to Bergetto*
BANDITTI [OFFICERS, SERVANTS etc.].

Women

ANNABELLA, *daughter to Florio*
HIPPOLITA, *wife to Richardetto*
PHILOTIS, *his niece*
PUTANA, *tutoress to Annabella*

The Scene:

PARMA

ACT ONE

SCENE ONE

Enter FRIAR *and* GIOVANNI.

FRIAR: Dispute no more in this, for know, young man,
    These are no school-points; nice philosophy
    May tolerate unlikely arguments,
    But Heaven admits no jest; wits that presum'd
    On wit too much, by striving how to prove
    There was no God, with foolish grounds of art
    Discover'd first the nearest way to hell,
    And fill'd the world with devilish atheism.
    Such questions, youth, are fond; for better 'tis
    To bless the sun than reason why it shines;   *10*
    Yet He thou talk'st of is above the sun.
    No more; I may not hear it.

GIOVANNI: Gentle father,
    To you I have unclasp'd my burdened soul,
    Emptied the storehouse of my thoughts and heart,
    Made myself poor of secrets, have not left
    Another word untold, which hath not spoke
    All what I ever durst or think or know;
    And yet is here the comfort I shall have?
    Must I not do what all men else may, love?

FRIAR: Yes, you may love, fair son.

GIOVANNI: Must I not praise   *20*

2. *school-points:* topics for academic debate.   *nice:* subtle.
4. *admits:* allows.   6. *art:* learning.
9. *questions:* discussions.   *fond:* foolish.

27

That beauty which, if fram'd anew, the gods
Would make a god of if they had it there,
And kneel to it as I do kneel to them?

FRIAR: Why, foolish madman!

GIOVANNI: Shall a peevish sound,
A customary form from man to man,
Of brother and of sister, be a bar
'Twixt my perpetual happiness and me?
Say that we had one father, say one womb
(Curse to my joys) gave both us life and birth;
30   Are we not therefore each to other bound
So much the more by nature, by the links
Of blood, of reason – nay, if you will have't,
Even of religion – to be ever one,
One soul, one flesh, one love, one heart, one all?

FRIAR: Have done, unhappy youth, for thou art lost.

GIOVANNI: Shall then, for that I am her brother born,
My joys be ever banish'd from her bed?
No, father; in your eyes I see the change
Of pity and compassion; from your age,
40   As from a sacred oracle, distils
The life of counsel; tell me, holy man,
What cure shall give me ease in these extremes?

FRIAR: Repentance, son, and sorrow for this sin;
For thou hast mov'd a Majesty above
With thy unranged (almost) blasphemy.

GIOVANNI: O, do not speak of that, dear confessor.

FRIAR: Art thou, my son, that miracle of wit
Who once, within these three months, wert esteem'd
A wonder of thine age throughout Bononia?

24. *peevish:* trifling.   25. *customary form:* conventional formality.
36. *for that:* because.   45. *unranged:* disordered.
49. *Bononia:* Bologna (university town).

How did the university applaud   50
Thy government, behaviour, learning, speech,
Sweetness, and all that could make up a man!
I was proud of my tutelage, and chose
Rather to leave my books than part with thee.
I did so, but the fruits of all my hopes
Are lost in thee as thou art in thyself.
O Giovanni, hast thou left the schools
Of knowledge to converse with lust and death?
For death waits on thy lust. Look through the world,
And thou shalt see a thousand faces shine   60
More glorious than this idol thou ador'st.
Leave her, and take thy choice; 'tis much less sin,
Though in such games as those they lose that win.

GIOVANNI: It were more ease to stop the ocean
From floats and ebbs than to dissuade my vows.

FRIAR: Then I have done, and in thy wilful flaws
Already see thy ruin; Heaven is just.
Yet hear my counsel.

GIOVANNI: As a voice of life.

FRIAR: Hie to thy father's house; there lock thee fast
Alone within thy chamber; then fall down   70
On both thy knees, and grovel on the ground;
Cry to thy heart, wash every word thou utter'st
In tears, and, if't be possible, of blood;
Beg Heaven to cleanse the leprosy of lust
That rots thy soul; acknowledge what thou art,
A wretch, a worm, a nothing; weep, sigh, pray
Three times a day, and three times every night.
For seven days' space do this, then if thou find'st

51. *government*: self-conduct.   57. *Giovanni*: four syllables.
65. *floats*: floods.   *vows*: ? prayers.
66. *wilful flaws*: obstinate outbursts of passion. See note.

29

No change in thy desires, return to me:
80 I'll think on remedy. Pray for thyself
At home, whilst I pray for thee here. – Away,
My blessing with thee, we have need to pray.
GIOVANNI: All this I'll do to free me from the rod
Of vengeance; else I'll swear my fate's my god.
Exeunt.

SCENE TWO

Enter GRIMALDI *and* VASQUES *ready to fight.*

VASQUES: Come sir, stand to your tackling; if you prove craven, I'll make you run quickly.
GRIMALDI: Thou art no equal match for me.
VASQUES: Indeed, I never went to the wars to bring home news, nor cannot play the mountebank for a meal's meat and swear I got my wounds in the field. See you these grey hairs? They'll not flinch for a bloody nose. Wilt thou to this gear?
GRIMALDI: Why slave, think'st thou I'll balance my
10 reputation with a cast-suit? Call thy master; he shall know that I dare –
VASQUES: Scold like a cot-quean – that's your profession. Thou poor shadow of a soldier, I will make thee know my master keeps servants thy betters in quality and performance. Com'st thou to fight or prate?
GRIMALDI: Neither with thee. I am a Roman and a gentleman, one that have got mine honour with expense of blood.

1. *tackling:* weapons.   3. *equal:* i.e. socially.
8. *gear:* business (the fight).
10. *cast-suit:* servant (wearing master's cast-off clothing).
12. *cot-quean:* vulgar, scolding woman.

VASQUES: You are a lying coward and a fool. Fight, or
  by these hilts I'll kill thee. – Brave my lord! – You'll   *20*
  fight?
GRIMALDI: Provoke me not, for if thou dost –
VASQUES: Have at you.
    They fight; GRIMALDI *hath the worst.*
    Enter FLORIO, DONADO, SORANZO.
FLORIO: What mean these sudden broils so near my doors?
  Have you not other places but my house
  To vent the spleen of your disordered bloods?
  Must I be haunted still with such unrest
  As not to eat or sleep in peace at home?
  Is this your love, Grimaldi? Fie, 'tis naught.
DONADO: And Vasques, I may tell thee 'tis not well   *30*
  To broach these quarrels. You are ever forward
  In seconding contentions.
    Enter above ANNABELLA *and* PUTANA.
FLORIO: What's the ground?
SORANZO: That, with your patience, signiors, I'll resolve.
  This gentleman, whom fame reports a soldier,
  – For else I know not – rivals me in love
  To Signior Florio's daughter, to whose ears
  He still prefers his suit to my disgrace,
  Thinking the way to recommend himself
  Is to disparage me in his report.
  But know, Grimaldi, though maybe thou art   *40*
  My equal in thy blood, yet this bewrays
  A lowness in thy mind, which wert thou noble,
  Thou wouldst as much disdain as I do thee
  For this unworthiness. And on this ground,
  I will'd my servant to correct thy tongue,

20. *Brave:* challenge.   32. *ground:* subject of the quarrel.
41. *blood:* breeding.   *bewrays:* reveals.

Holding a man so base no match for me.

VASQUES: And had not your sudden coming not prevented us, I had let my gentleman blood under the gills; I should have wormed you, sir, for running mad.

50 GRIMALDI: I'll be reveng'd, Soranzo.

VASQUES: On a dish of warm broth to stay your stomach – do, honest innocence, do; spoon-meat is a wholesomer diet than a Spanish blade.

GRIMALDI: I'll remember this.

SORANZO: I fear thee not, Grimaldi.

Exit GRIMALDI.

FLORIO: My Lord Soranzo, this is strange to me,
Why you should storm, having my word engag'd:
Owing her heart, what need you doubt her ear?
Losers may talk by law of any game.

60 VASQUES: Yet the villain of words, Signior Florio, may be such as would make any unspleened dove choleric; blame not my lord in this.

FLORIO: Be you more silent.
I would not for my wealth my daughter's love
Should cause the spilling of one drop of blood.
Vasques, put up: let's end this fray in wine.

Exeunt [FLORIO, DONADO, SORANZO *and* VASQUES].

PUTANA: How like you this, child? Here's threat'ning, challenging, quarrelling and fighting on every side, and all is for your sake. You had need look to yourself, 70 charge; you'll be stolen away sleeping else shortly.

ANNABELLA: But, tut'ress, such a life gives no content

48. *gills:* slang term for fleshy part under jaws and ears.
52. *spoon-meat:* i.e. food for a baby.
58. *Owing:* possessing.
60. *of words:* i.e. as opposed to action.
61. *Unspleened:* not liable to anger. See note.
66. *put up:* i.e. his sword.

To me; my thoughts are fix'd on other ends.
Would you would leave me.

PUTANA: Leave you? No marvel else. Leave me no leaving, charge; this is love outright. Indeed, I blame you not; you have choice fit for the best lady in Italy.

ANNABELLA: Pray do not talk so much.

PUTANA: Take the worst with the best, there's Grimaldi the soldier, a very well-timbered fellow. They say he is a Roman, nephew to the Duke of Montferrato; they say   80
he did good service in the wars against the Milanese. But faith, charge, I do not like him, an't be for nothing but for being a soldier. Not one amongst twenty of your skirmishing captains but have some privy maim or other that mars their standing upright. I like him the worse, he crinkles so much in the hams. Though he might serve if there were no more men, yet he's not the man I would choose.

ANNABELLA: Fie, how thou prat'st.

PUTANA: As I am a very woman, I like Signior Soranzo   90
well. He is wise, and what is more, rich; and what is more than that, kind; and what is more than all this, a nobleman. Such a one, were I the fair Annabella myself, I would wish and pray for. Then, he is bountiful; besides, he is handsome, and, by my troth, I think wholesome (and that's news in a gallant of three and twenty); liberal, that I know; loving, that you know; and a man sure, else he could never ha' purchased such a good name with Hippolita, the lusty widow, in her husband's lifetime: and 'twere but for that report, sweetheart, would 'a were   100
thine. Commend a man for his qualities, but take a

79. *well-timbered:* well-built.   84. *privy:* secret.
85. *standing upright:* with sexual meaning.
95. *wholesome:* healthy (without venereal disease).

33

husband as he is a plain-sufficient, naked man. Such a one is for your bed and such a one is Signior Soranzo, my life for't.

ANNABELLA: Sure the woman took her morning's draught too soon.

Enter [below] BERGETTO *and* POGGIO.

PUTANA: But look, sweetheart, look what thing comes now. Here's another of your ciphers to fill up the number. O brave old ape in a silken coat! Observe.

110 BERGETTO: Did'st thou think, Poggio, that I would spoil my new clothes and leave my dinner to fight?

POGGIO: No sir, I did not take you for so arrant a baby.

BERGETTO: I am wiser than so; for I hope, Poggio, thou never heard'st of an elder brother that was a coxcomb, did'st, Poggio?

POGGIO: Never indeed, sir, as long as they had either land or money left them to inherit.

BERGETTO: Is it possible, Poggio? O, monstrous! Why, I'll undertake with a handful of silver to buy a headful

120 of wit at any time. But, sirrah, I have another purchase in hand: I shall have the wench mine uncle says. I will but wash my face, and shift socks, and then have at her, i'faith! – Mark my pace, Poggio.

[Walks affectedly.]

POGGIO: Sir. – *[Aside]* I have seen an ass and a mule trot the Spanish pavan with a better grace I know not how often.

*Exeunt [*BERGETTO *and* POGGIO*].*

ANNABELLA: This idiot haunts me too.

PUTANA: Ay, ay, he needs no description. The rich magnifico that is below with your father, charge, Signior

122. *shift:* change.   125. *pavan:* stately dance.

Donado his uncle, for that he means to make this his 130
cousin a golden calf, thinks that you will be a right
Israelite, and fall down to him presently; but I hope I
have tutored you better. They say a fool's bauble is a
lady's playfellow, yet you having wealth enough, you
need not cast upon the dearth of flesh at any rate. Hang
him, innocent!

    Enter GIOVANNI *[below].*

ANNABELLA: But see, Putana, see: what blessed shape
  Of some celestial creature now appears?
  What man is he, that with such sad aspect
  Walks careless of himself? 140

PUTANA: Where?

ANNABELLA: Look below.

PUTANA: O, 'tis your brother, sweet –

ANNABELLA: Ha?

PUTANA: 'Tis your brother.

ANNABELLA: Sure 'tis not he; that is some woeful thing
  Wrapp'd up in grief, some shadow of a man.
  Alas, he beats his breast, and wipes his eyes
  Drown'd all in tears. Methinks I hear him sigh.
  Let's down, Putana, and partake the cause; 150
  I know my brother in the love he bears me
  Will not deny me partage in his sadness.
  My soul is full of heaviness and fear.

    Exit [with PUTANA].

GIOVANNI: Lost, I am lost! My fates have doom'd my
  death.
  The more I strive, I love; the more I love,
  The less I hope. I see my ruin certain.

---

130. *for that:* because.   131. *cousin:* nephew.
133. *bauble:* stick carried by court fool (with sexual innuendo).
136. *innocent:* natural fool.   152. *partage:* share.

What judgement or endeavours could apply
To my incurable and restless wounds
I throughly have examin'd, but in vain.
160 O, that it were not in religion sin
To make our love a god and worship it.
I have even wearied Heaven with prayers, dried up
The spring of my continual tears, even starv'd
My veins with daily fasts. What wit or art
Could counsel I have practis'd; but alas,
I find all these but dreams and old men's tales
To fright unsteady youth. I'm still the same:
Or I must speak or burst; 'tis not, I know,
My lust, but 'tis my fate that leads me on.
170 Keep fear and low, faint-hearted shame with slaves.
I'll tell her that I love her, though my heart
Were rated at the price of that attempt.
O me! She comes.

    Enter ANNABELLA *and* PUTANA.

ANNABELLA: Brother!
GIOVANNI [*aside*]:   If such a thing
  As courage dwell in men, ye heavenly powers,
  Now double all that virtue in my tongue.
ANNABELLA: Why brother, will you not speak to me?
GIOVANNI: Yes, how d'ee, sister?
ANNABELLA: Howsoever I am, methinks you are not
  well.
PUTANA: Bless us, why are you so sad, sir?
180 GIOVANNI: Let me entreat you leave us awhile, Putana;
  Sister, I would be private with you.
ANNABELLA: Withdraw, Putana.
PUTANA: I will. [*Aside*] If this were any other company

159. *throughly:* thoroughly.   170. *Keep fear:* let fear dwell.

for her, I should think my absence an office of some
credit; but I will leave them together.
   Exit PUTANA.

GIOVANNI: Come sister, lend your hand, let's walk
   together.
I hope you need not blush to walk with me;
Here's none but you and I.

ANNABELLA: How's this?

GIOVANNI: Faith, I mean no harm.   190

ANNABELLA: Harm?

GIOVANNI: No, good faith; how is't with 'ee?

ANNABELLA [*aside*]: I trust he be not frantic. – I am very
   well, brother.

GIOVANNI: Trust me but I am sick, I fear so sick
'Twill cost my life.

ANNABELLA: Mercy forbid it; 'tis not so I hope.

GIOVANNI: I think you love me, sister.

ANNABELLA: Yes, you know I do.

GIOVANNI: I know't indeed. – Y'are very fair.   200

ANNABELLA: Nay then, I see you have a merry sickness.

GIOVANNI: That's as it proves; the poets feign (I read)
That Juno for her forehead did exceed
All other goddesses; but I durst swear
Your forehead exceeds hers as hers did theirs.

ANNABELLA: Troth, this is pretty.

GIOVANNI: Such a pair of stars
As are thine eyes would, like Promethean fire,
If gently glanc'd, give life to senseless stones.

ANNABELLA: Fie upon 'ee!

GIOVANNI: The lily and the rose, most sweetly strange,   210

184–5. *of some credit:* deserving payment.
202. *feign:* fable.
210. *strange:* at enmity.

    Upon your dimpled cheeks do strive for change.
    Such lips would tempt a saint; such hands as those
    Would make an anchorite lascivious.

ANNABELLA: D'ee mock me or flatter me?

GIOVANNI: If you would see a beauty more exact
    Than art can counterfeit or nature frame,
    Look in your glass and there behold your own.

ANNABELLA: O, you are a trim youth!

GIOVANNI: Here.
    Offers his dagger to her.

220 ANNABELLA: What to do?

GIOVANNI: And here's my breast; strike home.
    Rip up my bosom, there thou shalt behold
    A heart, in which is writ the truth I speak.
    Why stand 'ee?

ANNABELLA: Are you earnest?

GIOVANNI: Yes, most earnest.
    You cannot love?

ANNABELLA: Whom?

GIOVANNI: Me. My tortur'd soul
    Hath felt affliction in the heat of death.
    O, Annabella, I am quite undone;
    The love of thee, my sister, and the view
    Of thy immortal beauty hath untun'd
230 All harmony both of my rest and life.
    Why d'ee not strike?

ANNABELLA: Forbid it, my just fears!
    If this be true, 'twere fitter I were dead.

GIOVANNI: True, Annabella; 'tis no time to jest.
    I have too long suppress'd the hidden flames

211. *change:* replacement of one by the other.
218. *trim:* fine (ironical).
230. *rest and life:* ? sleeping and waking.

That almost have consum'd me; I have spent
Many a silent night in sighs and groans,
Ran over all my thoughts, despis'd my fate,
Reason'd against the reasons of my love,
Done all that smooth-cheek'd virtue could advise,
But found all bootless; 'tis my destiny   240
That you must either love or I must die.

ANNABELLA: Comes this in sadness from you?

GIOVANNI: Let some mischief
Befall me soon if I dissemble aught.

ANNABELLA: You are my brother Giovanni.

GIOVANNI: You,
My sister Annabella; I know this:
And could afford you instance why to love
So much the more for this; to which intent
Wise nature first in your creation meant
To make you mine; else't had been sin and foul
To share one beauty to a double soul.   250
Nearness in birth or blood doth but persuade
A nearer nearness in affection.
I have ask'd counsel of the holy church
Who tells me I may love you; and 'tis just,
That since I may, I should; and will, yes, will.
Must I now live, or die?

ANNABELLA: Live, thou hast won
The field and never fought; what thou hast urg'd
My captive heart had long ago resolv'd.
I blush to tell thee – but I'll tell thee now –
For every sigh that thou hast spent for me,   260
I have sigh'd ten; for every tear, shed twenty:
And not so much for that I lov'd, as that

240. *bootless:* unavailing.   242. *in sadness:* in all seriousness.
246. *instance:* proof.

I durst not say I lov'd, nor scarcely think it.

GIOVANNI: Let not this music be a dream, ye gods,
For pity's sake, I beg 'ee.

ANNABELLA: On my knees,
    She kneels.
Brother, even by our mother's dust, I charge you,
Do not betray me to your mirth or hate;
Love me or kill me, brother.

GIOVANNI: On my knees,
    He kneels.
Sister, even by my mother's dust, I charge you,
Do not betray me to your mirth or hate;
Love me or kill me, sister.

ANNABELLA: You mean good sooth, then?

GIOVANNI: In good troth I do,
And so do you, I hope: say, I'm in earnest.

ANNABELLA: I'll swear't, I.

GIOVANNI: And I, and by this kiss,
    Kisses her.
Once more, yet once more; now let's rise by this.
I would not change this minute for Elysium.
What must we now do?

ANNABELLA: What you will.

GIOVANNI: Come then;
After so many tears as we have wept,
Let's learn to court in smiles, to kiss and sleep.
    Exeunt.

272. *sooth:* truth.

SCENE THREE

Enter FLORIO *and* DONADO.

FLORIO: Signior Donado, you have said enough;
 I understand you, but would have you know
 I will not force my daughter 'gainst her will.
 You see I have but two, a son and her;
 And he is so devoted to his book,
 As I must tell you true, I doubt his health:
 Should he miscarry, all my hopes rely
 Upon my girl. As for worldly fortune,
 I am, I thank my stars, bless'd with enough.
 My care is how to match her to her liking;   10
 I would not have her marry wealth but love,
 And if she like your nephew, let him have her;
 Here's all that I can say.

DONADO: Sir, you say well,
 Like a true father, and for my part, I,
 If the young folks can like ('twixt you and me),
 Will promise to assure my nephew presently
 Three thousand florins yearly during life,
 And after I am dead my whole estate.

FLORIO: 'Tis a fair proffer, sir. Meantime, your nephew
 Shall have free passage to commence his suit;   20
 If he can thrive, he shall have my consent.
 So for this time I'll leave you, signior.
  Exit.

DONADO: Well,
 Here's hope yet, if my nephew would have wit,
 But he is such another dunce, I fear

6. *doubt:* am apprehensive about.
7. *miscarry:* come to harm. 16. *presently:* straightaway.

41

He'll never win the wench. When I was young
I could have done't i'faith, and so shall he
If he will learn of me; and in good time
He comes himself.

    Enter BERGETTO *and* POGGIO.

How now, Bergetto, whither away so fast?

30 BERGETTO: O uncle, I have heard the strangest news that
ever came out of the mint, have I not, Poggio?

POGGIO: Yes indeed, sir.

DONADO: What news, Bergetto?

BERGETTO: Why, look ye, uncle, my barber told me just
now that there is a fellow come to town who undertakes
to make a mill go without the mortal help of any water
or wind, only with sandbags: and this fellow hath a
strange horse, a most excellent beast, I'll assure you,
uncle (my barber says), whose head, to the wonder of
40 all Christian people, stands just behind where his tail is;
is't not true, Poggio?

POGGIO: So the barber swore, forsooth.

DONADO: And you are running thither?

BERGETTO: Ay forsooth, uncle.

DONADO: Wilt thou be a fool still? Come, sir, you shall
not go; you have more mind of a puppet-play than on
the business I told ye: why, thou great baby, wilt never
have wit? Wilt make thyself a may-game to all the world?

POGGIO: Answer for yourself, master.

50 BERGETTO: Why, uncle, should I sit at home still, and not
go abroad to see fashions like other gallants?

DONADO: To see hobby-horses! What wise talk, I pray,
had you with Annabella when you were at Signior
Florio's house?

36. *mortal:* emphatic expletive (used with negatives).
48. *may-game:* object of mirth.

BERGETTO: O, the wench! Uds sa'me, uncle, I tickled her
with a rare speech, that I made her almost burst her belly
with laughing.

DONADO: Nay, I think so; and what speech was't?

BERGETTO: What did I say, Poggio?

POGGIO: Forsooth, my master said that he loved her   60
almost as well as he loved parmesan, and swore – I'll be
sworn for him – that she wanted but such a nose as his
was to be as pretty a young woman as any was in Parma.

DONADO: O, gross!

BERGETTO: Nay, uncle, then she asked me whether my
father had any more children than myself, and I said,
'No, 'twere better he should have had his brains knocked
out first.'

DONADO: This is intolerable.

BERGETTO: Then said she, 'Will Signior Donado, your   70
uncle, leave you all his wealth?'

DONADO: Ha! that was good. Did she harp upon that
string?

BERGETTO: Did she harp upon that string? Ay, that she
did. I answered, 'Leave me all his wealth? Why, woman,
he hath no other wit; if he had, he should hear on't to
his everlasting glory and confusion; I know,' quoth I,
'I am his white boy, and will not be gulled'; and with
that she fell into a great smile, and went away. Nay,
I did fit her.   80

DONADO: Ah, sirrah, then I see there is no changing of
nature. Well, Bergetto, I fear thou wilt be a very ass still.

BERGETTO: I should be sorry for that, uncle.

55. *Uds sa'me:* God save me (oath).
61. *parmesan:* cheese of Parma.
77. *glory:* presumably a malapropism.
78. *white boy:* favourite.
80. *fit her:* give her an apt answer.

DONADO: Come, come you home with me; since you are
no better a speaker, I'll have you write to her after some
courtly manner and enclose some rich jewel in the letter.

BERGETTO: Ay, marry, that will be excellent.

DONADO: Peace, innocent.
Once in my time I'll set my wits to school;

90   If all fail, 'tis but the fortune of a fool.

BERGETTO: Poggio, 'twill do, Poggio.

   Exeunt.

ACT TWO

Enter GIOVANNI *and* ANNABELLA, *as from their chamber.*

GIOVANNI: Come, Annabella, no more sister now,
　　But love, a name more gracious; do not blush,
　　Beauty's sweet wonder, but be proud to know
　　That yielding thou hast conquer'd, and inflam'd
　　A heart whose tribute is thy brother's life.

ANNABELLA: And mine is his. O, how these stol'n
　　contents
　　Would print a modest crimson on my cheeks
　　Had any but my heart's delight prevail'd.

GIOVANNI: I marvel why the chaster of your sex
　　Should think this pretty toy call'd maidenhead 　　　　*10*
　　So strange a loss when being lost 'tis nothing,
　　And you are still the same.

ANNABELLA:　　　　　　　　'Tis well for you;
　　Now you can talk.

GIOVANNI:　　　　　Music as well consists
　　In th'ear as in the playing.

ANNABELLA:　　　　　　　O, y'are wanton;
　　Tell on't, y'are best, do.

GIOVANNI:　　　　　　Thou wilt chide me then.
　　Kiss me: so; thus hung Jove on Leda's neck,
　　And suck'd divine ambrosia from her lips.
　　I envy not the mightiest man alive,
　　But hold myself in being king of thee

2. *love:* lover.　　6. *contents:* pleasures.　　10. *toy:* trifle.

45

20 More great than were I king of all the world.
But I shall lose you, sweetheart.

ANNABELLA: But you shall not.

GIOVANNI: You must be married, mistress.

ANNABELLA: Yes, to whom?

GIOVANNI: Some one must have you.

ANNABELLA: You must.

GIOVANNI: Nay, some other.

ANNABELLA: Now prithee, do not speak so; without
    jesting,
You'll make me weep in earnest.

GIOVANNI: What, you will not.
But tell me, sweet, canst thou be dar'd to swear
That thou wilt live to me and to no other?

ANNABELLA: By both our loves I dare, for didst thou
    know,
My Giovanni, how all suitors seem
30 To my eyes hateful, thou wouldst trust me then.

GIOVANNI: Enough, I take thy word. Sweet, we must part;
Remember what thou vow'st; keep well my heart.

ANNABELLA: Will you be gone?

GIOVANNI: I must.

ANNABELLA: When to return?

GIOVANNI: Soon.

ANNABELLA: Look you do.

GIOVANNI: Farewell.
    Exit.

ANNABELLA: Go where thou wilt, in mind I'll keep thee
    here;
And where thou art, I know I shall be there.
Guardian!
    Enter PUTANA.

PUTANA: Child, how is't child? Well, thank Heaven, ha?

46

ANNABELLA: O guardian, what a paradise of joy
    Have I pass'd over!   40

PUTANA: Nay, what a paradise of joy have you passed
    under! Why, now I commend thee, charge; fear nothing,
    sweetheart. What though he be your brother? Your
    brother's a man I hope, and I say still, if a young wench
    feel the fit upon her, let her take anybody, father or
    brother, all is one.

ANNABELLA: I would not have it known for all the world.

PUTANA: Nor I, indeed, for the speech of the people; else
    'twere nothing.

FLORIO [within]: Daughter Annabella!   50

ANNABELLA: O me! My father, – Here, sir. – Reach my
    work.

FLORIO [within]: What are you doing?

ANNABELLA: So; let him come now.
    Enter FLORIO, RICHARDETTO, *like a doctor of physic,*
    and PHILOTIS *with a lute in her hand.*

FLORIO: So hard at work, that's well; you lose no time.
    Look, I have brought you company: here's one,
    A learned doctor, lately come from Padua,
    Much skill'd in physic; and for that I see
    You have of late been sickly, I entreated
    This reverend man to visit you some time.

ANNABELLA: Y'are very welcome sir.

RICHARDETTO: I thank you, mistress.
    Loud fame in large report hath spoke your praise,   60
    As well for virtue as perfection;
    For which I have been bold to bring with me
    A kinswoman of mine, a maid, for song
    And music one perhaps will give content;

48. *for:* on account of.   52. *work:* needlework.
61. *perfection:* accomplishment.   64. *one:* one who.

Please you to know her.

ANNABELLA: They are parts I love,
And she for them most welcome.

PHILOTIS: Thank you, lady.

FLORIO: Sir, now you know my house, pray make not
    strange,
And if you find my daughter need your art,
I'll be your paymaster.

RICHARDETTO: Sir, what I am
She shall command.

70 FLORIO: You shall bind me to you.
Daughter, I must have conference with you
About some matters that concerns us both.
Good master doctor, please you but walk in;
We'll crave a little of your cousin's cunning.
I think my girl hath not quite forgot
To touch an instrument; she could have done't;
We'll hear them both.

RICHARDETTO: I'll wait upon you, sir.
    Exeunt.

SCENE TWO

Enter SORANZO *in his study reading a book.*

SORANZO: 'Love's measure is extreme, the comfort pain,
The life unrest, and the reward disdain.'
What's here? Look't o'er again. 'Tis so, so writes
This smooth, licentious poet in his rhymes.

65. *parts:* abilities.
67. *make not strange:* do not be distant.
68. *art:* skill (as doctor).
74. *cousin's:* niece's.   *cunning:* skill.

48

But Sannazar, thou liest, for had thy bosom
Felt such oppression as is laid on mine,
Thou wouldst have kiss'd the rod that made thee
   smart.
To work then, happy muse, and contradict
What Sannazar hath in his envy writ.
'Love's measure is the mean, sweet his annoys,   *10*
His pleasure's life, and his reward all joys.'
Had Annabella liv'd when Sannazar
Did in his brief encomium celebrate
Venice, that queen of cities, he had left
That verse which gain'd him such a sum of gold,
And for one only look from Annabel
Had writ of her and her diviner cheeks.
O, how my thoughts are –
VASQUES [*within*]: Pray forbear; in rules of civility, let me
give notice on't: I shall be taxed of my neglect of duty *20*
and service.
SORANZO: What rude intrusion interrupts my peace?
Can I be nowhere private?
VASQUES [*within*]: Troth, you wrong your modesty.
SORANZO: What's the matter, Vasques? Who is't?
   Enter HIPPOLITA *and* VASQUES.
HIPPOLITA: 'Tis I.
Do you know me now? Look, perjur'd man, on her
Whom thou and thy distracted lust have wrong'd;
Thy sensual rage of blood hath made my youth
A scorn to men and angels, and shall I   *30*
Be now a foil to thy unsated change?

8. *happy:* skilful, felicitous.   9. *envy:* ill-will.
14. *left:* given up.   20. *taxed of:* blamed for.
29. *rage:* violent passion.
31. *foil:* background.   *change:* caprice, changing humour.

Thou know'st, false wanton, when my modest fame
Stood free from stain or scandal, all the charms
Of hell or sorcery could not prevail
Against the honour of my chaster bosom.
Thine eyes did plead in tears, thy tongue in oaths
Such and so many that a heart of steel
Would have been wrought to pity as was mine:
And shall the conquest of my lawful bed,
40   My husband's death urg'd on by his disgrace,
My loss of womanhood, be ill rewarded
With hatred and contempt? No; know, Soranzo,
I have a spirit doth as much distaste
The slavery of fearing thee, as thou
Dost loathe the memory of what hath past.

SORANZO: Nay, dear Hippolita –

HIPPOLITA: Call me not dear,
Nor think with supple words to smooth the grossness
Of my abuses; 'tis not your new mistress,
Your goodly Madam Merchant, shall triumph
50   On my dejection; tell her thus from me,
My birth was nobler and by much more free.

SORANZO: You are too violent.

HIPPOLITA: You are too double
In your dissimulation. See'st thou this,
This habit, these black mourning weeds of care?
'Tis thou art cause of this and hast divorc'd
My husband from his life and me from him,
And made me widow in my widowhood.

SORANZO: Will you yet hear?

HIPPOLITA: More of thy perjuries?

43. *distaste:* dislike.
44. *fearing:* mistrusting.
50. *dejection:* humiliation.

Thy soul is drown'd too deeply in those sins;
Thou need'st not add to th'number.

SORANZO: Then I'll leave you;   60
You are past all rules of sense.

HIPPOLITA: And thou of grace.

VASQUES: Fie, mistress, you are not near the limits of
reason; if my lord had a resolution as noble as virtue
itself, you take the course to unedge it all. – Sir, I beseech
you do not perplex her; griefs, alas, will have a vent.
I dare undertake Madam Hippolita will now freely hear
you.

SORANZO: Talk to a woman frantic! Are these the fruits
of your love?

HIPPOLITA: They are the fruits of thy untruth, false man.   70
Didst thou not swear, whilst yet my husband liv'd,
That thou wouldst wish no happiness on earth
More than to call me wife? Didst thou not vow,
When he should die, to marry me? For which,
The devil in my blood and thy protests
Caus'd me to counsel him to undertake
A voyage to Leghorn, for that we heard
His brother there was dead, and left a daughter
Young and unfriended, who, with much ado,
I wish'd him to bring hither; he did so,   80
And went; and as thou know'st died on the way.
Unhappy man to buy his death so dear
With my advice! yet thou for whom I did it
Forget'st thy vows and leav'st me to my shame.

SORANZO: Who could help this?

HIPPOLITA: Who? Perjur'd man, thou couldst,
If thou hadst faith or love.

62. *not near:* beyond.   64. *unedge:* blunt.
75. *protests:* protestations.

SORANZO: You are deceiv'd;
    The vows I made – if you remember well –
    Were wicked and unlawful; 'twere more sin
    To keep them than to break them; as for me,
90 I cannot mask my penitence. Think thou
    How much thou hast digress'd from honest shame
    In bringing of a gentleman to death
    Who was thy husband, such a one as he,
    So noble in his quality, condition,
    Learning, behaviour, entertainment, love,
    As Parma could not show a braver man.
VASQUES: You do not well, this was not your promise.
SORANZO: I care not; let her know her monstrous life.
    Ere I'll be servile to so black a sin
100 I'll be accurs'd. – Woman, come here no more,
    Learn to repent and die; for by my honour,
    I hate thee and thy lust; you have been too foul.
        [Exit.]
VASQUES [aside]: This part has been scurvily play'd.
HIPPOLITA: How foolishly this beast contemns his fate,
    And shuns the use of that which I more scorn
    Than I once lov'd, his love. But let him go;
    My vengeance shall give comfort to his woe.
        She offers to go away.
VASQUES: Mistress, mistress, Madam Hippolita, pray a
    word or two.
110 HIPPOLITA: With me, sir?
VASQUES: With you if you please.
HIPPOLITA: What is't?
VASQUES: I know you are infinitely moved now, and you

91. *shame:* modesty.   103. *scurvily play'd:* badly acted.
104. *contemns:* despises.
107. *his woe:* my woe caused by him.

52

think you have cause; some I confess you have, but sure
not so much as you imagine.

HIPPOLITA: Indeed?

VASQUES: O, you were miserably bitter, which you
followed even to the last syllable. Faith, you were somewhat too shrewd; by my life, you could not have took
my lord in a worse time since I first knew him. Tomorrow *120*
you shall find him a new man.

HIPPOLITA: Well, I shall wait his leisure.

VASQUES: Fie, this is not a hearty patience; it comes sourly
from you; troth, let me persuade you for once.

HIPPOLITA [*aside*]: I have it and it shall be so: thanks,
opportunity! – Persuade me to what?

VASQUES: Visit him in some milder temper. O, if you
could but master a little your female spleen, how might
you win him!

HIPPOLITA: He will never love me. Vasques, thou hast *130*
been a too trusty servant to such a master, and I believe
thy reward in the end will fall out like mine.

VASQUES: So perhaps, too.

HIPPOLITA: Resolve thyself it will. Had I one so true, so
truly honest, so secret to my counsels as thou hast been to
him and his, I should think it a slight acquittance, not
only to make him master of all I have, but even of myself.

VASQUES: O, you are a noble gentlewoman.

HIPPOLITA: Wilt thou feed always upon hopes? Well,
I know thou art wise and seest the reward of an old *140*
servant daily what it is.

VASQUES: Beggary and neglect.

HIPPOLITA: True, but Vasques, wert thou mine, and
wouldst be private to me and my designs, I here protest

119. *shrewd:* shrewish.   134. *Resolve:* assure.
136. *acquittance:* discharge of debt.

53

myself and all what I can else call mine should be at thy dispose.

VASQUES [aside]: Work you that way, old mole? Then I have the wind of you. – I were not worthy of it by any desert that could lie within my compass: if I could –

150 HIPPOLITA: What then?

VASQUES: I should then hope to live in these my old years with rest and security.

HIPPOLITA: Give me thy hand; now promise but thy silence
And help to bring to pass a plot I have,
And here in sight of Heaven – that being done –
I make thee lord of me and mine estate.

VASQUES: Come, you are merry; this is such a happiness that I can neither think or believe.

HIPPOLITA: Promise thy secrecy and 'tis confirm'd.

160 VASQUES: Then here I call our good genii for witnesses, whatsoever your designs are or against whomsoever, I will not only be a special actor therein, but never disclose it till it be effected.

HIPPOLITA: I take thy word, and with that, thee for mine;
Come then, let's more confer of this anon.
On this delicious bane my thoughts shall banquet;
Revenge shall sweeten what my griefs have tasted.
Exeunt.

148. *have ... you:* see what you are aiming at.

SCENE THREE

Enter RICHARDETTO *and* PHILOTIS.

RICHARDETTO: Thou seest, my lovely niece, these
    strange mishaps,
  How all my fortunes turn to my disgrace,
  Wherein I am but as a looker-on,
  Whiles others act my shame and I am silent.
PHILOTIS: But uncle, wherein can this borrowed shape
  Give you content?
RICHARDETTO: I'll tell thee, gentle niece.
  Thy wanton aunt in her lascivious riots
  Lives now secure, thinks I am surely dead
  In my late journey to Leghorn for you,
  As I have caus'd it to be rumour'd out.   *10*
  Now would I see with what an impudence
  She gives scope to her loose adultery,
  And how the common voice allows hereof:
  Thus far I have prevail'd.
PHILOTIS: Alas, I fear
  You mean some strange revenge.
RICHARDETTO: O, be not troubled;
  Your ignorance shall plead for you in all.
  But to our business: what, you learn'd for certain
  How Signior Florio means to give his daugher
  In marriage to Soranzo?
PHILOTIS: Yes, for certain.
RICHARDETTO: But how find you young Annabella's
    love   *20*
  Inclin'd to him?

5. *shape:* disguise.   13. *how . . . hereof:* what gossip makes of it.
16. *plead . . . all:* act as your defence.

55

PHILOTIS:　　　　For aught I could perceive,
She neither fancies him or any else.

RICHARDETTO: There's mystery in that which time must
show.
　She us'd you kindly?

PHILOTIS:　　　　　　Yes.

RICHARDETTO:　　　　　And crav'd your company?

PHILOTIS: Often.

RICHARDETTO: 'Tis well, it goes as I could wish.
I am the doctor now, and as for you,
None knows you. If all fail not we shall thrive.
But who comes here?

　　Enter GRIMALDI.

　　　　　　　　I know him, 'tis Grimaldi,
A Roman and a soldier, near allied
30　Unto the Duke of Montferrato, one
Attending on the nuncio of the pope
That now resides in Parma, by which means
He hopes to get the love of Annabella.

GRIMALDI: Save you, sir.

RICHARDETTO:　　　And you, sir.

GRIMALDI:　　　　　　　I have heard
Of your approv'd skill which through the city
Is freely talked of, and would crave your aid.

RICHARDETTO: For what, sir?

GRIMALDI:　　　　　　Marry, sir, for this –
But I would speak in private.

RICHARDETTO:　　　　　Leave us, cousin.

　　Exit PHILOTIS.

GRIMALDI: I love fair Annabella and would know
40　Whether in arts there may not be receipts
To move affection.

　40. *receipts*: recipes (love potions).

RICHARDETTO: Sir, perhaps there may,
  But these will nothing profit you.
GRIMALDI: Not me?
RICHARDETTO: Unless I be mistook, you are a man
  Greatly in favour with the cardinal.
GRIMALDI: What of that?
RICHARDETTO: In duty to his grace,
  I will be bold to tell you, if you seek
  To marry Florio's daughter, you must first
  Remove a bar 'twixt you and her.
GRIMALDI: Who's that?
RICHARDETTO: Soranzo is the man that hath her heart,
  And while he lives, be sure you cannot speed.   50
GRIMALDI: Soranzo? What, mine enemy? Is't he?
RICHARDETTO: Is he your enemy?
GRIMALDI: The man I hate
  Worse than confusion;
  I'll kill him straight.
RICHARDETTO: Nay then, take mine advice,
  Even for his grace's sake, the cardinal:
  I'll find a time when he and she do meet,
  Of which I'll give you notice, and, to be sure
  He shall not 'scape you, I'll provide a poison
  To dip your rapier's point in. If he had
  As many heads as Hydra had, he dies.   60
GRIMALDI: But shall I trust thee, doctor?
RICHARDETTO: As yourself;
  Doubt not in aught. Thus shall the fates decree:
  By thee Soranzo falls that ruin'd me.
    Exeunt.

  50. *speed:* succeed.

SCENE FOUR

Enter DONADO, BERGETTO *and* POGGIO.

DONADO: Well, sir, I must be content to be both your secretary and your messenger myself; I cannot tell what this letter may work, but as sure as I am alive, if thou come once to talk with her, I fear thou wilt mar whatsoever I make.

BERGETTO: You make, uncle? Why, am not I big enough to carry mine own letter, I pray?

DONADO: Ay, ay, carry a fool's head o'thy own. Why, thou dunce, wouldst thou write a letter and carry it thyself?

BERGETTO: Yes, that I would, and read it to her with my own mouth, for you must think, if she will not believe me myself when she hears me speak, she will not believe another's handwriting. O, you think I am a blockhead, uncle. No, sir; Poggio knows I have indited a letter myself, so I have.

POGGIO: Yes truly, sir; I have it in my pocket.

DONADO: A sweet one, no doubt; pray let's see't.

BERGETTO: I cannot read my own hand very well, Poggio. Read it, Poggio.

DONADO: Begin.

POGGIO *(reads)*: 'Most dainty and honey-sweet mistress, I could call you fair, and lie as fast as any that loves you, but my uncle being the elder man, I leave it to him, as more fit for his age and the colour of his beard; I am wise enough to tell you I can bourd where I see occasion, or if you like my uncle's wit better than mine, you shall

26. *bourd*: jest (with pun on 'board' = accost).

marry me; if you like mine better than his, I will marry
you in spite of your teeth; so, commending my best parts
to you, I rest,   30

> Yours upwards and downwards,
> or you may choose,
> Bergetto.'

BERGETTO: Aha! here's stuff, uncle.

DONADO: Here's stuff indeed to shame us all. Pray, whose
advice did you take in this learned letter?

POGGIO: None, upon my word, but mine own.

BERGETTO: And, mine uncle, believe it, nobody's else;
'twas mine own brain, I thank a good wit for't.

DONADO: Get you home, sir, and look you keep within   40
doors till I return.

BERGETTO: How? That were a jest indeed; I scorn it
i'faith.

DONADO: What, you do not?

BERGETTO: Judge me, but I do now.

POGGIO: Indeed, sir, 'tis very unhealthy.

DONADO: Well sir, if I hear any of your apish running to
motions and fopperies till I come back, you were as good
not. Look to't!

Exit DONADO.

BERGETTO: Poggio, shall's steal to see this horse with the   50
head in's tail?

POGGIO: Ay, but you must take heed of whipping.

BERGETTO: Dost take me for a child, Poggio? Come,
honest Poggio.

Exeunt.

48. *motions:* puppet shows.

59

SCENE FIVE

Enter FRIAR *and* GIOVANNI.

FRIAR: Peace, thou hast told a tale whose every word
    Threatens eternal slaughter to the soul.
    I'm sorry I have heard it; would mine ears
    Had been one minute deaf before the hour
    That thou cam'st to me. O young man, castaway,
    By the religious number of mine order,
    I day and night have wak'd my aged eyes
    Above my strength to weep on thy behalf:
    But Heaven is angry, and be thou resolv'd
10   Thou art a man remark'd to taste a mischief;
    Look for't; though it come late it will come sure.
GIOVANNI: Father, in this you are uncharitable;
    What I have done I'll prove both fit and good.
    It is a principle, which you have taught
    When I was yet your scholar, that the frame
    And composition of the mind doth follow
    The frame and composition of the body;
    So where the body's furniture is beauty,
    The mind's must needs be virtue; which allowed,
20   Virtue itself is reason but refin'd,
    And love the quintessence of that. This proves
    My sister's beauty being rarely fair
    Is rarely virtuous; chiefly in her love,
    And chiefly in that love, her love to me.
    If hers to me, then so is mine to her,
    Since in like causes are effects alike.

6. *number:* ? group. See note.
10. *remark'd:* marked out.   *mischief:* calamity.

60

FRIAR: O ignorance in knowledge! Long ago,
How often have I warn'd thee this before?
Indeed, if we were sure there were no deity,
Nor Heaven nor hell, then to be led alone   30
By nature's light – as were philosophers
Of elder times – might instance some defence.
But 'tis not so. Then, madman, thou wilt find
That nature is in Heaven's positions blind.

GIOVANNI: Your age o'errules you; had you youth like mine,
You'd make her love your heaven, and her divine.

FRIAR: Nay, then, I see th'art too far sold to hell;
It lies not in the compass of my prayers
To call thee back; yet let me counsel thee:
Persuade thy sister to some marriage.   40

GIOVANNI: Marriage? Why, that's to damn her; that's to prove
Her greedy of variety of lust.

FRIAR: O fearful! If thou wilt not, give me leave
To shrive her, lest she should die unabsolv'd.

GIOVANNI: At your best leisure, father, then she'll tell you
How dearly she doth prize my matchless love;
Then you will know what pity 'twere we two
Should have been sunder'd from each other's arms.
View well her face, and in that little round
You may observe a world of variety: 50
For colour, lips; for sweet perfumes, her breath;
For jewels, eyes; for threads of purest gold,
Hair; for delicious choice of flowers, cheeks;
Wonder in every portion of that form;
Hear me but speak, and you will swear the spheres

32. *Of elder times:* i.e. before revealed religion.
34. *in Heaven's positions:* about Heaven's doctrines.

Make music to the citizens in Heaven.
But, father, what is else for pleasure fram'd,
Lest I offend your ears, shall go unnam'd.

FRIAR: The more I hear, I pity thee the more,
60   That one so excellent should give those parts
All to a second death. What I can do
Is but to pray; and yet I could advise thee
Wouldst thou be rul'd.

GIOVANNI: In what?

FRIAR: Why, leave her yet;
The throne of mercy is above your trespass,
Yet time is left you both –

GIOVANNI: To embrace each other,
Else let all time be struck quite out of number;
She is like me, and I like her, resolv'd.

FRIAR: No more! I'll visit her. This grieves me most,
Things being thus, a pair of souls are lost.
    Exeunt.

SCENE SIX

Enter FLORIO, DONADO, ANNABELLA, PUTANA.

FLORIO: Where's Giovanni?

ANNABELLA: Newly walk'd abroad,
And, as I heard him say, gone to the Friar,
His reverend tutor.

FLORIO: That's a blessed man,
A man made up of holiness; I hope
He'll teach him how to gain another world.

DONADO: Fair gentlewoman, here's a letter sent
To you from my young cousin. I dare swear

60. *parts:* attributes.   61. *second death:* damnation.

He loves you in his soul; would you could hear
Sometimes what I see daily, sighs and tears,
As if his breast were prison to his heart.   10

FLORIO: Receive it, Annabella.

ANNABELLA: Alas, good man.

DONADO: What's that she said?

PUTANA: An't please you, sir, she said, 'Alas, good man'.
Truly, I do commend him to her every night before her
first sleep because I would have her dream of him, and
she hearkens to that most religiously.

DONADO: Say'st so? God-a-mercy, Putana, there's something for thee, and prithee do what thou canst on his
behalf; sha'not be lost labour, take my word for't.   20

PUTANA: Thank you most heartily, sir; now I have a
feeling of your mind, let me alone to work.

ANNABELLA: Guardian!

PUTANA: Did you call?

ANNABELLA: Keep this letter.

DONADO: Signior Florio, in any case bid her read it
instantly.

FLORIO: Keep it for what? Pray read it me hereright.

ANNABELLA: I shall sir.
  She reads.

DONADO: How d'ee find her inclin'd, signior?   30

FLORIO: Troth, sir, I know not how; not all so well
As I could wish.

ANNABELLA: Sir, I am bound to rest your cousin's
  debtor;
The jewel I'll return, for if he love,
I'll count that love a jewel.

DONADO: Mark you that? –

22. *feeling:* 1. understanding 2. feeling of coin.
28. *hereright:* straightaway.

Nay, keep them both, sweet maid.

ANNABELLA: You must excuse me;
Indeed I will not keep it.

FLORIO: Where's the ring,
That which your mother in her will bequeath'd,
And charg'd you on her blessing not to give't
40 To any but your husband? Send back that.

ANNABELLA: I have it not.

FLORIO: Ha! Have it not? Where is't?

ANNABELLA: My brother in the morning took it from me,
Said he would wear't today.

FLORIO: Well, what do you say
To young Bergetto's love? Are you content
To match with him? Speak.

DONADO: There's the point indeed.

ANNABELLA [aside]: What shall I do? I must say
something now.

FLORIO: What say? Why d'ee not speak?

ANNABELLA: Sir, with your leave,
Please you to give me freedom?

FLORIO: Yes, you have it.

ANNABELLA: Signior Donado, if your nephew mean
50 To raise his better fortunes in his match,
The hope of me will hinder such a hope;
Sir, if you love him, as I know you do,
Find one more worthy of his choice than me.
In short, I'm sure I sha' not be his wife.

DONADO: Why, here's plain dealing; I commend thee
for't,
And all the worst I wish thee is Heaven bless thee!
Your father yet and I will still be friends,
Shall we not, Signior Florio?

FLORIO: Yes, why not?

Look, here your cousin comes.

Enter BERGETTO *and* POGGIO.

DONADO [*aside*]: O coxcomb! What doth he make here? *60*

BERGETTO: Where's my uncle, sirs?

DONADO: What's the news now?

BERGETTO: Save you, uncle, save you! You must not think
I come for nothing, masters. – And how, and how is't?
What, you have read my letter? Ah, there I – tickled you
i'faith.

POGGIO: But 'twere better you had tickled her in another
place.

BERGETTO: Sirrah sweetheart, I'll tell thee a good jest, and
riddle what 'tis. *70*

ANNABELLA: You say you'd tell me.

BERGETTO: As I was walking just now in the street, I met
a swaggering fellow would needs take the wall of me,
and because he did thrust me, I very valiantly called him
rogue. He thereupon bade me draw; I told him I had
more wit than so, but when he saw that I would not, he
did so maul me with the hilts of his rapier that my head
sung whilst my feet capered in the kennel.

DONADO [*aside*]: Was ever the like ass seen?

ANNABELLA: And what did you all this while? *80*

BERGETTO: Laugh at him for a gull till I see the blood run
about mine ears, and then I could not choose but find in
my heart to cry; till a fellow with a broad beard – they
say he is a new-come doctor – called me into his house
and gave me a plaster. Look you, here 'tis. And, sir, there
was a young wench washed my face and hands most
excellently; i'faith, I shall love her as long as I live for't.
Did she not, Poggio?

73. *take* . . . *me:* push me off the pavement.
78. *kennel:* gutter.   81. *gull:* fool.

POGGIO: Yes, and kissed him too.

90 BERGETTO: Why, la now, you think I tell a lie, uncle, I warrant.

DONADO: Would he that beat thy blood out of thy head had beaten some wit into it, for I fear thou never wilt have any.

BERGETTO: O uncle, but there was a wench would have done a man's heart good to have looked on her. – By this light, she had a face methinks worth twenty of you, Mistress Annabella!

DONADO: Was ever such a fool born?

100 ANNABELLA: I am glad she liked you, sir.

BERGETTO: Are you so? By my troth, I thank you forsooth.

FLORIO: Sure 'twas the doctor's niece that was last day with us here.

BERGETTO: 'Twas she, 'twas she!

DONADO: How do you know that, simplicity?

BERGETTO: Why, does not he say so? If I should have said no, I should have given him the lie, uncle, and so have deserved a dry beating again. I'll none of that.

FLORIO: A very modest, well-behaved young maid
As I have seen.

DONADO: Is she indeed?

110 FLORIO: Indeed,
She is, if I have any judgement.

DONADO: Well sir, now you are free, you need not care for sending letters; now you are dismissed, your mistress here will none of you.

BERGETTO: No? Why, what care I for that? I can have wenches enough in Parma for half-a-crown apiece, cannot I, Poggio?

POGGIO: I'll warrant you, sir.

100. *liked:* pleased.   108. *dry:* severe.

DONADO: Signior Florio,
  I thank you for your free recourse you gave   *120*
  For my admittance; and to you, fair maid,
  That jewel I will give you 'gainst your marriage. –
  Come, will you go, sir?
BERGETTO: Ay, marry will I. Mistress, farewell, mistress;
  I'll come again tomorrow. Farewell, mistress.
      Exeunt DONADO, BERGETTO *and* POGGIO.
      Enter GIOVANNI.
FLORIO: Son, where have you been? What, alone, alone
      still?
  I would not have it so; you must forsake
  This over-bookish humour. Well, your sister
  Hath shook the fool off.
GIOVANNI: 'Twas no match for her.
FLORIO: 'Twas not indeed; I meant it nothing less;   *130*
  Soranzo is the man I only like. –
  Look on him, Annabella. Come, 'tis supper-time,
  And it grows late.
      Exit FLORIO.
GIOVANNI: Whose jewel's that?
ANNABELLA: Some sweetheart's.
GIOVANNI: So I think.
ANNABELLA: A lusty youth, Signior Donado gave it me
  To wear against my marriage.
GIOVANNI: But you shall not wear it;
  Send it him back again.
ANNABELLA: What, you are jealous?
GIOVANNI: That you shall know anon at better leisure:
  Welcome, sweet night, the evening crowns the day.
      Exeunt.

  122. *'gainst*: in expectation of.

ACT THREE

SCENE ONE

Enter BERGETTO *and* POGGIO.

BERGETTO: Does my uncle think to make me a baby still?
No, Poggio, he shall know I have a sconce now.

POGGIO: Ay, let him not bob you off like an ape with an
apple.

BERGETTO: 'Sfoot, I will have the wench if he were ten
uncles, in despite of his nose, Poggio.

POGGIO: Hold him to the grindstone and give not a jot of
ground. She hath in a manner promised you already.

BERGETTO: True, Poggio, and her uncle the doctor swore
10   I should marry her.

POGGIO: He swore, I remember.

BERGETTO: And I will have her, that's more. Didst see the
codpiece-point she gave me, and the box of marmalade?

POGGIO: Very well, and kissed you, that my chops watered
at the sight on't. There's no way but to clap up a marriage
in hugger-mugger.

BERGETTO: I will do't, for I tell thee, Poggio, I begin to
grow valiant methinks, and my courage begins to rise.

POGGIO: Should you be afraid of your uncle?

20 BERGETTO: Hang him, old doting rascal! No, I say I will
have her.

POGGIO: Lose no time then.

2. *sconce:* head.   3. *bob:* fob.
13. *codpiece-point:* tagged lace for fastening codpiece.
16. *in hugger-mugger:* in secret.

BERGETTO: I will beget a race of wise men and constables
that shall cart whores at their own charges, and break
the duke's peace ere I have done myself. – Come away.
Exeunt.

SCENE TWO

Enter FLORIO, GIOVANNI, SORANZO, ANNABELLA,
PUTANA *and* VASQUES.

FLORIO: My lord Soranzo, though I must confess
The proffers that are made me have been great
In marriage of my daughter, yet the hope
Of your still rising honours have prevail'd
Above all other jointures; here she is;
She knows my mind; speak for yourself to her. –
And hear you, daughter, see you use him nobly;
For any private speech I'll give you time.
Come, son, and you the rest, let them alone;
Agree they as they may.

SORANZO: I thank you, sir.   10
GIOVANNI [*aside*]: Sister, be not all woman, think on me.
SORANZO: Vasques.
VASQUES: My lord?
SORANZO: Attend me without.
      Exeunt all except SORANZO *and* ANNABELLA.
ANNABELLA: Sir, what's your will with me?
SORANZO: Do you not know
What I should tell you?
ANNABELLA: Yes, you'll say you love me.
SORANZO: And I'll swear it, too; will you believe it?
ANNABELLA: 'Tis no point of faith.
      Enter GIOVANNI *above.*

18. *point of faith:* article of belief necessary for salvation.

SORANZO: Have you not will to love?
ANNABELLA: Not you.
SORANZO: Whom then?
ANNABELLA   That's as the fates infer.
GIOVANNI [*aside*]: Of those I'm regent now.
20 SORANZO: What mean you, sweet?
ANNABELLA: To live and die a maid.
SORANZO: O, that's unfit.
GIOVANNI [*aside*]: Here's one can say that's but a
    woman's note.
SORANZO: Did you but see my heart, then you would
    swear –
ANNABELLA: That you were dead.
GIOVANNI [*aside*]:   That's true, or somewhat near it.
SORANZO: See you these true love's tears?
ANNABELLA: No.
GIOVANNI [*aside*]:   Now she winks.
SORANZO: They plead to you for grace.
ANNABELLA: Yet nothing speak.
SORANZO: O grant my suit!
ANNABELLA: What is 't?
SORANZO: To let me live –
ANNABELLA: Take it.
SORANZO: – Still yours.
ANNABELLA: That is not mine to give.
GIOVANNI [*aside*]: One such another word would kill
    his hopes.
30 SORANZO: Mistress, to leave those fruitless strifes of wit,
    Know I have lov'd you long and lov'd you truly;
    Not hope of what you have but what you are
    Have drawn me on; then let me not in vain

19. *infer:* bring about.   20. *mean:* intend to do.
25. *winks:* turns a blind eye.   28. *Still:* ever.

Still feel the rigour of your chaste disdain.
I'm sick, and sick to th'heart.

ANNABELLA: Help, aqua-vitae!

SORANZO: What mean you?

ANNABELLA: Why, I thought you had been sick.

SORANZO: Do you mock my love?

GIOVANNI [aside]:   There sir, she was too nimble.

SORANZO [aside]: 'Tis plain, she laughs at me. – These
   scornful taunts
Neither become your modesty or years.

ANNABELLA: You are no looking-glass, or if you were,   *40*
I'd dress my language by you.

GIOVANNI [aside]:   I'm confirm'd.

ANNABELLA: To put you out of doubt, my lord,
   methinks
Your common sense should make you understand,
That if I lov'd you or desir'd your love,
Some way I should have given you better taste:
But since you are a nobleman, and one
I would not wish should spend his youth in hopes,
Let me advise you here to forbear your suit,
And think I wish you well, I tell you this.

SORANZO: Is't you speak this?

ANNABELLA: Yes, I myself; yet know –   *50*
Thus far I give you comfort – if mine eyes
Could have pick'd out a man, amongst all those
That sued to me, to make a husband of,
You should have been that man. Let this suffice;
Be noble in your secrecy and wise.

GIOVANNI [aside]: Why, now I see she loves me.

ANNABELLA: One word more:
As ever virtue liv'd within your mind,

35. *aqua-vitae*: spirits as restorative.

As ever noble course were your guide,
As ever you would have me know you lov'd me,
60 Let not my father know hereof by you;
If I hereafter find that I must marry,
It shall be you or none.

SORANZO: I take that promise.

ANNABELLA: O, O, my head!

SORANZO: What's the matter? Not well?

ANNABELLA: O, I begin to sicken.

GIOVANNI [aside]: Heaven forbid!
    Exit from above.

SORANZO: Help, help! Within there, ho!
    Look to your daughter, Signior Florio!
    Enter FLORIO, GIOVANNI, PUTANA.

FLORIO: Hold her up, she swoons.

70 GIOVANNI: Sister, how d'ee?

ANNABELLA: Sick. – Brother, are you there?

FLORIO: Convey her to her bed instantly, whilst I send for
    a physician; quickly, I say.

PUTANA: Alas, poor child.
    Exeunt all except SORANZO.
    Enter VASQUES.

VASQUES: My lord.

SORANZO: O, Vasques, now I doubly am undone,
    Both in my present and my future hopes:
    She plainly told me that she could not love,
    And thereupon soon sicken'd, and I fear
80   Her life's in danger.

VASQUES [aside]: By'r lady, sir, and so is yours, if you knew
    all. – 'Las, sir, I am sorry for that; maybe 'tis but the
    maid's-sickness, an overflux of youth; and then, sir, there

---

83. *maid's-sickness:* chlorosis. See note.
    overflux: overflow.

is no such present remedy as present marriage. But hath
she given you an absolute denial?

SORANZO: She hath, and she hath not; I'm full of grief;
But what she said I'll tell thee as we go.

Exeunt.

SCENE THREE

Enter GIOVANNI *and* PUTANA.

PUTANA: O sir, we are all undone, quite undone, utterly
undone, and shamed for ever! Your sister, O your
sister!

GIOVANNI: What of her? For Heaven's sake, speak; how
does she?

PUTANA: O, that ever I was born to see this day.

GIOVANNI: She is not dead, ha? Is she?

PUTANA: Dead? No, she is quick; 'tis worse, she is with
child. You know what you have done; Heaven forgive'ee! 'Tis too late to repent now, Heaven help us.   *10*

GIOVANNI: With child? How dost thou know't?

PUTANA: How do I know't? Am I at these years ignorant
what the meanings of qualms and water-pangs be? Of
changing of colours, queasiness of stomachs, pukings,
and another thing that I could name? Do not – for her
and your credit's sake – spend the time in asking how,
and which way, 'tis so. She is quick upon my word; if
you let a physician see her water y'are undone.

GIOVANNI: But in what case is she?

84. *present:* immediate.
8. *quick:* 1. alive 2. pregnant.
19. *case:* condition.

20 PUTANA: Prettily amended; 'twas but a fit which I soon
    espied, and she must look for often henceforward.
  GIOVANNI: Commend me to her, bid her take no care;
    Let not the doctor visit her, I charge you;
    Make some excuse till I return. – O me!
    I have a world of business in my head. –
    Do not discomfort her. –
    How does this news perplex me! – If my father
    Come to her, tell him she's recover'd well;
    Say 'twas but some ill diet; d'ee hear, woman?
30 Look you to't.
  PUTANA: I will sir.
    Exeunt.

SCENE FOUR

Enter FLORIO *and* RICHARDETTO.

FLORIO: And how d'ee find her, sir?
RICHARDETTO: Indifferent well;
    I see no danger, scarce perceive she's sick,
    But that she told me she had lately eaten
    Melons, and as she thought, those disagreed
    With her young stomach.
FLORIO: Did you give her aught?
RICHARDETTO: An easy surfeit-water, nothing else.
    You need not doubt her health; I rather think
    Her sickness is a fulness of her blood –
    You understand me?

20. *prettily:* fortunately.   22. *take no care:* do not worry.
1. *Indifferent:* fairly.
6. *easy surfeit-water:* mild cure for indigestion.

74

FLORIO: I do; you counsel well,
   And once within these few days will so order't,   *10*
   She shall be married ere she know the time.

RICHARDETTO: Yet let not haste, sir, make unworthy
     choice;
   That were dishonour.

FLORIO: Master doctor, no,
   I will not do so neither. In plain words,
   My Lord Soranzo is the man I mean.

RICHARDETTO: A noble and a virtuous gentleman.

FLORIO: As any is in Parma. Not far hence
   Dwells Father Bonaventure, a grave friar,
   Once tutor to my son; now at his cell
   I'll have 'em married.

RICHARDETTO: You have plotted wisely.   *20*

FLORIO: I'll send one straight to speak with him tonight.

RICHARDETTO: Soranzo's wise, he will delay no time.

FLORIO: It shall be so.
     Enter FRIAR *and* GIOVANNI.

FRIAR: Good peace be here and love.

FLORIO: Welcome, religious friar, you are one
   That still bring blessing to the place you come to.

GIOVANNI: Sir, with what speed I could, I did my best
   To draw this holy man from forth his cell
   To visit my sick sister, that with words
   Of ghostly comfort in this time of need
   He might absolve her, whether she live or die.   *30*

FLORIO: 'Twas well done, Giovanni; thou herein
   Hast showed a Christian's care, a brother's love. –
   Come, father, I'll conduct you to her chamber,
   And one thing would entreat you.

FRIAR: Say on, sir.

29. *ghostly:* spiritual.

FLORIO: I have a father's dear impression,
   And wish before I fall into my grave
   That I might see her married, as 'tis fit;
   A word from you, grave man, will win her more
   Than all our best persuasions.

FRIAR: Gentle sir,
40   All this I'll say, that Heaven may prosper her.
   Exeunt.

SCENE FIVE

Enter GRIMALDI.

GRIMALDI: Now if the doctor keep his word, Soranzo,
   Twenty to one you miss your bride; I know
   'Tis an unnoble act, and not becomes
   A soldier's valour; but in terms of love,
   Where merit cannot sway, policy must.
   I am resolv'd; if this physician
   Play not on both hands, then Soranzo falls.
   Enter RICHARDETTO.

RICHARDETTO: You are come as I could wish. This very
      night,
   Soranzo, 'tis ordain'd, must be affied
10   To Annabella; and, for aught I know,
   Married.

GRIMALDI: How!

RICHARDETTO: Yet your patience:
   The place, 'tis Friar Bonaventure's cell.
   Now I would wish you to bestow this night

35. *dear impression:* loving notion.
5. *policy:* low cunning.   7. *on both hands:* as a double agent.
9. *affied:* affianced.

76

In watching thereabouts; 'tis but a night;
If you miss now tomorrow I'll know all.

GRIMALDI: Have you the poison?

RICHARDETTO: Here 'tis in this box;
Doubt nothing, this will do't. In any case,
As you respect your life, be quick and sure.

GRIMALDI: I'll speed him.

RICHARDETTO: Do; away! for 'tis not safe
You should be seen much here. – Ever my love!   20

GRIMALDI: And mine to you.

Exit GRIMALDI.

RICHARDETTO: So, if this hit, I'll laugh and hug
    revenge;
And they that now dream of a wedding-feast
May chance to mourn the lusty bridegroom's ruin.
But to my other business. – Niece Philotis!

Enter PHILOTIS.

PHILOTIS: Uncle?

RICHARDETTO: My lovely niece, you have bethought
    'ee?

PHILOTIS: Yes, and as you counsel'd,
Fashion'd my heart to love him, but he swears
He will tonight be married; for he fears
His uncle else, if he should know the drift,   30
Will hinder all and call his coz to shrift.

RICHARDETTO: Tonight? Why, best of all! But let me
    see –
I ha' – yes – so it shall be: in disguise
We'll early to the friar's, I have thought on't.

Enter BERGETTO *and* POGGIO.

PHILOTIS: Uncle, he comes.

RICHARDETTO: Welcome, my worthy coz!

22. *hit:* succeed.   31. *shrift:* confession, revelation.

BERGETTO: Lass, pretty lass, come buss, lass! – Aha,
    Poggio!
    [*Kisses her.*]

POGGIO: There's hope of this yet.

RICHARDETTO: You shall have time enough; withdraw a
    little,
40 We must confer at large.

BERGETTO: Have you not sweetmeats or dainty devices
    for me?

PHILOTIS: You shall have enough, sweetheart.

BERGETTO: Sweetheart! Mark that, Poggio. By my troth,
    I cannot choose but kiss thee once more for that word
    'sweetheart'. Poggio, I have a monstrous swelling about
    my stomach, whatsoever the matter be.

POGGIO: You shall have physic for't sir.

RICHARDETTO: Time runs apace.

POGGIO: Time's a blockhead.

RICHARDETTO: Be rul'd; when we have done what's fit
50 to do,
    Then you may kiss your fill and bed her too.
    Exeunt.

SCENE SIX

Enter the FRIAR *sitting in a chair,* ANNABELLA *kneeling
and whispering to him, a table before them and wax-lights;
she weeps and wrings her hands.*

FRIAR: I am glad to see this penance, for believe me
    You have unripp'd a soul so foul and guilty,
    As I must tell you true, I marvel how

2. *unripp'd*: exposed.

The earth hath borne you up. But weep, weep on,
These tears may do you good; weep faster yet,
Whiles I do read a lecture.
ANNABELLA: Wretched creature!
FRIAR: Ay, you are wretched, miserably wretched,
  Almost condemn'd alive. There is a place
  – List, daughter – in a black and hollow vault,
  Where day is never seen; there shines no sun,   10
  But flaming horror of consuming fires;
  A lightless sulphur chok'd with smoky fogs
  Of an infected darkness; in this place
  Dwell many thousand, thousand sundry sorts
  Of never-dying deaths; there damned souls
  Roar without pity; there are gluttons fed
  With toads and adders; there is burning oil
  Pour'd down the drunkard's throat; the usurer
  Is forc'd to sup whole draughts of molten gold;
  There is the murderer forever stabb'd,   20
  Yet can he never die; there lies the wanton
  On racks of burning steel, whiles in his soul
  He feels the torment of his raging lust.
ANNABELLA: Mercy, O mercy!
FRIAR: There stands these wretched things
  Who have dream'd out whole years in lawless sheets
  And secret insults, cursing one another:
  Then you will wish each kiss your brother gave
  Had been a dagger's point; then you shall hear
  How he will cry, 'O would my wicked sister
  Had first been damn'd when she did yield to lust!' –   30
  But soft, methinks I see repentance work
  New motions in your heart. Say, how is't with you?
ANNABELLA: Is there no way left to redeem my miseries?

6. *read a lecture*: deliver a reprimand.

FRIAR: There is, despair not; Heaven is merciful,
And offers grace even now: 'tis thus agreed,
First, for your honour's safety that you marry
The Lord Soranzo; next, to save your soul,
Leave off this life, and henceforth live to him.

ANNABELLA: Ay me!

FRIAR: Sigh not; I know the baits of sin
40   Are hard to leave. O, 'tis a death to do't.
Remember what must come. Are you content?

ANNABELLA: I am.

FRIAR: I like it well; we'll take the time. –
Who's near us there?

    Enter FLORIO, GIOVANNI.

FLORIO: Did you call, father?

FRIAR: Is Lord Soranzo come?

FLORIO: He stays below.

FRIAR: Have you acquainted him at full?

FLORIO: I have,
And he is overjoy'd.

FRIAR: And so are we:
Bid him come near.

GIOVANNI [*aside*]:   My sister weeping, ha?
I fear this friar's falsehood. – I will call him.
    Exit.

FLORIO: Daughter, are you resolv'd?

50 ANNABELLA: Father, I am.
    Enter GIOVANNI, SORANZO *and* VASQUES.

FLORIO: My Lord Soranzo, here
Give me your hand, for that I give you this.
    [*Joins their hands.*]

SORANZO: Lady, say you so too?

42. *take the time:* seize the opportunity.

ANNABELLA: I do and vow
   To live with you and yours.
FRIAR: Timely resolv'd:
   My blessing rest on both; more to be done,
   You may perform it on the morning sun.
      Exeunt.

SCENE SEVEN

Enter GRIMALDI *with his rapier drawn and a dark lantern.*

GRIMALDI: 'Tis early night as yet, and yet too soon
   To finish such a work; here I will lie
   To listen who comes next.
      He lies down.
      Enter BERGETTO *and* PHILOTIS *disguised, and after*
      RICHARDETTO *and* POGGIO.
BERGETTO: We are almost at the place, I hope, sweetheart.
GRIMALDI [*aside*]: I hear them near, and heard one say
   'sweetheart'.
   'Tis he; now guide my hand, some angry justice,
   Home to his bosom. – Now have at you, sir!
      Strikes BERGETTO *and exit.*
BERGETTO: O help, help! Here's a stitch fallen in my guts.
   O for a flesh-tailor quickly! – Poggio!
PHILOTIS: What ails my love?   10
BERGETTO: I am sure I cannot piss forward and backward,
   and yet I am wet before and behind. Lights, lights! ho
   lights!
PHILOTIS: Alas, some villain here has slain my love.

S.D. *dark-lantern:* designed to give off little light.
9. *flesh-tailor:* surgeon.

RICHARDETTO: O Heaven forbid it! Raise up the next
neighbours
Instantly, Poggio, and bring lights.
   Exit POGGIO.
How is't Bergetto? Slain? It cannot be!
Are you sure y'are hurt?

BERGETTO: O, my belly seethes like a porridge-pot; some
20   cold water, I shall boil over else; my whole body is in a
sweat that you may wring my shirt. Feel here – Why,
Poggio!
   Enter POGGIO *with Officers and lights and halberts.*

POGGIO: Here. – Alas, how do you?

RICHARDETTO: Give me a light. What's here? All blood!
O sirs,
Signior Donado's nephew now is slain.
Follow the murderer with all the haste
Up to the city; he cannot be far hence.
Follow, I beseech you.

OFFICERS: Follow, follow, follow!
   Exeunt Officers.

RICHARDETTO: Tear off thy linen, coz, to stop his
30   wounds. –
Be of good comfort, man.

BERGETTO: Is all this mine own blood? Nay then, good-
night with me. Poggio, commend me to my uncle, dost
hear? Bid him for my sake make much of this wench.
O – I am going the wrong way sure, my belly aches so –
O farewell, Poggio – O – O –
   Dies.

PHILOTIS: O, he is dead!

POGGIO: How? Dead?

RICHARDETTO: He's dead indeed.
'Tis now too late to weep, let's have him home,

And with what speed we may, find out the murderer.

POGGIO: O my master, my master, my master!   *40*

Exeunt.

SCENE EIGHT

Enter VASQUES *and* HIPPOLITA.

HIPPOLITA: Betrothed?

VASQUES: I saw it.

HIPPOLITA: And when's the marriage day?

VASQUES: Some two days hence.

HIPPOLITA: Two days? Why, man, I would but wish two hours
To send him to his last and lasting sleep.
And Vasques, thou shalt see, I'll do it bravely.

VASQUES: I do not doubt your wisdom, nor, I trust, you my secrecy. I am infinitely yours.

HIPPOLITA: I will be thine in spite of my disgrace.   *10*
So soon? O wicked man! I durst be sworn
He'd laugh to see me weep.

VASQUES: And that's a villainous fault in him.

HIPPOLITA: No, let him laugh, I'm arm'd in my resolves:
Be thou still true.

VASQUES: I should get little by treachery against so hopeful a preferment as I am like to climb to.

HIPPOLITA: Even to my bosom, Vasques. Let my youth
Revel in these new pleasures; if we thrive,
He now hath but a pair of days to live.   *20*
Exeunt.

16. *against:* in exchange for.   18. *my youth:* i.e. Soranzo.

SCENE NINE

Enter FLORIO, DONADO, RICHARDETTO, POGGIO
and Officers.

FLORIO: 'Tis bootless now to show yourself a child,
Signior Donado; what is done is done;
Spend not the time in tears but seek for justice.

RICHARDETTO: I must confess, somewhat I was in fault,
That had not first acquainted you what love
Past 'twixt him and my niece, but as I live,
His fortune grieves me as it were mine own.

DONADO: Alas, poor creature, he meant no man harm,
That I am sure of.

FLORIO: I believe that too. –
10   But stay, my masters, are you sure you saw
The murderer pass here?

OFFICER: And it please you, sir, we are sure we saw a
ruffian, with a naked weapon in his hand all bloody, get
into my lord cardinal's grace's gate, that we are sure of;
but for fear of his grace, bless us, we durst go no further.

DONADO: Know you what manner of man he was?

OFFICER: Yes, sure, I know the man; they say 'a is a
soldier, he that loved your daughter, sir, an't please ye;
'twas he for certain.

FLORIO: Grimaldi, on my life!

20   OFFICER: Ay, ay, the same.

RICHARDETTO: The cardinal is noble, he no doubt
Will give true justice.

DONADO: Knock someone at the gate.

1. *bootless:* pointless.

POGGIO: I'll knock, sir.

   POGGIO *knocks.*

SERVANT *(within)*: What would 'ee?

FLORIO: We require speech with the lord cardinal
  About some present business; pray inform
  His grace that we are here.

   Enter CARDINAL *and* GRIMALDI.

CARDINAL: Why, how now, friends! What saucy mates
    are you
  That know nor duty nor civility?
  Are we a person fit to be your host?   30
  Or is our house become your common inn
  To beat our doors at pleasure? What such haste
  Is yours as that it cannot wait fit times?
  Are you the masters of this commonwealth
  And know no more discretion? O, your news
  Is here before you: you have lost a nephew,
  Donado, last night by Grimaldi slain.
  Is that your business? Well, sir, we have knowledge
    on't.
  Let that suffice.

GRIMALDI: In presence of your grace,
  In thought I never meant Bergetto harm;   40
  But Florio, you can tell with how much scorn
  Soranzo, back'd with his confederates,
  Hath often wrong'd me; I, to be reveng'd,
  For that I could not win him else to fight,
  Had thought by way of ambush to have kill'd him,
  But was unluckily therein mistook;
  Else he had felt what late Bergetto did;
  And though my fault to him were merely chance,

---

26. *present:* urgent.   28. *saucy mates:* insolent fellows.
37. *last night:* this night.

Yet humbly I submit me to your grace,
To do with me as you please.
　　[*Kneels.*]
50　CARDINAL:　　　　　　　　Rise up, Grimaldi. –
　　You citizens of Parma, if you seek
　　For justice, know, as nuncio from the pope,
　　For this offence I here receive Grimaldi
　　Into his holiness' protection.
　　He is no common man but nobly born,
　　Of prince's blood, though you sir, Florio,
　　Thought him too mean a husband for your daughter.
　　If more you seek for, you must go to Rome,
　　For he shall thither. Learn more wit, for shame;
60　Bury your dead. – Away, Grimaldi – leave 'em!
　　　　Exeunt CARDINAL *and* GRIMALDI.
　　DONADO: Is this a churchman's voice? Dwells justice
　　　　here?
　　FLORIO: Justice is fled to Heaven and comes no nearer.
　　Soranzo! Was't for him? O impudence!
　　Had he the face to speak it and not blush?
　　Come, come, Donado, there's no help in this,
　　When cardinals think murder's not amiss.
　　Great men may do their wills, we must obey,
　　But Heaven will judge them for't another day.
　　　　Exeunt.

59. *wit*: commonsense.

ACT FOUR

SCENE ONE

A Banquet. Hautboys. Enter the FRIAR, GIOVANNI,
ANNABELLA, PHILOTIS, SORANZO, DONADO,
FLORIO, RICHARDETTO, PUTANA *and* VASQUES.

FRIAR: These holy rites perform'd, now take your times
   To spend the remnant of the day in feast;
   Such fit repasts are pleasing to the saints
   Who are your guests, though not with mortal eyes
   To be beheld. – Long prosper in this day,
   You happy couple, to each other's joy!
SORANZO: Father, your prayer is heard; the hand of
      goodness
   Hath been a shield for me against my death,
   And, more to bless me, hath enrich'd my life
   With this most precious jewel; such a prize   10
   As earth hath not another like to this.
   Cheer up, my love, and gentlemen, my friends,
   Rejoice with me in mirth; this day we'll crown
   With lust cups to Annabella's health.
GIOVANNI *(aside)*: O torture! Were the marriage yet
      undone!
   Ere I'd endure this sight, to see my love
   Clipp'd by another, I would dare confusion,
   And stand the horror of ten thousand deaths.
VASQUES: Are you not well, sir?

S.D. *Hautboys:* oboes.
17. *Clipp'd:* embraced.   *confusion:* destruction.

87

GIOVANNI: Prithee, fellow, wait;
20 I need not thy officious diligence.

FLORIO: Signior Donado, come, you must forget
   Your late mishaps and drown your cares in wine.

SORANZO: Vasques!

VASQUES: My lord?

SORANZO: Reach me that weighty bowl –
   Here, brother Giovanni, here’s to you;
   Your turn comes next though now a bachelor;
   Here’s to your sister’s happiness and mine.

GIOVANNI: I cannot drink.

SORANZO: What?

GIOVANNI: ’Twill indeed offend me.

ANNABELLA: Pray do not urge him if he be not willing.
   Hautboys.

FLORIO: How now, what noise is this?

30 VASQUES: O sir, I had forgot to tell you: certain young
   maidens of Parma, in honour to Madam Annabella’s
   marriage, have sent their loves to her in a masque, for
   which they humbly crave your patience and silence.

SORANZO: We are much bound to them, so much the more
   As it comes unexpected; guide them in.
      Enter HIPPOLITA *and Ladies in* [*masks and*] *white robes,*
      with garlands of willows. Music and a dance.
   Thanks, lovely virgins; now might we but know
   To whom we have been beholding for this love,
   We shall acknowledge it.

HIPPOLITA: Yes, you shall know.
   [*Unmasks.*]
   What think you now?

ALL: Hippolita!

19. *wait:* wait on the guests.
29. *noise:* music.

88

HIPPOLITA: 'Tis she,
  Be not amaz'd; nor blush, young lovely bride,   40
  I come not to defraud you of your man.
  'Tis now no time to reckon up the talk
  What Parma long hath rumour'd of us both;
  Let rash report run on; the breath that vents it
  Will, like a bubble, break itself at last.
  But now to you, sweet creature, lend's your hand;
  Perhaps it hath been said that I would claim
  Some interest in Soranzo, now your lord.
  What I have right to do his soul knows best:
  But in my duty to your noble worth,   50
  Sweet Annabella, and my care of you,
  Here take, Soranzo, take this hand from me:
  I'll once more join what by the holy church
  Is finish'd and allow'd. Have I done well?

SORANZO: You have too much engag'd us.

HIPPOLITA: One thing more.
  That you may know my single charity,
  Freely I here remit all interest
  I e'er could claim, and give you back your vows;
  And to confirm't, reach me a cup of wine. –
  My Lord Soranzo, in this draught I drink   60
  Long rest t'ee! – Look to it, Vasques.

VASQUES: Fear nothing.
    He gives her a poisoned cup; she drinks.

SORANZO: Hippolita, I thank you and will pledge
  This happy union as another life. –
  Wine, there!

44. *rash report:* swift gossip.
55. *engag'd:* pun 1. enlisted our gratitude 2. affianced.
56. *single charity:* outstanding love.
63. *pledge:* drink to.

VASQUES: You shall have none, neither shall you pledge
her.

HIPPOLITA: How?

VASQUES: Know now, Mistress She-Devil, your own
mischievous treachery hath killed you; I must not marry
70   you.

HIPPOLITA: Villain!

ALL: What's the matter?

VASQUES: Foolish woman, thou art now like a fire-brand
that hath kindled others and burnt thyself. *Troppo sperar,
inganna*, thy vain hope hath deceived thee, thou are but
dead; if thou hast any grace, pray.

HIPPOLITA: Monster!

VASQUES: Die in charity, for shame! – This thing of malice,
this woman, had privately corrupted me with promise
80   of marriage, under this politic reconciliation to poison
my lord, whiles she might laugh at his confusion on his
marriage-day. I promised her fair, but I knew what my
reward should have been, and would willingly have
spared her life, but that I was acquainted with the danger
of her disposition, and now have fitted her a just payment
in her own coin. There she is; she hath yet — and end
thy days in peace, vile woman; as for life, there's no
hope, think not on't.

ALL: Wonderful justice!

RICHARDETTO: Heaven, thou art righteous.

90 HIPPOLITA: O, 'tis true;
I feel my minute coming. Had that slave
Kept promise – O, my torment! – thou this hour
Hadst died, Soranzo – heat above hell fire! –
Yet ere I pass away – cruel, cruel flames! –
Take here my curse amongst you: may thy bed

75. *but*: almost.   80. *under*: under the cloak of.

Of marriage be a rack unto thy heart,
Burn blood and boil in vengeance – O my heart,
My flame's intolerable! – mayst thou live
To father bastards, may her womb bring forth
Monsters, and die together in your sins,   100
Hated, scorn'd and unpitied – O! – O! –
   Dies.

FLORIO: Was e'er so vile a creature.

RICHARDETTO: Here's the end
  Of lust and pride.

ANNABELLA: It is a fearful sight.

SORANZO: Vasques, I know thee now a trusty servant,
  And never will forget thee. – Come, my love,
  We'll home, and thank the Heavens for this escape.
  Father and friends, we must break up this mirth;
  It is too sad a feast.

DONADO: Bear hence the body.

FRIAR: Here's an ominous change;
  Mark this, my Giovanni, and take heed;   110
  I fear the event: that marriage seldom's good
  Where the bride-banquet so begins in blood.
    Exeunt.

SCENE TWO

Enter RICHARDETTO *and* PHILOTIS.

RICHARDETTO: My wretched wife, more wretched in her
    shame
  Than in her wrongs to me, hath paid too soon
  The forfeit of her modesty and life;
  And I am sure, my niece, though vengeance hover,

111. *event*: outcome.

Keeping aloof yet from Soranzo's fall,
Yet he will fall, and sink with his own weight.
I need not now – my heart persuades me so –
To further his confusion; there is One
Above begins to work, for as I hear,
Debates already 'twixt his wife and him
Thicken and run to head; she, as 'tis said,
Slightens his love and he abandons hers.
Much talk I hear; since things go thus, my niece,
In tender love and pity of your youth,
My counsel is, that you should free your years
From hazard of these woes, by flying hence
To fair Cremona, there to vow your soul
In holiness a holy votaress.
Leave me to see the end of these extremes.
All human worldly courses are uneven;
No life is blessed but the way to Heaven.

PHILOTIS: Uncle, shall I resolve to be a nun?

RICHARDETTO: Ay, gentle niece, and in your hourly
prayers,
Remember me, your poor, unhappy uncle.
Hie to Cremona, now, as fortune leads,
Your home your cloister, your best friends your beads.
Your chaste and single life shall crown your birth;
Who dies a virgin lives a saint on earth.

PHILOTIS: Then farewell, world, and worldly thoughts,
adieu!
Welcome, chaste vows, myself I yield to you.
Exeunt.

---

10. *Debates*: quarrels.
11. *Thicken . . . head*: come to bursting point.
12. *Slightens*: slights.

SCENE THREE

Enter SORANZO *unbraced, and* ANNABELLA *dragged in.*

SORANZO: Come, strumpet, famous whore; were every
    drop
  Of blood that runs in thy adulterous veins
  A life, this sword – dost see't? – should in one blow
  Confound them all. Harlot, rare, notable harlot,
  That with thy brazen face maintainst thy sin,
  Was there no man in Parma to be bawd
  To your loose, cunning whoredom else but I?
  Must your hot itch and pleurisy of lust,
  The heyday of your luxury, be fed
  Up to a surfeit, and could none but I   *10*
  Be picked out to be cloak to your close tricks,
  Your belly-sports? Now I must be the dad
  To all that gallimaufrey that's stuff'd
  In thy corrupted, bastard-bearing womb?
  Say, must I?
ANNABELLA: Beastly man! Why, 'tis thy fate:
  I sued not to thee; for, but that I thought
  Your over-loving lordship would have run
  Mad on denial, had ye lent me time,
  I would have told 'ee in what case I was;
  But you would needs be doing.

---

s.d. *unbraced:* with part of clothing unfastened. See note.
4. *confound:* destroy. See note.
5. *maintainst:* persist in.
8. *pleurisy:* excess.
9. *heyday . . . luxury:* height of your lechery.
11. *close:* secret.
13. *gallimaufrey:* jumble, hodge podge.

20 SORANZO: Whore of whores!
Dar'st thou tell me this?
ANNABELLA: O yes, why not?
You were deceiv'd in me; 'twas not for love
I chose you but for honour; yet know this:
Would you be patient yet and hide your shame,
I'd see whether I could love you.
SORANZO: Excellent quean!
Why, art thou not with child?
ANNABELLA: What needs all this
When 'tis superfluous? I confess I am.
SORANZO: Tell me by whom.
ANNABELLA: Soft, sir, 'twas not in my bargain.
Yet somewhat, sir, to stay your longing stomach,
30 I'm content t'acquaint you with: the man,
The more than man that got this sprightly boy
– For 'tis a boy; therefore glory that, sir,
Your heir shall be a son –
SORANZO: Damnable monster!
ANNABELLA: Nay, and you will not hear, I'll speak no
more.
SORANZO: Yes, speak, and speak thy last.
ANNABELLA: A match, a match!
This noble creature was in every part
So angel-like, so glorious, that a woman
Who had not been but human, as was I,
Would have kneel'd to him and have begg'd for love.
40 You! Why, you are not worthy once to name
His name without true worship, or, indeed,
Unless you kneel'd, to hear another name him.
SORANZO: What was he call'd?

25. *excellent quean:* pre-eminent whore.
35. *A match:* agreed!

ANNABELLA: We are not come to that.
  Let it suffice that you shall have the glory
  To father what so brave a father got.
  In brief, had not this chance fall'n out as't doth,
  I never had been troubled with a thought
  That you had been a creature; but for marriage,
  I scarce dream yet of that.

SORANZO: Tell me his name.

ANNABELLA: Alas, alas, there's all!   50
  Will you believe?

SORANZO: What?

ANNABELLA: You shall never know.

SORANZO: How!

ANNABELLA: Never; if you do, let me be curs'd.

SORANZO: Not know it, strumpet? I'll rip up thy heart
  And find it there.

ANNABELLA: Do, do.

SORANZO: And with my teeth,
  Tear the prodigious lecher joint by joint.

ANNABELLA: Ha, ha, ha! the man's merry!

SORANZO: Dost thou laugh?
  Come, whore, tell me your lover, or by truth,
  I'll hew thy flesh to shreds! Who is't?

ANNABELLA *(sings)*: *Che morte più dolce che morire per*
  amore.

SORANZO: Thus will I pull thy hair, and thus I'll drag   60
  Thy lust-be-leper'd body through the dust.
  Yet tell his name.

ANNABELLA *(sings)*: *Morendo in gratia Dei, morirei senza*
  dolore.

SORANZO: Dost thou triumph? The treasure of the earth
  Shall not redeem thee; were there kneeling kings

55. *prodigious*: unnatural.

Did beg thy life, or angels did come down
To plead in tears, yet should not all prevail
Against my rage! Dost thou not tremble yet?

ANNABELLA: At what? To die? No, be a gallant
hangman;

70 I dare thee to the worst; strike, and strike home;
I leave revenge behind and thou shalt feel’t.

SORANZO: Yet tell me ere thou diest, and tell me truly,
Knows thy old father this?

ANNABELLA: No, by my life!

SORANZO: Wilt thou confess, and I will spare thy life?

ANNABELLA: My life? I will not buy my life so dear.

SORANZO: I will not slack my vengeance.

    Enter VASQUES.

VASQUES: What d’ee mean, sir?

SORANZO: Forbear, Vasques; such a damned whore
Deserves no pity.

80 VASQUES: Now the gods forfend! And would you be her
executioner, and kill her in your rage, too? O, ’twere
most unmanlike. She is your wife; what faults hath been
done by her before she married you were not against you.
Alas, poor lady, what hath she committed which any
lady in Italy in the like case would not? Sir, you must be
ruled by your reason and not by your fury; that were
unhuman and beastly.

SORANZO: She shall not live.

VASQUES: Come, she must. You would have her confess
90 the author of her present misfortunes, I warrant ’ee; ’tis
an unconscionable demand, and she should lose the
estimation that I, for my part, hold of her worth, if she
had done it. Why, sir, you ought not, of all men living,

69. *hangman:* executioner.   76. *slack:* be remiss in.
80. *forfend:* forbid.

to know it. Good sir, be reconciled; alas, good gentlewoman!

ANNABELLA: Pish, do not beg for me; I prize my life
As nothing. If the man will needs be mad,
Why, let him take it.

SORANZO: Vasques, hear'st thou this?

VASQUES: Yes, and commend her for it. In this she shows
the nobleness of a gallant spirit, and beshrew my heart,   *100*
but it becomes her rarely! – [*Aside to* SORANZO] Sir,
in any case smother your revenge; leave the scenting out
your wrongs to me; be ruled as you respect your honour
or you mar all. – [*Aloud*] Sir, if ever my service were of
any credit with you, be not so violent in your distractions.
You are married now; what a triumph might the report
of this give to other neglected suitors; 'tis as manlike to
bear extremities as godlike to forgive.

SORANZO: O Vasques, Vasques, in this piece of flesh,
This faithless face of hers, had I laid up   *110*
The treasure of my heart. – Hadst thou been virtuous,
Fair, wicked woman, not the matchless joys
Of life itself had made me wish to live
With any saint but thee. Deceitful creature,
How hast thou mock'd my hopes, and in the shame
Of thy lewd womb even buried me alive?
I did too dearly love thee.

VASQUES *(aside)*: This is well. Follow this temper with
some passion; be brief and moving, 'tis for the purpose.

SORANZO: Be witness to my words thy soul and thoughts,   *120*
And tell me, didst not think that in my heart,
I did too superstitiously adore thee?

---

102. *in any case:* by any means.   118. *temper:* strain.
119. *passion:* sorrowful emotion.
122. *too superstitiously:* with excessive observance.

ANNABELLA: I must confess, I know you lov'd me well.

SORANZO: And wouldst thou use me thus? O Annabella,
Be thus assur'd, whatsoe'er the villain was
That thus hath tempted thee to this disgrace,
Well he might lust, but never lov'd like me.
He doted on the picture that hung out
Upon thy cheeks to please his humorous eye,
130 Not on the part I lov'd, which was thy heart,
And as I thought, thy virtues.

ANNABELLA: O my lord!
These words wound deeper than your sword could do.

VASQUES: Let me not ever take comfort, but I begin to
weep myself, so much I pity him. Why, madam, I knew
when his rage was over-past, what it would come to.

SORANZO: Forgive me, Annabella; though thy youth
Hath tempted thee above thy strength to folly,
Yet will not I forget what I should be,
And what I am, a husband; in that name
140 Is hid divinity. If I do find
That thou wilt yet be true, here I remit
All former faults and take thee to my bosom.

VASQUES: By my troth, and that's a point of noble
charity.

ANNABELLA: Sir, on my knees –
[Kneels.]

SORANZO: Rise up; you shall not kneel.
Get you to your chamber; see you make no show
Of alteration; I'll be with you straight.
My reason tells me now that 'tis as common

129. *Humorous:* capricious.
137. *strength:* i.e. of moral purpose.
141. *remit:* pardon.
143. *point:* conclusion, decision.

To err in frailty as to be a woman.
Go to your chamber.
　　Exit ANNABELLA.

VASQUES: So, this was somewhat to the matter. What do *150*
you think of your heaven of happiness now, sir?

SORANZO: I carry hell about me; all my blood
Is fir'd in swift revenge.

VASQUES: That may be, but know you how, or on whom?
Alas, to marry a great woman, being made great in the
stock to your hand, is a usual sport in these days; but to
know what ferret it was that haunted your cony-berry,
there's the cunning.

SORANZO: I'll make her tell herself, or –

VASQUES: Or what? You must not do so. Let me yet *160*
persuade your sufferance a little while; go to her, use
her mildly, win her, if it be possible, to a voluntary, to
a weeping tune. For the rest, if all hit I will not miss my
mark. Pray, sir, go in; the next news I tell you shall
be wonders.

SORANZO: Delay in vengeance gives a heavier blow.
　　Exit.

VASQUES: Ah, sirrah, here's work for the nonce! I had a
suspicion of a bad matter in my head a pretty while ago;
but after my madam's scurvy looks here at home, her
waspish perverseness and loud fault-finding, then I *170*
remembered the proverb, that where hens crow and
cocks hold their peace, there are sorry houses. 'Sfoot!
if the lower parts of a she-tailor's cunning can cover such
a swelling in the stomach, I'll never blame a false stitch

155. *great* (2nd): pregnant.
156. *stock*: body.　　*to your hand*: ready for you.
157. *cony-berry*: rabbit-warren.
162. *voluntary*: 1. spontaneous confession 2. improvised piece of music.

in a shoe whiles I live again. Up and up so quick? And so
quickly, too? 'Twere a fine policy to learn by whom this
must be known. And I have thought on't – here's the
way or none. –

Enter PUTANA.

What, crying, old mistress? Alas, alas, I cannot blame 'ee;
180   we have a lord, Heaven help us, is so mad as the devil
himself, the more shame for him!

PUTANA: O, Vasques, that ever I was born to see this day!
Doth he use thee so too, sometimes, Vasques?

VASQUES: Me? Why, he makes a dog of me; but if some
were of my mind, I know what we would do. As sure
as I am an honest man, he will go near to kill my lady
with unkindness. Say she be with child, is that such a
matter for a young woman of her years to be blamed
for?

PUTANA: Alas, good heart, it is against her will full sore.

190 VASQUES: I durst be sworn, all his madness is for that she
will not confess whose 'tis, which he will know; and
when he doth know it, I am so well acquainted with his
humour, that he will forget all straight. Well, I could
wish she would in plain terms tell all, for that's the way
indeed.

PUTANA: Do you think so?

VASQUES: Foh, I know't, provided that he did not win
her to't by force. He was once in a mind that you could
tell, and meant to have wrung it out of you, but I
200 somewhat pacified him for that; yet sure you know a
great deal.

PUTANA: Heaven forgive us all! I know a little, Vasques.

VASQUES: Why should you not? Who else should? Upon

198. *in a mind:* of the opinion.

my conscience, she loves you dearly, and you would not
betray her to any affliction for the world.

PUTANA: Not for all the world, by my faith and troth,
Vasques.

VASQUES: 'Twere pity of your life if you should, but in this
you should both relieve her present discomforts, pacify
my lord, and gain yourself everlasting love and prefer-   210
ment.

PUTANA: Dost think so, Vasques?

VASQUES: Nay, I know't. Sure 'twas some near and entire
friend?

PUTANA: 'Twas a dear friend, indeed, but –

VASQUES: But what? Fear not to name him; my life
between you and danger. Faith, I think 'twas no base
fellow?

PUTANA: Thou wilt stand between me and harm?

VASQUES: 'Ud's pity, what else? You shall be rewarded,   220
too, trust me.

PUTANA: 'Twas even no worse than her own brother.

VASQUES: Her brother Giovanni, I warrant 'ee!

PUTANA: Even he, Vasques, as brave a gentleman as ever
kissed fair lady. O they love most perpetually.

VASQUES: A brave gentleman, indeed! Why, therein
I commend her choice. – Better and better! – You are
sure 'twas he?

PUTANA: Sure; and you shall see, he will not be long from
her too.   230

VASQUES: He were to blame if he would; but may I
believe thee?

PUTANA: Believe me? Why, dost think I am a Turk or Jew?
No, Vasques, I have known their dealings too long to
belie them now.

220. *'Ud's:* God's

VASQUES: Where are you? There within, sirs!
Enter Banditti.

PUTANA: How now, what are these?

VASQUES: You shall know presently. – Come, sirs, take
me this old, damnable hag, gag her instantly, and put
240 out her eyes. Quickly, quickly!

PUTANA: Vasques, Vasques!

VASQUES: Gag her, I say. 'Sfoot, d'ee suffer her to prate?
What, d'ee fumble about? Let me come to her. – I'll help
your old gums, you toad-bellied bitch! [*Gags her.*] Sirs,
carry her closely into the coalhouse, and put her eyes out
instantly. If she roars, slit her nose; d'ee hear, be speedy
and sure.
Exeunt [Banditti] with PUTANA.
Why this is excellent and above expectation! Her own
brother! O horrible! To what a height of liberty in
250 damnation hath the devil trained our age! Her brother!
Well, there's yet but a beginning. I must to my lord and
tutor him better in his points of vengeance. Now I see
how a smooth tale goes beyond a smooth tail. But soft –
What thing comes next?
Enter GIOVANNI.
Giovanni! As I would wish. My belief is strengthened;
'tis as firm as winter and summer.

GIOVANNI: Where's my sister?

VASQUES: Troubled with a new sickness, my lord; she's
somewhat ill.

260 GIOVANNI: Took too much of the flesh, I believe.

VASQUES: Troth, sir, and you I think have e'en hit it. But
my virtuous lady –

245. *closely:* secretly.   249. *liberty:* licence.
250. *trained:* seduced.
260. *Took . . . flesh:* 1. eaten too much meat 2. had too much sexual
experience.

GIOVANNI: Where's she?

VASQUES: In her chamber. Please you visit her; she is
  alone. [GIOVANNI *gives him money*.] Your liberality hath
  doubly made me your servant, and ever shall ever.

  Exit GIOVANNI.

  Enter SORANZO.

  Sir, I am made a man; I have plied my cue with cunning
  and success. I beseech you, let's be private.

SORANZO: My lady's brother's come; now he'll know all.

VASQUES: Let him know't; I have made some of them fast   *270*
  enough. How have you dealt with my lady?

SORANZO: Gently, as thou hast counsell'd. O, my soul
  Runs circular in sorrow for revenge.
  But Vasques, thou shalt know –

VASQUES: Nay, I will know no more, for now comes your
  turn to know. I would not talk so openly with you. Let
  my young master take time enough and go at pleasure;
  he is sold to death, and the devil shall not ransom him.
  Sir, I beseech you, your privacy.

SORANZO: No conquest can gain glory of my fear.   *280*

  Exeunt.

  265. *liberality:* 1. generosity 2. sexual licence.

ACT FIVE

SCENE ONE

Enter ANNABELLA *above.*

ANNABELLA: Pleasures, farewell, and all ye thriftless
    minutes
  Wherein false joys have spun a weary life.
  To these my fortunes now I take my leave.
  Thou precious Time, that swiftly rid'st in post
  Over the world, to finish up the race
  Of my last fate, here stay thy restless course,
  And bear to ages that are yet unborn
  A wretched woeful woman's tragedy.
  My conscience now stands up against my lust,
10 With depositions character'd in guilt,
  And tells me I am lost.
    Enter FRIAR [*below*].
                Now I confess,
  Beauty that clothes the outside of the face
  Is cursed if it be not cloth'd with grace.
  Here like a turtle, mew'd up in a cage,
  Unmated, I converse with air and walls,
  And descant on my vile unhappiness.
  O Giovanni, that hast had the spoil
  Of thine own virtues and my modest fame,

---

1. *thriftless:* unprofitable.   4. *in post:* with haste.
9. *against:* to witness against.
10. *character'd:* inscribed.   *guilt:* pun? 1. guilt 2. gilt.
14. *turtle:* turtle-dove.   *mew'd up:* imprisoned.

Would thou hadst been less subject to those stars
That luckless reign'd at my nativity: 20
O would the scourge due to my black offence
Might pass from thee, that I alone might feel
The torment of an uncontrolled flame!

FRIAR [*aside*]: What's this I hear?

ANNABELLA: That man, that blessed friar,
Who join'd in ceremonial knot my hand
To him whose wife I now am, told me oft
I trod the path to death, and showed me how.
But they who sleep in lethargies of lust
Hug their confusion, making Heaven unjust,
And so did I.

FRIAR [*aside*]:   Here's music to the soul.   30

ANNABELLA: Forgive me, my good genius, and this once
Be helpful to my ends. Let some good man
Pass this way, to whose trust I may commit
This paper double-lin'd with tears and blood;
Which being granted, here I sadly vow
Repentance, and a leaving of that life
I long have died in.

FRIAR: Lady, Heaven hath heard you,
And hath by providence ordain'd that I
Should be his minister for your behoof.

ANNABELLA: Ha, what are you?

FRIAR: Your brother's friend, the friar;   40
Glad in my soul that I have liv'd to hear
This free confession 'twixt your peace and you.
What would you, or to whom? Fear not to speak.

ANNABELLA: Is Heaven so bountiful? Then I have found
More favour than I hop'd. Here, holy man –
   Throws a letter.

35. *sadly*. solemnly.   39. *behoof*: benefit.

Commend me to my brother; give him that,
That letter; bid him read it and repent,
Tell him that I – imprison'd in my chamber,
Barr'd of all company, even of my guardian,
50 Who gives me cause of much suspect – have time
To blush at what hath pass'd; bid him be wise,
And not believe the friendship of my lord.
I fear much more than I can speak. Good father,
The place is dangerous and spies are busy;
I must break off – You'll do't?

FRIAR: Be sure I will;
And fly with speed. – My blessing ever rest
With thee, my daughter; live to die more blessed.
    Exit FRIAR.

ANNABELLA: Thanks to the Heavens, who have
    prolong'd my breath
To this good use: now I can welcome death.
    Exit.

SCENE TWO

Enter SORANZO *and* VASQUES.

VASQUES: Am I to be believed now? First, marry a
    strumpet that cast herself away upon you but to laugh
    at your horns, to feast on your disgrace, riot in your
    vexations, cuckold you in your bridebed, waste your
    estate upon panders and bawds!

SORANZO: No more, I say, no more!

VASQUES: A cuckold is a goodly tame beast, my lord.

SORANZO: I am resolv'd; urge not another word;
    My thoughts are great, and all as resolute

50. *suspect:* suspicion.   9. *great:* passionate.

As thunder; in mean time I'll cause our lady   10
To deck herself in all her bridal robes,
Kiss her, and fold her gently in my arms.
Begone! – yet hear you, are the banditti ready
To wait in ambush?

VASQUES: Good sir, trouble not yourself about other
business than your own resolution; remember that time
lost cannot be recalled.

SORANZO: With all the cunning words thou canst, invite
The states of Parma to my birthday's feast;
Haste to my brother-rival and his father,   20
Entreat them gently, bid them not to fail.
Be speedy and return.

VASQUES: Let not your pity betray you till my coming
back; think upon incest and cuckoldry.

SORANZO: Revenge is all the ambition I aspire:
To that I'll climb or fall; my blood's on fire.
    Exeunt.

SCENE THREE

Enter GIOVANNI.

GIOVANNI: Busy opinion is an idle fool
That as a school rod keeps a child in awe,
Frights the unexperienc'd temper of the mind:
So did it me, who ere my precious sister
Was married thought all taste of love would die
In such a contract; but I find no change
Of pleasure in this formal law of sports.

19. *states:* nobles.   1. *opinion:* common beliefs.

She is still one to me, and every kiss
As sweet and as delicious as the first
10 I reap'd when yet the privilege of youth
Entitled her a virgin. O, the glory
Of two united hearts like hers and mine!
Let poring bookmen dream of other worlds;
My world and all of happiness is here,
And I'd not change it for the best to come;
A life of pleasure is Elysium.
    Enter FRIAR.
Father, you enter on the jubilee
Of my retir'd delights. Now I can tell you,
The hell you oft have prompted, is nought else
20 But slavish and fond, superstitious fear;
And I could prove it too –
FRIAR: Thy blindness slays thee.
Look there, 'tis writ to thee.
    Gives the letter.
GIOVANNI: From whom?
FRIAR: Unrip the seals and see;
The blood's yet seething hot, that will anon
Be frozen harder than congeal'd coral.
Why d'ee change colour, son?
GIOVANNI: 'Fore Heaven, you make
Some petty devil factor 'twixt my love
And your religion-masked sorceries.
Where had you this?
FRIAR: Thy conscience, youth, is sear'd,
Else thou wouldst stoop to warning.
30 GIOVANNI: 'Tis her hand.

17. *jubilee:* joyful celebration. See note.
19. *prompted:* suggested.   20. *fond:* foolish.
27. *factor:* agent.   29. *sear'd:* dried up.

I know't; and 'tis all written in her blood.
She writes I know not what. Death? I'll not fear
An armed thunderbolt aim'd at my heart.
She writes we are discovered – pox on dreams
Of low, faint-hearted cowardice! Discovered?
The devil we are! Which way is't possible?
Are we grown traitors to our own delights?
Confusion take such dotage! 'Tis but forg'd.
This is your peevish chattering, weak old man.

    Enter VASQUES.

Now sir, what news bring you?   40

VASQUES: My lord, according to his yearly custom keeping
this day a feast in honour of his birthday, by me invites
you thither. Your worthy father, with the pope's
reverend nuncio and other magnificoes of Parma, have
promised their presence. Wilt please you to be of the
number?

GIOVANNI: Yes, tell him I dare come.

VASQUES: 'Dare come'?

GIOVANNI: So I said; and tell him more, I will come.

VASQUES: These words are strange to me.   50

GIOVANNI: Say I will come.

VASQUES: You will not miss?

GIOVANNI: Yet more? I'll come! Sir, are you answer'd?

VASQUES: So I'll say. – My service to you.

    Exit VASQUES.

FRIAR: You will not go, I trust.

GIOVANNI: Not go? For what?

FRIAR: O, do not go! This feast – I'll gage my life –
Is but a plot to train you to your ruin.
Be rul'd: you sha' not go.

GIOVANNI: Not go? Stood Death

56. *gage:* stake.   57. *train:* lure.

Threat'ning his armies of confounding plagues,
60   With hosts of dangers hot as blazing stars,
I would be there. Not go? Yes, and resolve
To strike as deep in slaughter as they all.
For I will go.
FRIAR: Go where thou wilt; I see
The wildness of thy fate draws to an end,
To a bad fearful end; I must not stay
To know thy fall; back to Bononia I
With speed will haste and shun this coming blow.
Parma, farewell; would I had never known thee,
Or aught of thine. Well, young man, since no prayer
70   Can make thee safe, I leave thee to despair.
    Exit FRIAR.
GIOVANNI: Despair or tortures of a thousand hells –
All's one to me; I have set up my rest.
Now, now, work serious thoughts on baneful plots;
Be all a man, my soul; let not the curse
Of old prescription rend from me the gall
Of courage, which enrols a glorious death.
If I must totter like a well-grown oak,
Some under-shrubs shall in my weighty fall
Be crush'd to splits: with me they all shall perish.
    Exit.

SCENE FOUR

Enter SORANZO, VASQUES, *and Banditti.*

SORANZO: You will not fail, or shrink in the attempt?
VASQUES: I will undertake for their parts. Be sure, my

72. *set . . . rest:* come to the point of hazarding all (metaphor from
card-game).
79. *splits:* splinters.

masters, to be bloody enough, and as unmerciful as if
you were preying upon a rich booty on the very mountains of Liguria. For your pardons, trust to my lord; but
for your reward, you shall trust none but your own
pockets.

ALL BANDITTI: We'll make a murder.

SORANZO: Here's gold, here's more; want nothing; what
  you do
Is noble, and an act of brave revenge.   10
I'll make ye rich banditti, and all free.

ALL: Liberty, liberty!

VASQUES: Hold! Take every man a vizard; when ye are
  withdrawn, keep as much silence as you can possibly.
  You know the watchword, till which be spoken, move
  not; but when you hear that, rush in like a stormy flood;
  I need not instruct ye in your own profession.

ALL: No, no, no!

VASQUES: In then; your ends are profit and preferment.
  Away.   20
    Exeunt Banditti.

SORANZO: The guests will all come, Vasques?

VASQUES: Yes, sir; and now let me a little edge your
  resolution. You see nothing is unready to this great work
  but a great mind in you: call to your remembrance your
  disgraces, your loss of honour, Hippolita's blood; and
  arm your courage in your own wrongs; so shall you
  best right those wrongs in vengeance which you may
  truly call your own.

SORANZO: 'Tis well; the less I speak the more I burn,
And blood shall quench that flame.   30

VASQUES: Now you begin to turn Italian. This beside –

13. *vizard:* mask.   22. *edge:* sharpen.

when my young incest-monger comes, he will be sharp
set on his old bit: give him time enough, let him have
your chamber and bed at liberty; let my hot hare have
law ere he be hunted to his death, that if it be possible, he
may post to hell in the very act of his damnation.

Enter GIOVANNI.

SORANZO: It shall be so; and see, as we would wish,
He comes himself first – Welcome, my much-lov'd
    brother,
Now I perceive you honour me; y'are welcome,
But where's my father?

40 GIOVANNI: With the other states,
Attending on the nuncio of the pope,
To wait upon him hither. How's my sister?

SORANZO: Like a good housewife, scarcely ready yet.
Y'are best walk to her chamber.

GIOVANNI: If you will.

SORANZO: I must expect my honourable friends;
Good brother, get her forth.

GIOVANNI: You are busy, sir.

Exit GIOVANNI.

VASQUES: Even as the great devil himself would have it;
let him go and glut himself in his own destruction.

Flourish.

Hark, the nuncio is at hand. Good sir, be ready to receive
50 him.

Enter CARDINAL, FLORIO, DONADO, RICHARDETTO
    and Attendants.

SORANZO: Most reverend lord, this grace hath made me
    proud

32–3. *be . . . bit:* have keen appetite for.
35. *law:* start given to hare before chase begins.
36. *post:* hurry.   40. *father:* i.e. father-in-law.   45. *expect:* await.

That you vouchsafe my house; I ever rest
Your humble servant for this noble favour.
CARDINAL: You are our friend, my lord; his holiness
Shall understand how zealously you honour
Saint Peter's vicar in his substitute.
Our special love to you.
SORANZO: Signiors, to you
My welcome, and my ever best of thanks
For this so memorable courtesy.
Pleaseth your grace to walk near?
CARDINAL: My lord, we come   60
To celebrate your feast with civil mirth,
As ancient custom teacheth: we will go.
SORANZO: Attend his grace there! Signiors, keep your
    way.
    Exeunt.

SCENE FIVE

Enter GIOVANNI *and* ANNABELLA *lying on a bed.*

GIOVANNI: What, chang'd so soon? Hath your new
    sprightly lord
Found out a trick in night-games more than we
Could know in our simplicity? Ha! is't so?
Or does the fit come on you to prove treacherous
To your past vows and oaths?
ANNABELLA: Why should you jest
At my calamity without all sense
Of the approaching dangers you are in?
GIOVANNI: What danger's half so great as thy revolt?
Thou art a faithless sister, else thou know'st
Malice, or any treachery beside,   10

Would stoop to my bent brows. Why, I hold fate
Clasp'd in my fist, and could command the course
Of time's eternal motion, hadst thou been
One thought more steady than an ebbing sea.
And what? You'll now be honest? That's resolv'd?

ANNABELLA: Brother, dear brother, know what I have
    been,
And know that now there's but a dining-time
'Twixt us and our confusion: let's not waste
These precious hours in vain and useless speech.
20 Alas, these gay attires were not put on
But to some end; this sudden solemn feast
Was not ordain'd to riot in expense;
I that have now been chamber'd here alone,
Barr'd of my guardian, or of any else,
Am not for nothing at an instant freed
To fresh access; be not deceiv'd my brother,
This banquet is an harbinger of death
To you and me; resolve yourself it is,
And be prepar'd to welcome it.

GIOVANNI: Well then,
30 The schoolmen teach that all this globe of earth
Shall be consum'd to ashes in a minute.

ANNABELLA: So I have read too.

GIOVANNI: But 'twere somewhat strange
To see the waters burn; could I believe
This might be true, I could believe as well
There might be hell or Heaven.

ANNABELLA: That's most certain.

GIOVANNI: A dream, a dream! Else in this other world
We should know one another.

28. *resolve*: assure.
30. *schoolmen*: medieval theologians.

ANNABELLA: So we shall.
GIOVANNI: Have you heard so?
ANNABELLA: For certain.
GIOVANNI: But d'ee think
 That I shall see you there, you look on me?
 May we kiss one another, prate or laugh,   *40*
 Or do as we do here?
ANNABELLA: I know not that;
 But good, for the present, what d'ee mean
 To free yourself from danger? Some way think
 How to escape; I'm sure the guests are come.
GIOVANNI: Look up, look here; what see you in my
  face?
ANNABELLA: Distraction and a troubled countenance.
GIOVANNI: Death and a swift repining wrath. – Yet
  look,
 What see you in mine eyes?
ANNABELLA: Methinks you weep.
GIOVANNI: I do indeed; these are the funeral tears
 Shed on your grave; these furrowed up my cheeks *50*
 When first I lov'd and knew not how to woo.
 Fair Annabella, should I here repeat
 The story of my life, we might lose time.
 Be record, all the spirits of the air
 And all things else that are, that day and night,
 Early and late, the tribute which my heart
 Hath paid to Annabella's sacred love
 Hath been these tears which are her mourners now:
 Never till now did Nature do her best
 To show a matchless beauty to the world,   *60*
 Which in an instant, ere it scarce was seen,
 The jealous Destinies requir'd again.

 42. *good:* i.e. good brother.   *mean:* intend to do.

Pray, Annabella, pray; since we must part,
Go thou white in thy soul to fill a throne
Of innocence and sanctity in Heaven.
Pray, pray, my sister.

ANNABELLA: Then I see your drift. –
Ye blessed angels, guard me!

GIOVANNI: So say I.
Kiss me; if ever after-times should hear
Of our fast-knit affections, though perhaps
70 The laws of conscience and of civil use
May justly blame us, yet when they but know
Our loves, that love will wipe away that rigour,
Which would in other incests be abhorr'd.
Give me your hand; how sweetly life doth run
In these well-coloured veins! How constantly
These palms do promise health! But I could chide
With Nature for this cunning flattery.
Kiss me again – forgive me.

ANNABELLA: With my heart.

GIOVANNI: Farewell.

ANNABELLA: Will you be gone?

GIOVANNI: Be dark, bright sun,
80 And make this midday night, that thy gilt rays
May not behold a deed will turn their splendour
More sooty than the poets feign their Styx.
One other kiss, my sister.

ANNABELLA: What means this?

GIOVANNI: To save thy fame and kill thee in a kiss.
     Stabs her.
Thus die, and die by me and by my hand.
Revenge is mine; honour doth love command.

ANNABELLA: O brother, by your hand!

GIOVANNI: When thou art dead,

116

I'll give my reasons for't; for to dispute
With thy (even in thy death) most lovely beauty
Would make me stagger to perform this act   *90*
Which I most glory in.

ANNABELLA: Forgive him, Heaven – and me my sins;
    farewell.
Brother unkind, unkind – Mercy, great Heaven –
    O! – O! –
    Dies.

GIOVANNI: She's dead, alas good soul! The hapless fruit
That in her womb receiv'd its life from me
Hath had from me a cradle and a grave.
I must not dally. This sad marriage-bed,
In all her best, bore her alive and dead.
Soranzo, thou hast miss'd thy aim in this;   *100*
I have prevented now thy reaching plots
And kill'd a love, for whose each drop of blood
I would have pawn'd my heart. Fair Annabella,
How over-glorious art thou in thy wounds,
Triumphing over infamy and hate!
Shrink not, courageous hand, stand up, my heart,
And boldly act my last and greater part.
    Exit with the body.

93. *unkind:* unnatural (and cruel).
101. *prevented:* forestalled.   *reaching:* far-reaching*

SCENE SIX

A banquet. Enter CARDINAL, FLORIO, DONADO,
SORANZO, RICHARDETTO, VASQUES *and Attendants;*
they take their places.

VASQUES: Remember, sir, what you have to do; be wise
and resolute.

SORANZO: Enough; my heart is fix'd. – Pleaseth your
grace
To taste these coarse confections? Though the use
Of such set entertainments more consists
In custom than in cause, yet, reverend sir,
I am still made your servant by your presence.

CARDINAL: And we your friend.

SORANZO: But where's my brother, Giovanni?
Enter GIOVANNI *with a heart upon his dagger.*

GIOVANNI: Here, here, Soranzo; trimm'd in reeking
10   blood
That triumphs over death; proud in the spoil
Of love and vengeance! Fate, or all the powers
That guide the motions of immortal souls
Could not prevent me.

CARDINAL: What means this?

FLORIO: Son Giovanni!

SORANZO: Shall I be forestalled?

GIOVANNI: Be not amaz'd; if your misgiving hearts
Shrink at an idle sight, what bloodless fear
20   Of coward passion would have seiz'd your senses
Had you beheld the rape of life and beauty
Which I have acted? My sister, O, my sister!

FLORIO: Ha! What of her?

GIOVANNI: The glory of my deed
  Darken'd the midday sun, made noon as night.
  You came to feast, my lords, with dainty fare;
  I came to feast too, but I digg'd for food
  In a much richer mine than gold or stone
  Of any value balanc'd; 'tis a heart,
  A heart, my lords, in which is mine entomb'd.
  Look well upon't; d'ee know't?   30

VASQUES: What strange riddle's this?

GIOVANNI: 'Tis Annabella's heart, 'tis; why d'ee startle?
  I vow 'tis hers; this dagger's point plough'd up
  Her fruitful womb, and left to me the fame
  Of a most glorious executioner.

FLORIO: Why, madman, art thyself?

GIOVANNI: Yes, father, and that times to come may
    know
  How as my fate I honoured my revenge,
  List, father, to your ears I will yield up
  How much I have deserv'd to be your son.   40

FLORIO: What is't thou say'st?

GIOVANNI: Nine moons have had their changes,
  Since I first throughly view'd and truly lov'd
  Your daughter and my sister.

FLORIO: How! – Alas,
  My lords, he's a frantic madman!

GIOVANNI: Father, no.
  For nine months' space in secret I enjoy'd
  Sweet Annabella's sheets; nine months I liv'd
  A happy monarch of her heart and her.
  Soranzo, thou know'st this; thy paler cheek
  Bears the confounding print of thy disgrace;
  For her too fruitful womb too soon bewray'd   50

50. *bewray'd*: revealed.

119

The happy passage of our stol'n delights,
And made her mother to a child unborn.
CARDINAL: Incestuous villain!
FLORIO: O, his rage belies him.
GIOVANNI: It does not; 'tis the oracle of truth;
I vow it is so.
SORANZO: I shall burst with fury!
Bring the strumpet forth.
VASQUES: I shall, sir.
          Exit VASQUES.
GIOVANNI: Do, sir. – Have you all no faith
To credit yet my triumphs? Here I swear
By all that you call sacred, by the love
60   I bore my Annabella whilst she liv'd,
These hands have from her bosom ripp'd this heart.
          Enter VASQUES.
Is't true or no, sir?
VASQUES: 'Tis most strangely true.
FLORIO: Cursed man! – have I liv'd to –
          Dies.
CARDINAL: Hold up, Florio. –
Monster of children, see what thou hast done,
Broke thy old father's heart. – Is none of you
Dares venture on him?
GIOVANNI: Let 'em. O, my father,
How well his death becomes him in his griefs!
Why, this was done with courage; now survives
None of our house but I, gilt in the blood
70   Of a fair sister and a hapless father.
SORANZO: Inhuman scorn of men, hast thou a thought
T'outlive thy murders?

51. *passage:* course.
53. *rage . . . him:* madness makes him lie.

GIOVANNI: Yes, I tell thee, yes;
  For in my fists I bear the twists of life.
  Soranzo, see this heart which was thy wife's?
  Thus I exchange it royally for thine,
    [*Stabs him.*]
  And thus and thus! Now brave revenge is mine.

VASQUES: I cannot hold any longer. – You, sir, are you
  grown insolent in your butcheries? Have at you!

GIOVANNI: Come, I am arm'd to meet thee.
    [*They*] *fight,* [*and* GIOVANNI *is wounded.*]

VASQUES: No, will it not be yet? If this will not, another   80
  shall. Not yet? I shall fit you anon. – Vengeance!
    Enter Banditti [*and fight* GIOVANNI].

GIOVANNI: Welcome, come more of you whate'er you
  be;
  I dare your worst –
  O, I can stand no longer; feeble arms,
  Have you so soon lost strength?

VASQUES: Now you are welcome, sir! – Away, my
  masters, all is done, shift for yourselves! Your reward is
  your own, shift for yourselves!

BANDITTI: Away, away!
    Exeunt Banditti.

VASQUES: How d'ee, lord? See you this? How is't?   90

SORANZO: Dead; but in death well pleased that I have
  liv'd
  To see my wrongs reveng'd on that black devil.
  O Vasques, to thy bosom let me give
  My last of breath: let not that lecher live – O! –
    Dies.

VASQUES: The reward of peace and rest be with him, my
  ever dearest lord and master.

GIOVANNI: Whose hand gave me this wound?

VASQUES: Mine, sir; I was your first man. Have you
  enough?

100 GIOVANNI: I thank thee; thou hast done for me but what
  I would have else done on myself. Art sure
  Thy lord is dead?

VASQUES: O, impudent slave! As sure as I am sure to see
  thee die.

CARDINAL: Think on thy life and end and call for mercy.

GIOVANNI: Mercy? Why, I have found it in this justice.

CARDINAL: Strive yet to cry for Heaven.

GIOVANNI: O, I bleed fast.
  Death, thou art a guest long look'd for; I embrace
  Thee and thy wounds. O, my last minute comes!

110 Where'er I go, let me enjoy this grace:
  Freely to view my Annabella's face.
      Dies.

DONADO: Strange miracle of justice!

CARDINAL: Raise up the city; we shall be murdered all.

VASQUES: You need not fear, you shall not; this strange
  task being ended I have paid the duty to the son which
  I have vowed to the father.

CARDINAL: Speak, wretched villain, what incarnate fiend
  Hath led thee on to this?

VASQUES: Honesty, and pity of my master's wrongs; for
120 know, my lord, I am by birth a Spaniard, brought forth
  my country in my youth by Lord Soranzo's father whom,
  whilst he lived, I served faithfully; since whose death
  I have been to this man, as I was to him. What I have
  done is duty, and I repent nothing but that the loss of my
  life had not ransomed his.

CARDINAL: Say, fellow, know'st thou any yet unnam'd
  Of counsel in this incest?

VASQUES: Yes, an old woman, sometimes guardian to this
murdered lady.

CARDINAL: And what's become of her?   *130*

VASQUES: Within this room she is, whose eyes, after her
confession, I caused to be put out, but kept alive to
confirm what from Giovanni's own mouth you have
heard. Now, my lord, what I have done you may judge
of, and let your own wisdom be a judge in your own
reason.

CARDINAL: Peace! First, this woman chief in these
  effects,
My sentence is that forthwith she be ta'en
Out of the city, for example's sake,
There to be burnt to ashes.

DONADO: 'Tis most just.   *140*

CARDINAL: Be it your charge, Donado; see it done.

DONADO: I shall.

VASQUES: What for me? If death, 'tis welcome. I have
been honest to the son as I was to the father.

CARDINAL: Fellow, for thee, since what thou didst was
  done
Not for thyself, being no Italian,
We banish thee forever, to depart
Within three days; in this we do dispense
With grounds of reason, not of thine offence.

VASQUES: 'Tis well; this conquest is mine; and I rejoice *150*
that a Spaniard outwent an Italian in revenge.

  Exit VASQUES.

CARDINAL: Take up these slaughter'd bodies; see them
  buried,

128. *sometimes:* formerly.
137. *chief . . . effects:* principal in these events.
148–9. *dispense with:* pardon.

123

And all the gold and jewels, or whatsoever
Confiscate by the canons of the church,
We seize upon to the pope's proper use.

RICHARDETTO [*discovers himself*]: Your grace's pardon;
    thus long I liv'd disguis'd
To see the effect of pride and lust at once
Brought both to shameful ends.

CARDINAL: What, Richardetto whom we thought for
    dead?

DONADO: Sir, was it you –

RICHARDETTO: Your friend.

160 CARDINAL: We shall have time
To talk at large of all, but never yet
Incest and murder have so strangely met.
Of one so young, so rich in nature's store,
Who could not say, 'Tis pity she's a whore?

    Exeunt.

155. *proper*: own.

FINIS

[Printer's Apology, 1633]

The general commendation deserved by the actors in their presentment of this tragedy may easily excuse such few faults as are escaped in the printing. A common charity may allow him the ability of spelling whom a secure confidence assures that he cannot ignorantly err in the application of sense.

THE
BROKEN
HEART.

A Tragedy.

ACTED
By the K I N G S Majesties Seruants
at the priuate House in the
B L A C K - F R I E R S.

Fide Honor.

LONDON:
Printed by *I. B.* for H V G H B E E S T O N, and are to
be sold at his Shop, neere the *Castle* in
Corne-hill. 1 6 3 3.

THE EPISTLE DEDICATORY

*To The Most Worthy Deserver of the
noblest titles in honour, William, Lord Craven,
Baron of Hampstead-Marshall.*

My Lord:

The glory of a great name, acquired by a greater glory of action, hath in all ages lived the truest chronicle to his own memory. In the practice of which argument, your growth to perfection (even in youth) hath appeared so sincere, so unflattering a penman, that posterity cannot with more delight read the merit of noble en-   5
deavours, than noble endeavours merit thanks from posterity to be read with delight. Many nations, many eyes have been witnesses of your deserts, and loved them: be pleased, then, with the freedom of your own nature, to admit one, amongst all, particularly into the list of such as honour a fair example of nobility. There is a kind   10
of humble ambition, not uncommendable, when the silence of study breaks forth into discourse, coveting rather encouragement than applause; yet herein censure commonly is too severe an auditor, without the moderation of an able patronage. I have ever been slow in courtship of greatness, not ignorant of such defects   15
as are frequent to opinion; but the justice of your inclination to industry emboldens my weakness of confidence to relish an experience of your mercy, as many brave dangers have tasted of your courage. Your lordship strove to be known to the world (when the world knew you least) by voluntary but excellent   20
attempts: like allowance I plead of being known to your lordship (in this low presumption) by tendering, to a favourable entertain-ment, a devotion offered from a heart, that can be as truly sensible of any least respect as ever profess the owner in my best, my readiest services. A lover of your natural love to virtue,   25

JOHN FORD

16. *opinion*: self-conceit.   22-3. *entertainment*: reception.

The Scene: SPARTA

*The Speakers' names fitted to their
Qualities.*

AMYCLAS,	*Common to the Kings of Laconia*
ITHOCLES, Honour of loveliness,	*A favourite*
ORGILUS, Angry,	*Son to Crotolon*
BASSANES, Vexation,	*A jealous nobleman*
ARMOSTES, An appeaser,	*A councillor of state*
CROTOLON, Noise,	*Another councillor*
PROPHILUS, Dear,	*Friend to Ithocles*
NEARCHUS, Young Prince,	*Prince of Argos*
TECNICUS, Artist,	*A philosopher*
HEMOPHIL, Glutton, ⎫ GRONEAS, Tavern-haunter, ⎭	*Two courtiers*
AMELUS, Trusty,	*Friend to Nearchus*
PHULAS, Watchful,	*Servant to Bassanes*
CALANTHA, Flower of beauty,	*The King's daughter*
PENTHEA, Complaint,	*Sister to Ithocles*
EUPHRANEA, Joy,	*A maid of honour*
CHRISTALLA, Crystal, ⎫ PHILEMA, A kiss, ⎭	*Maids of honour*
GRAUSIS, Old bedlam,	*Overseer of Penthea*

Persons Included

THRASUS, Fierceness,	*Father of Ithocles [already dead]*
APLOTES, Simplicity,	*Orgilus so disguised*

THE PROLOGUE

Our scene is Sparta. He whose best of art
Hath drawn this piece calls it *The Broken Heart*.
The title lends no expectation here
Of apish laughter, or of some lame jeer
At place or persons; no pretended clause   5
Of jests fit for a brothel courts applause
From vulgar admiration. Such low songs,
Tun'd to unchaste ears, suit not modest tongues.
The Virgin Sisters then deserv'd fresh bays
When innocence and sweetness crown'd their lays;   10
Then vices gasp'd for breath, whose whole commerce
Was whipp'd to exile by unblushing verse.
This law we keep in our presentment now,
Not to take freedom more than we allow.
What may be here thought a fiction, when time's youth   15
Wanted some riper years was known a truth;
In which, if words have cloth'd the subject right,
You may partake a pity with delight.

9. *Virgin Sisters*: the Muses.   *bays*: garland awarded to poets.
13. *presentment*: presentation.   16. *Wanted*: lacked.

ACT ONE

SCENE ONE

Enter CROTOLON *and* ORGILUS.

CROTOLON: Dally not further; I will know the reason
   That speeds thee to this journey.

ORGILUS: Reason, good sir?
   I can yield many.

CROTOLON: Give me one, a good one;
   Such I expect, and ere we part must have.
   Athens? Pray why to Athens? You intend not
   To kick against the world, turn cynic, stoic,
   Or read the logic lecture, or become
   An Areopagite, and judge in causes
   Touching the commonwealth? For as I take it,
   The budding of your chin cannot prognosticate   10
   So grave an honour.

ORGILUS: All this I acknowledge.

CROTOLON: You do? Then, son, if books and love of
     knowledge
   Inflame you to this travel, here in Sparta
   You may as freely study.

ORGILUS: 'Tis not that, sir.

CROTOLON: Not that, sir? As a father I command thee
   To acquaint me with the truth.

ORGILUS: Thus I obey 'ee:
   After so many quarrels as dissention,

7. *read . . . lecture:* study logic.
10. *The . . . chin:* i.e. lack of beard, youth.

Fury and rage had broach'd in blood, and sometimes
With death to such confederates as sided
20   With now dead Thrasus and yourself, my lord,
Our present king, Amyclas, reconcil'd
Your eager swords and seal'd a gentle peace.
Friends you profess'd yourselves, which to confirm,
A resolution for a lasting league
Betwixt your families was entertain'd,
By joining in a Hymenean bond
Me and the fair Penthea, only daughter
To Thrasus.

CROTOLON: What of this?

ORGILUS: Much, much, dear sir,
A freedom of converse, an interchange
30   Of holy and chaste love, so fix'd our souls
In a firm growth of union, that no time
Can eat into the pledge. We had enjoy'd
The sweets our vows expected, had not cruelty
Prevented all those triumphs we prepar'd for,
By Thrasus his untimely death.

CROTOLON: Most certain.

ORGILUS: From this time sprouted up that poisonous
      stalk
Of aconite, whose ripened fruit hath ravish'd
All health, all comfort of a happy life;
For Ithocles her brother, proud of youth,
40   And prouder in his power, nourish'd closely
The memory of former discontents.
To glory in revenge, by cunning partly,

26. *Hymenean bond:* i.e. marriage.
29–32. *A freedom . . . pledge:* i.e. a betrothal.
37. *aconite:* wolfsbane, poisonous plant.
40. *closely:* secretly.

Partly by threats, 'a woos at once and forces
His virtuous sister to admit a marriage
With Bassanes, a nobleman in honour
And riches, I confess, beyond my fortunes.

CROTOLON: All this is no sound reason to importune
My leave for thy departure.

ORGILUS: Now it follows.
Beauteous Penthea, wedded to this torture
By an insulting brother, being secretly   50
Compell'd to yield her virgin freedom up
To him who never can usurp her heart
Before contracted mine, is now so yok'd
To a most barbarous thraldom, misery,
Affliction, that he savours not humanity
Whose sorrow melts not into more than pity
In hearing but her name.

CROTOLON: As how, pray?

ORGILUS: Bassanes,
The man that calls her wife, considers truly
What heaven of perfections he is lord of,
By thinking fair Penthea his; this thought   60
Begets a kind of monster-love, which love
Is nurse unto a fear so strong and servile,
As brands all dotage with a jealousy.
All eyes who gaze upon that shrine of beauty,
He doth resolve, do homage to the miracle;
Someone, he is assur'd, may now or then –
If opportunity but sort – prevail.
So much out of a self-unworthiness

43. *at once:* suddenly.   44. *admit:* consent to.
50. *insulting:* arrogant.
55. *savours not humanity:* is barely human.
65. *resolve:* conclude.   67. *sort:* come about.

His fears transport him, not that he finds cause
70 In her obedience but his own distrust.

CROTOLON: You spin out your discourse.

ORGILUS: My griefs are violent;
For knowing how the maid was heretofore
Courted by me, his jealousies grow wild
That I should steal again into her favours
And undermine her virtues, which the gods
Know I nor dare nor dream of. Hence, from hence
I undertake a voluntary exile:
First, by my absence to take off the cares
Of jealous Bassanes; but chiefly, sir,
80 To free Penthea from a hell on earth;
Lastly, to lose the memory of something
Her presence makes to live in me afresh.

CROTOLON: Enough, my Orgilus, enough. To Athens;
I give a full consent. – Alas, good lady! –
We shall hear from thee often?

ORGILUS: Often.

CROTOLON: See,
Thy sister comes to give a farewell.

        Enter EUPHRANEA.

EUPHRANEA: Brother.

ORGILUS: Euphranea, thus upon thy cheeks I print
A brother's kiss, more careful of thine honour,
Thy health, and thy well-doing than my life.
90 Before we part, in presence of our father,
I must prefer a suit to 'ee.

EUPHRANEA: You may style it,
My brother, a command.

ORGILUS: That you will promise
To pass never to any man, however worthy,

91. *prefer*: present.

136

Your faith, till with our father's leave
I give a free consent.

CROTOLON: An easy motion;
I'll promise for her, Orgilus.

ORGILUS: Your pardon;
Euphranea's oath must yield me satisfaction.

EUPHRANEA: By Vesta's sacred fires I swear.

CROTOLON: And I
By great Apollo's beams join in the vow,
Not without thy allowance to bestow her   100
On any living.

ORGILUS: Dear Euphranea,
Mistake me not. Far, far 'tis from my thought,
As far from any wish of mine, to hinder
Preferment to an honourable bed
Or fitting fortune. Thou art young and handsome,
And 'twere injustice – more, a tyranny –
Not to advance thy merit. Trust me, sister,
It shall be my first care to see thee match'd
As may become thy choice and our contents.
I have your oath.

EUPHRANEA: You have. But mean you, brother,   110
To leave us as you say?

CROTOLON: Ay, ay, Euphranea;
He has just grounds direct him. I will prove
A father and a brother to thee.

EUPHRANEA: Heaven
Does look into the secrets of all hearts.
Gods, you have mercy with 'ee, else –

CROTOLON: Doubt nothing
Thy brother will return in safety to us.

95. *motion:* proposal.   109. *contents:* satisfaction.
115. *nothing:* not. See note.

137

ORGILUS: Souls sunk in sorrows never are without
  'em;
  They change fresh airs, but bear their griefs about 'em.
    Exeunt.

SCENE TWO

Flourish. Enter AMYCLAS *the King,* ARMOSTES, PRO-
PHILUS, *and attendants.*

AMYCLAS: The Spartan gods are gracious; our humility
  Shall bend before their altars and perfume
  Their temples with abundant sacrifice.
  See, lords, Amyclas your old king is ent'ring
  Into his youth again. I shall shake off
  This silver badge of age, and change this snow
  For hairs as gay as are Apollo's locks.
  Our heart leaps in new vigour.
ARMOSTES: May old time
  Run back to double your long life, great sir.
10 AMYCLAS: It will, it must, Armostes. Thy bold nephew,
  Death-braving Ithocles, brings to our gates
  Triumphs and peace upon his conquering sword.
  Laconia is a monarchy at length;
  Hath in this latter war trod underfoot
  Messene's pride; Messene bows her neck
  To Lacedemon's royalty. O, 'twas
  A glorious victory, and doth deserve
  More than a chronicle: a temple, lords,
  A temple to the name of Ithocles. –
  Where didst thou leave him, Prophilus?
20 PROPHILUS: At Pephon,

Most gracious sovereign. Twenty of the noblest
Of the Messenians there attend your pleasure
For such conditions as you shall propose
In settling peace and liberty of life.

AMYCLAS: When comes your friend the general?

PROPHILUS: He promis'd
To follow with all speed convenient.

   Enter CROTOLON, CALANTHA, CHRISTALLA,
   PHILEMA, *and* EUPHRANEA.

AMYCLAS: Our daughter. – Dear Calantha, the happy
   news,
The conquest of Messene, hath already
Enrich'd thy knowledge.

CALANTHA: With the circumstance
And manner of the fight related faithfully   30
By Prophilus himself. But pray, sir, tell me,
How doth the youthful general demean
His actions in these fortunes?

PROPHILUS: Excellent princess,
Your own fair eyes may soon report a truth
Unto your judgement, with what moderation,
Calmness of nature, measure, bounds and limits
Of thankfulness and joy 'a doth digest
Such amplitude of his success, as would
In others moulded of a spirit less clear
Advance 'em to comparison with heaven.   40
But Ithocles –

CALANTHA: Your friend –

PROPHILUS: He is so, madam,
In which the period of my fate consists.
He in this firmament of honour stands
Like a star fix'd, not mov'd with any thunder

32. *demean:* conduct.   42. *period:* high point.

    Of popular applause or sudden lightning
    Of self-opinion. He hath serv'd his country
    And thinks 'twas but his duty.
CROTOLON: You describe
    A miracle of man.
AMYCLAS: Such, Crotolon,
    On forfeit of a king's word, thou wilt find him. –
    Flourish.
50 Hark, warning of his coming. All attend him.
    Enter ITHOCLES, HEMOPHIL, *and* GRONEAS; *the rest*
    of the Lords ushering him in.
AMYCLAS: Return into these arms, thy home, thy
    sanctuary,
    Delight of Sparta, treasure of my bosom,
    Mine own, own Ithocles.
ITHOCLES: Your humblest subject.
ARMOSTES: Proud of the blood I claim an interest in
    As brother to thy mother, I embrace thee,
    Right noble nephew.
ITHOCLES: Sir, your love's too partial.
CROTOLON: Our country speaks by me, who by thy
    valour,
    Wisdom and service, shares in this great action,
    Returning thee, in part of thy due merits,
    A general welcome.
60 ITHOCLES: You exceed in bounty.
CALANTHA: Christalla, Philema, the chaplet! – Ithocles,
    Upon the wings of fame, the singular
    And chosen fortune of an high attempt
    Is borne so past the view of common sight,
    That I myself, with mine own hands, have wrought

59. *in part of*: in part payment for.
61. *chaplet*: victor's garland.

To crown thy temples this provincial garland.
Accept, wear, and enjoy it as our gift
Deserv'd, not purchas'd.

THOCLES: Y'are a royal maid.

AMYCLAS: She is in all our daughter.

THOCLES: Let me blush,
Acknowledging how poorly I have serv'd,   70
What nothings I have done compar'd with th'honours
Heap'd on the issue of a willing mind.
In that lay mine ability, that only.
For who is he so sluggish from his birth,
So little worthy of a name or country,
That owes not out of gratitude for life
A debt of service, in what kind soever
Safety or counsel of the commonwealth
Requires for payment?

CALANTHA: 'A speaks truth.

THOCLES: Whom heaven
Is pleas'd to style victorious, there, to such,   80
Applause runs madding, like the drunken priests
In Bacchus's sacrifices, without reason,
Voicing the leader-on a demi-god,
Whenas indeed each common soldier's blood
Drops down as current coin in that hard purchase
As his, whose much more delicate condition
Hath suck'd the milk of ease. Judgement commands,
But resolution executes. I use not,
Before this royal presence, these fit slights
As in contempt of such as can direct.   90

66. *provincial:* awarded to conqueror of a province.
73. *that:* i.e. a willing mind.
85. *current:* sterling, opposite of counterfeit.
89. *fit slights:* fitting self-deprecations.

My speech hath other end, not to attribute
All praise to one man's fortune which is strengthed
By many hands. For instance, here is Prophilus,
A gentleman – I cannot flatter truth –
Of such desert; and, though in other rank,
Both Hemophil and Groneas were not missing
To wish their country's peace. For, in a word,
All there did strive their best, and 'twas our duty.

AMYCLAS: Courtiers turn soldiers? We vouchsafe our hand.

    [*They kiss his hand.*]

  Observe your great example.

100 HEMOPHIL: With all diligence.

GRONEAS: Obsequiously and hourly.

AMYCLAS: Some repose
After these toils are needful. We must think on
Conditions for the conquered; they expect 'em.
On! – Come, my Ithocles.

EUPHRANEA [*to* PROPHILUS *who takes her arm*]: Sir, with your favour,
I need not a supporter.

PROPHILUS: Fate instructs me.

  Exeunt, except for HEMOPHIL, GRONEAS, CHRISTALLA
  and PHILEMA. HEMOPHIL *stays* CHRISTALLA;
  GRONEAS, PHILEMA.

CHRISTALLA: With me?

PHILEMA: Indeed, I dare not stay.

HEMOPHIL: Sweet lady,
Soldiers are blunt. – Your lip.

CHRISTALLA: Fie, this is rudeness!
You went not hence such creatures.

    100. *Observe:* pay respect to.
    103. *expect:* await.

GRONEAS: Spirit of valour
  Is a mounting nature.
PHILEMA: It appears so.
  Pray, in earnest, how many men apiece   110
  Have you two been the death of?
GRONEAS: Faith, not many;
  We were compos'd of mercy.
HEMOPHIL: For our daring
  You heard the general's approbation
  Before the king.
CHRISTALLA: You wish'd your country's peace;
  That show'd your charity. Where are your spoils
  Such as the soldier fights for?
PHILEMA: They are coming.
CHRISTALLA: By the next carrier, are they not?
GRONEAS: Sweet Philema,
  When I was in the thickest of mine enemies,
  Slashing off one man's head, another's nose,
  Another's arms and legs –
PHILEMA: And all together –   120
GRONEAS: Then would I with a sigh, remember thee,
  And cry, 'Dear Philema, 'tis for thy sake
  I do these deeds of wonder!' Dost not love me
  With all thy heart now?
PHILEMA: Now as heretofore.
  I have not put my love to use; the principal
  Will hardly yield an interest.
GRONEAS: By Mars,
  I'll marry thee.
PHILEMA: By Vulcan, y'are forsworn,
  Except my mind do alter strangely.

125. *to use:* out at interest.
127. *forsworn:* perjured.   128. *Except:* unless.

GRONEAS: One word.

CHRISTALLA: You lie beyond all modesty. Forbear me.

130 HEMOPHIL: I'll make thee mistress of a city; 'tis
Mine own by conquest.

CHRISTALLA: By petition; sue for't
In forma pauperis. City? Kennel. Gallants,
Off with your feathers; put on aprons, gallants;
Learn to reel, thrum, or trim a lady's dog,
And be good, quiet souls of peace, hobgoblins.

HEMOPHIL: Christalla!

CHRISTALLA: Practise to drill hogs, in hope
To share in the acorns. Soldiers? Corn-cutters,
But not so valiant; they ofttimes draw blood
Which you durst never do. When you have practis'd

140 More wit or more civility, we'll rank 'ee
I'th'list of men. Till then, brave things at arms,
Dare not to speak to us. – Most potent Groneas.

PHILEMA: And Hemophil the hardy – at your services.

Exeunt CHRISTALLA *and* PHILEMA.

GRONEAS: They scorn us as they did before we went.

HEMOPHIL: Hang 'em! Let us scorn them and be
reveng'd.

GRONEAS: Shall we?

HEMOPHIL: We will; and when we slight them
thus
Instead of following them, they'll follow us.
It is a woman's nature.

GRONEAS: 'Tis a scurvy one.

Exeunt.

132. *In . . . pauperis:* as a pauper.
   Kennel: ? gutter ? doghouse.
134. *reel, thrum:* wind thread, weave.
137. *Corn-cutters:* people who cut corns on feet.
141. *list:* catalogue.

SCENE THREE

Enter TECNICUS, *a philosopher; and* ORGILUS *disguised like a scholar of his.*

TECNICUS: Tempt not the stars, young man; thou canst not play
  With the severity of fate. This change
  Of habit and disguise in outward view
  Hides not the secrets of thy soul within thee
  From their quick-piercing eyes, which dive at all times
  Down to thy thoughts. In thy aspect I note
  A consequence of danger.

ORGILUS: Give me leave,
  Grave Tecnicus, without foredooming destiny,
  Under thy roof to ease my silent griefs,
  By applying to my hidden wounds the balm   10
  Of thy oraculous lectures. If my fortune
  Run such a crooked byway as to wrest
  My steps to ruin, yet thy learned precepts
  Shall call me back and set my footings straight.
  I will not court the world.

TECNICUS: Ah, Orgilus,
  Neglects in young men of delights and life
  Run often to extremities. They care not
  For harms to others who contemn their own.

ORGILUS: But I, most learned artist, am not so much
  At odds with nature that I grudge the thrift   20
  Of any true deserver; nor doth malice

---

7. *consequence:* inference.   8. *foredooming:* prejudging.
18. *contemn:* despise.   19. *artist:* scholar.
20. *thrift:* success.   21. *malice:* discouragement.

Of present hopes so check them with despair,
As that I yield to thought of more affliction
Than what is incident to frailty. Wherefore,
Impute not this retired course of living
Some little time, to any other cause
Than what I justly render: the information
Of an unsettled mind, as the effect
Must clearly witness.

TECNICUS: Spirit of truth inspire thee.

30   On these conditions I conceal thy change,
And willingly admit thee for an auditor.
I'll to my study.

ORGILUS: I to contemplations
In these delightful walks.

    [*Exit* TECNICUS.]

                      Thus metamorphos'd,
I may without suspicion harken after
Penthea's usage and Euphranea's faith.
Love, thou art full of mystery! The deities
Themselves are not secure in searching out
The secrets of those flames, which hidden waste
A breast made tributary to the laws

40   Of beauty. Physic yet hath never found
A remedy to cure a lover's wound.
Ha! Who are those that cross yon private walk
Into the shadowing grove in amorous foldings?

    PROPHILUS *passeth over, supporting* EUPHRANEA, *and*
    whispering.

My sister; O, my sister! 'Tis Euphranea

---

24. *frailty:* human frailty.
27. *information:* spiritual instruction.
31. *auditor:* student.   43. *foldings:* embraces.
s.d. *passeth over:* walks over stage and exits on other side.

With Prophilus, supported too! I would
It were an apparition. Prophilus
Is Ithocles his friend. It strangely puzzles me.
Again? Help me, my book; this scholar's habit
Must stand my privilege. My mind is busy,
Mine eyes and ears are open.
    Walks by, reading.
    Enter again PROPHILUS *and* EUPHRANEA.

PROPHILUS: Do not waste   *50*
The span of this stol'n time, lent by the gods
For precious use, in niceness. Bright Euphranea,
Should I repeat old vows, or study new,
For purchase of belief to my desires –

ORGILUS [*aside*]: Desires?

PROPHILUS: – My service, my integrity, –

ORGILUS [*aside*]: That's better.

PROPHILUS: – I should but repeat a lesson
Oft conn'd without a prompter but thine eyes.
My love is honourable.

ORGILUS [*aside*]:   So was mine
To my Penthea; chastely honourable.

PROPHILUS: Nor wants there more addition to my wish   *60*
Of happiness than having thee a wife,
Already sure of Ithocles a friend,
Firm and unalterable.

ORGILUS [*aside*]:   But a brother
More cruel than the grave.

EUPHRANEA: What can you look for
In answer to your noble protestations
From an unskilful maid, but language suited
To a divided mind?

49. *stand my privilege:* be my right (for being here).
52. *niceness:* coyness.

ORGILUS [*aside*]:   Hold out, Euphranea.

EUPHRANEA: Know, Prophilus, I never undervalued,
From the first time you mentioned worthy love,
70   Your merit, means or person. It had been
A fault of judgement in me, and a dulness
In my affections, not to weigh and thank
My better stars that offered me the grace
Of so much blissfulness. For to speak truth,
The law of my desires kept equal pace
With yours, nor have I left that resolution.
But only in a word, whatever choice
Lives nearest in my heart must first procure
Consent both from my father and my brother,
Ere he can own me his.

80 ORGILUS [*aside*]:   She is forsworn else.

PROPHILUS: Leave me that task.

EUPHRANEA: My brother, ere he parted
To Athens, had my oath.

ORGILUS [*aside*]:   Yes, yes, 'a had sure.

PROPHILUS: I doubt not with the means the court supplies
But to prevail at pleasure.

ORGILUS [*aside*]:   Very likely.

PROPHILUS: Meantime, best, dearest, I may build my
     hopes
On the foundation of thy constant suff'rance
In any opposition.

EUPHRANEA: Death shall sooner
Divorce life and the joys I have in living,
Than my chaste vows from truth.

PROPHILUS: On thy fair hand
I seal the like.

90 ORGILUS [*aside*]: There is no faith in woman.

86–7 *suff'rance In*: steadfastness in the face of.

Passion, O, be contain'd! My very heartstrings
Are on the tenters.

EUPHRANEA: Sir, we are overheard.
Cupid protect us! 'Twas a stirring, sir,
Of someone near.

PROPHILUS: Your fears are needless, lady.
None have access into these private pleasures
Except some near in court, or bosom student
From Tecnicus his oratory, granted
By special favour lately from the king
Unto the grave philosopher.

EUPHRANEA: Methinks
I hear one talking to himself. I see him.   100

PROPHILUS: 'Tis a poor scholar, as I told you, lady,

ORGILUS [*aside*]: I am discovered – [*Aloud*] Say it: is it
    possible
With a smooth tongue, a leering countenance,
Flattery, or force of reason (I come t'ee, sir)
To turn or to appease the raging sea?
Answer to that. – Your art? What art to catch
And hold fast in a net the sun's small atoms?
No, no; they'll out, they'll out. Ye may as easily
Outrun a cloud driven by a northern blast
As fiddle-faddle so. Peace, or speak sense.   110

EUPHRANEA: Call you this thing a scholar? 'Las, he's
    lunatic.

PROPHILUS: Observe him, sweet; 'tis but his recreation.

ORGILUS: But will you hear a little? You are so tetchy,
You keep no rule in argument. Philosophy
Works not open impossibilities
But natural conclusions. – Mew! Absurd!

92. *tenters*: hooks for stretching cloth.   97. *oratory*: lecture hall.
112. *Observe*: humour.   116. *Mew!*: rubbish!

The metaphysics are but speculations
Of the celestial bodies, or such accidents
As not mix'd perfectly, in the air engender'd,
120   Appear to us unnatural; that's all. –
Prove it. – Yet, with a reverence to your gravity,
I'll baulk illiterate sauciness, submitting
My sole opinion to the touch of writers.
PROPHILUS: Now let us fall in with him.
ORGILUS: Ha, ha, ha!
These apish boys, when they but taste the grammates
And principles of theory, imagine
They can oppose their teachers. Confidence
Leads many into errors.
PROPHILUS: By your leave, sir.
EUPHRANEA: Are you a scholar, friend?
ORGILUS: I am, gay creature,
130   With pardon of your deities, a mushroom
On whom the dew of heaven drops now and then;
The sun shines on me too, I thank his beams;
Sometimes I feel their warmth, and eat and sleep.
PROPHILUS: Does Tecnicus read to thee?
ORGILUS: Yes, forsooth;
He is my master surely. Yonder door
Opens upon his study.
PROPHILUS: Happy creatures!
Such people toil not, sweet, in heats of state,
Nor sink in thaws of greatness; their affections
Keep order with the limits of their modesty;
140   Their love is love of virtue. – What's thy name?
ORGILUS: Aplotes, sumptuous master; a poor wretch.
EUPHRANEA: Dost thou want anything?

123. *touch:* test.   125. *grammates:* rudiments.
134. *read to:* teach.   139. *modesty:* moderation.

ORGILUS: Books, Venus, books.

PROPHILUS: Lady, a new conceit comes in my thought,
  And most available for both our comforts.

EUPHRANEA: My lord?

PROPHILUS: Whiles I endeavour to deserve
  Your father's blessing to our loves, this scholar
  May daily at some certain hours attend
  What notice I can write of my success
  Here in this grove, and give it to your hands;
  The like from you to me. So can we never,   150
  Barr'd of our mutual speech, want sure intelligence.
  And thus our hearts may talk when our tongues
    cannot.

EUPHRANEA: Occasion is most favourable; use it.

PROPHILUS: Aplotes, wilt thou wait us twice a day,
  At nine i'th'morning and at four at night,
  Here in this bower, to convey such letters
  As each shall send to other? Do it willingly,
  Safely, and secretly, and I will furnish
  Thy study, or what else thou canst desire.

ORGILUS: Jove, make me thankful, thankful, I beseech
    thee,   160
  Propitious Jove. I will prove sure and trusty.
  You will not fail me books?

PROPHILUS: Nor aught besides
  Thy heart can wish. This lady's name's Euphranea,
  Mine Prophilus.

ORGILUS: I have a pretty memory;
  It must prove my best friend. I will not miss
  One minute of the hours appointed.

143. *conceit:* idea.   144. *available:* advantageous.
147. *attend:* await.   151. *sure intelligence:* certain information.
164. *pretty:* fine.

PROPHILUS: Write
  The books thou wouldst have bought thee in a note,
  Or take thyself some money.
ORGILUS: No, no money;
  Money to scholars is a spirit invisible;
170 We dare not finger it. Or books, or nothing.
PROPHILUS: Books of what sort thou wilt. Do not forget
  Our names.
ORGILUS: I warrant 'ee, I warrant 'ee.
PROPHILUS: Smile, Hymen, on the growth of our
    desires;
  We'll feed thy torches with eternal fires.
    Exeunt [PROPHILUS *and* EUPHRANEA].
ORGILUS: Put out thy torches, Hymen, or their light
  Shall meet a darkness of eternal night.
  Inspire me, Mercury, with swift deceits;
  Ingenious fate has leapt into mine arms,
  Beyond the compass of my brain. Mortality
180 Creeps on the dung of earth, and cannot reach
  The riddles which are purpos'd by the gods.
  Great acts best write themselves in their own stories;
  They die too basely who outlive their glories.
    Exit.

  180. *reach:* comprehend.

ACT TWO

SCENE ONE

Enter BASSANES *and* PHULAS.

BASSANES: I'll have that window next the street damm'd
    up;
  It gives too full a prospect to temptation,
  And courts a gazer's glances. There's a lust
  Committed by the eye that sweats and travails,
  Plots, wakes, contrives, till the deformed bear-whelp,
  Adultery, be lick'd into the act,
  The very act. That light shall be damm'd up,
  D'ee hear, sir?
PHULAS: I do hear, my lord; a mason
  Shall be provided suddenly.
BASSANES: Some rogue,
  Some rogue of your confederacy, factor   10
  For slaves and strumpets, to convey close packets
  From this spruce springal and the tother youngster,
  That gaudy earwig, or my lord, your patron,
  Whose pensioner you are. I'll tear thy throat out,
  Son of a cat, ill-looking hound's-head; rip up
  Thy ulcerous maw if I but scent a paper,
  A scroll, but half as big as what can cover
  A wart upon thy nose, a spot, a pimple,
  Directed to my lady. It may prove

7. *light:* window.
9. *suddenly:* at once.
10. *factor:* agent.
11. *close packets:* secret missives.
12. *springal:* youth.
13. *earwig:* flatterer (creeps into ear).

20   A mystical preparative to lewdness.

PHULAS: Care shall be had; I will turn every thread
    About me to an eye. – [*Aside*] Here's a sweet life!

BASSANES: The city housewives, cunning in the traffic
    Of chamber-merchandise, set all at price
    By wholesale, yet they wipe their mouths, and simper,
    Cull, kiss, and cry 'sweetheart', and stroke the head
    Which they have branch'd, and all is well again:
    Dull clods of dirt, who dare not feel the rubs
    Stuck on their foreheads!

PHULAS: 'Tis a villainous world,
    One cannot hold his own in't.

30 BASSANES: Dames at court
    Who flaunt in riots run another bias:
    Their pleasure heaves the patient ass that suffers
    Up on the stilts of office, titles, incomes;
    Promotion justifies the shame and sues for't.
    Poor honour! thou are stabb'd and bleed'st to death
    By such unlawful hire. The country mistress
    Is yet more wary, and in blushes hides
    Whatever trespass draws her troth to guilt.
    But all are false. On this truth I am bold:

40   No woman but can fall, and doth, or would. –
    Now for the newest news about the city;
    What blab the voices, sirrah?

PHULAS: O, my lord,
    The rarest, quaintest, strangest, tickling news
    That ever –

20. *mystical*: secret.
26. *Cull*: embrace.
27. *branch'd*: furnished with cuckold's horns.
28. *rubs*: obstacles, unevennesses (term from bowls).
31. *riots*: extravagant living.
    bias: direction (term from bowls).

BASSANES: Heyday! Up and ride me, rascal!
    What is't?
PHULAS: Forsooth, they say, the king has mew'd
    All his grey beard, instead of which is budded
    Another of a pure carnation colour,
    Speckled with green and russet.
BASSANES: Ignorant block!
PHULAS: Yes truly, and 'tis talk'd about the streets,
    That since Lord Ithocles came home, the lions   50
    Never left roaring, at which noise the bears
    Have danc'd their very hearts out.
BASSANES: Dance out thine, too.
PHILUS: Besides, Lord Orgilus is fled to Athens
    Upon a fiery dragon, and 'tis thought
    'A never can return.
BASSANES: Grant it, Apollo.
PHULAS: Moreover, please your lordship, 'tis reported
    For certain that whoever is found jealous
    Without apparent proof that 's wife is wanton,
    Shall be divorc'd. But this is but she-news;
    I had it from a midwife. I have more yet.   60
BASSANES: Antic, no more; idiots and stupid fools
    Grate my calamities. Why, to be fair
    Should yield presumption of a faulty soul!
    Look to the doors.
PHULAS [aside]:   The horn of plenty crest him.
        Exit PHULAS.
BASSANES: Swarms of confusion huddle in my thoughts
    In rare distemper. Beauty! O, it is
    An unmatch'd blessing or a horrid curse.

---

45. *mew'd:* moulted.   61. *Antic:* fool.   62. *Grate:* irritate.
63. *yield presumption:* cause suspicion.
64. *horn of plenty:* confusion of cornucopia and cuckold's horns.

Enter PENTHEA *and* GRAUSIS, *an old lady.*

She comes, she comes. So shoots the morning forth,
Spangled with pearls of transparent dew.
70   The way to poverty is to be rich,
As I in her am wealthy, but for her
In all contents a bankrupt. – Lov'd Penthea,
How fares my heart's best joy?

GRAUSIS: In sooth not well,
She is so over-sad.

BASSANES: Leave chattering, magpie. –
Thy brother is return'd, sweet, safe and honour'd
With a triumphant victory. Thou shalt visit him;
We will to court, where, if it be thy pleasure,
Thou shalt appear in such a ravishing lustre
Of jewels above value, that the dames
80   Who brave it there, in rage to be outshin'd,
Shall hide them in their closets, and unseen,
Fret in their tears, whiles every wond'ring eye
Shall crave none other brightness but thy presence.
Choose thine own recreations, be a queen
Of what delights thou fanciest best, what company,
What place, what times, do anything, do all things
Youth can command, so thou wilt chase these clouds
From the pure firmament of thy fair looks.

GRAUSIS: Now 'tis well said, my lord. – What, lady?
Laugh,
Be merry, time is precious.

90 BASSANES [*aside*]:   Furies whip thee!

PENTHEA: Alas, my lord, this language to your handmaid
Sounds as would music to the deaf. I need
No braveries nor cost of art to draw
The whiteness of my name into offence.

80. *brave it:* display their finery.

156

Let such, if any such there are, who covet
A curiosity of admiration,
By laying out their plenty to full view,
Appear in gaudy outsides. My attires
Shall suit the inward fashion of my mind,
From which, if your opinion nobly plac'd   *100*
Change not the livery your words bestow,
My fortunes with my hopes are at the highest.

BASSANES: This house, methinks, stands somewhat too
    much inward;
  It is too melancholy. We'll remove
  Nearer the court. Or what thinks my Penthea
  Of the delightful island we command?
  Rule me as thou canst wish.

PENTHEA: I am no mistress;
  Whither you please I must attend; all ways
  Are alike pleasant to me.

GRAUSIS: Island? Prison.
  A prison is as gaysome. We'll no islands.   *110*
  Marry out upon 'em! Whom shall we see there?
  Seagulls, and porpoises, and water-rats,
  And crabs, and mews, and dogfish? Goodly gear
  For a young lady's dealing, or an old one's.
  On no terms islands; I'll be stew'd first.

BASSANES [*aside to* GRAUSIS]:   Grausis,
  You are a juggling bawd! – This sadness, sweetest,
  Becomes not youthful blood. – [*Aside to* GRAUSIS]
    I'll have you pounded! –
    For my sake put on a more cheerful mirth;

96. *curiosity of admiration:* desire for admiration of others.
101. *livery:* ? delivery (of property into one's possession. Legal term).
113. *mews:* gulls.
116. *juggling:* cheating.   117. *pounded:* locked up.

Thou't mar thy cheeks, and make me old in griefs.
   – [*Aside to* GRAUSIS] Damnable bitch-fox!
120 GRAUSIS: I am thick of hearing
   Still when the wind blows southerly. What think 'ee
   If your fresh lady breed young bones, my lord?
   Would not a chopping boy d'ee good at heart?
   But as you said –
BASSANES [*aside*]: I'll spit thee on a stake,
   Or chop thee into collops.
GRAUSIS: Pray speak louder.
   Sure, sure, the wind blows south still.
PENTHEA: Thou prat'st madly.
BASSANES: 'Tis very hot; I sweat extremely.
   Enter PHULAS.
                                   – Now?

PHULAS: A herd of lords, sir.
BASSANES: Ha?
PHULAS: A flock of ladies.
BASSANES: Where?
PHULAS: Shoals of horses.
BASSANES: Peasant, how?
PHULAS: Caroches
130 In drifts – th'one enter, th'other stand without, sir.
   And now I vanish.
       Exit PHULAS.
       Enter PROPHILUS, HEMOPHIL, GRONEAS, CHRIST-
       ALLA, *and* PHILEMA.
PROPHILUS: Noble Bassanes.
BASSANES: Most welcome, Prophilus, ladies, gentlemen,
   To all my heart is open, you all honour me, –

123. *chopping*: strapping.   125. *collops*: slices (of meat).
129. *caroches*: luxurious coaches.
130. *drifts*: herds.

   [*Aside*] A tympany swells in my head already –
Honour me bountifully. – [*Aside*] How they flutter,
Wagtails and jays together.

PROPHILUS: From your brother,
By virtue of your love to him, I require
Your instant presence, fairest.

PENTHEA: He is well, sir?

PROPHILUS: The gods preserve him ever. Yet, dear
   beauty,
I find some alteration in him lately,   140
Since his return to Sparta. My good lord,
I pray use no delay.

BASSANES: We had not needed
An invitation if his sister's health
Had not fallen into question. – Haste, Penthea,
Slack not a minute. – Lead the way, good Prophilus,
I'll follow step by step.

PROPHILUS: Your arm, fair madam.
   Exeunt all except BASSANES *and* GRAUSIS.

BASSANES: One word with your old bawdship. Th'hadst
   been better
Rail'd at the sins thou worshipp'st than have thwarted
My will. I'll use thee cursedly.

GRAUSIS: You dote;
You are beside yourself. A politician   150
In jealousy? No, y'are too gross, too vulgar.
Pish, teach not me my trade; I know my cue.
My crossing you sinks me into her trust,
By which I shall know all. My trade's a sure one.

BASSANES: Forgive me, Grausis; 'twas consideration
I relish'd not. But have a care now.

134. *tympany:* tumour. See note.   150. *politician:* schemer.
155–6. *consideration . . . not:* point I did not consider.

GRAUSIS: Fear not;
  I am no new-come-to't.
BASSANES: Thy life's upon it,
  And so is mine. My agonies are infinite.
    Exeunt.

SCENE TWO

  Enter ITHOCLES *alone.*

ITHOCLES: Ambition? 'Tis of viper's breed; it gnaws
  A passage through the womb that gave it motion.
  Ambition, like a seeled dove, mounts upward,
  Higher and higher still to perch on clouds,
  But tumbles headlong down with heavier ruin.
  So squibs and crackers fly into the air;
  Then only breaking with a noise, they vanish
  In stench and smoke. Morality applied
  To timely practice keeps the soul in tune,
10 At whose sweet music all our actions dance.
  But this is form of books, and school tradition;
  It physics not the sickness of a mind
  Broken with griefs. Strong fevers are not eas'd
  With counsel but with best receipts and means.
  Means, speedy means and certain – that's the cure.
    Enter ARMOSTES *and* CROTOLON.
ARMOSTES: You stick, Lord Crotolon, upon a point
  Too nice and too unnecessary. Prophilus
  Is every way desertful. I am confident

  3. *seeled:* with eyelids sewn together. See note.
  6. *crackers:* fireworks.   9. *timely practice:* present business.
  11. *form of books:* bookish behaviour.
  14. *receipts:* recipes.   17. *nice:* scrupulous.

Your wisdom is too ripe to need instruction
From your son's tutelage.

CROTOLON: Yet not so ripe,   20
My Lord Armostes, that it dares to dote
Upon the painted meat of smooth persuasion,
Which tempts me to a breach of faith.

ITHOCLES: Not yet
Resolv'd, my lord? Why, if your son's consent
Be so available, we'll write to Athens
For his repair to Sparta. The king's hand
Will join with our desires; he had been mov'd to't.

ARMOSTES: Yes, and the king himself importun'd
    Crotolon
For a dispatch.

CROTOLON: Kings may command; their wills
Are laws not to be questioned.

ITHOCLES: By this marriage   30
You knit an union so devout, so hearty,
Between your loves to me and mine to yours,
As if mine own blood had an interest in it;
For Prophilus is mine and I am his.

CROTOLON: My lord, my lord.

ITHOCLES: What, good sir? Speak your thought.

CROTOLON: Had this sincerity been real once,
My Orgilus had not been now unwiv'd,
Nor your lost sister buried in a bride-bed.
Your uncle here, Armostes, knows this truth,
For had your father Thrasus liv'd – but peace   40
Dwell in his grave; I have done.

ARMOSTES: Y'are bold and bitter.

ITHOCLES: 'A presses home the injury; it smarts.

22. *painted*: fraudulent.

No reprehensions, uncle, I deserve 'em. –
Yet, gentle sir, consider what the heat
Of an unsteady youth, a giddy brain,
Green indiscretion, flattery of greatness,
Rawness of judgement, wilfulness in folly,
Thoughts vagrant as the wind and as uncertain,
Might lead a boy in years to. 'Twas a fault,
50   A capital fault, for then I could not dive
Into the secrets of commanding love;
Since when, experience by the extremities – in others –
Hath forc'd me to collect. And trust me, Crotolon,
I will redeem those wrongs with any service
Your satisfaction can require for current.

ARMOSTES: Thy acknowledgement is satisfaction.
  What would you more?

CROTOLON: I'm conquer'd; if Euphranea
  Herself admit the motion, let it be so.
  I doubt not my son's liking.

ITHOCLES: Use my fortunes,
60   Life, power, sword, and heart; all are your own.
      Enter BASSANES, PROPHILUS, CALANTHA, PENTHEA,
        EUPHRANEA, CHRISTALLA, PHILEMA *and* GRAUSIS.

ARMOSTES: The princess with your sister.

CALANTHA: I present 'ee
  A stranger here in court, my lord, for did not
  Desire of seeing you draw her abroad,
  We had not been made happy in her company.

ITHOCLES: You are a gracious princess. – Sister, wedlock
  Holds too severe a passion in your nature,
  Which can engross all duty to your husband,

50. *capital*: deadly.   53. *collect*: draw conclusions.
55. *for current*: as evidence of sincerity.
58. *admit*: accept.

Without attendance on so dear a mistress. —
'Tis not my brother's pleasure, I presume,
T'immure her in a chamber.

BASSANES: 'Tis her will;   70
She governs her own hours. Noble Ithocles,
We thank the gods for your success and welfare.
Our lady had of late been indispos'd,
Else we had waited on you with the first.

ITHOCLES: How does Penthea now?

PENTHEA: You best know, brother,
From whom my healths and comforts are deriv'd.

BASSANES [aside]: I like the answer well; 'tis sad and
   modest.
There may be tricks yet, tricks. — Have an eye,
   Grausis.

CALANTHA: Now, Crotolon, the suit we join'd in must
   not
Fall by too long demur.

CROTOLON: 'Tis granted, princess,   80
For my part.

ARMOSTES: With condition that his son
Favour the contract.

CALANTHA: Such delay is easy. —
The joys of marriage make thee, Prophilus,
A proud deserver of Euphranea's love,
And her of thy desert.

PROPHILUS: Most sweetly gracious.

BASSANES: The joys of marriage are the heaven on
   earth,
Life's paradise, great princess, the soul's quiet,
Sinews of concord, earthly immortality,
Eternity of pleasures; no restoratives

68. *mistress*: i.e. Calantha.   77. *sad*: sober.

90 Like to a constant woman. – [*Aside*] But where is she?
'Twould puzzle all the gods but to create
Such a new monster. – I can speak by proof,
For I rest in Elysium; 'tis my happiness.

CROTOLON: Euphranea, how are you resolv'd – speak freely –
In your affections to this gentleman?

EUPHRANEA: Nor more nor less than as his love assures me;
Which (if your liking with my brother's warrants)
I cannot but approve in all points worthy.

CROTOLON: So, so; I know your answer.

ITHOCLES: 'T had been pity
100 To sunder hearts so equally consented.

    Enter HEMOPHIL.

HEMOPHIL: The king, Lord Ithocles, commands your presence, –
And, fairest princess, yours.

CALANTHA: We will attend him.

    Enter GRONEAS.

GRONEAS: Where are the lords? All must unto the king
Without delay. The prince of Argos –

CALANTHA: Well, sir?

GRONEAS: Is coming to the court, sweet lady.

CALANTHA: How!
The Prince of Argos?

GRONEAS: 'Twas my fortune, madam,
T'enjoy the honour of these happy tidings.

ITHOCLES: Penthea.

PENTHEA: Brother?

ITHOCLES: Let me an hour hence
Meet you alone within the palace grove;

___

97. *warrants*: sanctions.

I have some secret with you. [*To* PROPHILUS] Prithee
  friend,   110

  Conduct her thither, and have special care
  The walks be clear'd of any to disturb us.
PROPHILUS: I shall.
BASSANES [*aside*]: How's that?
ITHOCLES: Alone, pray be alone. –
  I am your creature, princess. – On, my lords.
    Exeunt [*all except*] BASSANES.
BASSANES: Alone, alone? What means that word 'alone'?
  Why might not I be there? – Hum! – He's her brother;
  Brothers and sisters are but flesh and blood,
  And this same whoreson court-ease is temptation
  To a rebellion in the veins. – Besides,
  His fine friend Prophilus must be her guardian.   120
  Why may not he dispatch a business nimbly
  Before the other come? – Or pand'ring, pand'ring
  For one another? Be't to sister, mother,
  Wife, cousin, anything 'mongst youths of mettle
  Is in request. It is so – stubborn fate!
  But if I be a cuckold and can know it,
  I will be fell and fell.
    Enter GRONEAS.
GRONEAS: My lord, y'are call'd for.
BASSANES: Most heartily I thank ye. Where's my wife,
  pray?
GRONEAS: Retir'd amongst the ladies.
BASSANES: Still I thank'ee.
  There's an old waiter with her; saw you her too?   130
GRONEAS: She sits i'th' presence lobby fast asleep, sir.
BASSANES: Asleep? Sleep, sir?

125. *in request*: fashionable. *stubborn*: harsh.
127. *fell*: cruel.   130. *waiter*: attendant (Grausis).

GRONEAS: Is your lordship troubled?
You will not to the king?
BASSANES: Your humblest vassal.
GRONEAS: Your servant, my good lord.
BASSANES: I wait your footsteps.
    Exeunt.

SCENE THREE

[Enter] PROPHILUS *[and]* PENTHEA.

PROPHILUS: In this walk, lady, will your brother find you.
    And with your favour, give me leave a little
    To work a preparation. In his fashion,
    I have observ'd of late some kind of slackness
    To such alacrity as nature once
    And custom took delight in; sadness grows
    Upon his recreations, which he hoards
    In such a willing silence that to question
    The grounds will argue little skill in friendship
    And less good manners.
10 PENTHEA: Sir, I'm not inquisitive
    Of secrecies without an invitation.
PROPHILUS: With pardon, lady, not a syllable
    Of mine implies so rude a sense. The drift –
        Enter ORGILUS *[disguised]*.
    Do thy best
    To make this lady merry for an hour.
ORGILUS: Your will shall be a law, sir.
        Exit [PROPHILUS].
PENTHEA: Prithee leave me;

---

3. *fashion*: way of life.   8. *willing*: determined.

I have some private thoughts I would account with;
Use thou thine own.

ORGILUS: Speak on, fair nymph, our souls
Can dance as well to music of the spheres
As any's who have feasted with the gods.   20

PENTHEA: Your school terms are too troublesome.

ORGILUS: What heaven
Refines mortality from dross of earth,
But such as uncompounded beauty hallows
With glorified perfection?

PENTHEA: Set thy wits
In a less wild proportion.

ORGILUS: Time can never
On the white table of unguilty faith
Write counterfeit dishonour. Turn those eyes,
The arrows of pure love, upon that fire
Which once rose to a flame, perfum'd with vows
As sweetly scented as the incense smoking   30
On Vesta's altars; virgin tears, like
The holiest odours, sprinkled dews to feed 'em
And to increase their fervour.

PENTHEA: Be not frantic.

ORGILUS: All pleasures are but mere imagination
Feeding the hungry appetite with steam
And sight of banquet, whilst the body pines,
Not relishing the real taste of food.
Such is the leanness of a heart divided
From intercourse of troth – contracted loves.
No horror should deface that precious figure   40
Seal'd with the lively stamp of equal souls.

21. *school terms*: scholastic jargon.
23. *uncompounded*: unmixed, pure.
25. *proportion*: order.   26. *table*: tablet.   34. *mere*: absolute.

PENTHEA: Away! Some fury hath bewitch'd thy tongue;
  The breath of ignorance that flies from thence
  Ripens a knowledge in me of afflictions
  Above all suff'rance. Thing of talk, be gone,
  Be gone without reply.

ORGILUS: Be just, Penthea,
  In thy commands. When thou send'st forth a doom
  Of banishment, know first on whom it lights.
  Thus I take off the shroud in which my cares
50 Are folded up from view of common eyes.
    [*Removes his scholar's gown.*]
  What is thy sentence next?

PENTHEA: Rash man, thou layest
  A blemish on mine honour with the hazard
  Of thy too desperate life. Yet I profess,
  By all the laws of ceremonious wedlock,
  I have not given admittance to one thought
  Of female change since cruelty enforc'd
  Divorce betwixt my body and my heart.
  Why would you fall from goodness thus?

ORGILUS: O rather,
  Examine me how I could live to say
60 I have been much, much wrong'd. 'Tis for thy sake
  I put on this imposture. Dear Penthea,
  If thy soft bosom be not turn'd to marble,
  Thou't pity our calamities. My interest
  Confirms me thou art mine still.

PENTHEA: Lend your hand.
  With both of mine I clasp it thus, thus kiss it,
  Thus kneel before ye.
    [*Kneels.*]

47. *doom:* judgement.   56. *change:* changefulness.

ORGILUS: You instruct my duty.
  [*Kneels.*]
PENTHEA: We may stand up. Have you aught else to
  urge
  Of new demand? As for the old, forget it;
  'Tis buried in an everlasting silence,
  And shall be, shall be ever. What more would ye?   *70*
ORGILUS: I would possess my wife; the equity
  Of very reason bids me.
PENTHEA: Is that all?
ORGILUS: Why, 'tis the all of me myself.
PENTHEA: Remove
  Your steps some distance from me. At this space
  A few words I dare change. But first put on
  Your borrowed shape.
    [ORGILUS *resumes his disguise.*]
ORGILUS: You are obey'd; 'tis done.
PENTHEA: How, Orgilus, by promise I was thine,
  The heavens do witness; they can witness, too,
  A rape done on my truth. How I do love thee
  Yet, Orgilus, and yet, must best appear   *80*
  In tendering thy freedom, for I find
  The constant preservation of thy merit,
  By thy not daring to attempt my fame
  With injury of any loose conceit,
  Which might give deeper wounds to discontents.
  Continue this fair race. Then, though I cannot
  Add to thy comfort, yet I shall more often

66. *instruct my duty:* teach me what to do.
75. *change:* exchange.
81. *tendering:* either 1. having concern for. or 2. offering.
    find: discover the true character of.
83. *attempt my fame:* attack my reputation.
84. *loose conceit:* wild idea.   86. *race:* course of action.

Remember from what fortune I am fallen,
And pity mine own ruin. Live, live happy,
90   Happy in thy next choice, that thou mayst people
This barren age with virtues in thy issue.
And oh, when thou art married, think on me
With mercy, not contempt. I hope thy wife,
Hearing my story, will not scorn my fall.
Now let us part.

ORGILUS: Part? Yet advise thee better.
Penthea is the wife to Orgilus,
And ever shall be.

PENTHEA: Never shall nor will.

ORGILUS: How!

PENTHEA: Hear me; in a word I'll tell thee why:
The virgin dowry which my birth bestow'd
100   Is ravish'd by another; my true love
Abhors to think that Orgilus deserv'd
No better favours than a second bed.

ORGILUS: I must not take this reason.

PENTHEA: To confirm it,
Should I outlive my bondage, let me meet
Another worse than this and less desir'd,
If of all the men alive thou shouldst but touch
My lip or hand again.

ORGILUS: Penthea, now
I tell'ee you grow wanton in my sufferance.
Come, sweet, th'art mine.

PENTHEA: Uncivil sir, forbear,
110   Or I can turn affection into vengeance.
Your reputation, if you value any,
Lies bleeding at my feet. Unworthy man,
If ever henceforth thou appear in language,

108. *wanton:* frolicsome, frivolous. *sufferance:* suffering.

Message or letter to betray my frailty,
I'll call thy former protestations lust,
And curse my stars for forfeit of my judgement.
Go thou, fit only for disguise and walks
To hide thy shame. This once I spare thy life.
I laugh at mine own confidence; my sorrows
By thee are made inferior to my fortunes.   120
If ever thou didst harbour worthy love,
Dare not to answer. My good genius guide me,
That I may never see thee more. Go from me.

ORGILUS: I'll tear my veil of politic French off,
And stand up like a man resolv'd to do;
Action, not words, shall show me. O, Penthea!
        Exit ORGILUS.

PENTHEA: 'A sigh'd my name sure as he parted from me;
I fear I was too rough. Alas, poor gentleman,
'A look'd not like the ruins of his youth
But like the ruins of those ruins. Honour,   130
How much we fight with weakness to preserve thee.
        Enter BASSANES *and* GRAUSIS.

BASSANES: Fie on thee! Damn thee, rotten maggot,
    damn thee!
Sleep? Sleep at court? And now? Aches, convulsions,
Impostumes, rheums, gouts, palsies clog thy bones
A dozen years more yet.

GRAUSIS: Now y'are in humours.

BASSANES: She's by herself; there's hope of that. She's
    sad, too;

116. *forfeit:* loss (of judgement about Orgilus' character).
119. *confidence:* trustfulness.
122. *good genius:* guardian angel.
124. *politic French:* cunning dissimulation. See note.
134. *Impostumes:* abscesses.
135. *in humours:* displeased.

She's in strong contemplation. Yes, and fix'd.
The signs are wholesome.

GRAUSIS: Very wholesome, truly.

BASSANES: Hold your chops, nightmare. – Lady, come.
   Your brother
140 I carried to his closet. You must thither.

PENTHEA: Not well, my lord?

BASSANES: A sudden fit; 'twill off;
   Some surfeit or disorder. How dost, dearest?

PENTHEA: Your news is none o'th'best.

   Enter PROPHILUS.

PROPHILUS: The chief of men,
   The excellent Ithocles, desires
   Your presence, madam.

BASSANES: We are hasting to him.

PENTHEA: In vain we labour in this course of life
   To piece our journey out at length, or crave
   Respite of breath; our home is in the grave.

BASSANES: Perfect philosophy. Then let us care
150 To live so that our reckonings may fall even
   When w'are to make account.

PROPHILUS: He cannot fear
   Who builds on noble grounds; sickness or pain
   Is the deserver's exercise, and such
   Your virtuous brother to the world is known.
   Speak comfort to him, lady; be all gentle.
   Stars fall but in the grossness of our sight;
   A good man dying, th'earth doth lose a light.

   Exeunt.

137. *fix'd:* composed.
150. *fall even:* having no balance or debt on either side.
153. *exercise:* habitual employment.

ACT THREE

SCENE ONE

Enter TECNICUS, *and* ORGILUS *in his own shape.*

TECNICUS: Be well advis'd; let not a resolution
  Of giddy rashness choke the breath of reason.
ORGILUS: It shall not, most sage master.
TECNICUS: I am jealous;
  For if the borrowed shape so late put on
  Inferr'd a consequence, we must conclude
  Some violent design of sudden nature
  Hath shook that shadow off, to fly upon
  A new-hatch'd execution. Orgilus,
  Take heed thou hast not, under our integrity,
  Shrouded unlawful plots. Our mortal eyes   10
  Pierce not the secrets of your heart; the gods
  Are only privy to them.
ORGILUS: Learned Tecnicus,
  Such doubts are causeless, and to clear the truth
  From misconceit, the present state commands me.
  The prince of Argos comes himself in person
  In quest of great Calantha for his bride,
  Our kingdom's heir. Besides, mine only sister,
  Euphranea, is dispos'd to Prophilus.
  Lastly, the king is sending letters for me
  To Athens for my quick repair to court.   20
  Please to accept these reasons.

3. *jealous:* suspicious.   8. *execution:* enterprise.
14. *misconceit:* misunderstanding.

TECNICUS: Just ones, Orgilus,
  Not to be contradicted. Yet beware
  Of an unsure foundation; no fair colours
  Can fortify a building faintly jointed.
  I have observ'd a growth in thy aspect
  Of dangerous extent, sudden, and – look to't –
  I might add, certain –
ORGILUS: My aspect? Could art
  Run through mine inmost thoughts, it should not sift
  An inclination there more than what suited
  With justice of mine honour.
30 TECNICUS: I believe it.
  But know then, Orgilus, what honour is:
  Honour consists not in a bare opinion
  By doing any act that feeds content,
  Brave in appearance 'cause we think it brave.
  Such honour comes by accident, not nature,
  Proceeding from the vices of our passion
  Which makes our reason drunk. But real honour
  Is the reward of virtue, and acquir'd
  By justice or by valour, which for basis
40 Hath justice to uphold it. He then fails
  In honour, who for lucre of revenge
  Commits thefts, murders, treasons and adulteries,
  With such like, by intrenching on just laws,
  Whose sov'reignty is best preserv'd by justice.
  Thus as you see, how honour must be grounded
  On knowledge, not opinion; for opinion
  Relies on probability and accident,
  But knowledge on necessity and truth.
  I leave thee to the fit consideration

24. *faintly*: weakly.   33. *feeds content*: satisfies vanity.
41. *lucre of*: gain of. See note.   46. *opinion*: fancy.

Of what becomes the grace of real honour, 50
Wishing success to all thy virtuous meanings.
ORGILUS: The gods increase thy wisdom, reverend
oracle,
And in thy precepts make me ever thrifty.
    Exit ORGILUS.
TECNICUS: I thank thy wish. – Much mystery of fate
Lies hid in that man's fortunes. Curiosity
May lead his actions into rare attempts.
But let the gods be moderators still;
No human power can prevent their will.
    Enter ARMOSTES.
From whence comes 'ee?
ARMOSTES: From King Amyclas. Pardon
My interruption of your studies. Here 60
In this seal'd box he sends a treasure dear
To him as his crown. 'A prays your gravity,
You would examine, ponder, sift and bolt
The pith and circumstance of every tittle
The scroll within contains.
TECNICUS: What is't, Armostes?
ARMOSTES: It is the health of Sparta, the king's life,
Sinews and safety of the commonwealth,
The sum of what the oracle deliver'd,
When last he visited the prophetic temple
At Delphos. What his reasons are for which, 70
After so long a silence, he requires
Your counsel now, grave man, his majesty
Will soon himself acquaint you with.
TECNICUS: Apollo
Inspire my intellect! – The Prince of Argos
Is entertain'd?

51. *meanings:* intentions.   58. *prevent:* forestall.   63. *bolt:* sift.

ARMOSTES: He is, and has demanded
Our princess for his wife, which I conceive
One special cause the king importunes you
For resolution of the oracle.

TECNICUS: My duty to the King, good peace to
       Sparta,
And fair day to Armostes.

80   ARMOSTES: Like to Tecnicus.
       Exeunt.

SCENE TWO

Soft music. A song.

Can you paint a thought? or number
Every fancy in a slumber?
Can you count soft minutes roving
From a dial's point by moving?
Can you grasp a sigh? or lastly
Rob a virgin's honour chastely?
  No, O, no; yet you may
Sooner do both that and this,
This and that, and never miss,
10   *Than by any praise display*
Beauty's beauty; such a glory
As beyond all fate, all story,
  All arms, all arts,
  All loves, all hearts,
Greater than those, or they,
  Do, shall, and must obey.

During which time, enters PROPHILUS, BASSANES,
PENTHEA, GRAUSIS, *passing over the stage;* BASSANES

78. *resolution:* interpretation.

and GRAUSIS *enter again softly, stealing to several stands,*
    and listen.

BASSANES: All silent, calm, secure. – Grausis, no creaking?
    No noise ? Dost hear nothing?

GRAUSIS: Not a mouse
    Or whisper of the wind.

BASSANES: The floor is matted,
    The bed-posts sure are steel and marble. Soldiers   20
    Should not affect, methinks, strains so effeminate.
    Sounds of such delicacy are but fawnings
    Upon the sloth of luxury; they heighten
    Cinders of covert lust up to a flame.

GRAUSIS: What do you mean, my lord? Speak low; that
    gabbling
    Of yours will but undo us.

BASSANES: Chamber combats
    Are felt, not heard.

PROPHILUS [*within*]: 'A wakes.

BASSANES: What's that?

ITHOCLES [*within*]:   Who's there?
    Sister? – All quit the room else.

BASSANES: 'Tis consented.
    Enter PROPHILUS.

PROPHILUS: Lord Bassanes, your brother would be
    private;
    We must forbear. His sleep hath newly left him.   30
    Please 'ee withdraw?

BASSANES: By any means; 'tis fit.

PROPHILUS: Pray gentlewoman, walk too.

GRAUSIS: Yes, I will, sir.
    Exeunt.

S.D. *Several stands:* separate positions.
21. *affect:* like.   23. *luxury:* lechery.

SCENE THREE

ITHOCLES *discovered in a chair, and* PENTHEA.

ITHOCLES: Sit nearer, sister, to me; nearer yet.
We had one father, in one womb took life,
Were brought up twins together, yet have liv'd
At distance like two strangers. I could wish
That the first pillow whereon I was cradl'd
Had prov'd to me a grave.

PENTHEA: You had been happy
Then had you never known that sin of life
Which blots all following glories with a vengeance,
For forfeiting the last will of the dead,
From whom you had your being.

10 ITHOCLES: Sad Penthea,
Thou canst not be too cruel. My rash spleen
Hath with a violent hand pluck'd from thy bosom
A lover-bless'd heart to grind it into dust,
For which mine's now a-breaking.

PENTHEA: Not yet, heaven,
I do beseech thee. First let some wild fires
Scorch, not consume it; may the heat be cherish'd
With desires infinite but hopes impossible.

ITHOCLES: Wrong'd soul, thy prayers are heard.

PENTHEA: Here, lo, I breathe,
A miserable creature led to ruin
By an unnatural brother.

20 ITHOCLES: I consume
In languishing affections for that trespass,
Yet cannot die.

PENTHEA: The handmaid to the wages

178

Of county toil drinks the untroubled streams
With leaping kids and with the bleating lambs,
And so allays her thirst secure, whiles I
Quench my hot sighs with fleetings of my tears.
ITHOCLES: The labourer doth eat his coarsest bread,
Earn'd with his sweat, and lies him down to sleep,
Whiles every bit I touch turns in digestion
To gall, as bitter as Penthea's curse.   30
Put me to any penance for my tyranny
And I will call thee merciful.
PENTHEA: Pray kill me,
Rid me from living with a jealous husband;
Then we will join in friendship, be again
Brother and sister. Kill me, pray. Nay, will 'ee?
ITHOCLES: How does thy lord esteem thee?
PENTHEA: Such an one
As only you have made me: a faith breaker,
A spotted whore. Forgive me. I am one
In act, not in desires, the gods must witness.
ITHOCLES: Thou dost belie thy friend.
PENTHEA: I do not, Ithocles;   40
For she that's wife to Orgilus and lives
In known adultery with Bassanes
Is at the best a whore. Wilt kill me now?
The ashes of our parents will assume
Some dreadful figure, and appear to charge
Thy bloody guilt, that has betray'd their name
To infamy in this reproachful match.
ITHOCLES: After my victories abroad, at home
I meet despair; ingratitude of nature
Hath made my actions monstrous. Thou shalt stand   50

25. *secure:* free from care.   26. *fleetings:* streams.
40. *belie:* misrepresent.

179

A deity, my sister, and be worshipp'd
For thy resolved martyrdom; wrong'd maids
And married wives shall to thy hallowed shrine
Offer their orisons, and sacrifice
Pure turtles crown'd with myrtle, if thy pity
Unto a yielding brother's pressure lend
One finger but to ease it.

PENTHEA: O, no more!

ITHOCLES: Death waits to waft me to the Stygian banks
And free me from this chaos of my bondage;
60   And till thou wilt forgive, I must endure.

PENTHEA: Who is the saint you serve?

ITHOCLES: Friendship, or nearness
Of birth to any but my sister, durst not
Have mov'd that question. 'Tis a secret, sister,
I dare not murmur to myself.

PENTHEA: Let me,
By your new protestations, I conjure 'ee,
Partake her name.

ITHOCLES: Her name? – 'Tis – 'tis – I dare not!

PENTHEA: All your respects are forg'd.

ITHOCLES: They are not. – Peace.
Calantha is the princess, the king's daughter,
Sole heir of Sparta. – Me most miserable!
70   Do I now love thee? For my injuries,
Revenge thyself with bravery, and gossip
My treasons to the king's ears. Do! Calantha
Knows it not yet, nor Prophilus, my nearest.

PENTHEA: Suppose you were contracted to her, would
      it not
Split even your very soul to see her father

55. *turtles:* turtle doves.
71. *with bravery:* in splendid fashion.

180

Snatch her out of your arms against her will
And force her on the Prince of Argos?

ITHOCLES: Trouble not
The fountains of mine eyes with thine own story;
I sweat in blood for't.

PENTHEA: We are reconcil'd.
Alas, sir, being children, but two branches   *80*
Of one stock, 'tis not fit we should divide.
Have comfort, you may find it.

ITHOCLES: Yes, in thee,
Only in thee, Penthea mine.

PENTHEA: If sorrows
Have not too much dull'd my infected brain,
I'll cheer invention for an active strain.

ITHOCLES: Mad man! Why have I wrong'd a maid so
    excellent?

    Enter BASSANES *with a poniard,* PROPHILUS, GRONEAS,
    HEMOPHIL *and* GRAUSIS.

BASSANES: I can forbear no longer; more, I will not!
Keep off your hands, or fall upon my point.
Patience is tir'd, for, like a slow-pac'd ass,
Ye ride my easy nature, and proclaim   *90*
My sloth to vengeance a reproach and property.

ITHOCLES: The meaning of this rudeness?

PROPHILUS: He's distracted.

PENTHEA: O, my griev'd lord!

GRAUSIS: Sweet lady, come not near him;
He holds his perilous weapon in his hand
To prick 'a cares not whom nor where, – see, see, see!

BASSANES: My birth is noble, though the popular blast
Of vanity, as giddy as thy youth,

85. *cheer . . . strain:* plan what to do.   S.D. *poniard:* dagger.
91. *reproach:* mark of disgrace. *property:* general characteristic.

181

Hath rear'd thy name up to bestride a cloud,
Or progress in the chariot of the sun.
100 I am no clod of trade to lackey pride,
Nor like your slave of expectation wait
The bawdy hinges of your doors, or whistle
For mystical conveyance to your bed-sports.
GRONEAS: Fine humours! They become him.
HEMOPHIL: How 'a stares,
Struts, puffs and sweats. Most admirable lunacy!
ITHOCLES: But that I may conceive the spirit of wine
Has took possession of your soberer custom,
I'd say you were unmannerly.
PENTHEA: Dear brother, –
BASSANES: Unmannerly? – Mew, kitling! Smooth
formality
110 Is usher to the rankness of the blood
But impudence bears up the train. Indeed, sir,
Your fiery mettle, or your springal blaze
Of huge renown, is no sufficient royalty
To print upon my forehead the scorn 'cuckold'.
ITHOCLES: His jealousy has robb'd him of his wits;
'A talks 'a knows not what.
BASSANES: Yes, and 'a knows
To whom 'a talks: to one that franks his lust
In swine-security of bestial incest.
ITHOCLES: Ha, devil!
BASSANES: I will halloo't, though I blush more
120 To name the filthiness than thou to act it.
ITHOCLES: Monster!

---

101. *wait:* attend.
105. *admirable:* amazing.
112. *springal:* youthful.
117. *franks:* crams. See note.
103. *mystical:* secret.
109. *kitling:* kitten.
113. *royalty:* warrant.

PROPHILUS: Sir, by our friendship –
PENTHEA: By our bloods,
  Will you quite both undo us, brother?
GRAUSIS: Out on him,
  These are his megrims, firks and melancholies.
HEMOPHIL: Well said, old touch-hole.
GRONEAS: Kick him out at doors.
PENTHEA: With favour, let me speak. – My lord, what
    slackness
  In my obedience hath deserv'd this rage?
  Except humility and silent duty
  Have drawn on your unquiet, my simplicity
  Ne'er studied your vexation.
BASSANES: Light of beauty,
  Deal not ungently with a desperate wound!   130
  No breach of reason dares make war with her
  Whose looks are sovereignty, whose breath is balm.
  O, that I could preserve thee in fruition
  As in devotion!
PENTHEA: Sir, may every evil
  Lock'd in Pandora's box show'r, in your presence,
  On my unhappy head, if, since you made me
  A partner in your bed, I have been faulty
  In one unseemly thought against your honour.
ITHOCLES: Purge not his griefs, Penthea.
BASSANES: Yes, say on,
  Excellent creature. – Good, be not a hindrance   140
  To peace and praise of virtue. – O, my senses
  Are charm'd with sounds celestial. – On, dear, on.

123. *firks:* caprices.
124. *touch-hole:* term of abuse (literally, ignition hole in breech of gun).
133. *fruition:* pleasurable possession.
140. *Good:* good sir (i.e. Ithocles).

I never gave you one ill word. Say, did I?
Indeed I did not.

PENTHEA: Nor, by Juno's forehead,
Was I e'er guilty of a wanton error.

BASSANES: A goddess! Let me kneel.

GRAUSIS: Alas, kind animal.

ITHOCLES: No, but for penance.

BASSANES: Noble sir, what is it?
With gladness I embrace it; yet pray let not
My rashness teach you to be too unmerciful.

ITHOCLES: When you shall show good proof that
150   manly wisdom,
Not oversway'd by passion or opinion,
Knows how to lead your judgement, then this lady,
Your wife, my sister, shall return in safety
Home to be guided by you; but till first
I can, out of clear evidence, approve it,
She shall be my care.

BASSANES: Rip my bosom up;
I'll stand the execution with a constancy.
This torture is unsufferable.

ITHOCLES: Well, sir,
I dare not trust her to your fury.

BASSANES: But
Penthea says not so.

160 PENTHEA: She needs no tongue
To plead excuse who never purpos'd wrong.

HEMOPHIL [to GRAUSIS]: Virgin of reverence and
antiquity,
Stay you behind.

GRONEAS: The court wants not your diligence.
Exeunt all except BASSANES *and* GRAUSIS.

146. *kind:* foolish.   155. *approve:* certify.

GRAUSIS: What will you do, my lord? My lady's gone;
  I am denied to follow.
BASSANES: I may see her,
  Or speak to her once more.
GRAUSIS: And feel her too, man.
  Be of good cheer; she's your own flesh and bone.
BASSANES: Diseases desperate must find cures alike.
  She swore she has been true.
GRAUSIS: True, on my modesty.
BASSANES: Let him want truth who credits not her vows.   *170*
  Much wrong I did her, but her brother infinite.
  Rumour will voice me the contempt of manhood,
  Should I run on thus. Some way I must try
  To outdo art, and cry a jealousy.
    Exeunt.

SCENE FOUR

  Flourish. Enter AMYCLAS, NEARCHUS *leading* CAL-
  ANTHA, ARMOSTES, CROTOLON, EUPHRANEA,
  CHRISTALLA, PHILEMA, *and* AMELUS.

AMYCLAS: Cousin of Argos, what the heavens have pleas'd
  In their unchanging counsels to conclude
  For both our kingdoms' weal, we must submit to.
  Nor can we be unthankful to their bounties,
  Who when we were even creeping to our grave,
  Sent us a daughter; in whose birth our hope
  Continues of succession. As you are
  In title next, being grandchild to our aunt,
  So we in heart desire you may sit nearest
  Calantha's love, since we have ever vow'd   *10*
  Not to enforce affection by our will,

But by her own choice to confirm it gladly.
NEARCHUS: You speak the nature of a right just father.
    I come not hither roughly to demand
    My cousin's thraldom but to free mine own.
    Report of great Calantha's beauty, virtue,
    Sweetness, and singular perfections, courted
    All ears to credit what I find was publish'd
    By constant truth; from which, if any service
20   Of my desert can purchase fair construction,
    This lady must command it.
CALANTHA: Princely sir,
    So well you know how to profess observance,
    That you instruct your hearers to become
    Practitioners in duty, of which number
    I'll study to be chief.
NEARCHUS: Chief, glorious virgin,
    In my devotions, as in all men's wonder.
AMYCLAS: Excellent cousin, we deny no liberty;
    Use thine own opportunities. – Armostes,
    We must consult with the philosophers;
    The business is of weight.
30 ARMOSTES: Sir, at your pleasure.
AMYCLAS: You told me, Crotolon, your son's return'd
    From Athens. Wherefore comes 'a not to court
    As we commanded?
CROTOLON: He shall soon attend
    Your royal will, great sir.
AMYCLAS: The marriage
    Between young Prophilus and Euphranea
    Tastes of too much delay.
CROTOLON: My lord.
AMYCLAS: Some pleasures

22. *observance:* courtship.

At celebration of it would give life
To th'entertainment of the prince our kinsman.
Our court wears gravity more than we relish.

ARMOSTES: Yet the heavens smile on all your high
    attempts   40
  Without a cloud.

CROTOLON: So may the gods protect us.

CALANTHA: A prince a subject?

NEARCHUS: Yes, to beauty's sceptre;
  As all hearts kneel, so mine.

CALANTHA: You are too courtly.
    [*Enter*] *to them* ITHOCLES, ORGILUS, PROPHILUS.

ITHOCLES: Your safe return to Sparta is most welcome.
  I joy to meet you here, and as occasion
  Shall grant us privacy, will yield you reasons
  Why I should covet to deserve the title
  Of your respected friend. For, without compliment,
  Believe it, Orgilus, 'tis my ambition.

ORGILUS: Your lordship may command me your poor
  servant.   50

ITHOCLES [*aside*]: So amorously close? – so soon? – my
  heart!

PROPHILUS: What sudden change is next?

ITHOCLES: Life to the king,
  To whom I here present this noble gentleman,
  New come from Athens. Royal sir, vouchsafe
  Your gracious hand in favour of his merit.

CROTOLON [*aside*]: My son preferr'd by Ithocles!

AMYCLAS: Our bounties
  Shall open to thee, Orgilus. For instance,
  Hark in thine ear: if out of those inventions

40. *high attempts:* noble enterprises.
56. *preferr'd:* presented.

Which flow in Athens thou hast there engross'd
60   Some rarity of wit to grace the nuptials
Of thy fair sister, and renown our court
In th'eyes of this young prince, we shall be debtor
To thy conceit. Think on't.

ORGILUS: Your highness honours me.

NEARCHUS: My tongue and heart are twins.

CALANTHA: A noble birth.
Becoming such a father. – Worthy Orgilus,
You are a guest most wish'd for.

ORGILUS: May my duty
Still rise in your opinion, sacred princess.

ITHOCLES: Euphranea's brother, sir, a gentleman
Well worthy of your knowledge.

NEARCHUS: We embrace him,
Proud of so dear acquaintance.

70   AMYCLAS: All prepare
For revels and disport. The joys of Hymen,
Like Phoebus in his lustre, puts to flight
All mists of dulness. Crown the hours with gladness.
No sounds but music, no discourse but mirth.

CALANTHA: Thine arm, I prithee, Ithocles. – Nay, good
My lord, keep on your way; I am provided.

NEARCHUS: I dare not disobey.

ITHOCLES: Most heavenly lady.
    Exeunt.

59. *engross'd:* acquired.   63. *conceit:* invention.

SCENE FIVE

Enter CROTOLON, ORGILUS.

CROTOLON: The king hath spoke his mind.
ORGILUS: His will he hath;
  But were it lawful to hold plea against
  The power of greatness, not the reason, haply
  Such undershrubs as subjects sometimes might
  Borrow of nature justice, to inform
  That licence sovereignty holds without check
  Over a meek obedience.
CROTOLON: How resolve you
  Touching your sister's marriage? Prophilus
  Is a deserving and a hopeful youth.
ORGILUS: I envy not his merit but applaud it;   10
  Could wish him thrift in all his best desires,
  And with a willingness inleague our blood
  With his, for purchase of full growth in friendship.
  He never touch'd on any wrong that malic'd
  The honour of our house, nor stirr'd our peace.
  Yet, with your favour, let me not forget
  Under whose wing he gathers warmth and comfort,
  Whose creature he is bound, made, and must live so.
CROTOLON: Son, son, I find in thee a harsh condition;
  No courtesy can win it; 'tis too rancorous.   20
ORGILUS: Good sir, be not severe in your construction:
  I am no stranger to such easy calms

2. *hold plea:* try an action at law.
5. *inform:* control.   6. *licence:* authority.
10. *envy:* hold malice towards.
14. *malic'd:* intended harm towards.

189

As sit in tender bosoms. Lordly Ithocles
Hath grac'd my entertainment in abundance;
Too humbly hath descended from that height
Of arrogance and spleen which wrought the rape
On griev'd Penthea's purity. His scorn
Of my untoward fortunes is reclaim'd
Unto a courtship, almost to a fawning.
30   I'll kiss his foot since you will have it so.
CROTOLON: Since I will have it so? Friend, I will have
    it so,
Without our ruin by your politic plots
Or wolf of hatred snarling in your breast.
You have a spirit, sir, have ye, a familiar
That posts i'th' air for your intelligence?
Some such hobgoblin hurried you from Athens,
For yet you come unsent for.
ORGILUS: If unwelcome,
I might have found a grave there.
CROTOLON: Sure your business
Was soon dispatch'd, or your mind alter'd quickly.
ORGILUS: 'Twas care, sir, of my health cut short my
40   journey;
For there a general infection
Threatens a desolation.
CROTOLON: And I fear
Thou hast brought back a worse infection with
    thee,
Infection of thy mind; which, as thou sayst,
Threatens the desolation of our family.
ORGILUS: Forbid it, our dear genius. I will rather

---

28. *untoward:* unprosperous. *reclaim'd:* subdued, modified.
35. *posts:* journeys.

Be made a sacrifice on Thrasus' monument,
Or kneel to Ithocles his son in dust,
Than woo a father's curse. My sister's marriage
With Prophilus is from my heart confirm'd.   50
May I live hated, may I die despis'd,
If I omit to further it in all
That can concern me.

CROTOLON: I have been too rough.
My duty to my king made me so earnest;
Excuse it, Orgilus.

ORGILUS: Dear sir.

Enter to them PROPHILUS, EUPHRANEA, ITHOCLES,
        GRONEAS, HEMOPHIL.

CROTOLON: Here comes
Euphranea, with Prophilus and Ithocles.

ORGILUS: Most honoured, ever famous.

ITHOCLES: Your true friend.
On earth not any truer. With smooth eyes
Look on this worthy couple; your consent
Can only make them one.

ORGILUS: They have it. – Sister,   60
Thou pawn'dst to me an oath, of which engagement
I never will release thee if thou aim'st
At any other choice than this.

EUPHRANEA: Dear brother,
At him or none.

CROTOLON: To which my blessing's added.

ORGILUS: Which till a greater ceremony perfect,
Euphranea lend thy hand. – Here take her, Prophilus,
Live long a happy man and wife. And further,
That these in presence may conclude an omen,

58. *smooth:* kindly.
61. *pawn'dst:* pledged.

Thus for a bridal song I close my wishes:

Comforts lasting, loves increasing,
Like soft hours never ceasing;
Plenty's pleasure, peace complying,
Without jars, or tongues envying;
Hearts by holy union wedded
More than theirs by custom bedded;
Fruitful issues; life so graced,
Not by age to be defaced;
Budding, as the year ensu'th,
Every spring another youth:
All what thought can add beside
Crown this bridegroom and this bride.

PROPHILUS: You have seal'd joy close to my soul. –
    Euphranea,
Now I may call thee mine.

ITHOCLES: I but exchange
One good friend for another.

ORGILUS: If these gallants
Will please to grace a poor invention
By joining with me in some slight device,
I'll venture on a strain my younger days
Have studied for delight.

HEMOPHIL: With thankful willingness
I offer my attendance.

GRONEAS: No endeavour
Of mine shall fail to show itself.

ITHOCLES: We will
All join to wait on thy directions, Orgilus.

ORGILUS: O, my good lord, your favours flow towards
A too unworthy worm. But as you please,
I am what you will shape me.

ITHOCLES: A fast friend.

CROTOLON: I thank thee, son, for this acknowledgement;
   It is a sight of gladness.
ORGILUS: But my duty.
   Exeunt.

SCENE SIX

Enter CALANTHA, PENTHEA, CHRISTALLA, PHILEMA.

CALANTHA: Whoe'er would speak with us, deny his
      entrance;
   Be careful of our charge.
CHRISTALLA: We shall, madam.
CALANTHA: Except the king himself, give none
      admittance,
   Not any.
PHILEMA: Madam, it shall be our care.
      Exeunt [CHRISTALLA *and* PHILEMA].
CALANTHA: Being alone, Penthea, you have granted
   The opportunity you sought, and might
   At all times have commanded.
PENTHEA: 'Tis a benefit
   Which I shall owe your goodness even in death for.
   My glass of life, sweet princess, hath few minutes
   Remaining to run down; the sands are spent;   10
   For by an inward messenger I feel
   The summons of departure short and certain.
CALANTHA: You feed too much your melancholy.
PENTHEA: Glories
   Of human greatness are but pleasing dreams
   And shadows soon decaying. On the stage

9. *glass:* hourglass.

Of my mortality, my youth hath acted
Some scenes of vanity, drawn out at length
By varied pleasures, sweeten'd in the mixture
But tragical in issue. Beauty, pomp,
20 With every sensuality our giddiness
Doth frame an idol, are unconstant friends
When any troubled passion makes assault
On the unguarded castle of the mind.

CALANTHA: Contemn not your condition for the proof
Of bare opinion only. To what end
Reach all these moral texts?

PENTHEA: To place before 'ee
A perfect mirror, wherein you may see
How weary I am of ling'ring life,
Who count the best a misery.

CALANTHA: Indeed,
30 You have no little cause; yet none so great
As to distrust a remedy.

PENTHEA: That remedy
Must be a winding-sheet, a fold of lead,
And some untrod-on corner in the earth.
Not to detain your expectation, princess,
I have an humble suit.

CALANTHA: Speak and enjoy it.

PENTHEA: Vouchsafe, then, to be my executrix,
And take that trouble on 'ee to dispose
Such legacies as I bequeath impartially.
I have not much to give; the pains are easy;
40 Heaven will reward your piety and thank it
When I am dead. For sure I must not live,
I hope I cannot.

19. *issue:* outcome.   20. *sensuality:* pleasure of the senses.
24. *contemn:* despise.

CALANTHA: Now beshrew thy sadness;
  Thou turnst me too much woman.
PENTHEA [*aside*]:   Her fair eyes
  Melt into passion. Then I have assurance
  Encouraging my boldness. – In this paper
  My will was character'd, which you, with pardon,
  Shall now know from mine own mouth.
CALANTHA: Talk on, prithee,
  It is a pretty earnest.
PENTHEA: I have left me
  But three poor jewels to bequeath. The first is
  My youth; for though I am much old in griefs,   *50*
  In years I am a child.
CALANTHA: To whom that?
PENTHEA: To virgin-wives, such as abuse not wedlock
  By freedom of desires, but covet chiefly
  The pledges of chaste beds for ties of love,
  Rather than ranging of their blood; and next,
  To married maids such as prefer the number
  Of honourable issue in their virtues,
  Before the flattery of delights by marriage:
  May those be ever young.
CALANTHA: A second jewel
  You mean to part with.
PENTHEA: 'Tis my fame, I trust   *60*
  By scandal yet untouch'd. This I bequeath
  To Memory, and Time's old daughter, Truth.
  If ever my unhappy name find mention
  When I am fall'n to dust, may it deserve
  Beseeming charity without dishonour.

44. *passion*: pity.   46. *character'd*: written.
48. *earnest*: foretaste.   55. *ranging*: roving.

CALANTHA: How handsomely thou play'st with harmless
    sport
  Of mere imagination. Speak the last;
  I strangely like thy will.
PENTHEA: This jewel, madam,
  Is dearly precious to me. You must use
70 The best of your discretion to employ
  The gift as I intend it.
CALANTHA: Do not doubt me.
PENTHEA: 'Tis long agone since first I lost my heart,
  Long I have liv'd without it, else for certain
  I should have given that too. But instead
  Of it, to great Calantha, Sparta's heir,
  By service bound and by affection vow'd,
  I do bequeath in holiest rites of love
  Mine only brother, Ithocles.
CALANTHA: What saidst thou?
PENTHEA: Impute not, heaven-blest lady, to ambition,
80 A faith as humbly perfect as the prayers
  Of a devoted suppliant can endow it.
  Look on him, princess, with an eye of pity;
  How like the ghost of what he late appear'd
  'A moves before you.
CALANTHA [aside]:   Shall I answer here
  Or lend my ear too grossly?
PENTHEA: First, his heart
  Shall fall in cinders, scorch'd by your disdain,
  Ere he will dare, poor man, to ope an eye
  On these divine looks, but with low-bent thoughts
  Accusing such presumption. As for words,
90 'A dares not utter any but of service;
  Yet this lost creature loves 'ee. Be a princess

  85. *grossly:* indelicately.

In sweetness as in blood; give him his doom,
Or raise him up to comfort.

CALANTHA: What new change
Appears in my behaviour, that thou dar'st
Tempt my displeasure?

PENTHEA: I must leave the world
To revel in Elysium, and 'tis just
To wish my brother some advantage here.
Yet by my best hopes, Ithocles is ignorant
Of this pursuit. But if you please to kill him,
Lend him one angry look or one harsh word,   *100*
And you shall soon conclude how strong a power
Your absolute authority holds over
His life and end.

CALANTHA: You have forgot, Penthea,
How still I have a father.

PENTHEA: But remember
I am a sister, though to me this brother
Hath been, you know, unkind; O, most unkind!

CALANTHA: Christalla, Philema, where are 'ee? – Lady,
Your check lies in my silence.

    Enter CHRISTALLA *and* PHILEMA.

BOTH: Madam, here.

CALANTHA: I think 'ee sleep, 'ee drones; wait on Penthea
Unto her lodging. – [*Aside*] Ithocles? Wrong'd lady!   *110*

PENTHEA: My reckonings are made even. Death or fate
Can now nor strike too soon, nor force too late.

    Exeunt.

108. *check:* reproof.

ACT FOUR

SCENE ONE

Enter ITHOCLES *and* ARMOSTES.

ITHOCLES: Forbear your inquisition. Curiosity
Is of too subtle and too searching nature;
In fears of love too quick, too slow of credit.
I am not what you doubt me.

ARMOSTES: Nephew, be then
As I would wish. All is not right. Good heaven
Confirm your resolutions for dependence
On worthy ends which may advance your quiet.

ITHOCLES: I did the noble Orgilus much injury,
But griev'd Penthea more. I now repent it,
10   Now, uncle, now! This 'now' is now too late.
So provident is folly in sad issue,
That after-wit, like bankrupts' debts, stand tallied
Without all possibilities of payment.
Sure he's an honest, very honest gentleman;
A man of single meaning.

ARMOSTES: I believe it.
Yet, nephew, 'tis the tongue informs our ears;
Our eyes can never pierce into the thoughts
For they are lodg'd too inward. But I question
No truth in Orgilus. – The princess, sir.

ITHOCLES: The princess? Ha!

4. *doubt me:* suspect me to be.   11. *provident:* fertile.
12. *after-wit:* wisdom after the event.
15. *of single meaning:* sincere, direct.

ARMOSTES: With her the Prince of Argos.   *20*

    Enter NEARCHUS *leading* CALANTHA; AMELUS,
    CHRISTALLA, PHILEMA.

NEARCHUS: Great fair one, grace my hopes with any
    instance

  Of livery from the allowance of your favour –
  This little spark.

    [*Indicating* CALANTHA's *ring.*]

CALANTHA: A toy.

NEARCHUS: Love feasts on toys,
  For Cupid is a child. Vouchsafe this bounty;
  It cannot be denied.

CALANTHA: You shall not value,
  Sweet cousin, at a price what I count cheap,
  So cheap, that let him take it who dares stoop for't,
  And give it at next meeting to a mistress;
  She'll thank him for't, perhaps.

    Casts it to ITHOCLES.

AMELUS: The ring, sir, is
  The princess's; I could have took it up.   *30*

ITHOCLES: Learn manners, prithee. – To the blessed
    owner,

  Upon my knees.

    [*Offers the ring to* CALANTHA.]

NEARCHUS: Y'are saucy.

CALANTHA: This is pretty.
  I am, belike, a mistress. Wondrous pretty.
  Let the man keep his fortune since he found it;
  He's worthy on't. – On, cousin.

ITHOCLES [*to* AMELUS]:   Follow, spaniel!
  I'll force 'ee to a fawning else.

AMELUS: You dare not.

    21–2. *instance of livery:* badge of service.

Exeunt all except ITHOCLES *and* ARMOSTES.

ARMOSTES: My lord, you were too forward.

ITHOCLES: Look 'ee, uncle:
 Some such there are whose liberal contents
 Swarm without care in every sort of plenty;
40 Who, after full repasts, can lay them down
 To sleep; and they sleep, uncle, in which silence
 Their very dreams present 'em choice of pleasures;
 Pleasures – observe me, uncle – of rare object:
 Here heaps of gold, there increments of honours,
 Now change of garments, then the votes of people,
 Anon varieties of beauties, courting
 In flatteries of the night, exchange of dalliance;
 Yet these are still but dreams. Give me felicity
 Of which my senses waking are partakers,
50 A real, visible, material happiness;
 And then too, when I stagger in expectance
 Of the least comfort that can cherish life.
 I saw it, sir, I saw it; for it came
 From her own hand.

ARMOSTES: The princess threw it t'ee.

ITHOCLES: True, and she said – well, I remember what.
 Her cousin prince would beg it.

ARMOSTES: Yes, and parted
 In anger at your taking on't.

ITHOCLES: Penthea!
 O, thou hast pleaded with a powerful language!
 I want a fee to gratify thy merit.
 But I will do –

ARMOSTES: What is't you say?

60 ITHOCLES: In anger,

---

38. *liberal contents:* unrestrained satisfactions.
59. *want . . . merit:* lack a fitting reward for your deserts.

In anger let him part; for, could his breath,
Like whirlwinds, toss such servile slaves as lick
The dust his footsteps print, into a vapour,
It durst not stir a hair of mine. It should not;
I'd rend it up by th'roots first. To be anything
Calantha smiles on is to be a blessing
More sacred than a petty prince of Argos
Can wish to equal, or in worth or title.

ARMOSTES: Contain yourself, my lord. Ixion aiming
To embrace Juno bosom'd but a cloud   70
And begat centaurs. 'Tis a useful moral:
Ambition hatch'd in clouds of mere opinion
Proves but in birth a prodigy.

ITHOCLES: I thank 'ee.
Yet with your licence, I should seem uncharitable
To gentler fate if, relishing the dainties
Of a soul's settled peace, I were so feeble
Not to digest it.

ARMOSTES: He deserves small trust
Who is not privy counsellor to himself.

      Enter NEARCHUS, ORGILUS, *and* AMELUS.

NEARCHUS: Brave me?

ORGILUS: Your excellence mistakes his temper,
For Ithocles, in fashion of his mind,   80
Is beautiful, soft, gentle, the clear mirror
Of absolute perfection.

AMELUS: Was't your modesty
Term'd any of the prince his servants 'spaniel'?
Your nurse sure taught you other language.

ITHOCLES: Language!

NEARCHUS: A gallant man at arms is here, a doctor

----

72. *mere opinion:* absolute self-conceit.
73. *prodigy:* monster.   85. *doctor:* man learned.

In feats of chivalry, blunt and rough spoken,
Vouchsafing not the fustian of civility
Which less rash spirits style good manners.

ITHOCLES: Manners!

ORGILUS: No more, illustrious sir; 'tis matchless Ithocles.

NEARCHUS: You might have understood who I am.

90 ITHOCLES: Yes,
I did – else – but the presence calm'd th'affront;
Y'are cousin to the princess.

NEARCHUS: To the king too,
A certain instrument that lent supportance
To your colossic greatness; to that king too,
You might have added.

ITHOCLES: There is more divinity
In beauty than in majesty.

ARMOSTES: O, fie, fie!

NEARCHUS: This odd youth's pride turns heretic in
      loyalty. –
Sirrah, low mushrooms never rival cedars.
      Exeunt NEARCHUS *and* AMELUS.

ITHOCLES: Come back! – What pitiful dull thing am I
100 So to be tamely scolded at? Come back!
Let him come back and echo once again
That scornful sound of mushroom. Painted colts,
Like heralds' coats gilt o'er with crowns and sceptres,
May bait a muzzled lion.

ARMOSTES: Cousin, cousin,
Thy tongue is not thy friend.

ORGILUS: In point of honour
Discretion knows no bounds. Amelus told me
'Twas all about a little ring.

87. *fustian:* bombast.
91. *presence:* i.e. of royalty.

202

ITHOCLES: A ring
  The princess threw away and I took up.
  Admit she threw't to me, what arm of brass
  Can snatch it hence? No, could 'a grind the hoop   110
  To powder, 'a might sooner reach my heart
  Than steal and wear one dust on't. – Orgilus,
  I am extremely wrong'd.
ORGILUS: A lady's favour
  Is not to be so slighted.
ITHOCLES: Slighted!
ARMOSTES: Quiet
  These vain unruly passions, which will render ye
  Into a madness.
ORGILUS: Griefs will have their vent.
    Enter TECNICUS.
ARMOSTES: Welcome. Thou com'st in season, reverend
    man,
  To pour the balsam of a suppling patience
  Into the festering wound of ill-spent fury.
ORGILUS [*aside*]: What makes he here?
TECNICUS: The hurts are yet but mortal 120
  Which shortly will prove deadly. To the king,
  Armostes, see in safety thou deliver
  This seal'd up counsel. Bid him with a constancy
  Peruse the secrets of the gods. – O Sparta,
  O Lacedemon! double-nam'd, but one
  In fate. When kingdoms reel – mark well my saw –
  Their heads must needs be giddy. Tell the king
  That henceforth he no more must enquire after
  My aged head; Apollo wills it so.
  I am for Delphos.

112. *dust:* particle.
118. *suppling:* healing.

130 ARMOSTES: Not without some conference
　　With our great master.
　　TECNICUS: Never more to see him;
　　A greater prince commands me. – Ithocles,
　　When youth is ripe, and age from time doth part,
　　The lifeless trunk shall wed the broken heart.
　　ITHOCLES: What's this, if understood?
　　TECNICUS: List, Orgilus:
　　Remember what I told thee long before;
　　These tears shall be my witness.
　　ARMOSTES: 'Las, good man.
　　TECNICUS: *Let craft with courtesy a while confer,*
　　　　　　Revenge proves its own executioner.
140 ORGILUS: Dark sentences are for Apollo's priests;
　　I am not Oedipus.
　　TECNICUS: My hour is come.
　　Cheer up the king; farewell to all. – O Sparta,
　　O Lacedemon!
　　　Exit TECNICUS.
　　ARMOSTES: If prophetic fire
　　Have warm'd this old man's bosom, we might construe
　　His words to fatal sense.
　　ITHOCLES: Leave to the powers
　　Above us the effects of their decrees;
　　My burden lies within me. Servile fears
　　Prevent no great effects. – Divine Calantha!
　　ARMOSTES: The gods be still propitious.
　　　Exeunt except ORGILUS.
　　ORGILUS: Something oddly
150 The bookman prated; yet 'a talk'd it weeping.
　　Let craft with courtesy a while confer,
　　Revenge proves its own executioner.

　　148. *prevent:* go before.

204

Con it again; for what? It shall not puzzle me;
'Tis dotage of a withered brain. – Penthea
Forbade me not her presence; I may see her
And gaze my fill. Why, see her then I may,
When, if I faint to speak, I must be silent.

    [*Exit.*]

SCENE TWO

Enter BASSANES, GRAUSIS *and* PHULAS.

BASSANES: Pray use your recreations; all the service
  I will expect is quietness amongst 'ee.
  Take liberty at home, abroad, at all times,
  And in your charities appease the gods
  Whom I with my distractions have offended.
GRAUSIS: Fair blessings on thy heart.
PHULAS [*aside*]:   Here's a rare change:
  My lord, to cure the itch, is surely gelded;
  The cuckold in conceit hath cast his horns.
BASSANES: Betake 'ee to your several occasions,
  And wherein I have heretofore been faulty,   10
  Let your constructions mildly pass it over.
  Henceforth I'll study reformation, – more
  I have not for employment.
GRAUSIS: O, sweet man!
  Thou art the very honeycomb of honesty.
PHULAS: The garland of goodwill. – Old lady, hold up
  Thy reverend snout and trot behind me softly,
  As it becomes a moile of ancient carriage.

    Exeunt except BASSANES.

8. *conceit:* imagination.   9. *several occasions:* different activities.
11. *constructions:* interpretations.

BASSANES: Beasts only capable of sense enjoy
    The benefit of food and ease with thankfulness;
20   Such silly creatures, with a grudging, kick not
    Against the portion nature hath bestow'd.
    But men, endow'd with reason and the use
    Of reason to distinguish from the chaff
    Of abject scarcity the quintessence,
    Soul, and elixir of the earth's abundance
    The treasures of the sea, the air, nay heaven,
    Repining at these glories of creation,
    Are verier beasts than beasts. And of those beasts
    The worst am I; I, who was made a monarch
30   Of what a heart could wish for, a chaste wife,
    Endeavour'd what in me lay to pull down
    That temple built for adoration only,
    And level't in the dust of causeless scandal.
    But to redeem a sacrilege so impious,
    Humility shall pour, before the deities
    I have incens'd, a largess of more patience
    Than their displeased altars can require.
    No tempests of commotion shall disquiet
    The calms of my composure.
    Enter ORGILUS.
ORGILUS: I have found thee,
40   Thou patron of more horrors than the bulk
    Of manhood, hoop'd about with ribs of iron,
    Can cram within thy breast. Penthea, Bassanes,
    Curs'd by thy jealousies, – more, by thy dotage –
    Is left a prey to words.
BASSANES: Exercise
    Your trials for addition to my penance;
    I am resolv'd.

18. *capable of sense:* possessing sensory faculties.

ORGILUS: Play not with misery
  Past cure. Some angry minister of fate hath
  Depos'd the empress of her soul, her reason,
  From its most proper throne; but, what's the miracle
  More new, I, I have seen it and yet live!   50

BASSANES: You may delude my senses, not my
    judgement;
  'Tis anchor'd into a firm resolution.
  Dalliance of mirth or wit can ne'er unfix it.
  Practise yet further.

ORGILUS: May thy death of love to her
  Damn all thy comforts to a lasting fast
  From every joy of life. Thou barren rock,
  By thee we have been split in ken of harbour.

    Enter ITHOCLES, PENTHEA, *her hair about her ears,*
    [ARMOSTES,] PHILEMA, CHRISTALLA.

ITHOCLES: Sister, look up, your Ithocles, your brother
  Speaks t'ee. Why do you weep? Dear, turn not from
    me. –
  Here is a killing sight; lo, Bassanes,   60
  A lamentable object.

ORGILUS: Man, dost see't?
  Sports are more gamesome; am I yet in merriment?
  Why dost not laugh?

BASSANES: Divine and best of ladies,
  Please to forget my outrage. Mercy ever
  Cannot but lodge under a roof so excellent.
  I have cast off that cruelty of frenzy
  Which once appear'd, impostor, and then juggled
  To cheat my sleeps of rest.

ORGILUS: Was I in earnest?

54. *Practise yet further:* try even harder.   57. *ken:* sight.
67. *impostor:* deceiving spirit. See note.

PENTHEA: Sure, if we were all sirens we should sing
    pitifully;
70   And 'twere a comely music when in parts
    One sung another's knell. The turtle sighs
    When he hath lost his mate, and yet some say
    'A must be dead first. 'Tis a fine deceit
    To pass away in a dream; indeed, I've slept
    With mine eyes open a great while. No falsehood
    Equals a broken faith. There's not a hair
    Sticks on my head but like a leaden plummet
    It sinks me to the grave. I must creep thither;
    The journey is not long.
ITHOCLES: But thou, Penthea,
80   Hast many years, I hope, to number yet
    Ere thou canst travel that way.
BASSANES: Let the swan first
    Be wrapp'd up in an everlasting darkness,
    Before the light of nature, chiefly form'd
    For the whole world's delight, feel an eclipse
    So universal.
ORGILUS: Wisdom, look 'ee,
    Begins to rave. – Art thou mad too, antiquity?
PENTHEA: Since I was first a wife, I might have been
    Mother to many pretty prattling babes.
    They would have smil'd when I smil'd, and, for certain,
90   I should have cried when they cried. – Truly, brother,
    My father would have pick'd me out a husband,
    And then my little ones had been no bastards.
    But 'tis too late for me to marry now,
    I am past child-bearing; 'tis not my fault.
BASSANES: Fall on me, if there be a burning Etna,

70. *in parts:* each taking an individual part.

And bury me in flames! Sweats hot as sulphur
Boil through my pores. Affliction hath in store
No torture like this.

ORGILUS: Behold a patience! –
Lay by thy whining, grey dissimulation;
Do something worth a chronicle. Show justice   *100*
Upon the author of this mischief; dig out
The jealousies that hatch'd this thraldom first
With thine own poniard. Every antic rapture
Can roar as thine does.

ITHOCLES: Orgilus, forbear.

BASSANES: Disturb him not; it is a talking motion
Provided for my torment. What a fool am I
To bandy passion! Ere I'll speak a word
I will look on and burst.

PENTHEA: I lov'd you once.

ORGILUS: Thou didst, wrong'd creature, in despite of
    malice;
For it I love thee ever.

PENTHEA: Spare your hand;   *110*
Believe me, I'll not hurt it.

ORGILUS: Pain my heart too.

PENTHEA: Complain not though I wring it hard. I'll
    kiss it;
O 'tis a fine soft palm. Hark in thine ear:
Like whom do I look, prithee? Nay, no whispering.
Goodness! we had been happy. Too much happiness
Will make folk proud, they say. – But that is he;
    Points at ITHOCLES.
And yet he paid for't home. Alas, his heart
Is crept into the cabinet of the princess;

103. *antic rapture:* clownish fit of passion (? ham emotion).
117. *home:* fully.

We shall have points and bride-laces. Remember
120 When we last gather'd roses in the garden,
I found my wits, but truly you lost yours.
That's he, and still 'tis he.

ITHOCLES: Poor soul, how idly
Her fancies guide her tongue.

BASSANES: Keep in, vexation,
And break not into clamour.

ORGILUS: She has tutor'd me;
Some powerful inspiration checks my laziness. –
Now let me kiss your hand, griev'd beauty.

PENTHEA: Kiss it. –
Alack, alack, his lips be wondrous cold;
Dear soul, h'as lost his colour. Have 'ee seen
A straying heart? All crannies! every drop
130 Of blood is turn'd to an amethyst,
Which married bachelors hang in their ears.

ORGILUS: Peace usher her into Elysium.
If this be madness, madness is an oracle.

    Exit ORGILUS.

ITHOCLES: Christalla, Philema, when slept my sister,
Her ravings are so wild?

CHRISTALLA: Sir, not these ten days.

PHILEMA: We watch by her continually. Besides,
We cannot any way pray her to eat.

BASSANES: O, misery of miseries!

PENTHEA: Take comfort;
You may live well and die a good old man.
140 By yea and nay, an oath not to be broken,

---

119. *points:* tagged laces used in dress.
    bride-laces: silks used to tie sprigs of rosemary, traditional at a
wedding.   122. *idly:* irrationally.   125. *checks:* reproves.

If you had join'd our hands once in the temple –
'Twas since my father died, for had he liv'd
He would have done't – I must have call'd you father.
O, my wrack'd honour, ruin'd by those tyrants,
A cruel brother and a desperate dotage!
There is no peace left for a ravish'd wife
Widow'd by lawless marriage. To all memory
Penthea's, poor Penthea's name is strumpeted;
But since her blood was season'd by the forfeit
Of noble shame with mixtures of pollution,   *150*
Her blood – 'tis just – be henceforth never heighten'd
With taste of sustenance. Starve; let that fullness
Whose pleurisy hath fever'd faith and modesty –
Forgive me; O, I faint!

ARMOSTES: Be not so wilful,
Sweet niece, to work thine own destruction.

ITHOCLES: Nature
Will call her daughter monster. – What? not eat?
Refuse the only ordinary means
Which are ordain'd for life? Be not, my sister,
A murd'ress to thyself. – Hearst thou this, Bassanes?

BASSANES: Foh! I am busy; for I have not thoughts   *160*
Enow to think. All shall be well anon;
'Tis tumbling in my head. There is a mastery
In art to fatten and keep smooth the outside;
Yes, and to comfort up the vital spirits
Without the help of food: fumes or perfumes,
Perfumes or fumes. Let her alone; I'll search out
The tricks on't.

PENTHEA: Lead me gently; heaven reward ye.
Griefs are sure friends; they leave, without control.

---

145. *desperate*: reckless.   153. *pleurisy*: excess.

Nor cure nor comforts for a leprous soul.
Exeunt the maids supporting PENTHEA.

170 BASSANES: I grant t'ee; and will put in practice instantly
What you shall still admire. 'Tis wonderful,
'Tis super-singular, not to be match'd;
Yet when I've done't, I've done't; ye shall all thank me.
Exit BASSANES.

ARMOSTES: The sight is full of terror.

ITHOCLES: On my soul
Lies such an infinite clog of massy dulness,
As that I have not sense enough to feel it.
See, uncle, th'augury thing returns again.
Shall's welcome him with thunder? We are haunted
And must use exorcism to conjure down
This spirit of malevolence.

180 ARMOSTES: Mildly, nephew.
Enter NEARCHUS *and* AMELUS.

NEARCHUS: I come not, sir, to chide your late disorder,
Admitting that th'inurement to a roughness
In soldiers of your years and fortunes, chiefly
So lately prosperous, hath not yet shook off
The custom of the war in hours of leisure;
Nor shall you need excuse since y'are to render
Account to that fair excellence, the princess,
Who in her private gallery expects it
From your own mouth alone. I am a messenger
But to her pleasure.

190 ITHOCLES: Excellent Nearchus,
Be prince still of my services, and conquer
Without the combat of dispute. I honour 'ee.

NEARCHUS: The king is on a sudden indispos'd;
Physicians are call'd for. 'Twere fit, Armostes,

171. *admire:* wonder at.

You should be near him.

ARMOSTES: Sir, I kiss your hands.
    Exeunt except NEARCHUS *and* AMELUS.

NEARCHUS: Amelus, I perceive Calantha's bosom
  Is warm'd with other fires than such as can
  Take strength from any fuel of the love
  I might address to her. Young Ithocles,
  Or ever I mistake, is lord ascendant   *200*
  Of her devotions, one, to speak him truly,
  In every disposition nobly fashioned.

AMELUS: But can your highness brook to be so rivall'd
  Considering th'inequality of the persons?

NEARCHUS: I can, Amelus; for affections injur'd
  By tyranny, or rigour of compulsion,
  Like tempest-threaten'd trees unfirmly rooted,
  Ne'er spring to timely growth. Observe, for instance,
  Life-spent Penthea and unhappy Orgilus.

AMELUS: How does your grace determine?

NEARCHUS: To be jealous *210*
  In public of what privately I'll further;
  And though they shall not know, yet they shall find it.
  Exeunt.

SCENE THREE

Enter HEMOPHIL *and* GRONEAS *leading* AMYCLAS,
and placing him in a chair, followed by ARMOSTES,
CROTOLON, *and* PROPHILUS.

AMYCLAS: Our daughter is not near?

ARMOSTES: She is retired, sir,
  Into her gallery.

AMYCLAS: Where's the prince our cousin?

PROPHILUS: New walk'd into the grove, my lord.

AMYCLAS: All leave us
  Except Armostes and you, Crotolon;
  We would be private.
PROPHILUS: Health unto your majesty.
    Exeunt PROPHILUS, HEMOPHIL, *and* GRONEAS.
AMYCLAS: What, Tecnicus is gone?
ARMOSTES: He is to Delphos;
  And to your royal hands presents this box.
AMYCLAS: Unseal it, good Armostes; therein lies
  The secrets of the oracle. Out with it;
10 Apollo live our patron. Read, Armostes.
ARMOSTES: *The plot in which the vine takes root*
       Begins to dry from head to foot;
       The stock soon withering, want of sap
       Doth cause to quail the budding grape;
       But from the neighbouring elm, a dew
       Shall drop and feed the plot anew.
AMYCLAS: That is the oracle; what exposition
  Makes the philosopher?
ARMOSTES: This brief one only;
  The plot is Sparta; the dried vine the king;
20 *The quailing grape his daughter; but the thing*
  Of most importance, not to be reveal'd,
  Is a near prince, the elm; the rest conceal'd.
                    Tecnicus.
AMYCLAS: Enough, although the opening of this riddle
  Be but itself a riddle, yet we construe
  How near our lab'ring age draws to a rest.
  But must Calantha quail too, that young grape
  Untimely budded? I could mourn for her;
  Her tenderness hath yet deserv'd no rigour
  So to be cross'd by fate.

    14. *quail:* dry up.   24. *opening:* interpretation.

ARMOSTES: You misapply, sir.   *30*
  With favour let me speak it what Apollo
  Hath clouded in hid sense. I here conjecture
  Her marriage with some neighb'ring prince, the dew
  Of which befriending elm shall ever strengthen
  Your subjects with a sovereignty of power.
CROTOLON: Besides, most gracious lord, the pith of
    oracles
  Is to be then digested, when th'events
  Expound their truth, not brought as soon to light
  As utter'd; truth is child of time, and herein
  I find no scruple, rather cause of comfort,   *40*
  With unity of kingdoms.
AMYCLAS: May it prove so
  For weal of this dear nation. – Where is Ithocles?
  Armostes, Crotolon, when this wither'd vine
  Of my frail carcass on the funeral pile
  Is fir'd into its ashes, let that young man
  Be hedg'd about still with your cares and loves.
  Much owe I to his worth, much to his service. –
  Let such as wait come in now.
ARMOSTES: All attend here.
    Enter ITHOCLES, CALANTHA, PROPHILUS, ORGILUS,
    EUPHRANEA, HEMOPHIL, *and* GRONEAS.
CALANTHA: Dear sir, king, father!
ITHOCLES: O, my royal master!
AMYCLAS: Cleave not my heart, sweet twins of my life's
    solace,   *50*
  With your forejudging fears. There is no physic
  So cunningly restorative to cherish
  The fall of age, or call back youth and vigour,

40. *scruple:* bothersome point.

As your consents in duty. I will shake off
This languishing disease of time, to quicken
Fresh pleasures in these drooping hours of sadness.
Is fair Euphranea married yet to Prophilus?

CROTOLON: This morning, gracious lord.

ORGILUS: This very morning;
Which, with your highness' leave, you may observe too.

60   Our sister looks, methinks, mirthful and sprightly,
As if her chaster fancy could already
Expound the riddle of her gain in losing
A trifle maids know only that they know not.
Pish! prithee blush not; 'tis but honest change
Of fashion in the garment, loose for strait,
And so the modest maid is made a wife.
Shrewd business, is't not, sister?

EUPHRANEA: You are pleasant.

AMYCLAS: We thank thee, Orgilus; this mirth becomes
thee. –
But wherefore sits the court in such a silence?

70   A wedding without revels is not seemly.

CALANTHA: Your late indisposition, sir, forbade it.

AMYCLAS: Be it thy charge, Calantha, to set forward
The bridal sports, to which I will be present;
If not, at least consenting. – Mine own Ithocles,
I have done little for thee yet.

ITHOCLES: Y'have built me
To the full height I stand in.

CALANTHA [aside]:   Now or never. –
May I propose a suit?

AMYCLAS: Demand and have it.

CALANTHA: Pray, sir, give me this young man and no
further
Account him yours than he deserves in all things

216

To be thought worthy mine; I will esteem him   *80*
  According to his merit.
AMYCLAS: Still th'art my daughter,
  Still grow'st upon my heart. – [*To* ITHOCLES] Give
    me thine hand. –
  Calantha, take thine own. In noble actions
  Thou'lt find him firm and absolute. – I would not
  Have parted with thee, Ithocles, to any
  But to a mistress who is all what I am.
ITHOCLES: A change, great king, most wish'd for 'cause
    the same.
CALANTHA: Th'art mine. – [*Aside to* ITHOCLES] Have
    I now kept my word?
ITHOCLES [*aside*]:   Divinely.
ORGILUS: Rich fortune's guard, the favour of a princess,
  Rock thee, brave man, in ever-crowned plenty;   *90*
  Y'are minion of the time, be thankful for it. –
  [*Aside*] Ho! here's a swinge in destiny. Apparent
  The youth is up on tiptoe, yet may stumble.
AMYCLAS: On to your recreations. – Now convey me
  Unto my bedchamber. – None on his forehead
  Wear a distempered look.
ALL: The gods preserve 'ee.
CALANTHA [*aside to* ITHOCLES]: Sweet, be not from my
    sight.
ITHOCLES [*aside to* CALANTHA]:   My whole felicity!
    Exeunt, carrying out of the king; ORGILUS *stays* ITHOCLES.
ORGILUS: Shall I be bold, my lord?
ITHOCLES: Thou canst not, Orgilus.
  Call me thine own, for Prophilus must henceforth
  Be all thy sister's; friendship, though it cease not   *100*

89. *guard:* guardianship.   91. *minion:* favourite.
92. *swinge in:* violent movement of.   *Apparent:* obviously.

    In marriage, yet is oft at less command
    Than when a single freedom can dispose it.
ORGILUS: Most right, my most good lord, my most
    great lord,
    My gracious princely lord, I might add, royal.
ITHOCLES: Royal? A subject royal?
ORGILUS: Why not, pray sir?
    The sovereignty of kingdoms in their nonage
    Stoop'd to desert, not birth; there's as much merit
    In clearness of affection, as in puddle
    Of generation. You have conquer'd love
110   Even in the loveliest; if I greatly err not,
    The son of Venus hath bequeath'd his quiver
    To Ithocles his manage, by whose arrows
    Calantha's breast is open'd.
ITHOCLES: Can't be possible?
ORGILUS: I was myself a piece of suitor once,
    And forward in preferment too; so forward,
    That speaking truth, I may without offence, sir,
    Presume to whisper that my hopes and – hark 'ee –
    My certainty of marriage stood assured
    With as firm footing, by your leave, as any's
    Now at this very instant – but –
120 ITHOCLES: 'Tis granted;
    And for a league of privacy between us,
    Read o'er my bosom and partake a secret:
    The princess is contracted mine.
ORGILUS: Still, why not?
    I now applaud her wisdom. When your kingdom
    Stands seated in your will secure and settled,

---

108. *clearness of affection:* purity of disposition.
    puddle: stagnant, muddy water.
123. *Still:* even so.

I dare pronounce you will be a just monarch;
Greece must admire and tremble.
ITHOCLES: Then the sweetness
 Of so imparadis'd a comfort, Orgilus,
 It is to banquet with the gods.
ORGILUS: The glory
 Of numerous children, potency of nobles,   *130*
 Bent knees, hearts pav'd to tread on.
ITHOCLES: With a friendship
 So dear, so fast as thine.
ORGILUS: I am unfitting
 For office, but for service.
ITHOCLES: We'll distinguish
 Our fortunes merely in the title; partners
 In all respects else but the bed.
ORGILUS: The bed?
 Forfend it, Jove's own jealousy – till lastly
 We slip down in the common earth together;
 And there our beds are equal, save some monument
 To show this was the king and this the subject.
  Soft sad music.
List, what sad sounds are these? Extremely sad ones. *140*
ITHOCLES: Sure from Penthea's lodgings.
ORGILUS: Hark, a voice too.
  A Song [within].
 O no more, no more; too late
 Sighs are spent; the burning tapers
 Of a life as chaste as fate,
 Pure as are unwritten papers,
  Are burnt out. No heat, no light
  Now remains; 'tis ever night.
 Love is dead; let lovers' eyes,
  Lock'd in endless dreams,

150　　*Th'extremes of all extremes,*
　　　Ope no more, for now love dies,
　　　　Now love dies, implying
　　Love's martyrs must be ever, ever dying.

ITHOCLES: O, my misgiving heart!

ORGILUS:　　　　　　　　　　　A horrid stillness
　　Succeeds this deathful air. Let's know the reason.
　　Tread softly; there is mystery in mourning.
　　　Exeunt.

SCENE FOUR

Enter CHRISTALLA *and* PHILEMA, *bringing in* PENTHEA
*in a chair, veiled; two other Servants placing two chairs,
one on the one side, and the other with an engine on the other.
The Maids sit down at her feet, mourning. The Servants go
out; meet them* ITHOCLES *and* ORGILUS.

SERVANT [*aside to* ORGILUS]: 'Tis done; that on her right
　　hand.

ORGILUS:　　　　　　　　　　　Good, begone.

ITHOCLES: Soft peace enrich this room.

ORGILUS:　　　　　　　　　　How fares the lady?

PHILEMA: Dead.

CHRISTALLA:　　Dead!

PHILEMA:　　　　　　Starv'd.

CHRISTALLA:　　　　　　　Starv'd!

ITHOCLES:　　　　　　　　　　Me miserable!

ORGILUS:　　　　　　　　　　　　Tell us,
　　How parted she from life?

PHILEMA:　　　　　　　She call'd for music,
　　And begg'd some gentle voice to tune a farewell

　　S.D. *engine*: contrivance. See note.

To life and griefs. Christalla touch'd the lute,
I wept the funeral song.

CHRISTALLA: Which scarce was ended,
But her last breath seal'd up these hollow sounds:
'O cruel Ithocles and injur'd Orgilus!'
So down she drew her veil, so died.

ITHOCLES: So died!   *10*

ORGILUS: Up; you are messengers of death; go from us.
Here's woe enough to court without a prompter.
Away; and hark ye, till you see us next,
No syllable that she is dead. Away!
Keep a smooth brow. –

     Exeunt PHILEMA *and* CHRISTALLA.
                My lord!

ITHOCLES: Mine only sister,
Another is not left me.

ORGILUS: Take that chair;
I'll seat me here in this; between us sits
The object of our sorrows. Some few tears
We'll part among us; I perhaps can mix
One lamentable story to prepare 'em.   *20*
There, there, sit there, my lord.

ITHOCLES: Yes, as you please.

    ITHOCLES *sits down and is caught in the engine.*
What means this treachery?

ORGILUS: Caught! You are caught,
Young master. 'Tis thy throne of coronation,
Thou fool of greatness. See, I take this veil off;
Survey a beauty wither'd by the flames
Of an insulting Phaeton, her brother.

ITHOCLES: Thou mean'st to kill me basely?

ORGILUS: I foreknew

The last act of her life, and train'd thee hither
To sacrifice a tyrant to a turtle.
30 You dreamt of kingdoms, did 'ee? how to bosom
The delicacies of a youngling princess,
How with this nod to grace that subtle courtier,
How with that frown to make this noble tremble,
And so forth; whiles Penthea's groans and tortures,
Her agonies, her miseries, afflictions
Ne'er touch'd upon your thought. As for my injuries,
Alas they were beneath your royal pity.
But yet they liv'd, thou proud man, to confound thee.
Behold thy fate, this steel.

    [*Draws a dagger.*]

ITHOCLES: Strike home! A courage
40 As keen as thy revenge shall give it welcome.
But prithee faint not; if the wound close up,
Tent it with double force and search it deeply.
Thou look'st that I should whine and beg compassion,
As loath to leave the vainness of my glories;
A statelier resolution arms my confidence,
To cozen thee of honour. Neither could I,
With equal trial of unequal fortune,
By hazard of a duel; 'twere a bravery
Too mighty for a slave intending murder.
50 On to the execution, and inherit
A conflict with thy horrors.

ORGILUS: By Apollo,
Thou talk'st a goodly language! For requital,
I will report thee to thy mistress richly.
And take this peace along: some few short minutes

---

28. *act:* 1. action 2. drama metaphor. *train'd:* lured.
42. *Tent:* probe.   46. *cozen:* cheat.
48. *bravery:* honour.

Determin'd, my resolves shall quickly follow
Thy wrathful ghost; then, if we tug for mastery,
Penthea's sacred eyes shall lend new courage.
Give me thy hand; be healthful in thy parting
From lost mortality. Thus, thus I free it.
   [*Stabs him.*]

ITHOCLES: Yet, yet I scorn to shrink.

ORGILUS: Keep up thy spirit;   60
  I will be gentle even in blood; to linger
  Pain, which I strive to cure, were to be cruel.
    [*Stabs him again.*]

ITHOCLES: Nimble in vengeance, I forgive thee. Follow
  Safety, with best success; o, may it prosper! –
  Penthea, by thy side thy brother bleeds:
  The earnest of his wrongs to thy forc'd faith,
  Thoughts of ambition, or delicious banquet,
  With beauty, youth, and love, together perish
  In my last breath, which on the sacred altar
  Of a long-look'd-for peace – now – moves – to
    heaven.   70
    He dies.

ORGILUS: Farewell, fair spring of manhood; henceforth
  welcome
  Best expectation of a noble suff'rance
  I'll lock the bodies safe, till what must follow
  Shall be approv'd. – Sweet twins, shine stars for ever.
  In vain they build their hopes whose life is shame;
  No monument lasts but a happy name.
    Exit ORGILUS.

55. *Determin'd:* concluded.   61. *linger:* prolong.
66. *earnest:* payment.   74. *approv'd:* confirmed.

ACT FIVE

SCENE ONE

Enter BASSANES *alone.*

BASSANES: Athens, to Athens I have sent, the nursery
    Of Greece for learning and the fount of knowledge;
    For here in Sparta there's not left amongst us
    One wise man to direct; we're all turn'd madcaps.
    'Tis said Apollo is the god of herbs;
    Then certainly he knows the virtue of 'em.
    To Delphos I have sent, too; if there can be
    A help for nature, we are sure yet.
       Enter ORGILUS.

ORGILUS: Honour
    Attend thy counsels ever.

BASSANES: I beseech thee
10   With all my heart, let me go from thee quietly;
    I will not aught to do with thee of all men.
    The doublers of a hare, or, in a morning,
    Salutes from a splay-footed witch, to drop
    Three drops of blood at th'nose just, and no more,
    Croaking of ravens, or the screech of owls
    Are not so boding mischief as thy crossing
    My private meditations. Shun me, prithee;
    And if I cannot love thee heartily,
    I'll love thee as well as I can.

ORGILUS: Noble Bassanes,
    Mistake me not.

20 BASSANES: Phew, then we shall be troubled.

Thou wert ordain'd my plague – heaven make me
   thankful,
And give me patience too, heaven, I beseech thee.
ORGILUS: Accept a league of amity; for henceforth,
  I vow by my best genius, in a syllable,
  Never to speak vexation. I will study
  Service and friendship with a zealous sorrow
  For my past incivility towards 'ee.
BASSANES: Heyday, good words, good words, I must
   believe 'em,
  And be a coxcomb for my labour.
ORGILUS: Use not
  So hard a language; your misdoubt is causeless.   30
  For instance, if you promise to put on
  A constancy of patience, such a patience
  As chronicle or history ne'er mentioned,
  As follows not example but shall stand
  A wonder and a theme for imitation,
  The first, the index pointing to a second,
  I will acquaint 'ee with an unmatch'd secret,
  Whose knowledge to your griefs shall set a period.
BASSANES: Thou canst not, Orgilus; 'tis in the power
  Of the gods only. Yet for satisfaction,   40
  Because I note an earnest in thine utterance
  Unforc'd and naturally free, be resolute
  The virgin-bays shall not withstand the lightning
  With a more careless danger than my constancy
  The full of thy relation; could it move
  Distraction in a senseless marble statue,

31. *For instance:* as illustration of this fact.
36. *index:* pointer.
42. *resolute:* resolved.
44. *more careless:* greater contempt of.

It should find me a rock. I do expect now
Some truth of unheard moment.

ORGILUS: To your patience
You must add privacy, as strong in silence
50   As mysteries lock'd up in Jove's own bosom.
BASSANES: A skull hid in the earth a treble age
Shall sooner prate.
ORGILUS: Lastly, to such direction
As the severity of a glorious Actaeon
Deserves to lead your wisdom and your judgement,
You ought to yield obedience.
BASSANES: With assurance
Of will and thankfulness.
ORGILUS: With manly courage
Please then to follow me.
BASSANES: Where'er, I fear not.
Exeunt.

SCENE TWO

Loud music. Enter GRONEAS *and* HEMOPHIL *leading*
EUPHRANEA; CHRISTALLA *and* PHILEMA *leading*
PROPHILUS; NEARCHUS *supporting* CALANTHA;
CROTOLON *and* AMELUS. *Cease loud music; all make
a stand.*

CALANTHA: We miss our servants Ithocles and Orgilus.
On whom attend they?
CROTOLON: My son, gracious princess,
Whisper'd some new device, to which these revels

48. *moment:* momentousness.   49. *privacy:* secrecy.
S.D. *make a stand:* take up formal positioning.
3. *device:* performance.

Should be but usher, wherein I conceive
Lord Ithocles and he himself are actors.

CALANTHA: A fair excuse for absence. As for Bassanes,
Delights to him are troublesome. Armostes
Is with the king?

CROTOLON: He is.

CALANTHA: On to the dance. –
Dear cousin, hand you the bride; the bridegroom must be
Entrusted to my courtship. – Be not jealous,   *10*
Euphranea; I shall scarcely prove a temptress. –
Fall to our dance.

Music. NEARCHUS *dance with* EUPHRANEA, PROPHILUS
with CALANTHA, CHRISTALLA *with* HEMOPHIL,
PHILEMA *with* GRONEAS. *Dance the first change, during
which enter* ARMOSTES.

ARMOSTES (*in* CALANTHA'*s ear*): The king your father's
dead.

CALANTHA: To the other change.

ARMOSTES: Is't possible?

Dance again. Enter BASSANES.

BASSANES [*in* CALANTHA'*s ear*]:   O, madam!
Penthea, poor Penthea's starv'd.

CALANTHA: Beshrew thee! –
Lead to the next.

BASSANES: Amazement dulls my senses.

Dance again. Enter ORGILUS.

ORGILUS [*in* CALANTHA'*s ear*]: Brave Ithocles is
murder'd, murder'd cruelly.

CALANTHA: How dull this music sounds! Strike up more
sprightly;

    9. *hand:* conduct by the hand.   S.D. *change:* round in dancing.

Our footings are not active like our heart
Which treads the nimbler measure.

ORGILUS: I am thunderstruck.
    Last change. Cease music.

20 CALANTHA: So, let us breathe awhile. Hath not this
    motion
    Rais'd fresher colour on your cheeks?

NEARCHUS: Sweet princess,
    A perfect purity of blood enamels
    The beauty of your white.

CALANTHA: We all look cheerfully;
    And, cousin, it is methinks a rare presumption
    In any who prefers our lawful pleasures
    Before their own sour censure, to interrupt
    The custom of this ceremony bluntly.

NEARCHUS: None dares, lady.

CALANTHA: Yes, yes; some hollow voice deliver'd to me
    How that the king was dead.

ARMOSTES: The king is dead.
30   That fatal news was mine; for in mine arms
    He breath'd his last, and with his crown bequeath'd 'ee
    Your mother's wedding ring, which here I tender.

CROTOLON: Most strange!

CALANTHA: Peace crown his ashes. We are
    queen, then.

NEARCHUS: Long live Calantha, Sparta's sovereign
    queen!

ALL: Long live the queen!

CALANTHA: What whispered Bassanes?

BASSANES: That my Penthea, miserable soul,
    Was starv'd to death.

CALANTHA: She's happy; she hath finish'd

A long and painful progress. – A third murmur
Pierc'd mine unwilling ears.

ORGILUS: That Ithocles
Was murder'd; rather butcher'd, had not bravery   *40*
Of an undaunted spirit, conquering terror,
Proclaim'd his last act triumph over ruin.

ARMOSTES: How? Murder'd?

CALANTHA: By whose hand?

ORGILUS: By mine; this weapon
Was instrument to my revenge. The reasons
Are just and known; quit him of these, and then
Never liv'd gentleman of greater merit,
Hope, or abiliment to steer a kingdom.

CROTOLON: Fie, Orgilus!

EUPHRANEA: Fie, brother!

CALANTHA: You have done it?

BASSANES: How it was done let him report, the forfeit
Of whose allegiance to our laws doth covet   *50*
Rigour of justice; but that done it is,
Mine eyes have been an evidence of credit
Too sure to be convinc'd. – Armostes, rend not
Thine arteries with hearing the bare circumstances
Of these calamities. Thou'st lost a nephew,
A niece, and I a wife. Continue man still;
Make me the pattern of digesting evils,
Who can outlive my mighty ones, not shrinking
At such a pressure as would sink a soul
Into what's most of death, the worst of horrors.   *60*
But I have seal'd a covenant with sadness,
And enter'd into bonds without condition,
To stand these tempests calmly. – Mark me, nobles,

45. *quit*: acquit.   47. *abiliment*: ability.
53. *convinc'd*: confuted.   57. *digesting*: enduring.

I do not shed a tear, not for Penthea.
Excellent misery!

CALANTHA: We begin our reign
With a first act of justice. – Thy confession,
Unhappy Orgilus, dooms thee a sentence.
But yet thy father's or thy sister's presence
Shall be excus'd. – Give, Crotolon, a blessing
70 To thy lost son. – Euphranea, take a farewell,
And both be gone.

CROTOLON: Confirm thee, noble sorrow,
In worthy resolution.

EUPHRANEA: Could my tears speak,
My griefs were slight.

ORGILUS: All goodness dwell amongst ye. –
Enjoy my sister, Prophilus; my vengeance
Aim'd never at thy prejudice.

CALANTHA: Now withdraw. –
Exeunt CROTOLON, PROPHILUS, *and* EUPHRANEA.
Bloody relater of thy stains in blood,
For that thou hast reported him, whose fortunes
And life by thee are both at once snatch'd from him,
With honourable mention, make thy choice
80 Of what death likes thee best; there's all our bounty. –
But to excuse delays, let me, dear cousin,
Entreat you and these lords see execution
Instant before 'ee part.

NEARCHUS: Your will commands us.

ORGILUS: One suit, just queen, my last: vouchsafe your
      clemency
That by no common hand I be divided
From this my humble frailty.

---

75. *thy prejudice:* harm to you.   80. *likes:* pleases.
81. *excuse:* obviate.   86. *humble frailty:* i.e. life.

CALANTHA: To their wisdoms,
  Who are to be spectators of thine end,
  I make the reference. Those that are dead
  Are dead; had they not now died, of necessity
  They must have paid the debt they ow'd to nature   *90*
  One time or other. – Use dispatch, my lords;
  We'll suddenly prepare our coronation.
        Exeunt CALANTHA, PHILEMA, CHRISTALLA.
ARMOSTES: 'Tis strange these tragedies should never
    touch on
  Her female pity.
BASSANES: She has a masculine spirit;
  And wherefore should I pule, and like a girl
  Put finger in the eye? Let's be all toughness,
  Without distinction betwixt sex and sex.
NEARCHUS: Now, Orgilus, thy choice?
ORGILUS: To bleed to death.
ARMOSTES: The executioner?
ORGILUS: Myself, no surgeon;
  I am well skill'd in letting blood. Bind fast   *100*
  This arm, that so the pipes may from their conduits
  Convey a full stream. Here's a skilful instrument;
      [*Shows his dagger.*]
  Only I am a beggar to some charity
  To speed me in this execution
  By lending th'other prick to th'tother arm,
  When this is bubbling life out.
BASSANES: I am for 'ee;
  It most concerns my art, my care, my credit. –
  Quick, fillet both his arms.
ORGILUS: Gramercy, friendship;

92. *suddenly:* at once.   104. *speed:* aid.   108. *fillet:* bind.

Such courtesies are real which flow cheerfully
110 Without an expectation of requital.
Reach me a staff in this hand. If a proneness
Or custom in my nature, from my cradle,
Had been inclin'd to fierce and eager bloodshed,
A coward guilt, hid in a coward quaking,
Would have betray'd fame to ignoble flight
And vagabond pursuit of dreadful safety.
But look upon my steadiness, and scorn not
The sickness of my fortune, which since Bassanes
Was husband to Penthea, had lain bedrid.
120 We trifle time in words. Thus I show cunning
In opening of a vein too full, too lively –
    [*Opens a vein.*]
ARMOSTES: Desperate courage!
NEARCHUS: Honourable infamy!
HEMOPHIL: I tremble at the sight.
GRONEAS: Would I were loose.
BASSANES: It sparkles like a lusty wine new broach'd;
The vessel must be sound from which it issues. –
Grasp hard this other stick; I'll be as nimble.
But prithee look not pale; have at 'ee, stretch out
Thine arm with vigour and unshook virtue.
    [*Opens another vein.*]
Good! O, I envy not a rival fitted
130 To conquer in extremities. This pastime
Appears majestical; some high-tun'd poem
Hereafter shall deliver to posterity
The writer's glory and his subject's triumph. –
How is't, man? Droop not yet.
ORGILUS: I feel no palsies;
On a pair-royal do I wait in death:

116. *dreadful*: full of dread.   120. *cunning*: skill.

232

My sovereign, as his liegeman; on my mistress,
As a devoted servant; and on Ithocles,
As if no brave, yet no unworthy enemy.
Nor did I use an engine to entrap
His life out of a slavish fear to combat   140
Youth, strength, or cunning, but for that I durst not
Engage the goodness of a cause on fortune,
By which his name might have outfac'd my
  vengeance.
O Tecnicus, inspir'd with Phoebus' fire,
I call to mind thy augury; 'twas perfect:
Revenge proves its own executioner.
When feeble man is bending to his mother,
The dust 'a was first fram'd on, thus he totters.
BASSANES: Life's fountain is dried up.
ORGILUS: So falls the standards
Of my prerogative in being a creature.   150
A mist hangs o'er mine eyes; the sun's bright splendour
Is clouded in an everlasting shadow.
Welcome, thou ice that sitt'st about my heart;
No heat can ever thaw thee.
    Dies.
NEARCHUS: Speech hath left him.
BASSANES: 'A has shook hands with time. His funeral urn
Shall be my charge. Remove the bloodless body.
The coronation must require attendance;
That past, my few days can be but one mourning.
    Exeunt.

142. *Engage:* stake.
148. *fram'd on:* composed of.
150. *prerogative:* natural advantage.

SCENE THREE

*An altar covered with white, two lights of virgin wax;
during which music of recorders. Enter four bearing*
ITHOCLES *on a hearse, or in a chair, in a rich robe, and
a crown on his head; place him on one side of the altar.
After him enter* CALANTHA *in a white robe, and crowned;*
EUPHRANEA, PHILEMA, CHRISTALLA, *in white;*
NEARCHUS, ARMOSTES, CROTOLON, PROPHILUS,
AMELUS, BASSANES, HEMOPHIL *and* GRONEAS.
CALANTHA *goes and kneels before the altar, the rest stand
off, the women kneeling behind. Cease recorders during her
devotions. Soft music.* CALANTHA *and the rest rise, doing
obeisance to the altar.*

CALANTHA: Our orisons are heard; the gods are merciful.
  Now tell me, you whose loyalties pays tribute
  To us your lawful sovereign, how unskilful
  Your duties or obedience is, to render
  Subjection to the sceptre of a virgin,
  Who have been ever fortunate in princes
  Of masculine and stirring composition.
  A woman has enough to govern wisely
  Her own demeanours, passions, and divisions.
10 A nation warlike and inur'd to practice
  Of policy and labour cannot brook
  A feminate authority. We therefore
  Command your counsel, how you may advise us
  In choosing of a husband whose abilities
  Can better guide this kingdom.

1. *orisons:* prayers.   3. *unskilful:* unwise.   9. *divisions:* inner strifes.

NEARCHUS: Royal lady,
  Your law is in your will.
ARMOSTES: We have seen tokens
  Of constancy too lately to mistrust it.
CROTOLON: Yet if your highness settle on a choice
  By your own judgement both allow'd and lik'd of,
  Sparta may grow in power, and proceed   20
  To an increasing height.
CALANTHA: Hold you the same mind?
BASSANES: Alas, great mistress, reason is so clouded
  With the thick darkness of my infinite woes
  That I forecast nor dangers, hopes, or safety.
  Give me some corner of the world to wear out
  The remnant of the minutes I must number,
  Where I may hear no sounds but sad complaints
  Of virgins who have lost contracted partners,
  Of husbands howling that their wives were ravish'd
  By some untimely fate, of friends divided   30
  By churlish opposition, or of fathers
  Weeping upon their children's slaughtered carcasses,
  Or daughters groaning o'er their fathers' hearses,
  And I can dwell there, and with these keep consort
  As musical as theirs. What can you look for
  From an old, foolish, peevish, doting man
  But craziness of age?
CALANTHA: Cousin of Argos.
NEARCHUS: Madam?
CALANTHA: Were I presently
  To choose you for my lord, I'll open freely
  What articles I would propose to treat on   40
  Before our marriage.
NEARCHUS: Name them, virtuous lady.

34. *consort:* harmony.

CALANTHA: I would presume you would retain the
    royalty
  Of Sparta in her own bounds. Then in Argos
  Armostes might be viceroy; in Messene
  Might Crotolon bear sway; and Bassanes –
BASSANES: I, queen? Alas! what I?
CALANTHA: Be Sparta's marshal.
  The multitudes of high employments could not
  But set a peace to private griefs. These gentlemen,
  Groneas and Hemophil, with worthy pensions
50 Should wait upon your person in your chamber.
  I would bestow Christalla on Amelus;
  She'll prove a constant wife. And Philema
  Should into Vesta's temple.
BASSANES: This is a testament;
  It sounds not like conditions on a marriage.
NEARCHUS: All this should be perform'd.
CALANTHA: Lastly, for Prophilus,
  He should be, cousin, solemnly invested
  In all those honours, titles and preferments
  Which his dear friend, and my neglected husband
  Too short a time enjoy'd.
PROPHILUS: I am unworthy
  To live in your remembrance.
60 EUPHRANEA: Excellent lady!
NEARCHUS: Madam, what means that word 'neglected
    husband'?
CALANTHA: Forgive me. – Now I turn to thee, thou
    shadow
  Of my contracted lord. – Bear witness all,
  I put my mother's wedding ring upon
  His finger; 'twas my father's last bequest.

42. *royalty*: sovereignty.

Thus I new marry him whose wife I am;
Death shall not separate us. O, my lords,
I but deceiv'd your eyes with antic gesture,
When one news straight came huddling on another
Of death, and death, and death. Still I danc'd forward,   70
But it struck home, and here, and in an instant.
Be such mere women, who with shrieks and outcries
Can vow a present end to all their sorrows,
Yet live to vow new pleasures, and outlive them.
They are the silent griefs which cut the heartstrings;
Let me die smiling.

NEARCHUS: 'Tis a truth too ominous.

CALANTHA: One kiss on these cold lips, my last. Crack,
     crack! –
     Argos now's Sparta's king. – Command the voices
     Which wait at th'altar now to sing the song
     I fitted for my end.

NEARCHUS: Sirs, the song.   80

     A Song.

ALL: *Glories, pleasures, pomps, delight, and ease,*
               Can but please
            Th'outward senses, when the mind
            Is untroubled or by peace refin'd.

1 [*voice*]: *Crowns may flourish and decay,*
            Beauties shine, but fade away.

2 [*voice*]: *Youth may revel, yet it must*
            Lie down in a bed of dust.

3 [*voice*]: *Earthly honours flow and waste,*
            Time alone doth change and last.   90

ALL: *Sorrows mingled with contents prepare*
               Rest for care;
            Love only reigns in death, though art

68. *antic gesture:* acting performance.

Can find no comfort for a broken heart.
  [CALANTHA *dies.*]
ARMOSTES: Look to the queen.
BASSANES: Her heart is broke indeed. –
  O, royal maid, would thou hadst miss'd this part;
  Yet 'twas a brave one. I must weep to see
  Her smile in death.
ARMOSTES: Wise Tecnicus! Thus said he:
  When youth is ripe and age from time doth part,
100 *The lifeless trunk shall wed the broken heart.*
  'Tis here fulfilled.
NEARCHUS: I am your king.
ALL: Long live
  Nearchus, king of Sparta!
NEARCHUS: Her last will
  Shall never be digress'd from. Wait in order
  Upon these faithful lovers as becomes us.
  The counsels of the gods are never known
  Till men can call th'effects of them their own.

FINIS

THE EPILOGUE

Where noble judgements and clear eyes are fix'd
To grace endeavour, there sits truth not mix'd
With ignorance. Those censures may command
Belief which talk not till they understand.
Let some say, 'This was flat'; some, 'Here the scene
Fell from its height'; another, that the mean
Was 'ill observ'd' in such a growing passion
As it transcended either state or fashion.
Some few may cry 'twas 'pretty well' or 'so,
But – ' and there shrug in silence. Yet we know   10
Our writer's aim was in the whole address'd
Well to deserve of *all* but please the *best*;
Which granted, by th'allowance of this strain,
The *Broken Heart* may be piec'd up again.

3. *censures:* opinion.
6. *the mean:* proper moderation.

THE
CHRONICLE
HISTORIE
OF
PERKIN WARBECK.

A Strange Truth.

Acted (some-times) by the Queenes
MAIESTIES Servants at the
Phœnix in *Drurie* lane.

Fide Honor.

LONDON,
Printed by *T. P.* for *Hugh Beeston,* and are to
be sold at his Shop, neere the *Castle* in
Cornehill. 1 6 3 4.

[DEDICATORY EPISTLE]

To The Rightly Honourable William Cavendish,
Earl of Newcastle, Viscount Mansfield, Lord Bolsover
and Ogle.

My Lord:

Out of the darkness of a former age (enlightened by a late both learned and an honourable pen) I have endeavoured to personate a great attempt, and in it a greater danger. In other labours you may read actions of antiquity discoursed; in this abridgement, find the actors themselves discoursing: in some kind, practised as well 5 what to speak, as speaking why to do. Your lordship is a most competent judge in expressions of such credit, commissioned by your known ability in examining and enabled by your knowledge in determining the monuments of time. Eminent titles may indeed inform who their owners are, not often what. To yours the 10 addition of that information in both cannot in any application be observed flattery, the authority being established by truth. I can only acknowledge the errors in writing mine own, the worthiness of the subject written being a perfection in the story, and of it. The custom of your lordship's entertainments, even to strangers, 15 is rather an example than a fashion: in which consideration, I dare not profess a curiosity, but am only studious that your lordship will please, amongst such as best honour your goodness, to admit into your noble construction

JOHN FORD

2. *personate:* describe.
5. *actors:* principals in the action.
7. *expressions:* representations.
9. *determining:* deciding which are.
15. *entertainments:* patronages.
17. *curiosity:* skill.

The Scene:

THE CONTINENT OF GREAT BRITAIN

The Persons Presented

HENRY VII, *King of England*
LORD DAUBENEY
SIR WILLIAM STANLEY, *King's chamberlain*
EARL OF OXFORD
EARL OF SURREY
RICHARD FOX, *Bishop of Durham*
URSWICK, *King's chaplain*
SIR ROBERT CLIFFORD
LAMBERT SIMNEL, *a falconer*
HIALAS, *a Spanish agent*
A CONSTABLE
Officers, Servingmen and Soldiers, an Executioner, a Confessor, a Post,
a Sheriff

JAMES IV, *King of Scotland*
EARL OF HUNTLY
EARL OF CRAWFORD
LORD DALYELL
MARCHMOUNT, *a herald*
Masquers, Attendants, a Sheriff, a Servant (attending Katherine),
a Herald

PERKIN WARBECK
FRION, *his Secretary*
JOHN A-WATER, *Mayor of Cork*
HERON, *a Mercer*
SKELTON, *a Tailor*
ASTLEY, *a Scrivener*

Women
LADY KATHERINE GORDON, *Wife to Perkin*
COUNTESS OF CRAWFORD
JANE DOUGLAS, *Lady Katherine's maid*

PROLOGUE

Studies have of this nature been of late
So out of fashion, so unfollow'd, that
It is become more justice to revive
The antic follies of the times than strive
To countenance wise industry. No want   5
Of art doth render wit or lame or scant
Or slothful in the purchase of fresh bays,
But want of truth in them who give the praise
To their self-love, presuming to outdo
The writer or, for need, the actors too.   10
But such this author's silence best befits,
Who bids them be in love with their own wits.
From him to clearer judgements we can say,
He shows a history couch'd in a play,
A history of noble mention, known,   15
Famous, and true; most noble cause our own;
Not forg'd from Italy, from France, from Spain,
But chronicled at home; as rich in strain
Of brave attempts as ever fertile rage
In action could beget to grace the stage.   20
We cannot limit scenes, for the whole land
Itself appear'd too narrow to withstand
Competitors for kingdoms. Nor is here
Unnecessary mirth forc'd, to endear
A multitude. On these two rests the fate   25
Of worthy expectation: Truth and State.

4. *antic:* grotesque.
7. *bays:* garland awarded to poets.
10. *for need:* if necessary.
19. *rage:* passion.
26. *State:* matter of state.

ACT ONE

SCENE ONE

Enter King HENRY, DURHAM, OXFORD, SURREY,
Sir WILLIAM STANLEY *(Lord Chamberlain), Lord*
DAUBENEY. *The king supported to his throne by*
STANLEY *and* DURHAM. *A Guard.*

KING HENRY: Still to be haunted, still to be pursued,
  Still to be frighted with false apparitions
  Of pageant majesty and new coin'd greatness,
  As if we were a mockery king in state,
  Only ordain'd to lavish sweat and blood
  In scorn and laughter to the ghosts of York,
  Is all below our merits; yet, my lords,
  My friends and counsellors, yet we sit fast
  In our own royal birthright. The rent face
  And bleeding wounds of England's slaughter'd people   *10*
  Have been by us, as by the best physician,
  At last both thoroughly cur'd and set in safety.
  And yet for all this glorious work of peace
  Oneself is scarce secure.
DURHAM: The rage of malice
  Conjures fresh spirits with the spells of York.
  For ninety years ten English kings and princes,
  Threescore great dukes and earls, a thousand lords
  And valiant knights, two hundred fifty thousand

---

s.D. *supported:* formally escorted.
3. *pageant:* mimic.
4. *mockery king:* counterfeit king.

Of English subjects have in civil wars
20 Been sacrific'd to an uncivil thirst
Of discord and ambition. This hot vengeance
Of the just powers above to utter ruin
And desolation had rain'd on, but that
Mercy did gently sheathe the sword of justice,
In lending to this blood-shrunk commonwealth
A new soul, new birth, in your sacred person.

DAUBENEY: Edward the Fourth after a doubtful fortune
Yielded to nature, leaving to his sons,
Edward and Richard, the inheritance
30 Of a most bloody purchase; these young princes
Richard the tyrant, their unnatural uncle,
Forc'd to a violent grave; so just is Heaven,
Him hath your majesty by your own arm,
Divinely strengthen'd, pull'd from his boar's sty
And struck the black usurper to a carcass:
Nor doth the house of York decay in honours,
Though Lancaster doth repossess his right;
For Edward's daughter is King Henry's queen,
A blessed union, and a lasting blessing
40 For this poor panting island, if some shreds,
Some useless remnant of the house of York
Grudge not at this content.

OXFORD: Margaret of Burgundy
Blows fresh coals of division.

SURREY: Painted fires
Without or heat to scorch or light to cherish.

DAUBENEY: York's headless trunk (her father), Edward's
        fate
(Her brother king), the smothering of her nephews
By tyrant Gloucester (brother to her nature),

25. *blood-shrunk:* shrunk through loss of blood.

Nor Gloucester's own confusion – all decrees
Sacred in Heaven – can move this woman-monster,
But that she still from the unbottom'd mine   50
Of devilish policies doth vent the ore
Of troubles and sedition.

OXFORD: In her age –
 Great sir, observe the wonder – she grows fruitful,
 Who in her strength of youth was always barren.
 Nor are her births as other mothers' are,
 At nine or ten months' end; she has been with child
 Eight or seven years at least; whose twins being born –
 A prodigy in nature! – even the youngest
 Is fifteen years of age at his first entrance,
 As soon as known i'th'world; tall striplings, strong   60
 And able to give battle unto kings,
 Idols of Yorkish malice.

OXFORD: And but idols;
 A steely hammer crushes 'em to pieces.

KING HENRY: Lambert, the eldest, lords, is in our service,
 Preferr'd by an officious care of duty
 From the scullery to a falconer – strange example!
 Which shows the difference between noble natures
 And the base-born. But for the upstart duke,
 The new-reviv'd York, Edward's second son,
 Murder'd long since i'th'tower, he lives again   70
 And vows to be your king.

STANLEY: The throne is fill'd, sir.

KING HENRY: True, Stanley, and the lawful heir sits
 on it.
 A guard of angels and the holy prayers

48. *confusion*: destruction.   50. *unbottom'd*: bottomless.
62. *but*: only.   65. *Preferr'd*: promoted.   *officious*: zealous.
68. *for*: as for.

Of loyal subjects are sure defence
Against all force and counsel of intrusion.
But now, my lords, put case some of our nobles,
Our 'great ones', should give countenance and courage
To trim Duke Perkin: you will all confess
Our bounties have unthriftily been scatter'd
Amongst unthankful men.

80 DAUBENEY: Unthankful beasts,
Dogs, villains, traitors!

KING HENRY: Daubeney, let the guilty
Keep silence; I accuse none, though I know
Foreign attempts against a state and kingdom
Are seldom without some great friends at home.

STANLEY: Sir, if no other abler reasons else
Of duty or allegiance could divert
A headstrong resolution, yet the dangers
So lately pass'd by men of blood and fortunes
In Lambert Simnel's party must command
90 More than a fear, a terror to conspiracy.
The high-born Lincoln, son to De la Pole,
The Earl of Kildare, Lord Geraldine,
Francis Lord Lovell, and the German baron,
Bold Martin Swart, with Broughton and the rest –
Most spectacles of ruin, some of mercy –
Are precedents sufficient to forewarn
The present times, or any that live in them,
What folly, nay, what madness 'twere to lift
A finger up in all defence but yours,
100 Which can be but imposturous in a title.

75. *counsel*: secret plan.   76. *put case*: suppose.
77. *countenance*: patronage.   78. *trim*: pretty (ironical).
88. *pass'd*: experienced.
100. *Which*: i.e. any defence other than Henry's.
        imposturous: fraudulent.

KING HENRY: Stanley, we know thou lov'st us, and thy
    heart
  Is figur'd on thy tongue; nor think we less
  Of any's here. How closely we have hunted
  This cub, since he unlodg'd, from hole to hole
  Your knowledge is our chronicle: first Ireland,
  The common stage of novelty, presented
  This gewgaw to oppose us; there the Geraldines
  And Butlers once again stood in support
  Of this colossic statue; Charles of France
  Thence call'd him into his protection,   110
  Dissembl'd him the lawful heir of England;
  Yet this was all but French dissimulation,
  Aiming at peace with us, which being granted
  On honourable terms on our part, suddenly
  This smoke of straw was pack'd from France again
  T'infect some grosser air; and now we learn,
  Maugre the malice of the bastard Neville,
  Sir Taylor, and a hundred English rebels,
  They're all retir'd to Flanders, to the dam
  That nurs'd this eager whelp, Margaret of Burgundy.   120
  But we will hunt him there, too; we will hunt him,
  Hunt him to death, even in the beldam's closet,
  Though the archduke were his buckler.

SURREY: She has styled him
  'The fair white rose of England'.

DAUBENEY: Jolly gentleman,
  More fit to be a swabber to the Flemish
  After a drunken surfeit.

    Enter URSWICK.

102. *figur'd:* represented.   103. *any's:* any that is.
111. *Dissembl'd him:* pretended he was.
117. *Maugre:* despite.

URSWICK: Gracious sovereign,
   Please you peruse this paper.
      [KING HENRY *reads.*]
DURHAM: The king's countenance
   Gathers a sprightly blood.
DAUBENEY: Good news, believe it.
KING HENRY: Urswick, thine ear – [*Aside to* URSWICK]
   Th'ast lodg'd him?
URSWICK: Strongly safe, sir.
KING HENRY: Enough. Is Barley come too?
130 URSWICK: No, my lord.
KING HENRY: No matter – phew, he's but a running
      weed,
   At pleasure to be pluck'd up by the roots;
   But more of this anon. – I have bethought me. –
   My lords, for reasons which you shall partake,
   It is our pleasure to remove our court
   From Westminster to th'Tower; we will lodge
   This very night there; give, Lord Chamberlain,
   A present order for it.
STANLEY [*aside*]:   The Tower! – I shall, sir.
KING HENRY: Come, my true, best, fast friends; these
      clouds will vanish,
140   The sun will shine at full, the heavens are clearing.
      Flourish. Exeunt.

   133. *bethought me:* decided.
   134. *partake:* share.

SCENE TWO

Enter HUNTLY *and* DALYELL.

HUNTLY: You trifle time, sir.
DALYELL: O, my noble lord,
  You conster my griefs to so hard a sense,
  That where the text is argument of pity,
  Matter of earnest love, your gloss corrupts it
  With too much ill-plac'd mirth.
HUNTLY: Much mirth, Lord Dalyell?
  Not so, I vow. Observe me, sprightly gallant.
  I know thou art a noble lad, a handsome,
  Descended from an honourable ancestry,
  Forward and active, dost resolve to wrestle
  And ruffle in the world by noble actions   10
  For a brave mention to posterity:
  I scorn not thy affection to my daughter,
  Not I, by good Saint Andrew; but this bugbear,
  This whoreson tale of honour – honour, Dalyell! –
  So hourly chats and tattles in mine ear
  The piece of royalty that is stitch'd up
  In my Kate's blood, that 'tis as dangerous
  For thee, young lord, to perch so near an eaglet,
  As foolish for my gravity to admit it.
  I have spoke all at once.
DALYELL: Sir, with this truth   20
  You mix such wormwood that you leave no hope
  For my disorder'd palate e'er to relish

2. *conster:* construe (accent on first syllable).
10. *ruffle:* do battle.   13. *bugbear:* fanciful object of fear.
15. *chats ... tattles:* chats of ... tattles of.   19. *admit:* allow.

255

A wholesome taste again. Alas, I know, sir,
What an unequal distance lies between
Great Huntly's daughter's birth and Dalyell's fortunes.
She's the king's kinswoman, plac'd near the crown,
A princess of the blood, and I a subject.

HUNTLY: Right, but a noble subject; put in that too.

DALYELL: I could add more; and in the rightest line
30   Derive my pedigree from Adam Mure,
A Scottish knight, whose daughter was the mother
To him who first begot the race of Jameses
That sway the sceptre to this very day.
But kindreds are not ours, when once the date
Of many years have swallowed up the memory
Of their originals: so pasture fields,
Neighbouring too near the ocean, are soop'd up
And known no more; for, stood I in my first
And native greatness, if my princely mistress
40   Vouchsaf'd me not her servant, 'twere as good
I were reduc'd to clownery, to nothing,
As to a throne of wonder.

HUNTLY [aside]:   Now by Saint Andrew,
A spark of metal! 'A has a brave fire in him.
I would 'a had my daughter, so I knew't not.
But must not be so, must not. – Well, young lord,
This will not do yet. If the girl be headstrong
And will not hearken to good counsel, steal her
And run away with her; dance galliards, do,
And frisk about the world to learn the languages;
50   'Twill be a thriving trade, you may set up by't.

34. *kindreds:* lineage.   *ours:* recognized.
37. *soop'd:* swallowed.
40. *Vouchsaf'd me not:* did not deign to let me be.
41. *clownery:* status of a peasant.
42. *As to:* ? as raised to.   48. *galliards:* quick, lively dances.

256

DALYELL: With pardon, noble Gordon, this disdain
  Suits not your daughter's virtue or my constancy.
HUNTLY: You are angry. – [*Aside*] Would 'a would
    beat me; I deserve it. –
  Dalyell, thy hand, w'are friends; follow thy courtship,
  Take thine own time and speak; if thou prevail'st
  With passion more than I can with my counsel,
  She's thine; nay, she is thine; 'tis a fair match,
  Free and allowed. I'll only use my tongue
  Without a father's power, use thou thine.
  Self do, self have; no more words; win and wear her.   60
DALYELL: You bless me; I am now too poor in thanks
  To pay the debt I owe you.
HUNTLY: Nay, th'art poor
  Enough. – [*Aside*] I love his spirit infinitely. –
  Look ye, she comes; to her now, to her, to her!
    Enter KATHERINE *and* JANE.
KATHERINE: The king commands your presence, sir.
HUNTLY: The gallant, –
  This, this, this lord, this servant, Kate, of yours –
  Desires to be your master.
KATHERINE: I acknowledge him
  A worthy friend of mine.
DALYELL: Your humblest creature.
HUNTLY [*aside*]: So, so, the game's afoot, I'm in cold
    hunting:
  The hare and hounds are parties.
DALYELL: Princely lady,   70
  How most unworthy I am to employ
  My services in honour of your virtues,
  How hopeless my desires are to enjoy

69. *in cold hunting:* i.e. the scent is dead.
70. *parties:* partners.

Your fair opinion, and much more your love,
Are only matter of despair, unless
Your goodness give large warrant to my boldness,
My feeble-wing'd ambition.

HUNTLY [*aside*]:   This is scurvy!

KATHERINE: My lord, I interrupt you not.

HUNTLY [*aside*]:   Indeed!
Now, on my life, she'll court him! – Nay, nay, on, sir.

80   DALYELL: Oft have I tun'd the lesson of my sorrows
To sweeten discord and enrich your pity,
But all in vain: here had my comforts sunk
And never ris'n again to tell a story
Of the despairing lover, had not now,
Even now, the earl your father –

HUNTLY [*aside*]:   'A means me, sure.

DALYELL: – After some fit disputes of your condition,
Your highness and my lowness, giv'n a licence
Which did not more embolden than encourage
My faulting tongue.

HUNTLY: How, how? how's that? embolden?
90   Encourage? I encourage ye? D'ee hear sir? –
A subtle trick, a quaint one! – Will you hear, man?
What did I say to you? Come, come to th'point.

KATHERINE: It shall not need, my lord.

HUNTLY: Then hear me, Kate. –
Keep you on that hand of her. I on this. –
Thou stand'st between a father and a suitor,
Both striving for an interest in thy heart:
He courts thee for affection, I for duty;
He as a servant pleads, but by the privilege
Of nature though I might command, my care

80. *lesson:* musical piece or exercise.   86. *disputes:* statements.
91. *quaint:* ingenious.   98–9. *by . . . command:* i.e. as a father.

Shall only counsel what it shall not force.   100
Thou canst but make one choice; the ties of marriage
Are tenures not at will but during life.
Consider whose thou art, and who: a princess,
A princess of the royal blood of Scotland,
In the full spring of youth and fresh in beauty.
The king that sits upon the throne is young
And yet unmarried, forward in attempts
On any least occasion to endanger
His person. Wherefore, Kate, as I am confident
Thou dar'st not wrong thy birth and education   110
By yielding to a common, servile rage
Of female wantonness, so I am confident
Thou wilt proportion all thy thoughts to side
Thy equals, if not equal thy superiors.
My Lord of Dalyell, young in years, is old
In honours but not eminent in titles
Or in estate that may support or add to
The expectation of thy fortunes. Settle
Thy will and reason by a strength of judgement;
For in a word, I give thee freedom; take it.   120
If equal fates have not ordain'd to pitch
Thy hopes above my height, let not thy passion
Lead thee to shrink mine honour in oblivion;
Thou art thine own; I have done.

DALYELL: O, y'are all oracle,
The living stock and root of truth and wisdom!

KATHERINE: My worthiest lord and father, the indulgence

102. *at will:* in one's power to change. *during:* for the duration of.
107. *attempts:* enterprises.   111. *rage:* passion.
112. *wantonness:* frivolous behaviour.
113. *side:* keep up with.   121. *equal:* impartial.
126. *indulgence:* kindness.

Of your sweet composition thus commands
The lowest of obedience; you have granted
A liberty so large, that I want skill
130   To choose without direction of example:
From which I daily learn, by how much more
You take off from the roughness of a father
By so much more I am engag'd to tender
The duty of a daughter. For respects
Of birth, degrees of title, and advancement,
I nor admire nor slight them; all my studies
Shall ever aim at this perfection only:
To live and die so, that you may not blush
In any course of mine to own me yours.

HUNTLY: Kate, Kate, thou grow'st upon my heart like
140   peace,
Creating every other hour a jubilee.

KATHERINE: To you, my Lord of Dalyell, I address
Some few remaining words: the general fame,
That speaks your merit even in vulgar tongues,
Proclaims it clear; but in the best, a precedent.

HUNTLY: Good wench, good girl, i'faith!

KATHERINE: For my part (trust me)
I value mine own worth at higher rate,
'Cause you are pleas'd to prize it. If the stream
Of your protested service – as you term it –
150   Run in a constancy more than a compliment,
It shall be my delight that worthy love
Leads you to worthy actions, and these guide ye
Richly to wed an honourable name;

127. *composition:* nature.   134. *respects:* considerations.
141. *jubilee:*occasion for rejoicing.   144. *speaks:* proclaims.
145. *best:* i.e. best tongues.   *precedent:* example.
149. *protested:* solemnly affirmed.

So every virtuous praise, in after ages,
Shall be your heir, and I, in your brave mention,
Be chronicled the mother of that issue,
That glorious issue.

HUNTLY [*aside*]: O, that I were young again!
She'd make me court proud danger, and suck spirit
From reputation.

KATHERINE: To the present motion,
Here's all that I dare answer: when a ripeness   160
Of more experience and some use of time
Resolves to treat the freedom of my youth
Upon exchange of troths, I shall desire
No surer credit of a match with virtue,
Than such as lives in you; meantime, my hopes are
Preserv'd secure in having you a friend.

DALYELL: You are a blessed lady, and instruct
Ambition not to soar a farther flight
Than in the perfum'd air of your soft voice.
My noble Lord of Huntly, you have lent   170
A full extent of bounty to this parley,
And for it, shall command your humblest servant.

HUNTLY: Enough; we are still friends, and will continue
A hearty love. – O, Kate, thou art mine own! –
No more; my Lord of Crawford.

Enter CRAWFORD.

CRAWFORD: From the king
I come, my Lord of Huntly, who in council
Requires your present aid.

HUNTLY: Some weighty business?

CRAWFORD: A secretary from a Duke of York,

155. *brave mention:* record of your brave deeds.
159. *motion:* proposal.   162. *treat:* bargain away.
163. *Upon:* upon the occasion of.   177. *present:* immediate.

The second son to the late English Edward,
180   Conceal'd I know not where these fourteen years,
Craves audience from our master, and 'tis said
The duke himself is following to the court.
HUNTLY: Duke upon duke! 'Tis well; 'tis well; here's
    bustling
For majesty. – My lord, I will along with ye.
CRAWFORD: My service, noble lady.
KATHERINE: Please ye walk, sir?
DALYELL [aside]: Times have their changes, sorrow makes
    men wise;
The sun itself must set as well as rise;
Then why not I? – Fair madam, I wait on ye.
    Exeunt.

SCENE THREE

Enter DURHAM, Sir ROBERT CLIFFORD, and URS-
WICK. Lights.

DURHAM: You find, Sir Robert Clifford, how securely
King Henry, our great master, doth commit
His person to your loyalty. You taste
His bounty and his mercy even in this,
That at a time of night so late, a place
So private as his closet, he is pleas'd
To admit you to his favour. Do not falter
In your discovery, but as you covet
A liberal grace and pardon for your follies,
10   So labour to deserve it, by laying open
All plots, all persons, that contrive against it.

---

1. *securely:* confidently.   8. *discovery:* disclosure.

URSWICK: Remember not the witchcraft or the magic,
The charms and incantations which the sorceress
Of Burgundy hath cast upon your reason!
Sir Robert, be your own friend now, discharge
Your conscience freely. All of such as love you
Stand sureties for your honesty and truth.
Take heed you do not dally with the king;
He is wise as he is gentle.

CLIFFORD: I am miserable
If Henry be not merciful.

URSWICK: The king comes.   20
    Enter KING HENRY.

KING HENRY: Clifford!

CLIFFORD [*kneels*]:   Let my weak knees rot on the earth,
If I appear as lep'rous in my treacheries
Before your royal eyes, as to mine own
I seem a monster, by my breach of truth.

KING HENRY: Clifford, stand up. For instance of thy
    safety
I offer thee my hand.

CLIFFORD: A sovereign balm
For my bruis'd soul, I kiss it with a greediness.
Sir, you are just master, but I –

KING HENRY: Tell me,
Is every circumstance thou has set down
With thine own hand within this paper true?   30
Is it a sure intelligence of all
The progress of our enemies' intents
Without corruption?

CLIFFORD: True, as I wish Heaven.
Or my infected honour white again.

25. *For instance:* as token.

KING HENRY: We know all, Clifford, fully, since this
    meteor,
    This airy apparition first discradled
    From Tournay into Portugal, and thence
    Advanc'd his fiery blaze for adoration
    To th'superstitious Irish; since, the beard
40   Of this wild comet, conjur'd into France,
    Sparkled in antic flames in Charles his court;
    But shrunk again from thence, and hid in darkness,
    Stole into Flanders, flourishing the rags
    Of painted power on the shore of Kent,
    Whence he was beaten back with shame and scorn,
    Contempt, and slaughter of some naked outlaws.
    But tell me, what new course now shapes Duke
    Perkin?
CLIFFORD: For Ireland, mighty Henry, so instructed
    By Stephen Frion, sometimes secretary
50   In the French tongue unto your sacred excellence,
    But Perkin's tutor now.
KING HENRY: A subtle villain,
    That Frion! Frion – you, my Lord of Durham,
    Knew well the man.
DURHAM: French both in heart and actions!
KING HENRY: Some Irish heads work in this mine of
    treason;
    Speak 'em!
CLIFFORD: Not any of the best; your fortune
    Hath dull'd their spleens; never had counterfeit
    Such a confused rabble of lost bankrupts
    For counsellors: first Heron, a broken mercer;

36. *discradled:* left the cradle.   37. *Tournay:* city in Flanders.
49. *sometimes:* formerly.   55. *Speak:* name.
58. *mercer:* seller of textiles.

Then John a-Water, sometimes Mayor of Cork;
Skelton a tailor, and a scrivener   60
Call'd Astley; and whate'er these list to treat of,
Perkin must hearken to. But Frion, cunning
Above these dull capacities, still prompts him
To fly to Scotland to young James the Fourth,
And sue for aid to him. This is the latest
Of all their resolutions.
KING HENRY: Still more Frion!
Pestilent adder, he will hiss out poison
As dang'rous as infectious. — We must match him.
Clifford, thou hast spoke home; we give thee life.
But Clifford, there are people of our own   70
Remain behind untold. Who are they, Clifford?
Name those and we are friends, and will to rest;
'Tis thy last task.
CLIFFORD: O sir, here I must break
A most unlawful oath to keep a just one.
KING HENRY: Well, well, be brief, be brief.
CLIFFORD: The first in rank
Shall be John Ratcliffe, Lord Fitzwater, then
Sir Simon Mountford and Sir Thomas Thwaites,
With William Daubeney, Cressoner, Astwood,
Worsley the Dean of Paul's, two other friars,
And Robert Ratcliffe.
KING HENRY: Churchmen are turn'd devils!   80
These are the principal?
CLIFFORD: One more remains
Unnamed, whom I could willingly forget.
KING HENRY: Ha, Clifford? one more?
CLIFFORD: Great sir, do not hear him;

60. *scrivener:* clerk.   69. *home:* satisfactorily.
71. *untold:* unmentioned.

265

For when Sir William Stanley, your Lord Chamberlain,
Shall come into the list, as he is chief,
I shall lose credit with ye; yet this lord,
Last nam'd, is first against you.

KING HENRY: Urswick, the light.
View well my face, sirs. Is there blood left in it?

DURHAM: You alter strangely, sir.

KING HENRY: Alter, lord bishop?
90 Why, Clifford stabb'd me, or I dream'd 'a stabb'd me. –
Sirrah, it is a custom with the guilty
To think they set their own stains off by laying
Aspersions on some nobler than themselves;
Lies wait on treasons, as I find it here.
Thy life again is forfeit; I recall
My word of mercy, for I know thou dar'st
Repeat the name no more.

CLIFFORD: I dare, and once more
Upon my knowledge name Sir William Stanley,
Both in his counsel and his purse the chief
100 Assistant to the feign'd Duke of York.

DURHAM: Most strange!

URSWICK: Most wicked!

KING HENRY: Yet again, once more.

CLIFFORD: Sir William Stanley is your secret enemy,
And if time fit, will openly profess it.

KING HENRY: Sir William Stanley? Who? Sir William
    Stanley?
My chamberlain, my counsellor, the love,
The pleasure of my court, my bosom friend,
The charge and controlment of my person,
The keys and secrets of my treasury,

94. *wait on:* accompany.   95. *recall:* call back.
107. *controlment of my person:* personal security.

The all of all I am! I am unhappy:
Misery of confidence! – Let me turn traitor   110
To mine own person, yield my sceptre up
To Edward's sister and her bastard duke!

DURHAM: You lose your constant temper.

KING HENRY: Sir William Stanley!
O, do not blame me. He! 'twas only he,
Who having rescued me in Bosworth field
From Richard's bloody sword, snatch'd from his head
The kingly crown, and plac'd it first on mine.
He never fail'd me. What have I deserv'd
To lose this good man's heart, or he his own?

URSWICK: The night doth waste; this passion ill becomes
     ye;   120
Provide against your danger.

KING HENRY: Let it be so.
Urswick, command straight Stanley to his chamber; –
'Tis well we are i'th'Tower; – set a guard on him. –
Clifford, to bed; you must lodge here tonight;
We'll talk with you tomorrow. – My sad soul
Divines strange troubles.

DAUBENEY [within]:   Ho! the king, the king!
I must have entrance.

KING HENRY: Daubeney's voice; admit him.
What new combustions huddle next to keep
Our eyes from rest? –

     Enter DAUBENEY.

               The news?

DAUBENEY: Ten thousand Cornish,
Grudging to pay your subsidies, have gathered   130
A head, led by a blacksmith and a lawyer;
They make for London, and to them is join'd

113. *constant temper:* even disposition.

Lord Audley; as they march their number daily
Increases; they are –

KING HENRY: Rascals! – Talk no more;
Such are not worthy of my thoughts tonight;
And if I cannot sleep I'll wake. – To bed.
When counsels fail and there's in man no trust,
Even then an arm from Heaven fights for the just.
   Exeunt.

ACT TWO

SCENE ONE

Enter above COUNTESS *of* CRAWFORD, KATHERINE, JANE, *with other ladies.*

COUNTESS: Come, ladies, here's a solemn preparation
 For entertainment of this English prince.
 The king intends grace more than ordinary;
 'Twere pity now if 'a should prove a counterfeit.
KATHERINE: Bless the young man, our nation would be
   laugh'd at
 For honest souls through Christendom! My father
 Hath a weak stomach to the business, madam,
 But that the king must not be cross'd.
COUNTESS: 'A brings
 A goodly troop, they say, of gallants with him;
 But very modest people, for they strive not   *10*
 To fame their names too much; their godfathers
 May be beholding to them, but their fathers
 Scarce owe them thanks; they are disguised princes,
 Brought up, it seems, to honest trades. No matter;
 They will break forth in season.
JANE: Or break out,
 For most of 'em are broken by report. –
   Flourish.
 The king!

6. *honest:* ingenuous.   11. *fame:* speak abroad the fame of.
15. *break forth:* be revealed.
   break out: ? as of skin-diseases, boils (Ure), ? escape.
16. *broken:* bankrupt.

KATHERINE: Let us observe 'em and be silent.

Enter KING JAMES, HUNTLY, CRAWFORD *and* DALYELL.

KING JAMES: The right of kings, my lords, extends not only

To the safe conservation of their own

20 But also to the aid of such allies

As change of time and state hath oftentimes

Hurl'd down from careful crowns, to undergo

An exercise of sufferance in both fortunes:

So English Richard, surnam'd Coeur-de-Lion,

So Robert Bruce, our royal ancestor,

Forc'd by the trial of the wrongs they felt,

Both sought and found supplies from foreign kings,

To repossess their own. Then grudge not, lords,

A much distressed prince; King Charles of France

30 And Maximilian of Bohemia both

Have ratified his credit by their letters.

Shall we then be distrustful? No; compassion

Is one rich jewel that shines in our crown,

And we will have it shine there.

HUNTLY: Do your will, sir.

KING JAMES: The young duke is at hand. Dalyell, from us

First greet him and conduct him on; then Crawford

Shall meet him next; and Huntly last of all

Present him to our arms. Sound sprightly music,

Whilst majesty encounters majesty.   *Hautboys.*

DALYELL *goes out, brings in* PERKIN [WARBECK] *at the door where* CRAWFORD *entertains him, and from*

---

22. *careful:* full of care.   23. *sufferance:* endurance.
27. *supplies:* reinforcements.   28. *grudge:* grudge help to.
S.D. *entertains:* receives.

CRAWFORD, HUNTLY *salutes him and presents him to
the king; they embrace;* PERKIN *in state retires some few
paces back; during which ceremony the noblemen slightly
salute* FRION, HERON *a mercer,* SKELTON *a tailor,*
ASTLEY *a scrivener, with* JOHN A-WATER, *all* PERKIN'S
followers. Salutations ended, cease music.

WARBECK: Most high, most mighty king! That now
 there stands   40
Before your eyes, in presence of your peers,
A subject of the rarest kind of pity
That hath in any age touch'd noble hearts,
The vulgar story of a prince's ruin
Hath made it too apparent. Europe knows,
And all the Western world, what persecution
Hath rag'd in malice against us, sole heir
To the great throne of old Plantagenets.
How from our nursery we have been hurried
Unto the sanctuary, from the sanctuary   50
Forc'd to the prison, from the prison hal'd
By cruel hands to the tormentor's fury,
Is register'd already in the volume
Of all men's tongues, whose true relation draws
Compassion, melted into weeping eyes
And bleeding souls; but our misfortunes since
Have rang'd a larger progress through strange lands,
Protected in our innocence by Heaven.
Edward the Fifth our brother, in his tragedy
Quench'd their hot thirst of blood, whose hire to
 murder   60
Paid them their wages of despair and horror;
The softness of my childhood smil'd upon

44. *vulgar:* widespread.   51. *hal'd:* dragged.
57. *progress:* journey (with ironic hint of royal progress).

The roughness of their task, and robb'd them farther
Of hearts to dare or hands to execute.
Great king, they spar'd my life, the butchers spar'd it;
Return'd the tyrant, my unnatural uncle,
A truth of my dispatch; I was convey'd
With secrecy and speed to Tournay, foster'd
By obscure means, taught to unlearn myself;
70   But as I grew in years I grew in sense
Of fear and of disdain, fear of the tyrant
Whose power sway'd the throne then; when disdain
Of living so unknown, in such a servile
And abject lowness, prompted me to thoughts
Of recollecting who I was, I shook off
My bondage, and made haste to let my aunt
Of Burgundy acknowledge me her kinsman,
Heir to the crown of England, snatch'd by Henry
From Richard's head, a thing scarce known i'th'world.
KING JAMES: My lord, it stands not with your counsel
80   now
To fly upon invectives; if you can
Make this apparent what you have discours'd
In every circumstance, we will not study
An answer but are ready in your cause.
WARBECK: You are a wise and just king, by the powers
Above reserv'd beyond all other aids
To plant me in mine own inheritance,
To marry these two kingdoms in a love
Never to be divorc'd while time is time.

66–7. *Return'd . . . truth:* reported the fact.
69. *unlearn myself:* forget my true identity.
80. *stands . . . counsel:* is not consistent with your purpose.
81. *fly upon:* resort to.
83. *study:* spend time thinking over.
86. *reserv'd:* appointed.

As for the manner first of my escape,   90
Of my conveyance next, of my life since,
The means and persons who were instruments,
Great sir, 'tis fit I overpass in silence,
Reserving the relation to the secrecy
Of your own princely ear, since it concerns
Some great ones living yet, and others dead
Whose issue might be question'd. For your bounty,
Royal magnificence to him that seeks it,
We vow hereafter to demean ourself
As if we were your own and natural brother,   100
Omitting no occasion in our person
To express a gratitude beyond example.
KING JAMES: He must be more than subject who can
    utter
The language of a king, and such is thine.
Take this for answer: be whate'er thou art,
Thou never shalt repent that thou hast put
Thy cause and person into my protection.
Cousin of York, thus once more we embrace thee;
Welcome to James of Scotland; for thy safety,
Know such as love thee not shall never wrong thee.   110
Come, we will taste awhile our court delights,
Dream hence afflictions past, and then proceed
To high attempts of honour. On, lead on!
Both thou and thine are ours, and we will guard ye.
Lead on!
    Exeunt all except ladies above.
COUNTESS: I have not seen a gentleman
Of a more brave aspect or goodlier carriage;
His fortunes move not him. – Madam, y'are passionate.

97. *issue*: offspring.   113. *attempts*: enterprises.
117. *passionate*: moved.

KATHERINE: Beshrew me, but his words have touch'd
    me home,
  As if his cause concern'd me. I should pity him
120 If 'a should prove another than he seems.
    Enter CRAWFORD [*above*].
CRAWFORD: Ladies, the king commands your presence
    instantly
  For entertainment of the duke.
KATHERINE: The duke
  Must then be entertain'd, the king obey'd;
  It is our duty.
COUNTESS: We will all wait on him.
    Exeunt.

SCENE TWO

Flourish. Enter KING HENRY, OXFORD, DURHAM,
SURREY.

KING HENRY: Have ye condemn'd my chamberlain?
DURHAM: His treasons
  Condemn'd him, sir, which were as clear and manifest
  As foul and dangerous; besides, the guilt
  Of his conspiracy press'd him so nearly,
  That it drew from him free confession
  Without an importunity.
KING HENRY: O, lord bishop,
  This argued shame and sorrow for his folly,
  And must not stand in evidence against
  Our mercy and the softness of our nature.
10 The rigour and extremity of law

118. *home:* deeply.   4. *nearly:* closely.

Is sometimes too too bitter, but we carry
A chancery of pity in our bosom.
I hope we may reprieve him from the sentence
Of death; I hope we may.

DURHAM: You may, you may;
And so persuade your subjects that the title
Of York is better, nay, more just and lawful
Than yours of Lancaster! So Stanley holds;
Which, if it be not treason in the highest,
Then we are traitors all, perjur'd and false,
Who have took oath to Henry and the justice   20
Of Henry's title; Oxford, Surrey, Daubeney,
With all your other peers of state and church,
Forsworn, and Stanley true alone to Heaven
And England's lawful heir!

OXFORD: By Vere's old honours,
I'll cut his throat dares speak it.

SURREY: 'Tis a quarrel
T'engage a soul in.

KING HENRY: What a coil is here,
To keep my gratitude sincere and perfect!
Stanley was once my friend and came in time
To save my life; yet, to say truth, my lords,
The man stay'd long enough t'endanger it: 30
But I could see no more into his heart
Than what his outward actions did present;
And for 'em have rewarded him so fully,
As that there wanted nothing in our gift
To gratify his merit, as I thought,
Unless I should divide my crown with him
And give him half, though now I well perceive
'Twould scarce have serv'd his turn without the whole.

26. *coil*: uproar.

But I am charitable, lords. Let justice
40   Proceed in execution whiles I mourn
The loss of one whom I esteem'd a friend.

DURHAM: Sir, he is coming this way.

KING HENRY: If 'a speak to me,
I could deny him nothing; to prevent it,
I must withdraw. Pray, lords, commend my favours
To his last peace which I with him will pray for.
That done, it doth concern us to consult
Of other following troubles.

    Exit.

OXFORD: I am glad
He's gone; upon my life, he would have pardon'd
The traitor had 'a seen him.

SURREY: 'Tis a king
Compos'd of gentleness.

50 DURHAM: Rare and unheard of;
But every man is nearest to himself,
And that the king observes; 'tis fit 'a should.

    Enter STANLEY, [*Confessor*], *Executioner*, URSWICK
    and DAUBENEY.

STANLEY: May I not speak with Clifford ere I shake
This piece of frailty off?

DAUBENEY: You shall, he's sent for.

STANLEY: I must not see the king?

DURHAM: From him, Sir William,
These lords and I am sent; he bade us say
That he commends his mercy to your thoughts,
Wishing the laws of England could remit
The forfeit of your life as willingly
60   As he would, in the sweetness of his nature,
Forget your trespass; but howe'er your body

57. *mercy:* compassion.

Fall into dust, he vows, the king himself
Doth vow, to keep a requiem for your soul,
As for a friend, close treasur'd in his bosom.

OXFORD: Without remembrance of your errors past
   I come to take my leave and wish you Heaven.

SURREY: And I; good angels guard ye.

STANLEY: O, the king,
   Next to my soul, shall be the nearest subject
   Of my last prayers. My grave Lord of Durham,
   My Lords of Oxford, Surrey, Daubeney, all,   70
   Accept from a poor dying man a farewell.
   I was as you once, great, and stood hopeful
   Of many flourishing years, but fate and time
   Have wheel'd about to turn me into nothing.
     Enter CLIFFORD.

DAUBENEY: Sir Robert Clifford comes, the man, Sir
   William,
   You so desire to speak with.

DURHAM: Mark their meeting.

CLIFFORD: Sir William Stanley, I am glad your
   conscience
   Before your end hath emptied every burden
   Which charg'd it, as that you can clearly witness
   How far I have proceeded in a duty   80
   That both concern'd my truth and the state's safety.

STANLEY: Mercy, how dear is life to such as hug it!
   Come hither. –
    Makes a cross on Clifford's face with his finger.
               By this token think on me.

CLIFFORD: This token? What? I am abus'd!

STANLEY: You are not.
   I wet upon your cheeks a holy sign,

68. *nearest:* most immediate.

The cross, the Christian's badge, the traitor's infamy.
Wear, Clifford, to thy grave this painted emblem:
Water shall never wash it off; all eyes
That gaze upon thy face shall read there written
90 A state-informer's character, more ugly
Stamp'd on a noble name than on a base.
The Heavens forgive thee. – Pray, my lords, no change
Of words; this man and I have us'd too many.

CLIFFORD: Shall I be disgrac'd
Without reply?

DURHAM: Give losers leave to talk;
His loss is irrecoverable.

STANLEY: Once more
To all a long farewell; the best of greatness
Preserve the king; my next suit is, my lords,
To be remember'd to my noble brother,
100 Derby, my much griev'd brother. O! persuade him
That I shall stand no blemish to his house
In chronicles writ in another age.
My heart doth bleed for him and for his sighs;
Tell him, he must not think the style of Derby,
Nor being husband to King Henry's mother,
The league with peers, the smiles of Fortune, can
Secure his peace above the state of man.
I take my leave to travel to my dust;
Subjects deserve their deaths whose kings are just.
Come, confessor. – [*To Executioner*] On with thy axe,
110   friend, on!
    [STANLEY *led off to execution.*]

CLIFFORD: Was I call'd hither by a traitor's breath
To be upbraided? Lords, the king shall know it.

90. *character:* sign, cipher.   92. *change:* exchange.
97. *best of greatness:* i.e. God.   104. *style:* title.

278

Enter KING HENRY *with a white staff.*

KING HENRY: The king doth know it, sir; the king hath
  heard
  What he or you could say. We have given credit
  To every point of Clifford's information,
  The only evidence 'gainst Stanley's head.
  'A dies for't; are you pleas'd?

CLIFFORD: I, pleas'd my lord?

KING HENRY: No echoes. For your service, we dismiss
  Your more attendance on the court; take ease
  And live at home; but as you love your life,   *120*
  Stir not from London without leave from us.
  We'll think on your reward. Away!

CLIFFORD: I go, sir.

  Exit CLIFFORD.

KING HENRY: Die all our griefs with Stanley. – Take
  this staff
  Of office, Daubeney; henceforth be our chamberlain.

DAUBENEY: I am your humblest servant.

KING HENRY: We are followed
  By enemies at home that will not cease
  To seek their own confusion: 'tis most true,
  The Cornish under Audley are march'd on
  As far as Winchester; but let them come,
  Our forces are in readiness, we'll catch 'em   *130*
  In their own toils.

DAUBENEY: Your army being muster'd
  Consist in all, of horse and foot, at least
  In number six and twenty thousand, men
  Daring and able, resolute to fight,
  And loyal in their truths.

KING HENRY: We know it, Daubeney.

  131. *toils:* snares.

For them we order thus: Oxford in chief,
Assisted by bold Essex and the earl
Of Suffolk, shall lead on the first battalia;
Be that your charge.

OXFORD: I humbly thank your majesty.

KING HENRY: The next division we assign to
140 Daubeney.
These must be men of action, for on those
The fortune of our fortunes must rely.
The last and main ourself commands in person,
As ready to restore the fight at all times,
As to consummate an assured victory.

DAUBENEY: The king is still oraculous.

KING HENRY: But Surrey,
We have employment of more toil for thee!
For our intelligence comes swiftly to us,
That James of Scotland late hath entertain'd
150 Perkin the counterfeit with more than common
Grace and respect, nay, courts him with rare favours.
The Scot is young and forward; we must look for
A sudden storm to England from the North;
Which to withstand, Durham shall post to Norham
To fortify the castle and secure
The frontiers against an invasion there.
Surrey shall follow soon with such an army,
As may relieve the bishop and encounter
On all occasions the death-daring Scots.
160 You know your charges all; 'tis now a time
To execute, not talk. Heaven is our guard still.
War must breed peace; such is the fate of kings.
 Exeunt.

146. *still oraculous:* ever divinely inspired.
159. *On all occasions:* at every opportunity.

SCENE THREE

Enter CRAWFORD *and* DALYELL.

CRAWFORD: 'Tis more than strange; my reason cannot answer
  Such argument of fine imposture, couch'd
  In witchcraft of persuasion, that it fashions
  Impossibilities as if appearance
  Could cozen truth itself. This dukeling mushroom
  Hath doubtless charm'd the king.

DALYELL: 'A courts the ladies,
  As if his strength of language chain'd attention
  By power of prerogative.

CRAWFORD: It madded
  My very soul to hear our master's motion:
10 What surety both of amity and honour
  Must of necessity ensue upon
  A match betwixt some noble of our nation
  And this brave prince forsooth.

DALYELL: 'Twill prove too fatal;
  Wise Huntly fears the threat'ning. Bless the lady
  From such a ruin!

CRAWFORD: How the council privy
  Of this young Phaeton do screw their faces
  Into a gravity their trades, good people,
  Were never guilty of! The meanest of 'em
  Dreams of at least an office in the state.

20 DALYELL: Sure not the hangman's; 'tis bespoke already
  For service to their rogueships. – Silence!

    Enter KING JAMES *and* HUNTLY.

6. *charm'd:* put a charm on.   8. *prerogative:* sovereign right.

KING JAMES: Do not
  Argue against our will; we have descended
  Somewhat, as we may term it, too familiarly
  From justice of our birthright to examine
  The force of your allegiance. – Sir, we have!
  But find it short of duty.

HUNTLY: Break my heart,
  Do, do, king! Have my services, my loyalty –
  Heaven knows untainted ever – drawn upon me
  Contempt now in mine age, when I but wanted
30 A minute of peace not to be troubled,
  My last, my long one? Let me be a dotard,
  A bedlam, a poor sot, or what you please
  To have me, so you will not stain your blood –
  Your own blood, royal sir, though mix'd with mine –
  By marriage of this girl to a straggler!
  Take, take my head, sir; whilst my tongue can wag
  It cannot name him other.

KING JAMES: Kings are counterfeits
  In your repute, grave oracle, not presently
  Set on their thrones, with sceptres in their fists.
40 But use your own detraction; 'tis our pleasure
  To give our cousin York for wife our kinswoman,
  The Lady Katherine. Instinct of sovereignty
  Designs the honour, though her peevish father
  Usurps our resolution.

HUNTLY: O, 'tis well,
  Exceeding well! I never was ambitious
  Of using congées to my daughter-queen.

29. *wanted:* lacked.   30–1. *peace . . . one:* i.e. death.
32. *bedlam:* lunatic.   38. *repute:* estimation.
43. *Designs:* points out.
44. *Usurps:* attempts unlawfully to change.   46. *congées:* obeisances.

A queen! perhaps a quean! – Forgive me, Dalyell,
Thou honourable gentleman. – None here
Dare speak one word of comfort?

DALYELL: Cruel misery!

CRAWFORD: The lady, gracious prince, maybe hath
     settled   50
Affection on some former choice.

DALYELL: Enforcement
Would prove but tyranny.

HUNTLY: I thank 'ee heartily.
Let any yeoman of our nation challenge
An interest in the girl; then the king
May add a jointure of ascent in titles
Worthy a free consent; now 'a pulls down
What old desert hath builded.

KING JAMES: Cease persuasions!
I violate no pawns of faiths, intrude not
On private loves. That I have play'd the orator
For kingly York to virtuous Kate her grant   60
Can justify, referring her contents
To our provision. The Welsh Harry henceforth
Shall therefore know, and tremble to acknowledge,
That not the painted idol of his policy
Shall fright the lawful owner from a kingdom.
We are resolv'd.

HUNTLY: Some of thy subjects' hearts,
King James, will bleed for this!

KING JAMES: Then shall their bloods
Be nobly spent. No more disputes! He is not
Our friend who contradicts us.

HUNTLY: Farewell, daughter!

---

47. *quean:* whore.
55. *jointure:* dowry.   *ascent:* one step back in genealogy. See note.

70 My care by one is lessened; thank the king for't.
    I and my griefs will dance now. – Look, lords, look!
    Here's hand in hand already!

KING JAMES: Peace, old frenzy! –

  Enter WARBECK *leading* KATHERINE, *complimenting;*
  COUNTESS *of* CRAWFORD, JANE, FRION, JOHN
  A-WATER, ASTLEY, HERON *and* SKELTON.

    How like a king 'a looks! Lords, but observe
    The confidence of his aspect! Dross cannot
    Cleave to so pure a metal; royal youth!
    Plantagenet undoubted!

HUNTLY: Ho! brave youth,
    But no Plantagenet by'r lady, yet,
    By red rose or by white.

WARBECK: An union this way
    Settles possession in a monarchy
80 Establish'd rightly, as is my inheritance. –
    [*To* KATHERINE] Acknowledge me but sovereign of
        this kingdom,
    Your heart, fair princess, and the hand of providence
    Shall crown you queen of me and my best fortunes.

KATHERINE: Where my obedience is, my lord, a duty,
    Love owes true service.

WARBECK: Shall I? –

KING JAMES: Cousin, yes,
    Enjoy her; from my hand accept your bride,
    And may they live at enmity with comfort,
    Who grieve at such an equal pledge of troths. –
    Y'are the prince's wife now.

KATHERINE: By your gift, sir.

WARBECK: Thus I take seizure of mine own.

    [*They embrace.*]

    79. *monarchy:* i.e. love of. See note.

KATHERINE: I miss yet   *90*
  A father's blessing; let me find it. – [*Kneels*] Humbly
  Upon my knees I seek it.
HUNTLY: I am Huntly,
  Old Alexander Gordon, a plain subject,
  Nor more nor less; and, lady, if you wish for
  A blessing, you must bend your knees to Heaven;
  For Heaven did give me you. Alas, alas,
  What would you have me say? May all the happiness
  My prayers ever sued to fall upon you
  Preserve you in your virtues. – Prithee, Dalyell,
  Come with me; for I feel thy griefs as full   *100*
  As mine; let's steal away and cry together.
DALYELL: My hopes are in their ruins.
      Exeunt HUNTLY *and* DALYELL.
KING JAMES: Good, kind Huntly
  Is overjoy'd. A fit solemnity
  Shall perfect these delights. Crawford, attend
  Our order for the preparation.
      Exeunt all except FRION, JOHN A-WATER, ASTLEY,
      HERON *and* SKELTON.
FRION: Now, worthy gentlemen, have I not followed
  My undertakings with success? Here's entrance
  Into a certainty above a hope.
HERON: Hopes are but hopes; I was ever confident, when I
  traded but in remnants, that my stars had reserved me *110*
  to the title of a viscount at least. Honour is honour
  though cut out of any stuffs.
SKELTON: My brother Heron hath right wisely delivered
  his opinion; for he that threads his needle with the sharp
  eyes of industry shall in time go through-stitch with the
  new suit of preferment.

112. *stuffs:* fabrics.   115. *go through-stitch with:* carry out completely.

ASTLEY: Spoken to the purpose, my fine-witted brother
    Skelton; for as no indenture but has its counterpawn, no
    noverint but his condition or defeasance; so no right but
120   may have claim, no claim but may have possession, any
    act of parliament to the contrary notwithstanding.
FRION: You are all read in mysteries of state
    And quick of apprehension, deep in judgement,
    Active in resolution; and 'tis pity
    Such counsel should lie buried in obscurity.
    But why in such a time and cause of triumph
    Stands the judicious Mayor of Cork so silent?
    Believe it, sir, as English Richard prospers,
    You must not miss employment of high nature.
130 JOHN A-WATER: If men may be credited in their mortality,
    which I dare not peremptorily aver, but they may, or
    not be; presumptions by this marriage are then, in sooth,
    of fruitful expectation. Or else I must not justify other
    men's belief, more than other should rely on mine.
FRION: Pith of experience! Those that have borne office,
    Weigh every word before it can drop from them.
    But, noble counsellors, since now the present
    Requires in point of honour – pray, mistake not –
    Some service to our lord, 'tis fit the Scots
140   Should not engross all glory to themselves
    At this so grand and eminent solemnity.
SKELTON: The Scots? The motion is defied. I had rather,
    for my part, without trial of my country, suffer persecu-
    tion under the pressing-iron of reproach, or let my skin
    be punch'd full of eyelet holes with the bodkin of derision.

118. *counterpawn:* second, fitting part of torn-through indenture.
119. *noverint:* bond. *defeasance:* clause stating how deed becomes void.
122. *mysteries:* arts.   130. *in their mortality:* as mere mortals.
133. *justify:* uphold.   134. *other:* others.   145. *eyelet-holes:* lace-holes

ASTLEY: I will sooner lose both my ears on the pillory of
forgery.

HERON: Let me first live a bankrupt, and die in the lousy
hole of hunger, without compounding for sixpence in
the pound.   150

JOHN A-WATER: If men fail not in their expectations, there
may be spirits also that digest no rude affronts, Master
Secretary Frion, or I am cozened, which is possible,
I grant.

FRION: Resolv'd like men of knowledge! At this feast then
In honour of the bride, the Scots, I know,
Will in some show, some mask or some device
Prefer their duties. Now it were uncomely
That we be found less forward for our prince
Than they are for their lady; and by how much   160
We outshine them in persons of account,
By so much more will our endeavours meet with
A livelier applause. Great emperors
Have for their recreations undertook
Such kind of pastimes. As for the conceit,
Refer it to my study; the performance,
You all shall share a thanks in; 'twill be grateful.

HERON: The motion is allowed. I have stole to a dancing-
school when I was a prentice.

ASTLEY: There have been Irish hubbubs when I have made   170
one too.

SKELTON: For fashioning of shapes and cutting a cross-caper
turn me off to my trade again.

---

149. *compounding:* settling to pay proportion to creditors.
161. *in:* in the eyes of.   165. *conceit:* informing idea of the masque.
167. *grateful:* pleasurable.   170. *hubbubs:* noisy entertainments.
170-1. *made one:* taken part.
172-3. *shapes, cutting a cross-caper:* 1. dance posture 2. tailoring effects.

JOHN A-WATER: Surely, there is, if I be not deceived, a
kind of gravity in merriment; as there is, or perhaps
ought to be, respect of persons in the quality of carriage
which is, as it is construed, either so or so.

FRION: Still you come home to me; upon occasion
I find you relish courtship with discretion;
180 And such are fit for statesmen of your merits.
Pray 'ee wait the prince, and in his ear acquaint him
With this design; I'll follow and direct 'ee.

Exeunt all except FRION.

O, the toil
Of humouring this abject scum of mankind!
Muddy-brain'd peasants! Princes feel a misery
Beyond impartial sufferance whose extremes
Must yield to such abettors; yet our tide
Runs smoothly without adverse winds. Run on!
Flow to a full sea! Time alone debates
190 Quarrels forewritten in the book of fates.

Exit.

178. *come home to me:* take my meaning.
     upon occasion: as opportunity arises.
186. *extremes:* extreme necessities.
189. *debates:* abates.

ACT THREE

SCENE ONE

Enter KING HENRY, *his gorget on, his sword, plume of feathers, leading-staff; and* URSWICK.

KING HENRY: How runs the time of day?

URSWICK: Past ten, my lord.

KING HENRY: A bloody hour will it prove to some
  Whose disobedience, like the sons o'th'earth,
  Throw a defiance 'gainst the face of Heaven.
  Oxford, with Essex and stout De la Pole,
  Have quieted the Londoners, I hope,
  And set them safe from fear?

URSWICK: They are all silent.

KING HENRY: From their own battlements they may
    behold
  Saint George's Fields o'erspread with armed men;
  Amongst whom, our own royal standard threatens   10
  Confusion to opposers. We must learn
  To practise war again in time of peace,
  Or lay our crown before our subjects' feet;
  Ha, Urswick, must we not?

URSWICK: The powers who seated
  King Henry on his lawful throne will ever
  Rise up in his defence.

KING HENRY: Rage shall not fright
  The bosom of our confidence; in Kent

s.d. *gorget*: throat armour. *leading-staff*: baton.

289

Our Cornish rebels, cozen'd of their hopes,
Met brave resistance by that country's earl,
20   George Aber'genny, Cobham, Poynings, Guildford,
And other loyal hearts; now, if Blackheath
Must be reserv'd the fatal tomb to swallow
Such stiff-neck'd abjects as with weary marches
Have travell'd from their homes, their wives and
   children,
To pay instead of subsidies their lives,
We may continue sovereign. Yet, Urswick,
We'll not abate one penny what in parliament
Hath freely been contributed; we must not;
Money gives soul to action. Our competitor,
30   The Flemish counterfeit, with James of Scotland,
Will prove what courage, need and want can nourish
Without the food of fit supplies. But Urswick,
I have a charm in secret that shall loose
The witchcraft wherewith young King James is bound,
And free it at my pleasure without bloodshed.
URSWICK: Your majesty's a wise king, sent from Heaven,
Protector of the just.
KING HENRY: Let dinner cheerfully
Be serv'd in; this day of the week is ours,
Our day of providence, for Saturday
40   Yet never fail'd in all my undertakings
To yield me rest at night.
      A Flourish.

                              What means this warning?
Good fate, speak peace to Henry.
      Enter DAUBENEY, OXFORD, *and Attendants.*
DAUBENEY: Live the king
Triumphant in the ruin of his enemies!

31. *prove:* find out by experience.   *need:* compulsion.

OXFORD: The head of strong rebellion is cut off,
  The body hew'd in pieces.
KING HENRY: Daubeney, Oxford,
  Minions to noblest fortunes, how yet stands
  The comfort of your wishes?
DAUBENEY: Briefly thus:
  The Cornish under Audley, disappointed
  Of flattered expectation, from the Kentish –
  Your majesty's right trusty liegemen – flew,   50
  Feather'd by rage and hearten'd by presumption,
  To take the field even at your palace gates,
  And face you in your chamber royal; arrogance
  Improv'd their ignorance, for they supposing
  – Misled by rumour – that the day of battle
  Should fall on Monday, rather brav'd your forces
  Than doubted any onset; yet this morning,
  When in the dawning I by your direction
  Strove to get Deptford-strand bridge, there I found
  Such a resistance as might show what strength   60
  Could make; here arrows hail'd in showers upon us
  A full yard long at least; but we prevail'd.
  My Lord of Oxford with his fellow peers,
  Environing the hill, fell fiercely on them
  On the one side, I on the other, till, great sir,
  – Pardon the oversight – eager of doing
  Some memorable act, I was engag'd
  Almost a prisoner, but was freed as soon
  As sensible of danger. Now the fight
  Began in heat, which quenched in the blood of   70
  Two thousand rebels and as many more

51. *Feather'd:* winged.   54. *Improv'd:* aggravated.
56. *brav'd:* treated with bravado.   57. *doubted:* suspected.
70. *quenched:* cooled down.

Reserv'd to try your mercy, have return'd
A victory with safety.

KING HENRY: Have we lost
An equal number with them?

OXFORD: In the total
Scarcely four hundred. Audley, Flammock, Joseph,
The ringleaders of this commotion,
Railed in ropes, fit ornaments for traitors,
Wait your determinations.

KING HENRY: We must pay
Our thanks where they are only due. O, lords,
80   Here is no victory, nor shall our people
Conceive that we can triumph in their falls.
Alas, poor souls! Let such as are escap'd,
Steal to the country back without pursuit:
There's not a drop of blood spilt but hath drawn
As much of mine; their swords could have wrought
    wonders
On their king's part who faintly were unsheath'd
Against their prince but wounded their own breasts.
Lords, we are debtors to your care, our payment
Shall be both sure and fitting your deserts.

90 DAUBENEY: Sir, will you please to see those rebels, heads
Of this wild monster-multitude?

KING HENRY: Dear friend,
My faithful Daubeney, no; on them our justice
Must frown in terror; I will not vouchsafe
An eye of pity to them. Let false Audley
Be drawn upon an hurdle from the Newgate

72. *Reserv'd*: set apart.   *return'd*: brought back (i.e. the fight has).
77. *Railed*: tied in a row.
86. *who*: which (i.e. the swords). *faintly*: weak-spiritedly.
95. *hurdle*: sledge on which prisoners were drawn.
    Newgate: Newgate prison.

To Tower-hill in his own coat of arms
Painted on paper, with the arms revers'd,
Defac'd and torn; there let him lose his head.
The lawyer and the blacksmith shall be hang'd,
Quarter'd, their quarters into Cornwall sent,   100
Examples to the rest, whom we are pleas'd
To pardon and dismiss from further quest.
My Lord of Oxford, see it done.

OXFORD: I shall, sir.

KING HENRY: Urswick!

URSWICK: My lord?

KING HENRY: To Dinham, our high-treasurer,
Say we command commissions be new granted
For the collection of our subsidies
Through all the west, and that speedily.
Lords, we acknowledge our engagements due
For your most constant services.

DAUBENEY: Your soldiers
Have manfully and faithfully acquitted   110
Their several duties.

KING HENRY: For it, we will throw
A largesse free amongst them which shall hearten
And cherish up their loyalties. More yet
Remains of like employment; not a man
Can be dismiss'd till enemies abroad,
More dangerous than these at home, have felt
The puissance of our arms. O, happy kings
Whose thrones are raised in their subjects' hearts.
     Exeunt.

102. *quest:* official enquiry.

SCENE TWO

Enter HUNTLY *and* DALYELL.

HUNTLY: Now, sir, a modest word with you, sad
    gentleman:
  Is not this fine, I trow, to see the gambols,
  To hear the jigs, observe the frisks, b'enchanted
  With the rare discord of bells, pipes and tabors,
  Hotch-potch of Scotch and Irish twingle-twangles,
  Like to so many quiristers of Bedlam
  Trolling a catch! The feasts, the manly stomachs,
  The healths in usquebaugh and bonny-clabber,
  The ale in dishes never fetch'd from China,
10 The hundred thousand knacks not to be spoken of, –
  And all this for King Oberon and Queen Mab, –
  Should put a soul int'ee. Look 'ee, good man,
  How youthful I am grown; but by your leave,
  This new queen-bride must henceforth be no more
  My daughter; no, by'r lady, 'tis unfit!
  And yet you see how I do bear this change, –
  Methinks courageously. Then shake off care
  In such a time of jollity.

DALYELL: Alas, sir,
  How can you cast a mist upon your griefs,
20 Which, howsoe'er you shadow, but present

4. *tabors:* drums.
5. *twingle-twangles:* sound of Gaelic harp.
6. *quiristers:* choiristers.
7. *Trolling a catch:* running over a song.
8. *usquebaugh:* whisky.
   bonny-clabber: Irish drink of sour buttermilk and beer.
10. *knacks:* delicacies.

To any judging eye the perfect substance
Of which mine are but counterfeits?

HUNTLY: Foh, Dalyell!
Thou interrupts the part I bear in music
To this rare bridal feast. Let us be merry;
Whilst flattering calms secure us against storms,
Tempests when they begin to roar put out
The light of peace and cloud the sun's bright eye
In darkness of despair; yet we are safe.

DALYELL: I wish you could as easily forget
The justice of your sorrows, as my hopes   30
Can yield to destiny.

HUNTLY: Pish! then I see
Thou dost not know the flexible condition
Of my ap'd nature; I can laugh, laugh heartily
When the gout cramps my joints; let but the stone
Stop in my bladder, I am straight a-singing;
The quartan fever shrinking every limb
Sets me a-cap'ring straight; do but betray me
And bind me a friend for ever. What? I trust
The losing of a daughter – though I doted
On every hair that grew to trim her head –   40
Admits not any pain like one of these!
Come, th'art deceiv'd in me. Give me a blow,
A sound blow on the face; I'll thank thee for't.
I love my wrongs; still tha'rt deceiv'd in me.

DALYELL: Deceiv'd? O, noble Huntly, my few years
Have learnt experience of too ripe an age
To forfeit fit credulity. Forgive

25. *secure . . . against:* make careless about.
33. *ap'd:* counterfeit, absurdly imitated. See note.
41. *Admits:* allows.
47. *fit credulity:* capacity for proper belief or disbelief.

My rudeness, I am bold.

HUNTLY: Forgive me first
A madness of ambition; by example
50   Teach me humility, for patience scorns
Lectures which schoolmen use to read to boys
Uncapable of injuries. Though old
I could grow tough in fury, and disclaim
Allegiance to my king; could fall at odds
With all my fellow peers that durst not stand
Defendants 'gainst the rape done on mine honour.
But kings are earthly gods; there is no meddling
With their annointed bodies; for their actions,
They only are accountable to Heaven.
60   Yet in the puzzle of my troubled brain
One antidote's reserv'd against the poison
Of my distractions; 'tis in thee t'apply it.

DALYELL: Name it! O, name it quickly, sir!

HUNTLY: A pardon
For my most foolish slighting thy deserts.
I have cull'd out this time to beg it; prithee
Be gentle; had I been so, thou hadst own'd
A happy bride, but now a castaway
And never child of mine more.

DALYELL: Say not so, sir;
It is not fault in her.

HUNTLY: The world would prate
70   How she was handsome; young I know she was,
Tender, and sweet in her obedience;
But lost now. What a bankrupt am I made
Of a full stock of blessings! – Must I hope
A mercy from thy heart?

50. *patience:* experience.   52. *of injuries:* of being injured.
66. *gentle:* generous.

DALYELL: A love, a service,
A friendship to posterity.
HUNTLY: Good angels
Reward thy charity! I have no more
But prayers left me now.
DALYELL: I'll lend you mirth, sir,
If you will be in consort.
HUNTLY: Thank ye truly.
I must! yes, yes, I must! Here's yet some ease –
A partner in affliction: look not angry.   80
DALYELL: Good, noble sir!
        Flourish.
HUNTLY: O, hark! We may be quiet.
The king and all the others come: a meeting
Of gaudy sights. This day's the last of revels;
Tomorrow sounds of war. Then new exchange:
Fiddles must turn to swords. Unhappy marriage!
        Enter KING JAMES, WARBECK *leading* KATHERINE,
        CRAWFORD, COUNTESS [*of* CRAWFORD] *and* JANE.
        HUNTLY *and* DALYELL *fall among them.*
KING JAMES: Cousin of York, you and your princely
        bride
Have liberally enjoy'd such soft delights
As a new-married couple could forethink;
Nor has our bounty shorten'd expectation.
But after all those pleasures of repose   90
Or amorous safety, we must rouse the ease
Of dalliance with achievements of more glory
Than sloth and sleep can furnish. Yet, for farewell,
Gladly we entertain a truce with time,
To grace the joint endeavours of our servants.

78. *consort:* harmony. See note.   81. *may:* must.
89. *shorten'd:* fallen short of.

WARBECK: My royal cousin, in your princely favour
The extent of bounty hath been so unlimited,
As only an acknowledgement in words
Would breed suspicion in our state and quality.
100 When we shall in the fulness of our fate –
Whose minister, necessity, will perfect –
Sit on our own throne, then our arms laid open
To gratitude, in sacred memory
Of these large benefits, shall twine them close
Even to our thoughts and heart without distinction.
Then James and Richard, being in effect
One person, shall unite and rule one people,
Divisible in title only.
KING JAMES: Seat ye. –
Are the presenters ready?
CRAWFORD: All are ent'ring.
HUNTLY [aside]: Dainty sport toward, Dalyell. Sit;
110   come sit!
Sit and be quiet; here are kingly bug's-words.
*Enter at one door four Scotch Antics accordingly habited;
enter at another four wild Irish in trowses, long-haired, and
accordingly habited. Music. The masquers dance.*
KING JAMES: To all, a general thanks!
WARBECK: In the next room
Take your own shapes again; you shall receive
Particular acknowledgement.
     [Exeunt the Masquers.]
KING JAMES: Enough
Of merriments. Crawford, how far's our army
Upon the march?

109. *presenters:* actors.   110. *toward:* about to take place.
111. *bug's-words:* swaggering language.
s.D. *Antics:* clowns.   *trowses:* tight-fitting drawers.

298

CRAWFORD: At Heydonhall, great king,
  Twelve thousand well prepar'd.
KING JAMES: Crawford, tonight
  Post thither. We in person with the prince
  By four o'clock tomorrow after dinner
  Will be wi'ee; speed away!
CRAWFORD: I fly, my lord.   120
    [*Exit.*]
KING JAMES: Our business grows to head now; where's
      your secretary,
  That he attends 'ee not to serve?
WARBECK: With Marchmount,
  Your herald.
KING JAMES: Good! The proclamation's ready;
  By that it will appear how the English stand
  Affected to your title. – Huntly, comfort
  Your daughter in her husband's absence; fight
  With prayers at home for us who for your honours
  Must toil in fight abroad.
HUNTLY: Prayers are the weapons
  Which men, so near their graves as I, do use.
  I've little else to do.
KING JAMES: To rest, young beauties!   130
  We must be early stirring, quickly part.
  A kingdom's rescue craves both speed and art.
  Cousins, good night.
    Flourish.
WARBECK: Rest to our cousin king.
KATHERINE: Your blessing, sir.
HUNTLY: Fair blessings on your highness! – Sure, you
      need 'em.
    Exeunt all except WARBECK, KATHERINE [*and* JANE].
  125. *Affected to:* disposed towards.

WARBECK: Jane, set the lights down and from us return
   To those in the next room this little purse;
   Say we'll deserve their loves.

JANE: It shall be done, sir.
   [*Exit.*]

WARBECK: Now, dearest, ere sweet sleep shall seal those
   eyes,
140 Love's precious tapers, give me leave to use
   A parting ceremony; for tomorrow
   It would be sacrilege to intrude upon
   The temple of thy peace. Swift as the morning
   Must I break from the down of thy embraces,
   To put on steel, and trace the paths which lead
   Through various hazards to a careful throne.

KATHERINE: My lord, I would fain go wi'ee; there's
   small fortune
   In staying here behind.

WARBECK: The churlish brow
   Of war, fair dearest, is a sight of horror
150 For ladies' entertainment. If thou hear'st
   A truth of my sad ending by the hand
   Of some unnatural subject, thou withal
   Shalt hear how I died worthy of my right
   By falling like a king; and in the close
   Which my last breath shall sound, thy name, thou
   fairest,
   Shall sing a requiem to my soul, unwilling
   Only of greater glory 'cause divided
   From such a heaven on earth as life with thee.
   But these are chimes for funerals; my business
160 Attends on fortune of a sprightlier triumph;

151. *truth:* report.
154. *close:* conclusion of piece of music.

For love and majesty are reconcil'd,
And vow to crown thee empress of the west.

KATHERINE: You have a noble language, sir; your right
In me is without question, and however
Events of time may shorten my deserts
In others' pity, yet it shall not stagger
Or constancy or duty in a wife.
You must be king of me, and my poor heart
Is all I can call mine.

WARBECK: But we will live,
Live, beauteous virtue, by the lively test   170
Of our own blood, to let the counterfeit
Be known the world's contempt.

KATHERINE: Pray do not use
That word; it carries fate in't. The first suit
I ever made, I trust your love will grant.

WARBECK: Without denial, dearest.

KATHERINE: That hereafter,
If you return with safety, no adventure
May sever us in tasting any fortune:
I ne'er can stay behind again.

WARBECK: Y'are lady
Of your desires and shall command your will.
Yet 'tis too hard a promise.

KATHERINE: What our destinies   180
Have rul'd out in their books we must not search
But kneel to.

WARBECK: Then to fear when hope is fruitless
Were to be desperately miserable,
Which poverty our greatness dares not dream of,

181. *rul'd out:* decreed. *search:* examine.
184. *poverty:* i.e. of spirit.

And much more scorns to stoop to. Some few minutes
Remain yet; let's be thrifty in our hopes.
   Exeunt.

SCENE THREE

Enter KING HENRY, HIALAS, *and* URSWICK.

KING HENRY: Your name is Pedro Hialas, a Spaniard?
HIALAS: Sir, a Castilian born.
KING HENRY: King Ferdinand
With wise Queen Isabel, his royal consort,
Write 'ee a man of worthy trust and candour.
Princes are dear to Heaven who meet with subjects
Sincere in their employments; such I find
Your commendation, sir. Let me deliver
How joyful I repute the amity
With your most fortunate master, who almost
10   Comes near a miracle in his success
Against the Moors who had devour'd his country,
Entire now to his sceptre. We, for our part,
Will imitate his providence, in hope
Of partage in the use on't. We repute
The privacy of his advisement to us
By you, intended an ambassador
To Scotland for a peace between our kingdoms,
A policy of love which well becomes
His wisdom and our care.

186. *thrifty:* flourishing.
7. *deliver:* declare.
12. *Entire . . . sceptre:* completely under his rule.
13. *providence:* foresight.
14. *partage . . . on't:* share in the profit of it.
    repute: think highly of.
15. *privacy . . . advisement:* his private advice.

HIALAS: Your majesty
  Doth understand him rightly.
KING HENRY: Else,   20
  Your knowledge can instruct me; wherein, sir,
  To fall on ceremony would seem useless,
  Which shall not need; for I will be as studious
  Of your concealment in our conference
  As any counsel shall advise.
HIALAS: Then sir,
  My chief request is, that on notice given
  At my dispatch in Scotland, you will send
  Some learned man of power and experience
  To join in treaty with me.
KING HENRY: I shall do it,
  Being that way well provided by a servant   30
  Which may attend 'ee ever.
HIALAS: If King James
  By any indirection should perceive
  My coming near your court, I doubt the issue
  Of my employment.
KING HENRY: Be not your own herald;
  I learn sometimes without a teacher.
HIALAS: Good days
  Guard all your princely thoughts.
KING HENRY: Urswick, no further
  Than the next open gallery attend him. –
  A hearty love go with you.
HIALAS: Your vow'd beadsman.
  Exeunt URSWICK *and* HIALAS.

  20. *Else:* if not.
  29. *join . . . me:* join me in the negotiations.
  30. *servant:* i.e. Fox, bishop of Durham.
  33. *doubt the issue:* have doubts about the success.
  38. *beadsman:* literally, one paid to pray for another.

KING HENRY: King Ferdinand is not so much a fox
40   But that a cunning huntsman may in time
Fall on the scent; in honourable actions
Safe imitation best deserves a praise.
    Enter URSWICK.
What, the Castilian's pass'd away?

URSWICK: He is,
And undiscover'd. The two hundred marks
Your majesty convey'd 'a gently purs'd
With a right modest gravity.

KING HENRY: What was't
'A mutter'd in the earnest of his wisdom?
'A spoke not to be heard. 'Twas about –

URSWICK: Warbeck:
How if King Henry were but sure of subjects,
50   Such a wild runagate might soon be cag'd,
No great ado withstanding.

KING HENRY: Nay, nay; something
About my son Prince Arthur's match.

URSWICK: Right, right, sir;
'A humm'd it out, how that King Ferdinand
Swore that the marriage 'twixt the Lady Catherine
His daughter and the Prince of Wales your son
Should never be consummated as long
As any Earl of Warwick liv'd in England,
Except by new creation.

KING HENRY: I remember;
'Twas so indeed. The king his master swore it?

URSWICK: Directly, as he said.

60 KING HENRY: An Earl of Warwick! –
Provide a messenger for letters instantly

47. *earnest:* seriousness.
50. *runagate:* vagabond.   60. *Directly:* exactly.

To Bishop Fox. Our news from Scotland creeps,
It comes so slow; we must have airy spirits;
Our time requires dispatch. – The Earl of Warwick!
Let him be son to Clarence, younger brother
To Edward: Edward's daughter is, I think,
Mother to our Prince Arthur. – Get a messenger.
 Exeunt.

SCENE FOUR

 Enter KING JAMES, WARBECK, CRAWFORD,
 DALYELL, HERON, ASTLEY, JOHN A-WATER,
 SKELTON *and Soldiers.*

KING JAMES: We trifle time against these castle walls;
 The English prelate will not yield. Once more
 Give him a summons.
  Parley.
  Enter above DURHAM *armed, a truncheon in his hand, and
 Soldiers.*
WARBECK: See, the jolly clerk
 Appears trimm'd like a ruffian.
KING JAMES: Bishop, yet
 Set ope the ports, and to your lawful sovereign,
 Richard of York, surrender up this castle,
 And he will take thee to his grace; else Tweed
 Shall overflow his banks with English blood,
 And wash the sand that cements those hard stones
 From their foundation.
10 DURHAM: Warlike King of Scotland,

S.D. *Parley:* drum or trumpet to summon conference with enemy.
4. *trimm'd:* dressed up.   5. *ports:* gates.

Vouchsafe a few words from a man enforc'd
To lay his book aside and clap on arms
Unsuitable to my age or my profession.
Courageous prince, consider on what grounds
You rend the face of peace, and break a league
With a confederate king that courts your amity.
For whom, too? For a vagabond, a straggler,
Not noted in the world by birth or name,
An obscure peasant, by the rage of hell
20 Loos'd from his chains to set great kings at strife.
What nobleman, what common man of note,
What ordinary subject hath come in,
Since first you footed on our territories,
To only feign a welcome? Children laugh at
Your proclamations, and the wiser pity
So great a potentate's abuse by one
Who juggles merely with the fawns and youth
Of an instructed compliment. Such spoils,
Such slaughters as the rapine of your soldiers
30 Already have committed is enough
To show your zeal in a conceited justice.
Yet, great king, wake not yet my master's vengeance;
But shake that viper off which gnaws your entrails.
I and my fellow subjects are resolv'd,
If you persist, to stand your utmost fury,
Till our last blood drop from us.
WARBECK: O sir, lend
No ear to this traducer of my honour! –
What shall I call thee, thou grey-bearded scandal,
That kick'st against the sovereignty to which

22. *come in:* i.e. in support.
27. *fawns:* servile cringes.   *youth:* newness.
28. *instructed:* i.e. not inborn.   31. *conceited:* imagined question of.

Thou owest allegiance? – Treason is bold-fac'd   40
And eloquent in mischief; sacred king,
Be deaf to his known malice.

DURHAM: Rather yield
Unto those holy motions which inspire
The sacred heart of an annointed body!
It is the surest policy in princes
To govern well their own than seek encroachment
Upon another's right.

CRAWFORD: The king is serious,
Deep in his meditations.

DALYELL: Lift them up
To Heaven, his better genius!

WARBECK: Can you study
While such a devil raves? O, sir!

KING JAMES: Well. – Bishop,   50
You'll not be drawn to mercy?

DURHAM: Conster me
In like case by a subject of your own.
My resolution's fix'd; King James be counsell'd:
A greater fate waits on thee.
    Exit DURHAM *with his followers.*

KING JAMES: Forage through
The country, spare no prey of life or goods.

WARBECK: O sir, then give me leave to yield to nature;
I am most miserable. Had I been
Born what this clergyman would by defame
Baffle belief with, I had never sought
The truth of mine inheritance with rapes   60
Of women, or of infants murdered, virgins

---

43. *motions:* inner promptings.   49. *study:* deeply meditate.
51–2. *Conster . . . own:* interpret me as though I were a subject of your own.
56. *nature:* natural feelings.   58. *defame:* defamation.

Deflowered, old men butchered, dwellings fir'd,
My land depopulated, and my people
Afflicted with a kingdom's devastation.
Show more remorse, great king, or I shall never
Endure to see such havoc with dry eyes.
Spare, spare my dear, dear England!

KING JAMES: You fool your piety.
Ridiculously, careful of an interest
Another man possesseth! Where's your faction?
70   Shrewdly the bishop guess'd of your adherents,
When not a petty burgess of some town,
No, not a villager hath yet appear'd
In your assistance. That should make 'ee whine,
And not your country's sufferance as you term it.

DALYELL: The king is angry.

CRAWFORD: And the passionate duke
Effeminately dolent.

WARBECK: The experience
In former trials, sir, both of mine own
Or other princes cast out of their thrones,
Have so acquainted me how misery
80   Is destitute of friends or of relief,
That I can easily submit to taste
Lowest reproof without contempt or words.

KING JAMES: An humble-minded man.

        [*Enter* FRION.]

                              Now, what intelligence
Speaks Master Secretary Frion?

FRION: Henry
Of England hath in open field o'erthrown

67. *fool:* make foolish.   74. *sufferance:* suffering.
76. *dolent:* sorrowful.
82. *contempt or words:* expressing contempt or giving verbal reproof.

The armies who oppos'd him in the right
Of this young prince.
KING JAMES: His subsidies, you mean!
More, if you have it.
FRION: Howard, Earl of Surrey,
Back'd by twelve earls and barons of the north,
An hundred knights and gentlemen of name,   90
And twenty thousand soldiers, is at hand
To raise your siege; Brooke, with a goodly navy,
Is admiral at sea; and Daubeney follows
With an unbroken army for a second.
WARBECK: 'Tis false; they come to side with us.
KING JAMES: Retreat;
We shall not find them stones and walls to cope with.
Yet, Duke of York – for such thou sayest thou art –
I'll try thy fortune to the height. To Surrey
By Marchmount I will send a brave defiance
For single combat; once a king will venture   100
His person to an earl, with condition
Of spilling lesser blood. Surrey is bold
And James resolv'd.
WARBECK: O rather, gracious sir,
Create me to this glory, since my cause
Doth interest this fair quarrel; valued least
I am his equal.
KING JAMES: I will be the man; –
March softly off; where victory can reap
A harvest crown'd with triumph, toil is cheap.
    Exeunt.

94. *for a second:* in support.   100. *once:* for once.
101–2. *with condition Of:* as agreement for.
104. *Create me to:* invest me with.   105. *Doth interest:* is involved in.

309

ACT FOUR

SCENE ONE

Enter SURREY, DURHAM, *Soldiers, with drums and colours.*

SURREY: Are all our braving enemies shrunk back,
Hid in the fogs of their distempered climate,
Not daring to behold our colours wave
In spite of this infected air? Can they
Look on the strength of Cundrestrine defac'd,
The glory of Heydonhall devasted, that
Of Edington cast down, the pile of Fulden
O'erthrown, and this, the strongest of their forts,
Old Ayton Castle, yielded and demolished,
And yet not peep abroad? The Scots are bold,
Hardy in battle; but it seems the cause
They undertake, considered, appears
Unjointed in the frame on't.

DURHAM: Noble Surrey,
Our royal master's wisdom is at all times
His fortune's harbinger, for then he draws
His sword to threaten war, his providence
Settles on peace, the crowning of an empire.
Trumpet.

SURREY: Rank all in order; 'tis a herald's sound;
Some message from King James. Keep a fix'd station.
Enter MARCHMOUNT *and another herald in their coats.*

***

6. *devasted:* devastated.   S.D. *coats:* i.e. heralds' coats.

MARCHMOUNT: From Scotland's awful majesty we come   20
    Unto the English general.

SURREY: To me?
    Say on.

MARCHMOUNT: Thus then: the waste and prodigal
    Effusion of so much guiltless blood,
    As in two potent armies of necessity
    Must glut the earth's dry womb, his sweet compassion
    Hath studied to prevent; for which to thee,
    Great Earl of Surrey, in a single fight
    He offers his own royal person, fairly
    Proposing these conditions only, that,
    If victory conclude our master's right,   30
    The earl shall deliver for his ransom
    The town of Berwick to him with the fishgarths;
    If Surrey shall prevail, the king will pay
    A thousand pounds down present for his freedom
    And silence further arms. So speaks King James.

SURREY: So speaks King James! so like a king 'a speaks.
    Heralds, the English general returns
    A sensible devotion from his heart,
    His very soul, to this unfellowed grace.
    For let the king know, gentle heralds, truly   40
    How his descent from his great throne to honour
    A stranger subject with so high a title
    As his compeer in arms hath conquered more
    Than any sword could do; for which, my loyalty
    Respected, I will serve his virtues ever

26. *studied:* made it his aim.
30. *conclude:* settle.
32. *fishgarths:* salmon-catching enclosures at Berwick.
34. *present:* immediately.
38. *sensible:* deeply felt.
39. *unfellowed:* unequalled.   45. *Respected:* taken into account.

In all humility. But Berwick, say,
Is none of mine to part with. In affairs
Of princes, subjects cannot traffic rights
Inherent to the crown. My life is mine,
50   That I dare freely hazard; and – with pardon
To some unbrib'd vainglory – if his majesty
Shall taste a change of fate, his liberty
Shall meet no articles. If I fall, falling
So bravely, I refer me to his pleasure
Without condition; and for this dear favour,
Say, if not countermanded, I will cease
Hostility unless provok'd.

MARCHMOUNT: This answer
We shall relate unpartially.

DURHAM: With favour,
Pray have a little patience. – [*Aside to* SURREY] Sir,
   you find
60   By these gay flourishes how wearied travail
Inclines to willing rest; here's but a prologue,
However confidently utter'd, meant
For some ensuing acts of peace. Consider
The time of year, unseasonableness of weather,
Charge, barrenness of profit, and occasion
Presents itself for honourable treaty,
Which we may make good use of. I will back
As sent from you, in point of noble gratitude,
Unto King James with these his heralds; you
70   Shall shortly hear from me, my lord, for order
Of breathing or proceeding; and King Henry –
Doubt not – will thank the service.

---

53. *meet no articles:* require no conditions.
71. *breathing:* pausing.

SURREY: To your wisdom,
  Lord bishop, I refer it.
DURHAM: Be it so, then.
SURREY: Heralds, accept this chain and these few crowns.
MARCHMOUNT: Our duty, noble general!
DURHAM: In part
  Of retribution for such princely love,
  My lord the general is pleased to show
  The king your master his sincerest zeal
  By further treaty by no common man:
  I will myself return with you.
SURREY: Y'oblige   *80*
  My faithfullest affections t'ee, lord bishop.
MARCHMOUNT: All happiness attend your lordship!
  [*Exeunt* DURHAM, MARCHMOUNT *and Herald.*]
SURREY: Come friends
  And fellow soldiers; we, I doubt, shall meet
  No enemies but woods and hills to fight with;
  Then 'twere as good to feed and sleep at home:
  We may be free from danger, not secure.
    Exeunt.

                      SCENE TWO

  Enter WARBECK *and* FRION.

WARBECK: Frion! O Frion! All my hopes of glory
  Are at a stand! The Scottish king grows dull,
  Frosty and wayward since this Spanish agent
  Hath mix'd discourses with him. They are private;

76. *retribution:* recompense.   86. *secure:* over-confident.
 2. *stand:* standstill.

                      313

I am not call'd to council now. Confusion
On all his crafty shrugs! I feel the fabric
Of my designs are tottering.
FRION: Henry's policies
Stir with too many engines.
WARBECK: Let his mines,
Shap'd in the bowels of the earth, blow up
10 Works rais'd for my defence, yet can they never
Toss into air the freedom of my birth,
Or disavow my blood Plantagenet's.
I am my father's son still; but O, Frion,
When I bring into count with my disasters
My wife's compartnership, my Kate's, my life's,
Then, then my frailty feels an earthquake. Mischief
Damn Henry's plots! I will be England's king,
Or let my aunt of Burgundy report
My fall in the attempt deserv'd our ancestors!
20 FRION: You grow too wild in passion; if you will
Appear a prince indeed, confine your will
To moderation.
WARBECK: What a saucy rudeness
Prompts this distrust! If I will appear?
Appear a prince? Death throttle such deceits
Even in their birth of utterance! cursed cozenage
Of trust! Ye make me mad; 'twere best, it seems,
That I should turn impostor to myself,
Be mine own counterfeit, belie the truth
Of my dear mother's womb, the sacred bed
30 Of a prince murdered and a living baffl'd.

8. *engines:* contrivances.
   mines: underground passages filled with explosives.
12. *disavow:* deny.
19. *deserv'd:* was worthy of.
30. *baffl'd:* disgraced.

314

FRION: Nay, if you have no ears to hear, I have
  No breath to spend in vain.
WARBECK: Sir, sir, take heed!
  Gold and the promise of promotion rarely
  Fail in temptation.
FRION: Why to me this?
WARBECK: Nothing;
  Speak what you will. We are not sunk so low
  But your advice may piece again the heart
  Which many cares have broken. You were wont
  In all extremities to talk of comfort;
  Have ye none left now? I'll not interrupt ye.
  Good, bear with my distractions. If King James   *40*
  Deny us dwelling here, next whither must I?
  I prithee, be not angry.
FRION: Sir, I told ye
  Of letters come from Ireland, how the Cornish
  Stomach their last defeat and humbly sue
  That with such forces as you could partake,
  You would in person land in Cornwall, where
  Thousands will entertain your title gladly.
WARBECK: Let me embrace thee, hug thee! Th'ast
    reviv'd
  My comforts. If my cousin king will fail,
  Our cause will never.
      Enter JOHN A-WATER, HERON, ASTLEY [*and*] SKELTON.
                      Welcome, my tried friends.   *50*
  You keep your brains awake in our defence. –
  Frion, advise with them of these affairs,
  In which be wondrous secret; I will listen
  What else concerns us here. Be quick and wary.
      Exit.

36. *piece:* put together.   44. *Stomach:* resent.

ASTLEY: Ah, sweet young prince! Secretary, my fellow counsellors and I have consulted, and jump all in one opinion directly, that if this Scotch garboils do not fadge to our minds, we will pell-mell run amongst the Cornish choughs presently and in a trice.

60 SKELTON: 'Tis but going to sea and leaping ashore, cut ten or twelve thousand unnecessary throats, fire seven or eight towns, take half-a-dozen cities, get into the market place, crown him Richard the Fourth, and the business is finished.

JOHN A-WATER: I grant ye, quoth I, so far forth as men may do, no more than men may do; for it is good to consider, when consideration may be to the purpose; otherwise, still you shall pardon me: little said is soon amended.

70 FRION: Then you conclude the Cornish action surest?

HERON: We do so, and doubt not but to thrive abundantly. Ho! my masters, had we known of the commotion when we set sail out of Ireland, the land had been ours ere this time.

SKELTON: Pish, pish! 'tis but forbearing being an earl or a duke a month or two longer. I say, and say it again, if the work go not on apace, let me never see new fashion more. I warrant ye, I warrant ye, we will have it so, and so it shall be.

80 ASTLEY: This is but a cold phlegmatic country, not stirring enough for men of spirit; give me the heart of England for my money.

SKELTON: A man may batten there in a week only with hot loaves and butter, and a lusty cup of muscadine and

57. *garboils:* tumult.   57-8. *fadge . . . minds:* go as we wish.
83. *batten:* grow fat.
84. *muscadine:* muscatel, sweet wine.

sugar at breakfast, though he make never a meal all the
month after.

JOHN A-WATER: Surely, when I bore office, I found by
experience that to be much troublesome was to be much
wise and busy. I have observed how filching and bragging
has been the best service in these last wars, and therefore 90
conclude peremptorily on the design in England. If
things and things may fall out, as who can tell what or
how, but the end will show it.

FRION: Resolv'd like men of judgement! Here to linger
More time is but to lose it. Cheer the prince,
And haste him on to this; on this depends
Fame in success, or glory in our ends.
    Exeunt.

SCENE THREE

Enter KING JAMES; DURHAM *and* HIALAS *on either side.*

HIALAS: France, Spain and Germany combine a league
Of amity with England; nothing wants
For settling peace through Christendom but love
Between the British monarchs, James and Henry.

DURHAM: The English merchants, sir, have been receiv'd
With general procession into Antwerp;
The emperor confirms the combination.

HIALAS: The king of Spain resolves a marriage
For Catherine his daughter with Prince Arthur.

DURHAM: France courts this holy contract.

HIALAS: What can hinder 10
A quietness in England –

DURHAM: But your suffrage

7. *combination*: alliance.

To such a silly creature, mighty sir,
As is but in effect an apparition,
A shadow, a mere trifle?

HIALAS: To this union
The good of both the church and commonwealth
Invite 'ee, –

DURHAM: To this unity a mystery
Of providence points out a greater blessing
For both these nations than our human reason
Can search into: King Henry hath a daughter,
The Princess Margaret; I need not urge
What honour, what felicity can follow
On such affinity 'twixt two Christian kings
Inleagu'd by ties of blood. But sure I am,
If you, sir, ratify the peace propos'd,
I dare both motion and effect this marriage
For weal of both the kingdoms.

KING JAMES: Dar'st thou, lord bishop?

DURHAM: Put it to trial, royal James, by sending
Some noble personage to the English court
By way of embassy.

HIALAS: Part of the business
Shall suit my mediation.

KING JAMES: Well, what Heaven
Hath pointed out to be, must be. You two
Are ministers, I hope, of blessed fate.
But herein only I will stand acquitted:
No blood of innocents shall buy my peace;
For Warbeck, as you nick him, came to me
Commended by the states of Christendom,
A prince, though in distress. His fair demeanour,

25. *motion:* purpose.   32. *ministers:* agents.
35. *nick:* call.

318

Lovely behaviour, unappalled spirit,
Spoke him not base in blood however clouded.
The brute beasts have both rocks and caves to fly to, *40*
And men the altars of the church. To us
He came for refuge: kings come near in nature
Unto the gods in being touch'd with pity.
Yet, noble friends, his mixture with our blood,
Even with our own, shall no way interrupt
A general peace; only I will dismiss him
From my protection, throughout my dominions
In safety, but not ever to return.

HIALAS: You are a just king.

DURHAM: Wise and herein happy.

KING JAMES: Nor will we dally in affairs of weight: *50*
Huntly, lord bishop, shall with you to England,
Ambassador from us; we will throw down
Our weapons; peace on all sides now! Repair
Unto our council; we will be soon with you.

HIALAS: Delay shall question no dispatch; Heaven
crown it.
    Exeunt DURHAM *and* HIALAS.

KING JAMES: A league with Ferdinand! A marriage
With English Margaret! A free release
From restitution for the late affronts!
Cessation from hostility! and all
For Warbeck not delivered but dismiss'd! *60*
We could not wish it better. – Dalyell!
    Enter DALYELL.

DALYELL: Here, sir.

KING JAMES: Are Huntly and his daughter sent for?

---

38. *Lovely:* loving.   39. *Spoke:* proclaimed.
44. *mixture . . . blood:* i.e. by marriage.
55. *question no dispatch:* not put in jeopardy the settlement.

DALYELL: Sent for
And come, my lord.

KING JAMES: Say to the English prince
We want his company.

DALYELL: He is at hand, sir.

Enter WARBECK, KATHERINE, JANE, FRION, HERON,
SKELTON, JOHN A-WATER, ASTLEY.

KING JAMES: Cousin, our bounty, favours, gentleness,
Our benefits, the hazard of our person,
Our people's lives, our land, hath evidenc'd
How much we have engag'd on your behalf.
How trivial and how dangerous our hopes
70 Appear, how fruitless our attempts in war,
How windy, rather smoky, your assurance
Of party shows, we might in vain repeat.
But now obedience to the mother church,
A father's care upon his country's weal,
The dignity of state, directs our wisdom
To seal an oath of peace through Christendom,
To which we are sworn already. 'Tis you
Must only seek new fortunes in the world,
And find an harbour elsewhere. As I promis'd
80 On your arrival, you have met no usage
Deserves repentance in your being here:
But yet I must live master of mine own.
However, what is necessary for you
At your departure, I am well content
You be accommodated with, provided
Delay prove not my enemy.

WARBECK: It shall not,
Most glorious prince. The fame of my designs

71. *windy:* unsubstantial.   72. *party:* support.

Soars higher than report of ease and sloth
Can aim at. I acknowledge all your favours
Boundless and singular, am only wretched,   90
In words as well as means, to thank the grace
That flow'd so liberally. Two empires firmly
You're lord of – Scotland, and Duke Richard's heart.
My claim to mine inheritance shall sooner
Fail than my life to serve you, best of kings.
And witness Edward's blood in me, I am
More loth to part with such a great example
Of virtue, than all other mere respects.
But, sir, my last suit is, you will not force
From me what you have given, this chaste lady,   100
Resolv'd on all extremes.
KATHERINE: I am your wife;
No human power can or shall divorce
My faith from duty.
WARBECK: Such another treasure
The earth is bankrupt of.
KING JAMES: I gave her, cousin,
And must avow the gift; will add withal
A furniture becoming her high birth
And unsuspected constancy. Provide
For your attendance. We will part good friends.
    Exeunt KING [JAMES] *and* DALYELL.
WARBECK: The Tudor hath been cunning in his plots;
His Fox of Durham would not fail at last.   110
But what? Our cause and courage are our own;
Be men, my friends, and let our cousin king

88. *report:* reputation.   98. *mere respects:* aspects whatsoever.
101. *Resolv'd . . . extremes:* determined to face all extremities.
105. *avow'd:* acknowledge.   106. *furniture:* provision.
107. *unsuspected:* not open to suspicion.

See how we follow fate as willingly
As malice follows us. Y'are all resolv'd
For the west parts of England?
ALL: Cornwall, Cornwall!
FRION: The inhabitants expect you daily.
WARBECK: Cheerfully
Draw all our ships out of the harbour, friends;
Our time of stay doth seem too long. We must
Prevent intelligence; about it suddenly!
120 ALL: A prince, a prince, a prince!
     Exeunt [HERON, SKELTON, ASTLEY *and* JOHN
     A-WATER].
WARBECK: Dearest, admit not into thy pure thoughts
The least of scruples which may charge their softness
With burden of distrust. Should I prove wanting
To noblest courage now, here were the trial:
But I am perfect, sweet; I fear no change
More than thy being partner in my sufferance.
KATHERINE: My fortunes, sir, have arm'd me to
     encounter
What chance soe'er they meet with. – Jane, 'tis fit
Thou stay behind, for whither wilt thou wander?
130 JANE: Never till death will I forsake my mistress;
Nor then, in wishing to die with 'ee gladly.
KATHERINE: Alas, good soul!
FRION: Sir, to your aunt of Burgundy
I will relate your present undertakings;
From her expect on all occasions welcome.
You cannot find me idle in your services.
WARBECK: Go, Frion, go! Wise men know how to
     soothe

119. *Prevent:* forestall. *intelligence:* news of our movements.
125. *perfect:* complete.   126. *More than:* other than.

322

Adversity, not serve it; thou hast waited
Too long on expectation. Never yet
Was any nation read of so besotted
In reason as to adore the setting sun.   *140*
Fly to the archduke's court; say to the duchess,
Her nephew, with fair Katherine his wife,
Are on their expectation to begin
The raising of an empire; if they fail,
Yet the report will never. Farewell, Frion!
   Exit FRION.
This man, Kate, has been true, though now of late
I fear too much familiar with the Fox.
   Enter HUNTLY *and* DALYELL.
HUNTLY: I come to take my leave. You need not doubt
My interest in this sometime child of mine.
She's all yours now, good sir. O poor, lost creature!   *150*
Heaven guard thee with much patience! If thou canst
Forget thy title to old Huntly's family,
As much of peace will settle in thy mind
As thou canst wish to taste but in thy grave.
Accept my tears yet, prithee; they are tokens
Of charity as true as of affection.
KATHERINE: This is the cruel'st farewell!
HUNTLY: Love, young gentleman,
This model of my griefs. She calls you husband:
Then be not jealous of a parting kiss;
It is a father's, not a lover's off'ring. –   *160*
Take it, my last. – I am too much a child!
Exchange of passion is to little use,
So I should grow too foolish. – Goodness guide thee.
   Exit HUNTLY.

145. *report:* good name.   154. *but:* except for.
158. *model:* epitome.   162. *passion:* grief.

KATHERINE: Most miserable daughter! – Have you
    aught
  To add, sir, to our sorrows?
DALYELL: I resolve,
  Fair lady, with your leave, to wait on all
  Your fortunes in my person, if your lord
  Vouchsafe me entertainment.
WARBECK: We will be bosom friends, most noble
    Dalyell,
170 For I accept this tender of your love
  Beyond ability of thanks to speak it. –
  Clear thy drown'd eyes, my fairest; time and industry
  Will show us better days or end the worst.
  Exeunt.

SCENE FOUR

Enter OXFORD *and* DAUBENEY.

OXFORD: No news from Scotland yet, my lord?
DAUBENEY: Not any
  But what King Henry knows himself. I thought
  Our armies should have march'd that way; his mind,
  It seems, is altered.
OXFORD: Victory attends
  His standard everywhere.
DAUBENEY: Wise princes, Oxford,
  Fight not alone with forces. Providence
  Directs and tutors strength, else elephants
  And barbed horses might as well prevail
  As the most subtle stratagems of war.

8. *barbed*: caparisoned.

OXFORD: The Scottish king show'd more than common
    bravery   10
  In proffer of a combat hand to hand
  With Surrey.
DAUBENEY: And but show'd it. Northern bloods
  Are gallant being fir'd, but the cold climate,
  Without good store of fuel, quickly freezeth
  The glowing flames.
OXFORD: Surrey, upon my life,
  Would not have shrunk an hair's-breadth.
DAUBENEY: May 'a forfeit
  The honour of an English name and nature
  Who would not have embrac'd it with a greediness
  As violent as hunger runs to food.
  'Twas an addition any worthy spirit   20
  Would covet, next to immortality,
  Above all joys of life. We all miss'd shares
  In that great opportunity.

    Enter KING HENRY *and* URSWICK *whispering.*

OXFORD: The king!
  See, 'a comes smiling.
DAUBENEY: O, the game runs smooth
  On his side then, believe it. Cards well shuffl'd
  And dealt with cunning bring some gamester thrift,
  But others must rise losers.
KING HENRY: The train takes?
URSWICK: Most prosperously.
KING HENRY: I knew it should not miss.
  He fondly angles who will hurl his bait
  Into the water 'cause the fish at first   30
  Plays round about the line and dares not bite. –

---

20. *addition:* mark of honour.   27. *train:* lure.   29. *fondly:* foolishly.

Lords, we may reign your king yet. Daubeney, Oxford,
Urswick, must Perkin wear the crown?

DAUBENEY: A slave!

OXFORD: A vagabond!

URSWICK: A glow-worm!

KING HENRY: Now, if Frion,
  His practis'd politician, wear a brain
  Of proof, King Perkin will in progress ride
  Through all his large dominions. Let us meet him,
  And tender homage. Ha, sirs? Liegemen ought
  To pay their fealty.

DAUBENEY: Would the rascal were,
40 With all his rabble, within twenty miles
  Of London!

KING HENRY: Farther off is near enough
  To lodge him in his home. I'll wager odds,
  Surrey and all his men are either idle,
  Or hasting back; they have not work, I doubt,
  To keep them busy.

DAUBENEY: 'Tis a strange conceit, sir.

KING HENRY: Such voluntary favours as our people
  In duty aid us with we never scatter'd
  On cobweb parasites, or lavish'd out
  In riot or a needless hospitality;
50 No undeserving favourite doth boast
  His issues from our treasury; our charge
  Flows through all Europe, proving us but steward
  Of every contribution, which provides
  Against the creeping canker of disturbance.
  Is it not rare then, in this toil of state
  Wherein we are embark'd with breach of sleep,

36. *Of proof*: of tested power.
42. *lodge*: discover (hunting term).   51. *issues*: money.

Cares, and the noise of trouble, that our mercy
Returns nor thanks nor comfort? Still the West
Murmur and threaten innovation,
Whisper our government tyrannical,   60
Deny us what is ours, nay, spurn their lives,
Of which they are but owners by our gift.
It must not be.

OXFORD: It must not, should not.
    Enter a Post.

KING HENRY: So then –
    To whom?

POST: This packet to your sacred majesty.

KING HENRY: Sirrah, attend without.
    [*Exit the Post.*]

OXFORD: New from the North, upon my life!

DAUBENEY: Wise Henry
    Divines aforehand of events; with him
    Attempts and execution are one act.

KING HENRY: Urswick, thine ear. – Frion is caught; the
    man
    Of cunning is outreach'd: we must be safe.   70
    Should reverend Morton, our archbishop, move
    To a translation higher yet, I tell thee
    My Durham owns a brain deserves that see.
    He's nimble in his industry, and mounting.
    Thou hear'st me?

URSWICK: And conceive your highness fitly.

KING HENRY: Daubeney and Oxford, since our army
    stands
    Entire, it were a weakness to admit

59. *innovation:* revolt.   S.D. *Post:* courier.
72. *translation:* promotion. See note to l.71.
75. *conceive:* understand.

327

The rust of laziness to eat amongst them.
Set forward toward Salisbury; the plains
80 Are most commodious for their exercise.
Ourself will take a muster of them there,
And or disband them with reward, or else
Dispose as best concerns us.

DAUBENEY: Salisbury?
Sir, all is peace at Salisbury.

KING HENRY: Dear friend,
The charge must be our own; we would a little
Partake the pleasure with our subjects' ease. –
Shall I entreat your loves?

OXFORD: Command our lives.

KING HENRY: Y'are men know how to do, not to
    forethink;
My bishop is a jewel, tried and perfect,
90 A jewel, lords. The post who brought these letters
Must speed another to the mayor of Exeter.
Urswick, dismiss him not.

URSWICK: He waits your pleasure.

KING HENRY: Perkin a king! A king!

URSWICK: My gracious lord?

KING HENRY: Thoughts, busied in the sphere of royalty,
Fix not on creeping worms without their stings,
Mere excrements of earth. The use of time
Is thriving safety and a wise prevention
Of ills expected. W'are resolved for Salisbury.
    Exeunt.

85. *charge:* responsibility.
96. *excrements:* superfluous outgrowths.   *use:* i.e. proper use.

SCENE FIVE

A general shout within.
Enter WARBECK, DALYELL, KATHERINE *and* JANE.

WARBECK: After so many storms as wind and seas
 Have threaten'd to our weather-beaten ships,
 At last, sweet fairest, we are safe arriv'd
 On our dear mother earth, ingrateful only
 To Heaven and us in yielding sustenance
 To sly usurpers of our throne and right.
 These general acclamations are an omen
 Of happy process to their welcome lord.
 They flock in troops, and from all parts with wings
 Of duty fly to lay their hearts before us.   10
 Unequall'd pattern of a matchless wife,
 How fares my dearest yet?
KATHERINE: Confirm'd in health;
 By which I may the better undergo
 The roughest face of change; but I shall learn
 Patience to hope, since silence courts affliction
 For comforts, to this truly noble gentleman,
 Rare, unexampled pattern of a friend,
 And my beloved Jane, the willing follower
 Of all misfortunes.
DALYELL: Lady, I return
 But barren crops of early protestations,   20
 Frost-bitten in the spring of fruitless hopes.
JANE: I wait but as the shadow to the body;
 For, madam, without you let me be nothing.

8. *process:* progress. 20. *protestations:* avowals.

WARBECK: None talk of sadness; we are on the way
Which leads to victory. Keep coward's thoughts
With desperate sullenness. The lion faints not
Lock'd in a grate, but loose, disdains all force
Which bars his prey; and we are lion-hearted,
Or else no king of beasts.
Another shout.

Hark how they shout,
30 Triumphant in our cause! Bold confidence
Marches on bravely, cannot quake at danger.
Enter SKELTON.

SKELTON: Save King Richard the Fourth, save thee, king
of hearts! The Cornish blades are men of mettle; have
proclaimed through Bodmin and the whole county my
sweet prince Monarch of England. Four thousand tall
yeomen, with bow and sword, already vow to live and
die at the foot of King Richard.
Enter ASTLEY.

ASTLEY: The mayor, our fellow counsellor, is servant for
an emperor. Exeter is appointed for the rendezvous, and
40 nothing wants to victory but courage and resolution.
*Sigillatum et datum decimo Septembris, anno regni regis primo
et cetera; confirmatum est.* All's cocksure.

WARBECK: To Exeter, to Exeter march on.
Commend us to our people; we in person
Will lend them double spirits; tell them so.

SKELTON and ASTLEY: King Richard, King Richard!
[*Exeunt* SKELTON *and* ASTLEY.]

WARBECK: A thousand blessings guard our lawful arms!
A thousand horrors pierce our enemies' souls!
Pale fear unedge their weapons' sharpest points,
50 And when they draw their arrows to the head,

26. *sullenness:* melancholy.   27. *grate:* cage.

330

Numbness shall strike their sinews. Such advantage
Hath Majesty in its pursuit of justice,
That on the proppers-up of Truth's old throne,
It both enlightens counsel and gives heart
To execution; whiles the throats of traitors
Lie bare before our mercy. O divinity
Of royal birth! How it strikes dumb the tongues
Whose prodigality of breath is brib'd
By trains to greatness. Princes are but men,
Distinguish'd in the fineness of their frailty,   60
Yet not so gross in beauty of the mind;
For there's a fire more sacred, purifies
The dross of mixture. Herein stands the odds:
Subjects are men on earth, kings men and gods.
    Exeunt.

60. *frailty:* mortal condition. *in:* because of.   63. *odds:* difference.

ACT FIVE

SCENE ONE

Enter KATHERINE *and* JANE *in riding suits, with one Servant.*

KATHERINE: It is decreed, and we must yield to fate,
Whose angry justice, though it threaten ruin,
Contempt and poverty, is all but trial
Of a weak woman's constancy in suffering.
Here, in a stranger's and an enemy's land,
Forsaken and unfurnish'd of all hopes
But such as wait on misery, I range
To meet affliction wheresoe'er I tread.
My train and pomp of servants is reduc'd
10 To one kind gentlewoman and this groom.
Sweet Jane, now whither must we?

JANE: To your ships,
Dear lady, and turn home.

KATHERINE: Home! I have none.
Fly thou to Scotland; thou hast friends will weep
For joy to bid thee welcome, but O, Jane,
My Jane, my friends are desperate of comfort
As I must be of them; the common charity,
Good people's alms, and prayers of the gentle
Is the revenue must support my state.
As for my native country, since it once
20 Saw me a princess in the height of greatness

7. *range:* wander.   15. *desperate:* without hope.
18. *state:* pun 1. condition 2. nation.

332

My birth allow'd me, here I make a vow
Scotland shall never see me, being fallen
Or lessened in my fortunes. Never, Jane,
Never to Scotland more will I return.
Could I be England's queen – a glory, Jane,
I never fawn'd on – yet the king who gave me,
Hath sent me with my husband from his presence;
Deliver'd us suspected to his nation;
Render'd us spectacles to time and pity.
And is it fit I should return to such   30
As only listen after our descent
From happiness enjoy'd to misery
Expected, though uncertain? Never, never!
Alas, why dost thou weep? and that poor creature
Wipe his wet cheeks too? Let me feel alone
Extremities who know to give them harbour.
Nor thou nor he has cause; you may live safely.

JANE: There is no safety whiles your dangers, madam,
Are every way apparent.

SERVANT: Pardon, lady;
I cannot choose but show my honest heart.   40
You were ever my good lady.

KATHERINE: O, dear souls!
Your shares in grief are too too much.

    Enter DALYELL.

DALYELL: I bring,
Fair princess, news of further sadness yet,
Than your sweet youth hath been acquainted with.

KATHERINE: Not more, my lord, than I can welcome.
    Speak it!
The worst, the worst I look for.

26. *gave me:* i.e. in marriage.   28. *Deliver'd:* presented.
31. *listen after:* endeavour to hear of.   40. *honest:* open.

DALYELL: All the Cornish
  At Exeter were by the citizens
  Repuls'd, encounter'd by the Earl of Devonshire
  And other worthy gentlemen of the country.
50 Your husband march'd to Taunton, and was there
  Affronted by King Henry's chamberlain,
  The king himself in person with his army
  Advancing nearer, to renew the fight
  On all occasions. But the night before
  The battles were to join, your husband privately,
  Accompanied with some few horse, departed
  From out the camp and posted none knows whither.
KATHERINE: Fled, without battle given?
DALYELL: Fled, but follow'd
  By Daubeney, all his parties left to taste
60 King Henry's mercy, for to that they yielded,
  Victorious without bloodshed.
KATHERINE: O, my sorrows!
  If both our lives had prov'd the sacrifice
  To Henry's tyranny we had fallen like princes
  And robb'd him of the glory of his pride.
DALYELL: Impute it not to faintness or to weakness
  Of noble courage, lady, but foresight;
  For by some secret friend he had intelligence
  Of being bought and sold by his base followers.
  Worse yet remains untold.
KATHERINE: No, no, it cannot.
70 DALYELL: I fear y'are betray'd; the Earl of Oxford
  Runs hot in your pursuit.
KATHERINE: 'A shall not need;
  We'll run as hot in resolution, gladly
  To make the earl our gaoler.

51. *affronted*: confronted.   55. *battles*: battalions.

334

JANE: Madam, madam!
  They come, they come!
    Enter OXFORD, *with followers.*

DALYELL: Keep back, or he who dares
  Rudely to violate the law of honour
  Runs on my sword.

KATHERINE: Most noble sir, forbear! –
  What reason draws you hither, gentlemen?
  Whom seek 'ee?

OXFORD: All stand off! – With favour, lady,
  From Henry, England's king, I would present
  Unto the beauteous princess, Katherine Gordon,   80
  The tender of a gracious entertainment.

KATHERINE: We are that princess whom your master
    king
  Pursues with reaching arms to draw into
  His power. Let him use his tyranny;
  We shall not be his subjects.

OXFORD: My commission
  Extends no further, excellentest lady,
  Than to a service. 'Tis King Henry's pleasure
  That you and all that have relation t'ee
  Be guarded as becomes your birth and greatness.
  For rest assur'd, sweet princess, that not aught   90
  Of what you do call yours shall find disturbance,
  Or any welcome other than what suits
  Your high condition.

KATHERINE: By what title, sir,
  May I acknowledge you?

OXFORD: Your servant, lady,
  Descended from the line of Oxford's earls,

83. *reaching:* far-reaching.

Inherits what his ancestors before him
Were owners of.

KATHERINE: Your king is herein royal,
That by a peer so ancient in desert
As well as blood commands us to his presence.

OXFORD: Invites 'ee, princess, not commands.

100 KATHERINE: Pray use
Your own phrase as you list. To your protection,
Both I and mine submit.

OXFORD: There's in your number
A nobleman whom fame hath bravely spoken.
To him the king my master bade me say
How willingly he courts his friendship; far
From an enforcement, more than what in terms
Of courtesy so great a prince may hope for.

DALYELL: My name is Dalyell.

OXFORD: 'Tis a name hath won
Both thanks and wonder from report, my lord;
110 The court of England emulates your merit
And covets to embrace 'ee.

DALYELL: I must wait on
The princess in her fortunes.

OXFORD: Will you please,
Great lady, to set forward?

KATHERINE: Being driven
By fate, it were in vain to strive with Heaven.
        Exeunt.

103. *spoken:* spoken of.
110. *emulates:* is jealous of.

SCENE TWO

Enter KING HENRY, SURREY, URSWICK, *and a guard of Soldiers.*

KING HENRY: The counterfeit, King Perkin, is escap'd;
    Escape, so let him! He is hedg'd too fast
    Within the circuit of our English pale
    To steal out of our ports or leap the walls
    Which guard our land; the seas are rough, and wider
    Than his weak arms can tug with. Surrey, henceforth
    Your king may reign in quiet: turmoils past,
    Like some unquiet dream, have rather busied
    Our fancy than affrighted rest of state.
    But Surrey, why in articling a peace   *10*
    With James of Scotland was not restitution
    Of losses, which our subjects did sustain
    By the Scotch inroads, questioned?
SURREY: Both demanded
    And urg'd, my lord, to which the king replied
    In modest merriment but smiling earnest
    How that our master Henry was much abler
    To bear the detriments than he repay them.
KING HENRY: The young man, I believe, spake honest
    truth;
    'A studies to be wise betimes. Has, Urswick,
    Sir Rhys ap Thomas and Lord Brooke our steward   *20*
    Return'd the western gentlemen full thanks
    From us for their tried loyalties?

9. *rest of state:* national peace.
10. *articling a peace:* arranging peace treaty.
17. *detriments:* losses.   19. *betimes:* early.

URSWICK: They have,
Which, as if health and life had reign'd amongst 'em,
With open hearts they joyfully receiv'd.

KING HENRY: Young Buckingham is a fair-natur'd
   prince,
Lovely in hopes and worthy of his father;
Attended by an hundred knights and squires
Of special name he tender'd humble service,
Which we must ne'er forget. And Devonshire's
   wounds,
30   Though slight, shall find sound cure in our respect.

Enter DAUBENEY, *with* WARBECK, HERON, JOHN
A-WATER, ASTLEY, SKELTON [*guarded*].

DAUBENEY: Life to the king, and safety fix his throne!
I here present you, royal sir, a shadow
Of majesty, but in effect a substance
Of pity; a young man in nothing grown
To ripeness but th'ambition of your mercy:
Perkin, the Christian world's strange wonder.

KING HENRY: Daubeney, we observe no wonder. I
   behold, 'tis true,
An ornament of nature, fine and polish'd,
A handsome youth indeed; but not admire him.
How came he to thy hands?

40 DAUBENEY: From sanctuary
At Beaulieu, near Southampton, register'd
With these few followers for persons privileg'd.

KING HENRY: I must not thank you, sir! You were to
   blame
To infringe the liberty of houses sacred.
Dare we be irreligious?

---

30. *respect:* esteem.   35. *ambition of:* strong desire for.
39. *admire:* wonder at.   42. *for:* as being.

DAUBENEY: Gracious lord,
  They voluntarily resign'd themselves
  Without compulsion.
KING HENRY: So! 'Twas very well,
  'Twas very, very well. – Turn now thine eyes,
  Young man, upon thyself and thy past actions:
  What revels in combustion through our kingdom   50
  A frenzy of aspiring youth hath danc'd,
  Till, wanting breath, thy feet of pride have slipp'd
  To break thy neck.
WARBECK: But not my heart; my heart
  Will mount till every drop of blood be frozen
  By death's perpetual winter. If the sun
  Of majesty be darken'd, let the sun
  Of life be hid from me in an eclipse
  Lasting and universal. Sir, remember
  There was a shooting in of light when Richmond,
  Not aiming at a crown, retir'd, and gladly,   60
  For comfort, to the Duke of Bretaine's court.
  Richard, who swayed the sceptre, was reputed
  A tyrant then; yet then a dawning glimmer'd
  To some few wand'ring remnants, promising day
  When first they ventur'd on a frightful shore
  At Milford Haven.
DAUBENEY: Whither speeds his boldness?
  Check his rude tongue, great sir.
KING HENRY: O, let him range.
  The player's on the stage still, 'tis his part;
  'A does but act. – What followed?
WARBECK: Bosworth Field,
  Where at an instant, to the world's amazement,   70
  A morn to Richmond and a night to Richard
  Appear'd at once. The tale is soon applied:

Fate, which crown'd these attempts when least assur'd,
Might have befriended others like resolv'd.

KING HENRY: A pretty gallant! Thus your aunt of
    Burgundy,
Your duchess aunt, inform'd her nephew; so
The lesson, prompted and well conn'd, was moulded
Into familiar dialogue, oft rehearsed
Till, learnt by heart, 'tis now receiv'd for truth.

80 WARBECK: Truth in her pure simplicity wants art
To put a feigned blush on; scorn wears only
Such fashion as commends to gazers' eyes
Sad ulcerated novelty, far beneath
The sphere of majesty. In such a court,
Wisdom and gravity are proper robes
By which the sovereign is best distinguish'd
From zanies to his greatness.

KING HENRY: Sirrah, shift
Your antic pageantry and now appear
In your own nature, or you'll taste the danger
Of fooling out of season.

90 WARBECK: I expect
No less than what severity calls justice
And politicians safety. Let such beg
As feed on alms; but if there can be mercy
In a protested enemy, then may it
Descend to these poor creatures, whose engagements
To th'bettering of their fortunes have incurr'd
A loss of all; to them if any charity
Flow from some noble orator, in death
I owe the fee of thankfulness.

---

78. *familiar:* easily understood.
87. *zanies to:* buffoon imitators of.
88. *antic pageantry:* clownish play-acting.   94. *protested:* declared.

KING HENRY: So brave!
What a bold knave is this! Which of these rebels   100
Has been the mayor of Cork?

DAUBENEY: This wise formality. –
Kneel to the king, 'ee rascals!

KING HENRY: Canst thou hope
A pardon where thy guilt is so apparent?

JOHN A-WATER: Under your good favours, as men are men
    they may err; for I confess respectively, in taking great
    parts, the one side prevailing, the other side must go down.
    Herein the point is clear – if the proverb hold, that
    hanging goes by destiny – that it is to little purpose to
    say this thing or that shall be thus or thus; for as the
    fates will have it, so it must be, and who can help it?   110

DAUBENEY: O blockhead! thou a privy-councillor?
    Beg life, and cry aloud, 'Heaven save King Henry'.

JOHN A-WATER: Everyman knows what is best, as it
    happens. For my own part, I believe it is true, if I be not
    deceived, that kings must be kings and subjects subjects.
    But which is which, you shall pardon me for that.
    Whether we speak or hold our peace, all are mortal, no
    man knows his end.

KING HENRY: We trifle time with follies.

[WARBECK's followers] ALL :   Mercy, mercy!

KING HENRY: Urswick, command the dukeling and
    these fellows   120
To Digby, the lieutenant of the Tower;
With safety let them be convey'd to London.
It is our pleasure no uncivil outrage,
Taunts or abuse be suffer'd to their persons.
They shall meet fairer law than they deserve.

101. *wise formality:* pompous idiot.
105. *respectively:* respectfully.

Time may restore their wits, whom vain ambition
Hath many years distracted.

WARBECK: Noble thoughts
Meet freedom in captivity. The Tower? –
Our childhood's dreadful nursery.

KING HENRY: No more!

URSWICK: Come, come; you shall have leisure to
130   bethink 'ee.

        Exit URSWICK, *with* WARBECK *and his* [*followers*].

KING HENRY: Was ever so much impudence in forgery?
The custom, sure, of being styl'd a king
Hath fasten'd in his thought that he is such.
But we shall teach the lad another language.
'Tis good we have him fast.

DAUBENEY: The hangman's physic
Will purge this saucy humour.

KING HENRY: Very likely;
Yet we could temper mercy with extremity,
Being not too far provok'd.

        Enter OXFORD, KATHERINE *in her richest attire,*
        [DALYELL,] JANE, *and attendants.*

OXFORD: Great sir, be pleas'd
With your accustomed grace to entertain
The Princess Katherine Gordon.

140 KING HENRY: Oxford, herein
We must beshrew thy knowledge of our nature.
A lady of her birth and virtues could not
Have found us so unfurnish'd of good manners
As not on notice given to have met her
Halfway in point of love. – Excuse, fair cousin,

130. *bethink'ee*: contemplate.   131. *forgery*: deceit.
137. *temper*: mix.   *extremity*: extreme severity.
141. *beshrew*: blame.

The oversight! O fie, you may not kneel;
'Tis most unfitting. First, vouchsafe this welcome,
A welcome to your own, for you shall find us
But guardian to your fortune and your honours.
KATHERINE: My fortunes and mine honours are weak
    champions   150
As both are now befriended, sir. However,
Both bow before your clemency.
KING HENRY: Our arms
Shall circle them from malice. – A sweet lady!
Beauty incomparable! Here lives majesty
At league with love.
KATHERINE: O sir, I have a husband.
KING HENRY: We'll prove your father, husband, friend
    and servant;
Prove what you wish to grant us. – Lords, be careful
A patent presently be drawn for issuing
A thousand pounds from our exchequer yearly
During our cousin's life. – Our queen shall be   160
Your chief companion, our own court your home,
Our subjects all your servants.
KATHERINE: But my husband?
KING HENRY: By all descriptions you are noble Dalyell,
Whose generous truth hath fam'd a rare observance.
We thank 'ee; 'tis a goodness gives addition
To every title boasted from your ancestry,
In all most worthy.
DALYELL: Worthier than your praises,
Right princely sir, I need not glory in.
KING HENRY: Embrace him, lords. – [To KATHERINE]
    Whoever calls you mistress

155. *At league with:* in alliance with.
164. *fam'd:* made renowned.   *observance:* devotion.

170 Is lifted in our charge. – A goodlier beauty
Mine eyes yet ne'er encounter'd.

KATHERINE: Cruel misery
Of fate! What rests to hope for?

KING HENRY: Forward, lords,
To London. – Fair, ere long I shall present 'ee
With a glad object, peace, and Huntly's blessing.
Exeunt.

SCENE THREE

Enter CONSTABLE *and officers,* WARBECK, URSWICK,
and LAMBERT SIMNEL *like a falconer* [*, followed by a
mob*]. *A pair of stocks.*

CONSTABLE: Make room there! Keep off, I require 'ee,
and none come within twelve foot of his majesty's new
stocks, upon pain of displeasure. – Bring forward the
malefactor. – Friend, you must to this gear, no remedy. –
Open the hole and in with his legs, just in the middle
hole, there, that hole. [WARBECK *is put in the stocks.*] –
Keep off or I'll commit you all. Shall not a man in
authority be obeyed? So, so, there; 'tis as it should be.
Put on the padlock and give me the key. – Off, I say;
10   keep off!

URSWICK: Yet, Warbeck, clear thy conscience. Thou
hast tasted
King Henry's mercy liberally. The law
Has forfeited thy life; an equal jury
Have doomed thee to the gallows. Twice, most
wickedly,

170. *charge:* care.   2. *his majesty's:* i.e. Warbeck's.
13. *forfeited:* confiscated.   *equal:* impartial.

Most desperately, hast thou escap'd the Tower,
Inveigling to thy party with thy witchcraft
Young Edward, Earl of Warwick, son to Clarence,
Whose head must pay the price of that attempt.
Poor gentleman, unhappy in his fate
And ruin'd by thy cunning! So a mongrel   20
May pluck the true stag down. Yet, yet confess
Thy parentage, for yet the king has mercy.
SIMNEL: You would be Dick the Fourth, very likely!
Your pedigree is publish'd; you are known
For Osbeck's son of Tournay, a loose runagate,
A landloper; your father was a Jew,
Turn'd Christian merely to repair his miseries.
Where's now your kingship?
WARBECK: Baited to my death?
Intolerable cruelty! I laugh at
The Duke of Richmond's practice on my fortunes.   30
Possession of a crown ne'er wanted heralds.
SIMNEL: You will not know who I am?
URSWICK: Lambert Simnel,
Your predecessor in a dangerous uproar;
But on submission, not alone receiv'd
To grace, but by the king vouchsaf'd his service.
SIMNEL: I would be Earl of Warwick, toil'd and ruffled
Against my master, leap'd to catch the moon,
Vaunted my name Plantagenet, as you do:
An earl, forsooth! Whenas in truth I was
As you are, a mere rascal. Yet his majesty   40
– A prince compos'd of sweetness, Heaven protect
     him –
Forgave me all my villainies, repriev'd

26. *landloper:* vagabond.   30. *practice:* intrigue.
36. *ruffled:* battled.

The sentence of a shameful end, admitted
My surety of obedience to his service.
And I am now his falconer, live plenteously,
Eat from the king's purse, and enjoy the sweetness
Of liberty and favour, sleep securely.
And is not this now better than to buffet
The hangman's clutches? or to brave the cordage
50 Of a tough halter which will break your neck?
So then the gallant totters. Prithee, Perkin,
Let my example lead thee; be no longer
A counterfeit; confess and hope for pardon.
  WARBECK: For pardon? Hold, my heartstrings, whiles
    contempt
Of injuries in scorn may bid defiance
To this base man's foul language. – Thou poor vermin!
How dar'st thou creep so near me? Thou, an earl?
Why, thou enjoy'st as much of happiness
As all the swinge of slight ambition flew at.
60 A dunghill was thy cradle. So a puddle,
By virtue of the sunbeams, breathes a vapour
To infect the purer air, which drops again
Into the muddy womb that first exhal'd it.
Bread, and a slavish ease, with some assurance
From the base beadle's whip, crown'd all thy hopes.
But, sirrah, ran there in thy veins one drop
Of such a royal blood as flows in mine,
Thou wouldst not change condition to be second
In England's state without the crown itself.
70 Coarse creatures are incapable of excellence.
But let the world, as all to whom I am

43. *admitted:* allowed.   48. *buffet:* contend with.
51. *totters:* swings.   55. *injuries:* calumnies.
59. *swinge:* impetus.   64–5. *assurance From:* security against.

This day a spectacle, to time deliver,
And by tradition fix posterity
Without another chronicle than truth,
How constantly my resolution suffer'd
A martyrdom of majesty!

SIMNEL: He's past
Recovery, a Bedlam cannot cure him.

URSWICK: Away, inform the king of his behaviour.

SIMNEL: Perkin, beware the rope; the hangman's coming.

URSWICK: If yet thou hast no pity of thy body,   80
Pity thy soul!

    Exit SIMNEL.

    Enter KATHERINE, JANE, DALYELL, *and* OXFORD.

JANE: Dear lady!

OXFORD: Whither will 'ee,
Without respect of shame?

KATHERINE: Forbear me, sir,
And trouble not the current of my duty. –
O my lov'd lord! Can any scorn be yours
In which I have no interest? – Some kind hand
Lend me assistance that I may partake
Th'infliction of this penance. – My life's dearest,
Forgive me, I have stay'd too long from tend'ring
Attendance on reproach; yet bid me welcome.

WARBECK: Great miracle of constancy! My miseries   90
Were never bankrupt of their confidence
In worst afflictions, till this; now I feel them.
Report and thy deserts, thou best of creatures,
Might to eternity have stood a pattern

73. *tradition:* i.e. the handing down of his story.
    fix: make certainly known to.
75. *constantly:* steadfastly.
89. *reproach:* disgrace (= Warbeck).
93. *Report:* reputation.

347

For every virtuous wife without this conquest.
Thou hast outdone belief, yet may their ruin
In after marriages be never pitied
To whom thy story shall appear a fable.
Why wouldst thou prove so much unkind to greatness,
100   To glorify thy vows by such a servitude?
I cannot weep, but trust me, dear, my heart
Is liberal of passion. – Harry Richmond,
A woman's faith hath robb'd thy fame of triumph!

OXFORD: Sirrah, leave off your juggling, and tie up
The devil that ranges in your tongue.

URSWICK: Thus witches
Possess'd, even to their deaths deluded, say
They have been wolves and dogs, and sail'd in
   eggshells
Over the sea, and rid on fiery dragons;
Pass'd in the air more than a thousand miles,
110   All in a night. The enemy of mankind
Is powerful but false, and falsehood confident.

OXFORD: Remember, lady, who you are. Come from
That impudent impostor.

KATHERINE: You abuse us;
For when the holy churchman join'd our hands,
Our vows were real then; the ceremony
Was not in apparition but in act. –
Be what these people term thee, I am certain
Thou art my husband. No divorce in Heaven
Has been sued out between us. 'Tis injustice
120   For any earthly power to divide us.

99. *greatness:* high social status. See note.
110. *enemy of mankind:* the devil.
116. *apparition:* appearance.
117. *Be what:* whatever.
119. *sued out:* applied for in court of law.

348

Or we will live, or let us die together.
There is a cruel mercy.
WARBECK: Spite of tyranny
We reign in our affections, blessed woman!
Read in my destiny the wrack of honour;
Point out, in my contempt of death, to memory
Some miserable happiness, since herein,
Even when I fell, I stood enthron'd a monarch
Of one chaste wife's troth, pure and uncorrupted.
Fair angel of perfection, immortality
Shall raise thy name up to an adoration,   130
Court every rich opinion of true merit,
And saint it in the calendar of virtue,
When I am turn'd into the selfsame dust
Of which I was first form'd.
OXFORD: The lord ambassador,
Huntly your father, madam, should 'a look on
Your strange subjection in a gaze so public,
Would blush on your behalf and wish his country
Unleft, for entertainment to such sorrow.
KATHERINE: Why art thou angry, Oxford? I must be
More peremptory in my duty. – Sir,   140
Impute it not unto immodesty
That I presume to press you to a legacy
Before we part for ever.
WARBECK: Let it be then
My heart, the rich remains of all my fortunes.
KATHERINE: Confirm it with a kiss, pray.
WARBECK: O, with that
I wish to breathe my last. Upon thy lips,

132. *saint it:* be accounted a saint.
138. *entertainment to:* experience of.
140. *peremptory:* resolute.

Those equal twins of comeliness, I seal
The testament of honourable vows.
Whoever be the man that shall unkiss
150 This sacred print next, may he prove more thrifty
In this world's just applause, not more desertful.

KATHERINE: By this sweet pledge of both our souls,
I swear
To die a faithful widow to thy bed;
Not to be forc'd or won. O, never, never!

Enter SURREY, DAUBENEY, HUNTLY *and*
CRAWFORD.

DAUBENEY: Free the condemned person, quickly free
him.
What, has 'a yet confess'd?

URSWICK: Nothing to purpose;
But still 'a will be king.

SURREY: Prepare your journey
To a new kingdom then. – Unhappy madam,
Wilfully foolish! – See, my lord ambassador,
160 Your lady daughter will not leave the counterfeit
In this disgrace of fate.

HUNTLY: I never pointed
Thy marriage, girl, but yet being married,
Enjoy thy duty to a husband freely.
Thy griefs are mine. I glory in thy constancy
And must not say I wish that I had miss'd
Some partage in these trials of a patience.

KATHERINE: You will forgive me, noble sir?

HUNTLY: Yes, yes,
In every duty of a wife and daughter
I dare not disavow thee. To your husband,

161. *disgrace:* disfavour.   *pointed:* arranged.
169. *disavow:* disown.

For such you are, sir, I impart a farewell   *170*
Of manly pity. What your life has pass'd through,
The dangers of your end will make apparent.
And I can add, for comfort to your sufferance,
No cordial but the wonder of your frailty
Which keeps so firm a station. We are parted.

WARBECK: We are. A crown of peace renew thy age,
Most honourable Huntly. – Worthy Crawford,
We may embrace; I never thought thee injury.

CRAWFORD: Nor was I ever guilty of neglect
Which might procure such thought. I take my leave,
sir.   *180*

WARBECK: To you, Lord Dalyell, what? Accept a sigh;
'Tis hearty and in earnest.

DALYELL: I want utterance;
My silence is my farewell.

KATHERINE: O – o –

JANE: Sweet madam,
What do you mean? – My lord, your hand!

DALYELL: Dear lady,
Be pleas'd that I may wait 'ee to your lodging.
  Exeunt DALYELL, KATHERINE, JANE.
  Enter Sheriff and officers; SKELTON, ASTLEY, HERON,
  and JOHN A-WATER *with halters about their necks.*

OXFORD: Look 'ee; behold your followers appointed
To wait on 'ee in death.

WARBECK: Why, peers of England,
We'll lead 'em on courageously. I read
A triumph over tyranny upon
Their several foreheads. – Faint not in the moment   *190*
Of victory! Our ends, and Warwick's head,
Innocent Warwick's head – for we are prologue

178. *thought:* intended.

351

But to his tragedy – conclude the wonder
Of Henry's fears. And then the glorious race
Of fourteen kings Plantagenets determines
In this last issue male. Heaven be obey'd.
Impoverish time of its amazement, friends,
And we will prove as trusty in our payments,
As prodigal to nature in our debts.

200   Death? Pish! 'tis but a sound, a name of air,
A minute's storm, or not so much. To tumble
From bed to bed, be massacred alive
By some physicians for a month or two
In hope of freedom from a fever's torments
Might stagger manhood. Here, the pain is past
Ere sensibly 'tis felt. Be men of spirit!
Spurn coward passion! So illustrious mention
Shall blaze our names and style us kings o'er death.

DAUBENEY: Away! – Impostor beyond precedent;
No chronicle records his fellow.
    Exeunt all Officers and Prisoners.

210 HUNTLY: I have
Not thoughts left; 'tis sufficient in such cases
Just laws ought to proceed.
    Enter KING HENRY, DURHAM, *and* HIALAS.

KING HENRY: We are resolv'd:
Your business, noble lords, shall find success
Such as your king importunes.

HUNTLY: You are gracious.

KING HENRY: Perkin, we are inform'd, is arm'd to die;
In that we'll honour him. Our lords shall follow
To see the execution. And from hence

195. *determines:* comes to an end.
206. *sensibly:* acutely.
208. *blaze:* proclaim.

We gather this fit use: that public states,
As our particular bodies, taste most good
In health when purged of corrupted blood.   *220*
    Exeunt.

218. *use:* moral benefit.

FINIS

EPILOGUE

Here has appear'd, though in a several fashion,
The threats of majesty, the strength of passion,
Hopes of an empire, change of fortunes – all
What can to theatres of greatness fall,
Proving their weak foundations. Who will please
Amongst such several sight, to censure these
No births abortive, nor a bastard brood –
Shame to a parentage or fosterhood –
May warrant by their loves all just excuses,
And often find a welcome to the Muses.

1. *several:* suitable to each.
6. *censure these:* judge these to be.
10. *to:* to the company of.

COMMENTARY AND NOTES

The references are to line numbers.
S.D. = Stage direction. S.P. = Speech prefix. Q. = Quarto.

'TIS PITY SHE'S A WHORE

SOURCES AND INFLUENCES

No definite source has been found for the mainplot of the play though some earlier treatments of the theme of brother–sister incest have been suggested. Incest crops up in a number of important plays of the period, including *Hamlet*, *The Revenger's Tragedy*, Beaumont and Fletcher's *A King and No King*, Tourneur's *The Atheist's Tragedy* and Massinger's *The Unnatural Combat*. None of these plays treats the incest sympathetically; in each it is a monstrous aberration, moral and/or psychological. Of particular interest is Middleton's *Women Beware Women*. The subplot (which contains an incest story) probably provided Ford with originals for the character-group of Bergetto, Poggio, Donado (and Annabella); and perhaps also suggested the bourgeois setting and atmosphere, which is unusual in Ford. The mainplot of *'Tis Pity She's a Whore* has a similar relationship with *Romeo and Juliet*, Shakespeare's Romeo, Juliet, Nurse and Friar Lawrence being repeated (with significant variations) in Giovanni, Annabella, Putana and Friar Bonaventure. In fact, verbal echoes show that Ford was working with Shakespeare's play freshly in mind.

[In Q. there is a commendatory poem by one Thomas Ellice.]

DEDICATORY EPISTLE

John Mordaunt: 1599–1642; a courtier, created first Earl of Peterborough in 1628; a general on the Parliament side at the outbreak of the civil war.

8. these . . . leisure: It is tempting to see this as Ford's acknowledgement that *'Tis Pity* is his first play; but no such thing may be intended.

ACT ONE

Scene One

At the outset, Ford presents the central moral and psychological problem of his play in the form of a dispute, but a dispute with questions on one side, statements and commands on the other. The effect is to show that the problem is incapable of being effectively explored by rational argument, and in any case the two sides can find no middle ground to provide them with a common language. It is a brilliant stroke of Ford's to counterpoint the explosive and counter-rational situation with the rhetoric and imagery of the academic relationship which had earlier joined the disputants in harmony. A gap already opens up between Giovanni and the world he formerly inhabited.

26. *Of . . . sister:* For greater effect, the actual nature of Giovanni's 'madness' is suspended till now. The effect might be to win some sympathy for Giovanni before an inevitably shocking disclosure. Even the syntax of the disclosure itself seems designed to lessen the blow by making it just a little vague.

28–34. Giovanni's argument in defence of his love – the first of several such arguments – is substantially repeated at I, ii, 248 ff.

43–5. Giovanni's sin is in fact a double one: the sin of incest, and the sin of blasphemy in his making a religion of his love. Cf. lines 20–3 and 59–61.

66. *flaws:* All editions read 'flames'.

83-4. *All ... god:* Giovanni's provision for failure sounds ominous and provides the first of the many references to fate in the play, references which could, in one interpretation, supply an explanation of the play's story and a condonation of the lovers' actions.

Scene Two

In an expansive scene, Ford sets in motion two of the play's four subplots as well as bringing to the point of consummation the central love-relationship. The device of Annabella and Putana's overseeing from the upper-stage allows Ford a *Troilus and Cressida* type of review of potential lovers. The poetry of Giovanni and Annabella's dialogue is in part conventional, courtly love poetry; but lines 212-13 have an unhealthy ring (reminding one of *Measure for Measure*); while the Juno comparison, as Morris points out, has added point when one remembers that Juno was Jupiter's sister as well as his wife. The swearing ritual at the end of the scene provides a sort of mock marriage, and it will dominate Giovanni's thoughts in the last but one scene of the play. Like most of Ford's heroes, Giovanni and Annabella blind themselves to a course of action which is likely to produce catastrophic results.

3. Grimaldi, a nobleman, would do himself a dishonour to fight with Vasques, a servant. No play of Ford's recognizes social distinctions more clearly than *'Tis Pity She's a Whore*. (Cf. II, ii, 48-51 and III, ix, 55-7.)

29. *Is ... love:* Grimaldi has already declared his love for Annabella to Florio.

48-9. *I ... mad:* An allusion to the practice of cutting the vermiform ligament in a dog's tongue as a preventive against rabies.

50. *I'll be revenged:* This is the first of a series of threats of revenge, mostly aimed at Soranzo. Revenge dominates the subplots and informs the catastrophe; but the play can hardly be considered to be about revenge, as the cursory handling of Richardetto will show.

54. *I'll . . . this:* This edition. Q. reads 'remember this' and subsequent editions 'Remember this'.

61. *unspleened dove:* The dove was commonly thought not to possess a spleen, the malfunctioning of which could cause melancholy disorders. The gall was supposed to draw choler from the liver and was therefore regarded as the source of anger, but gall and spleen were often confused. Cf. the expression 'pigeon-livered'.

114. *elder brother:* If Ford implies that Bergetto is an elder brother he has forgotten this by I, iii, 66–9.

131, 2. *golden calf, Israelite:* The reference is to Exodus, 32.

134–5. *you . . . rate:* 'You need not wager recklessly and accept Bergetto for fear you will have no other suitors' (Morris).

154. *Lost . . . death:* This provides an explicit answer to the last lines of scene i.

154–72. There is a certain amount of contradiction here as Giovanni (perfectly in character) at one moment accepts guilt, at another finds extenuation, and at another disbelieves in the whole system of sin and punishment: a pointer to the moral complexities of the whole play.

During 173 S.D. *Enter . . . Putana:* They have descended off-stage while Giovanni soliloquizes and now join him on the main stage.

207. *Promethean fire:* Prometheus, in classical mythology, brought fire from heaven to men.

219–23. This moment prefigures in reverse the last episode of the lovers' relationship.

253–4. *I . . . you:* There is some disagreement among critics as to whether Giovanni actually lies at this point. It has been argued that the Friar's failure to prove a case against him is taken by Giovanni as condonation of his love, but this is probably over-subtle. More likely, the character's lack of integrity at this point is an aspect of Ford's strategy of balancing sympathy with condemnation.

277. *What . . . will:* The childlike moment, following as it does a religious solemnity, indicates the depth of innocence which Ford recognizes as an ingredient in the relationship.

Scene Three

The scene establishes an unsolemn, even cosy ambience for what has gone before. Florio, who tells us in scene i that Soranzo is the acceptable suitor for Annabella, evidently tolerates Donado's importunities on behalf of his nephew in a friendly compliance. The subplot world of money-matches and venalities is often interpreted as a background intended to ennoble by contrast the unselfish idealism of Giovanni and Annabella. But in fact Florio, Donado and Bergetto are very much more attractive characters than their parallels in *Women Beware Women*, and Florio's intention to avoid forcing his daughter into a marriage against her will (lines 10–11) makes him a mouthpiece for a frequent sentiment of Ford. This part of the subplot material is intended to establish a sort of domestic normality, in order to stress the henceforward isolation of the main characters.

71–2. '*Will . . . wealth*': The interview referred to must have occurred before the play opened. Annabella's reported remark sounds distinctly out of character, and could suggest a stage early in Ford's composition of the play when Annabella was intended to use Bergetto as a cover for her exploits just as Isabella uses the Ward in *Women Beware Women*. But perhaps one should not examine too closely this comic nonsense.

ACT TWO

Scene One

It has been claimed that the love of Giovanni and Annabella is ethereal, never earthy; but the teasing exchange of the opening of the scene tactfully creates a mood in which sexual modesty is a thing of the past, and the moment is charged with the notion of joyous – and proud – sexual possession. Ford then earths the teasing in the coarseness of Putana who gives us a debased perspective on the lovers' relationship (the connexion between Putana and Juliet's nurse is very clear at this point). At the end of the scene, the unashamedly crude introduction of more subplot material forbodes a dramatic structure of opportunist invention rather than skilful organization.

13–14. *Music ... playing:* i.e. he enjoys talking about their love-making as much as doing it.

16–17. *thus ... lips:* Leda was approached by Jupiter in the form of a swan, and their offspring were Castor and Pollux, and Helen. Morris suggests that Giovanni chooses the myth as an example of unnatural union dignified by art.

43–6. *Your ... one:* Putana fails to distinguish between lust, the object of which is sex, and love, the object of which is somebody. At this moment one's sympathies are drawn to the higher sensitivity of the lovers.

55. Padua was famous for the medical school of its university.

57. *you ... sickly:* Presumably a sickliness brought on by her care for Giovanni. At I, iii, 5–6, we heard of Giovanni's similar affliction.

Scene Two

The scene introduces the last of the four subplots, another revenge story based on sexual jealousy. Brutality and egotism preclude sympathy from Soranzo and Hippolita, but in terms of integrity, Hippolita appears the more wronged (see note to lines 87–9). The presentation of Soranzo as the courtly lover in the first part of the scene and as the adulterer and murder-accomplice in the second provides one of Ford's double perspectives. But the effect is less subtle here than normally, and may merely be clumsy characterization.

5. *Sannazar:* Jacopo Sannazaro (c. 1456–1530), Italian poet and pastoralist (wrote *Arcadia*), was the author of an epigram praising Venice and was rewarded by the city (see lines 12–14).

19. *rules of civility:* Rules of civility constantly collide with passion in this play.

49. *Madam Merchant:* Italicized in Q. (and this may well follow Ford's MS). See note to I, ii, 3.

87–9. *The . . . them:* In Ford's world, a vow often has the potency of magic, however conventionally 'wrong' it appears. (The end of the play in part depends on this.) Soranzo, appearing to clear up a previous misdeed, commits a second one and appears merely hypocritical. This is the sort of rationalization of one's wishes, irrespective of an absolute morality, which in part colours Giovanni's position (and in this Ford's characterization importantly anticipates George Eliot's).

100. *accurs'd:* Bawcutt's emendation of Q.'s two readings: 'a Curse' (uncorrected) and 'a Coarse' (corrected).

Scene Three

The plots begin to intertwine, in this most Italianate of Ford's plays. Richardetto is an ambiguous figure in an unfortunate way – moral spokesman and righteous victim, he is also a contriver and (at second hand) a poisoner and murderer. He epitomizes the play's uneasy handling of the stock intrigue motifs of Jacobean tragedy.

32. *by which means:* Presumably 'By means of his influential position'.

49. *Soranzo . . . heart:* This is a deliberate lie in view of line 22 above. Richardetto sees the opportunity of using Grimaldi as Hippolita sees the opportunity of using Vasques in the previous scene.

63. *thee:* All editions read 'me'. 'Thee' makes better sense and avoids the awkward repetition.

Scene Four

After the duplicity and deceptions of the last scenes, the candour of the fool, Bergetto, has an engaging quality. One contrast seemingly at the back of Ford's mind in this play is that between innocence and sophistication. The love of Giovanni and Annabella in the first act is innocent, but fails to remain so.

Scene Five

Dialogues between Giovanni and the Friar punctuate the play and provide it with a system of thematic polarities – conventional morality and religious conformity versus individuality and free-thinking, discipline versus free expression, age versus youth and so on. The difficulty of deciding where Ford's sympathies lie argues either the skill with which things are balanced or his humanity before the problems posed.

6. *number:* Q. Gifford emended it to 'founder', 'members' is perhaps possible, and the whole line has been explained away as corrupt. Morris claims that 'the subdued oath would be an odd one', but Bonaventure's model, Friar Lawrence, similarly swears: 'By my holy order' (*Romeo and Juliet*, III, iii).

14–26: Giovanni's argument is neoplatonic in its terminology but is meant to sound like unconvincing logic-chopping. He is seeking to rationalize his forbidden love. His tone in the rest of the scene shows that he is more insolently confident of the right-ness of his position than desperate to convince himself or the Friar of the truth. Never again in the play will Giovanni waver in this confidence in his own power to choose between right and wrong.

41–2. *Marriage ... lust:* For the moment, Giovanni appears to achieve a higher ethical standard than his teacher; and critics have condemned the friar for his advocacy of marriage as a practical means of breaking up the incestuous relationship.

54. *form:* Dodsley's emendation of Q's 'throne'. Most editors retain 'throne'.

55–6. *the spheres ... Heaven:* An allusion to the notion that the planetary orbits, or spheres in their motion, produced the 'harmony' or 'music of the spheres', inaudible on the post-Fall earth. In some versions, the music was contributed by sirens, one in each sphere.

Scene Six

The end of the scene skilfully reminds the audience of the now domesticated nature of Giovanni and Annabella's relationship but hints at an internal threat to its very existence – Giovanni's jealousy. Annabella's bantering is misplaced and reveals the possessive nature of Giovanni's love.

4–5. *I . . . world:* The sort of dramatic irony that Ford rarely indulges in.

37–40. *Where's . . . that:* Florio's pushing of Bergetto's suit, when elsewhere and notably at the end of the scene he supports the claims of Soranzo, has been described variously as hypocrisy and tact. The importance of the ring as a love-symbol is stressed several times in Ford's plays (see especially *The Broken Heart*, IV, i, 27–35, where the same ironic implications appear).

ACT THREE

Scene One

Bergetto's revolt against family pressures in the matter of love relationships is a comic burlesque of the central situation of the play; and like the incestuous lovers, he has his own integrity. But it is a serious critical problem to decide how far the multiplying subplots are justified in the play and how far they are padding for a theme incapable of more extensive treatment.

34. *cart whores:* Prostitutes were exhibited in the street in carts as part of their punishment.

Scene Two

Annabella's mocking of Soranzo, followed by her more kindly attitude, anticipates the effect of a later dialogue in IV, iii. Giovanni's growing mistrust of his love is shown by his eavesdropping.

Soranzo is presented simply – and unconvincingly – as the courtly lover.

11. *be . . . woman:* Cf. Hamlet's 'Frailty, thy name is woman'. Giovanni's remark shows again the precarious nature of the relationship.

19–20. *That's . . . now:* This is part of Giovanni's growing *hubris* and it sorts ill with the lack of confidence in Annabella shown in line 11 (see note above). Earlier he had given himself up to Fate (I, i, 84 and ii, 154); now he sees himself in charge. The result is 'security', the Elizabethan notion of a culpable lack of anxiety, and, here, something akin to religious despair.

23–4. *Did . . . dead:* A playing with the literal and metaphorical meanings of 'heart' which anticipates the end of the play and recalls the same sort of imagery in I, ii.

45. *taste:* Annabella may mean 'knowledge', 'tasting' and 'knowing' being closely linked in the language (as in Milton). And the word 'test' (= 'evidence', 'proof') may also be involved.

68. *Look . . . Florio:* The line, given to Giovanni in Q. and to Soranzo by Gifford, is an echo of *Othello*, I, i. The parallel situation links the two moments in Ford's mind: the stolen daughter, given up to a monstrous love-match.

83. *maid's-sickness:* Chlorosis or 'green-sickness' (because of a greenish tinge in the complexion), an ailment prevalent in girls at the age of puberty. The same diagnosis is made in scene iv. See note to iv, 8.

Scene Three

Some of the details of the presentation of Annabella's pregnancy may be derived from *The Duchess of Malfi*, II, i (Giovanni's confusion is very like Antonio's), but Ford uses the episode (and Putana's directness of language) to convince us again of the physical nature of the lovers' relationship.

Scene Four

Dramatic irony figures strongly in this scene as plottings and motivations become inextricably tangled. In particular, the nature of (dis)honour, nobility, virtue, fatherly love and even religious piety is rendered ambiguous by the audience's growing misgivings about human percipience and judgement. The cross-purposes of the characters begin to make a comment on human insulation and egotism, the other (darker) side of proud integrity.

8. *fulness:* Q. and all subsequent editions. The next three lines make it evident that the two men are talking about maid's-sickness, and as this is a form of anaemia, 'fulness' (= 'perfection' or 'copiousness') seems the opposite of the required sense. Perhaps it should read 'foulness', although 'fulness' recalls 'overflux of youth' of ii, 83. In view of Giovanni's fears of the previous scene and explicit injunction that a doctor should not visit Annabella, it is possible that the audience is meant to think that Richardetto realizes the true position and is obliquely encouraging the (disastrous) match with Soranzo as a sort of revenge: a pre-arranged cuckoldom for his enemy should the Grimaldi plot fail. Otherwise, there is an inconsistency in the plot here of the sort that becomes frequent later on.

21. This might refer to Bonaventure, or, in view of the next line, Soranzo.

Scene Five

Philotis, unlike Annabella (and Giovanni) and Bergetto, appears as the type of the dutiful child. Love is seen as not merely a super-rational and tyrannical power but as something which can be learnt or cultivated. The older and wiser Annabella of iv, iii will also see this. Katherine of *Perkin Warbeck* is Ford's most important study of this attitude.

14–15. *'tis . . . all:* Morris paraphrases: 'You only risk waiting a night: if nothing happens I shall learn the full details tomorrow, and instruct you accordingly.'

38. S.P. *Poggio:* Bawcutt's emendation of Q.'s '*Phi.*' Gifford gives the line to Richardetto.

Scene Six

Annabella's repentance hardly convinces us as a serious moral readjustment, given the circumstances of her material position and the nature of the Friar's 'punishment' speech; but both Giovanni and Annabella are pragmatists with regard to ethical problems and one should not look for behaviour from them which accords with a coherent philosophy of life. The Friar's own moral position is most seriously called into doubt by his advice to Annabella to marry for her 'honour's safety' (line 36). In extenuation, it is argued that he is being practical and that he does not know that Annabella is pregnant. However, it is the new problem (of the pregnancy) which sent Giovanni to the Friar (scene iii). So he presumably does know (though one may be assuming a sort of consistency here which is often beyond dramatic requirements and is certainly beyond Ford's interests elsewhere in this play).

S.D.: Q. gives '*Enter the Fryar in his study, sitting in his chair . . .*'. It is usually assumed that this scene takes place in Annabella's bedroom and follows on III, iv, 33. However, the original idea was that the affiancement should take place at Bonaventure's cell, and Richardetto has given that information to Grimaldi. Nobody stresses a change of plan. It may be that Ford revised parts of this, catering for the complex plotting, and thus produced confusions. See notes to lines 45 and 55–6 below.

24–30. *There . . . lust:* Ford has been critized for not finding an apt 'punishment to fit the crime' for the incestuous, but one can see a Sartrian idea here of people being each other's hell, just as in the incest they had been each other's pleasure; and so the essentially medieval picture of hell is given a strikingly modern turn.

45. *He ... below:* This seems to be a clear reference to Florio's house, not Bonaventure's cell.

55-6. *more ... sun:* What has taken place is a formal affiancement. The Friar then looks forward to a church service in the morning as part of the ceremony or the wedding itself. The wedding celebration is described in the next scene (lines 3–4) as being arranged for two days hence, and this may be more evidence of rewriting.

Scene Seven

From mistaken motives and intricate plotting, the play now opens out into a series of casual slaughters, deaths put on by cunning, and purposes mistook, fallen on the inventors' heads. The effect on the structure of the play is to finish off the four subplots in the next five, crowded scenes. Bergetto's pathetic comic death has been often praised.

Scene Eight

10. *disgrace:* She presumably refers to her social disgrace in marrying a servant.

Scene Nine

Richardetto's blame for much of the trouble is lightly passed over. Ford clearly regards him as an aspect of the plotting of the play during these scenes, not as part of the play's moral structure. The Cardinal is a more difficult case and he represents a sort of tyranny which contributes to the impression of moral anarchy in the play: while private revenge is condemned, public justice fails to be carried out.

8. *Alas ... harm:* In a play which contains more than Ford's usually meagre allowance of malice and active enmity, Bergetto's epitaph is a significant footnote to his subplot.

56. *sir, Florio:* Q. reads 'Sir Florio', followed by all subsequent editions. If Q. is correct the Cardinal intends heavy irony by entitling the merchant whose bourgeois social position he is, at

the present moment, taking care to stress. I prefer to see a compositor's error and have emended accordingly.

62. *Justice ... nearer:* An allusion to the classical legend of Astraea, goddess of justice, who fled from earth at the end of the Golden Age and was placed among the stars as the constellation Virgo.

ACT FOUR

Scene One

Ford uses the convention of the murderous celebration twice in the play, here and in the last scene; but it is more than a cliché in the hands of a playright fascinated both by the formal occasion which confers ceremony on human activity, and by the destructive byproducts of the activity itself.

7. *hand of goodness:* Presumably a synonym for the hand of God, and therefore highly inappropriate in its suggestion that Bergetto's slaughter was God's means of saving Soranzo.

After 35 S.D. *with garlands of willows:* Willows were the symbol of disappointed love. Ford includes a masque-revenge of spurned lovers in *Love's Sacrifice*.

74–5. *Troppo ... inganna:* 'Too much hope deceives.'

86. *yet —— and end:* As in Q. There was evidently something missing or illegible in the copy-text.

94. *heat ... fire:* The fires of hell, a theoretical concept in the Friar's sermon (III, vi), seem now in the deaths of Bergetto (III, vii) and Hippolita to have been translated into real experience.

99. *flame's:* Q. reads 'Flame's'. The sense is odd and one might expect something more like 'pain's'. Perhaps the compositor misread 'shame's' (cf. first line next scene).

Scene Two

Richardetto's utterances start to gather an authority which suggests one solution to the play's moral problems. Sexuality itself may begin to seem the villain, creating irrational behaviour, destructive jealousy, and impiety. The Christian stoic answer is to refrain, with God's help (lines 27-8).

Scene Three

In fantastic contrast, violence and obscenity follow a scene of quiet resolution and resignation. Ford, it is claimed, is incapable of achieving the louder effects of human passion without falsity. But Soranzo's opening speech (like much of the scene) is a convincing mimicry of degrading sexual jealousy. Ford in part wrote this scene twice, here and in *Love's Sacrifice* (v, i) – the courageous heroine asserting the eternal validity of her love for another man before a husband of murderous intent. Annabella's softening, lines 123, 131, 145, strikes an unexpected note and one which anticipates her mood of the end of the play. But the reversal may appear too sudden, reminding us of the abrupt switches in the tragedies and tragi-comedies of Fletcher. The rest of the scene improbably crowds in various events and creates problems of chronology, and, more important, of character motivation. Is Giovanni's visit to Annabella intended to give the impression that the incestuous relationship continues after the wedding? This affects one's understanding of the 'repentance' of III, vi. See next note.

S.D. *unbraced:* This is usually taken as a symbol of mental turmoil and a comparison is made with *Hamlet*, II, i, 78. But the original intention may have been to present this as the night of the marriage, and 'unbraced' indicated Soranzo's rising from bed having discovered how he has been tricked. This makes immediate sense of lines 16-20 ('but ... doing'). However, IV, ii, 10-12 suggests a time-lag between IV, i and IV, iii, and there is a deal of other conflicting evidence about the chronology of the play. See notes to IV, iii, 254-66; v, i, 1-23; v, ii, 1; v, iii, 4-11.

4. *confound:* There may be involved in the sense of this the Latin root, 'fundere', meaning 'to pour out'.

22–3. *'twas . . . honour:* Cf. the Friar's reference to 'honour' at
III, vi, 36.

59. *Che . . . amore:* 'What death is sweeter than to die for love?'

64. *Morendo . . . dolore:* 'Dying in the grace of God, I should die
without sorrow'. 'Morirei' is Bawcutt's emendation of Q.'s
(corrected) 'morirere'. Neither this nor the Italian of line 59 has
been identified.

80–7. *Now . . . beastly:* Vasques' speech is a piece of double-talk
intended for Annabella's ears but containing truths aimed at
Soranzo who, by his passionate desire for crude retaliation, shows
ignobility and bestiality. Cf. lines 103–4 where Vasques is talking
about a revenge to restore honour which will involve punishing
the guilty man as well as Annabella. Soranzo is very different, as
an avenger, from the cool, honour-seeking Orgilus in *The Broken
Heart*.

255–66. The function of the episode is to give Vasques 'proof'
of the incestuous relationship so that he will not seem too credulous.
However, it is not clear if the audience is meant to assume that
the amatory relationship continues; and Vasques' 'she is alone'
(265–5) is odd because Soranzo has just gone to her. A lot of this
scene looks like patching and reshaping.

ACT FIVE

Scene One

The religious orthodoxy of Annabella's final conversion comes as
a surprise after the unease or contempt surrounding the religious
spokesmen of the play. In a complementary volte-face her love
for Giovanni is degraded by her to superficial infatuation. And yet
her generosity to Giovanni (lines 21–3) goes part way to deny
what she says.

1–23. It is not obvious if this is to be taken as a second repentance, psychological reasons for which remain unexplained, or the
continuance of that of III, vi, with the events hurrying on from the

marriage. In fact, Annabella in this speech is aware of the speed of time passing and I am inclined to see this as the continuation of the earlier repentance. But this involves disputable theories concerning 'long time' and 'short time' in the play which have yet to be examined.

47. *That letter:* Bawcutt claims that we do not know what is in the letter and assumes that it urges Giovanni to repent; but in v, iii we learn that its main burden is to warn Giovanni of the physical danger he is in from Soranzo.

Scene Two

1. *Am . . now:* This is an obvious continuation of iv, iii, making it difficult to argue a time-lag between iv, iii and v, i.

10–11. *I'll . . . robes:* Many touches in the presentation of Soranzo in Acts iv and v remind one of Othello, this not the least of them.

Scene Three

Giovanni's rapid exchange of emotions may suggest a disintegrating personality. Death-wish and enormous *hubris* seem mixed in his determination to walk into Soranzo's trap.

4–11. This suggests fairly strongly that the relationship of Annabella and Giovanni continues after the marriage, though it is possible to argue that the marriage and tragic end occupy only two days. A way out would be to suggest that Giovanni anticipates the delights of their kisses, and that his visit to his sister in iv, iii is a mistake of Ford's. In any case, the effect of the speech is to show the coarsening character of his love, and the extreme remarks of the end (lines 11–16) adumbrate the Marlovian hubris that he is suffering from.

17. *jubilee:* Bawcutt and Morris find the meaning unclear, but see *OED.*, sb.5.

25. *congeal'd coral:* It was erroneously thought that coral was a plant which hardened into its rigid form only when taken from the water.

37. *Are . . . delights:* In scene v Giovanni decides that Annabella is traitorous.

71–2. *Despair . . . me:* Again, Giovanni gives explicit voice to his 'security', a desperate and despairing state of mind from a religious and moral point of view. Giovanni's inurement to sin is like Macbeth's, and each of them develops a fierce courage which lacks real humanity. Their detachment from reality is in each case a sort of madness.

Scene Four

8–9. *what . . . revenge:* Soranzo's hiring of murderers in no way degrades his Italian notion of revenge for honour. In this, Soranzo's action is akin to Orgilus' use of the 'engine': each is unprepared to take the chance of fair combat because their revenge might then be thwarted and honour will remain unsatisfied (cf. *The Broken Heart*, v, ii, 139–43).

31. *turn Italian:* Italy had a reputation for the intensity of its feuding and revenge plotting. Cf. v, vi, 150–1.

35–6. *he . . . damnation:* Giovanni, killed in the middle of his sinning, would be damned at once, without chance to prepare himself for death. Comparison is often made with a similar sentiment in *Hamlet*, III, iii.

Scene Five

The scene owes something to Othello's murder of Desdemona, and this can help us sort out Giovanni's enigmatic and mixed motivations for killing Annabella. Her reform and marriage have betrayed their love, and the ritual sacrifice becomes the proper response to the vow sworn in I, ii. Critics have also claimed that he kills her to save her from further torture; kills her to revenge himself against his rival, Soranzo (he calls his action a revenge on three occasions in this and the last scene); kills her as a dog-in-the-manger act; and kills her because he is now a psycopath. All views are possible but none is in itself satisfying (see also note to line 86). The charge of madness, in any case, needs careful examination. (Ford entertains it as a point of view in the next scene.) Much depends on the tone of this most understated and restrained of Ford's poetry which provides a climax to one side of the play – its intense and subtle analysis of two people in a disastrous relationship. The outer action of the play receives an appropriately melodramatic climax in the next scene.

S.D. *Enter ... bed:* Either a 'discovery' (curtains drawn aside) or the bed was pushed out onto stage.

11–13. *Why ... motion:* Again, there is a Marlovian ring in these lines, and perhaps even a specific Marlovian echo: 'I hold the Fates bound fast in iron chains. And with my hand turn fortune's wheel about' (6 *Tamburlaine*).

82. *Styx:* A river in the classical underworld over which the shades of the departed were ferried by Charon.

86. *Revenge is mine: Vindicta mihi,* the classic cry of triumph of the Elizabethan stage revenger, Giovanni is best understood as revenging himself against both Soranzo and Annabella for marrying. He does not cease to love Annabella but must avenge his honour or his love will be degraded (cf. the similar problem of Penthea and Orgilus: Penthea can only do honour to her love for Orgilus by destroying the possibility for its fruition. See note to *The Broken Heart*, II, iii, 77–107).

106. *And ... part:* Giovanni's attitudinizing is beautifully caught in the play-acting metaphors. Again, a reference to *Othello* is apposite.

Scene Six

Giovanni's entry with a heart upon his dagger can be seen as ridiculous melodrama or profound symbol, decadent sensationalism or an economic summary of themes and images. Built into the scene are a series of 'interpretations' of the moment. Florio's charge of madness, lines 36 and 44, implies a judgement not on Giovanni's actions but on his apparently lunatic remarks. The characters question the validity of his claims, not the balance of his mind. The proof of his claims leaves Giovanni open to a moral charge which Ford's honesty would not allow to be blurred.

Giovanni dies as he lives, villain-hero of his story, claiming an afterlife only so that he can view Annabella's face. Death turns out to be the long looked-for answer to the problem of a life in which dictates of the heart run counter to social, ethical and religious demands of behaviour. Giovanni's self-sufficiency looks for justice, not mercy.

23–4. *The . . . night:* For Othello, the eclipse, which he painfully realizes never happens (v, ii), would symbolize death and disorder; for Giovanni it is part of his greater glory. Ford typically transmutes borrowed material.

69. *gilt:* Giovanni intends no pun here, but for the audience this recalls Annabella's 'character'd in guilt' of v, i, 10, and so the word in itself epitomizes the double perspective of this final scene: Giovanni's viewpoint and that of conventional morality. His guilt to him seems gilt, his brutality a glory, his madness a terrible sanity, the pathos of his father's death a becoming courage.

73. *twists of life:* The threads of life were spun by the Parcae and cut by them at the moment appointed for death. This is Giovanni's most splendid and deluded moment as he claims to control the power of death itself.

81. *Vengeance:* Evidently the watchword agreed upon in v, iv.

137. *this woman:* Usually taken to be Putana, but Annabella may be intended.

153–5. *And . . . use:* This is interpreted, alongside the Cardinal's failure to dispense true justice in III, ix, as a symptom of the corruption of the establishment in the play.

THE BROKEN HEART

SOURCES AND INFLUENCES

The lines in the Prologue

> What may be here thought a fiction, when Time's youth
> Wanted some riper years, was known a truth,

have invited scholars to look for an historical source for the play's story or for some aspect of that story. The relationship of Sir Philip Sidney and Penelope Rich has been seen behind that of Orgilus and Penthea, the 'engine', by which Orgilus catches Ithocles (IV, iv) has been traced to a Dutch incident of the sixteenth century (as well as to a play of Barnabe Barnes), and a story in Hoby's translation of *The Book of the Courtier* has been suggested as the original of Penthea's love-melancholy, constancy and death. But what the Prologue refers to has yet to be satisfactorily explained.

Sidney's *Arcadia* evidently supplied some of the atmosphere, a character-name, Amyclas, and hints for the story of Penthea and Orgilus; North's translation of Plutarch's 'Life of Lycurgus' provided something of the Spartan setting and Spartan *mores*; and the historical situation behind the play is the three wars between Sparta and Messenia, 743–453 B.C.

THE DEDICATORY EPISTLE

William, Lord Craven: 1606–97. Soldier of distinction, knighted, 1627, and created baron by Charles I. Commanded the English troops fighting for Gustavus Adolphus, 1631, and was a Royalist during the Civil War, when he supported Elizabeth, widowed daughter of James I. Created Earl of Craven by Charles II in 1664. Was a Fellow of the Royal Society.

THE SPEAKERS' NAMES

Most of the names, indicating the characters' qualities, are derived from Greek words and suggest a 'humorous', almost allegorical, approach to the play's construction. This fits the otherworldly atmosphere of the play but is distinctly unusual in tragedy. The following derivations are mostly from Anderson.

Amyclas: probably from *Arcadia* which includes a Spartan king so called.

Ithocles: unexplained.

Orgilus: 'inclined to anger'.

Bassanes: 'a trial or test'.

Armostes: 'one who arranges or governs'.

Crotolon: 'a rattling noise'.

Prophilus: ? 'dear' plus 'before'.

Nearchus: 'fresh' plus 'leader'.

Tecnicus: 'artistic'.

Hemophil: ? 'blood' plus 'fond of', a reference to gluttony or, ironically, to military prowess. The name is spelt 'Lemophil' in *The Speakers' Names* and the last scene of Q., a reading preferred by Morris and glossed 'lover of the wine-vat'.

Groneas: ? 'eaten out' or 'hole, hollow vessel'.

Amelus: Morris points out that this actually means 'neglectful'.

Phulas: 'to keep watch and ward, especially by night'.

Calantha: 'beauty' plus 'full bloom of a flower or plant'.

Penthea: 'to mourn, lament'.

Euphranea: 'one who cheers, gladdens'.

Christalla: 'ice, crystal'.

Philema: 'a kiss'.

Grausis: 'old woman'.

Thrasus: 'bold'.

Aplotes: 'simplicity'.

ACT ONE

Scene One

As in *'Tis Pity She's a Whore*, Ford begins the play in the middle of an argument to serve as a dramatic opening which will lead naturally into exposition. Orgilus in the latter part of the scene assumes power over his sister's marriage in order to create a situation parallel to that between Penthea and Ithocles. His aim, presumably, is deliberately not to exercise that power tyranically. The stated intention of visiting Athens is evidently disingenuous.

6–8. *cynic, stoic, Areopagite:* This is part of Ford's careful inclusion of apt detail. The Cynics and Stoics were sects of philosophers in ancient Greece; an Areopagite was a member of the Areopagus, the judicial court in Athens.

78–9: *First . . . Bassanes:* This is ambiguous, meaning either 'to take away Bassanes' anxieties' or 'to relieve myself of my anxieties about Bassanes'. The generosity of the former idea, unless Orgilus is thinking of improving Penthea's situation, seems unlikely.

98. *By . . . fires:* Vesta was the Roman goddess of the hearth. She was served by the Vestal virgins, and hence Euphranea's choice of the oath. References to the classical gods proliferate in the play and serve to establish the setting. Often, as here, they are associated with a solemn act of oath-swearing.

Scene Two

The world of Spartan politics and empire provides a public background for the private emotions and griefs which form the substance of the play. Ithocles, already presented in the first scene as the brother and as the destroyer of natural love, is carefully introduced here as the successful soldier, the man of the moment and the king's darling: the crucial position, in fact, for the *de casibus* tragedy. References to time and age at the beginning of the scene introduce the theme of the passing of time which will be seen as a determinant in the obstruction of love and happiness.

13. *Laconia:* An alternative name for Lacedemonia, the area controlled by the city of Sparta.

15. *Messene:* The capital city of Messenia, bordering province.

20. *Pephon:* A town in Laconia, near Messenia.

32–3. *How ... fortunes:* Calantha's question is significant, relating as it does to her incipient relationship with Ithocles, and to the theme of self-government which will receive extensive exploration in the play.

41. *Your friend:* Calantha's interjection is a well-aimed deflationary tactic which, like Crotolon's comment at lines 47–8, serves to make acceptable Prophilus' hyperboles and the atmosphere of deification in which Ithocles is awaited. The scene as a whole exemplifies Ford's use of shifting viewpoints which is so typical of his art.

61–8. The crowning ceremony anticipates a parallel episode at the end of the play. Parallelism becomes a significant technique in the play's strategy.

71–2. *What ... mind:* 'How little my achievements are, merely the offspring of good intentions, compared with the honours heaped on me.'

81–2. *like ... sacrifices:* The reference is to the bacchanals, the orgiastic celebrations of Bacchus which involved the celebrants' frenzied rushing over mountains and through woods, tearing to pieces wild creatures met on the way.

88–90. Ithocles, modestly deprecating the value of the leader whose commands others carry out, suddenly realizes the tactlessness of his remark in the presence of the nation's ruler.

100. *Observe ... example:* This is obscure and I have followed Anderson's note. Morris gives 'model yourselves on Ithocles'.

106 – end of scene: It is difficult to see why Ford arranged this clumsy piece of comic business, though it might serve as a parody of the courtly love-relationships which are beginning to appear (in Ithocles and Calantha, and Prophilus and Euphranea) in the main plot. The reflection of 'woman's nature' at the end anticipates in crude fashion what is to be a major concern of the play. The last few lines might suggest that Ford intended to develop this

foursome into a genuine subplot, but if so he lost interest or could not find room for it, and all four remain mere extras.

127, 7. *Mars, Vulcan:* Mars, the god of war, was found by Vulcan in adultery with Venus, Vulcan's wife.

Scene Three

The opening of the scene parallels scene i, and Tecnicus' anxieties about Orgilus point the way of future action and adumbrate the temperate way of life which the play supports. With important differences, Orgilus' overhearing of the courtship of Euphranea by Prophilus recalls Giovanni's overhearing of Annabella and Soranzo in *'Tis Pity She's a Whore*, III, ii. Almost in the way of Restoration comedy – which in structure *The Broken Heart* oddly anticipates – Euphranea and Prophilus conduct the one successful love-affair which acts as a foil to the two tragic love-affairs of the play. The message-passing plot in which Orgilus becomes involved – recalling Vindice's pandering for his sister in *The Revenger's Tragedy* – is the sort of intrigue motif which is unuseful for Ford's thematic concerns. The idea is simply dropped.

15–18. *Ah ... own:* Tecnicus' nicely taken point exposes the dangers of a stoicism which leads to insensitivity. As Calantha's story will illustrate, the control of one's feelings is not the same as the attenuation of one's emotional response.

35. The account of Orgilus' real motives brings together in this line two of the women whom the play – and in part Orgilus – will test. The third is Calantha. In this scene Euphranea passes the test (though Orgilus is confused about it) and remains true to her 'chaste vows'. Consequently, Ford is unable to use her positively in the rest of the play and she becomes from now on a secondary figure. Meanwhile, Orgilus finds himself unexpectedly tested as fate gives him the opportunity for revenge against Ithocles through Prophilus, but a revenge which will repeat Ithocles' own tyranny.

102–88. *Say ... errors:* Orgilus' 'antic disposition' takes the form of a scholastic argument. Morris suggests that he argues with a book, but perhaps he is giving both sides of a debate – i.e. arguing with himself – and only a slight shuffling of Q.'s punctuation brings this out.

141. *Aplotes:* The implications of Orgilus' chosen name are firstly 'madness' and secondly 'stoic simplicity', the opposite of the feverish yearnings of ordinary humanity. 'Aplotes' has characterized himself in lines 29–31.

173. *Hymen:* The god of love, usually represented as carrying a bridal torch.

177. *Mercury:* Doubly relevant as the messenger of the gods and as the god of eloquence and thieving (and hence most cunning).

ACT TWO

Scene One

The early part of the scene, before the entry of Penthea, owes much to *Volpone* and Jonson's conception of the jealous type in Corbaccio (*Volpone*, II, v). Phulas' 'news' (lines 42–60) comes from the same play. The holding back till Act II of two major characters, Penthea and Bassanes, indicates the sort of dramatic shape Ford is aiming at in a play without a single hero.

5–6. *till . . . act:* Mother bears, it was thought, literally licked their cubs into shape.

23–40. Bassanes' bitter invective against female sexual morality echoes many earlier railings in the 'malcontent' tragedies of the Jacobean stage. Ford's play, setting out to demonstrate the opposite truth, turns the formula on its head. The concreteness of description and the bold metaphors are untypical of Ford's style and suggest the texture of the verse of *The Revenger's Tragedy*.

77–119. *Thou . . . griefs:* Bassanes' indulgence to Penthea is presumably not a sincere kindness but a test of her temperament, as the 'asides' to Grausis show.

134. *tympany:* Intended as a symptom of Bassanes' disease of jealousy.

147-9. *Th'hadst ... will:* This is obscure and there may be textual corruption. Morris interprets: 'You would have been better off blaspheming against the vices you honour and serve'. Some editions emend 'sins' to 'saints'.

Scene Two

The Marlovian theme of ambition interests Ford as the sort of passion, like love and desire for revenge, which can lead a man from right conduct. At times, Ford seems willing to let the theme turn his play into a *de casibus* tragedy, but Ithocles' ambition is never made convincing, and if it were made so it would tend to devalue his love for Calantha. But IV, iv shows that the idea is never entirely forgotten. The concern for the marriage of Euphranea and Prophilus leads the play back into the more central interest of romantic love, and thence to its perversion in Bassanes' sexual jealousy.

1-2. *'tis ... motion:* It was believed that this is how the young viper was born. The image, as an analogue of destruction, is a common one in Renaissance literature.

3-5: The blinded pigeon was released in order to climb up and up until exhausted.

8-15. *Morality ... cure:* Ford often returns to the difficulty of applying a theoretical moral code to the problems of living. The images of music and dance as emblems of psychological and ethical harmony within the individual and society look forward, ulti-mately, to the wedding dance and funeral dirge in the last scenes of the play.

52. *experience ... others:* This is probably not sincere; the 'extremities' are from his own burgeoning feeling for Calantha.

99-100. *'T had ... consented:* This and his speech at lines 30-4 show that by his support of Euphranea's marriage, Ithocles hopes in part to expiate his sin in breaking the union of Euphranea's brother and Penthea, a renewal by proxy of the sort that Shakespeare employed in his last plays. But here no beneficent providence operates.

104. *Argos:* A town and state north-east of Laconia.

122–5. *Or . . . request:* Editors usually punctuate (thus giving a different sense): 'Or pand'ring/For one another (be't to sister, mother,/Wife, cousin, anything) 'mongst youths of mettle/Is in request'.

Scene Three

The climax of the act is the meeting of Penthea and Orgilus, and their dialogue, with its hints and delicacies, silences and cross-purposes, is perhaps one of the best, and certainly one of the most painful exchanges Ford wrote. Baffled frustration on the one side and steely constancy to a personally discovered ideal on the other, charges the scene with a tension that decorum just keeps from breaking into violent passion.

18–50. *Speak . . . eyes:* Orgilus continues his disguise of mad scholasticism as a way of gradually preparing Penthea for his self-disclosure. At the same time, his abstract language ennobles his feelings for Penthea's spiritual beauty.

64–7. *Lend . . . up:* It is utterly typical of Ford's characters to solemnize in ritual a moment like this. The action will be echoed in IV, ii. The intention of the ritual, here, is to undo the previous troth-plighting and thereby to stress the importance in which Penthea holds that previous troth-plighting.

77–107. This is the nub of Penthea's tragedy and it has been often misunderstood. She refuses Orgilus now not out of an excessive regard for the legality of her marriage with Bassanes but because that marriage has dishonoured her (it is a rape) and made her unworthy of Orgilus and their love. Lines 99–102 are crucial to Penthea's explanation of the position.

109–123. *Uncivil . . . me:* Penthea's anger is in large part insincere, as her speech following Orgilus' exit shows. Having failed to drive him off with persuasion she attempts scorn. Her real concern, throughout the scene, is to release Orgilus for marriage with another.

119–20. *my . . . fortunes:* Penthea appears to be saying that her sorrows are made less than her misfortunes would otherwise cause (because of Orgilus' behaviour).

124. *politic French:* 'French' is sometimes emended to 'frenzy' but this is not necessary. The phrase means 'cunning dissimulation' and the French were associated with dissembling (cf. *Perkin Warbeck*, I, i, 112).

146–7. A piece of stoic philosophy with which many Ford characters would agree. See note to lines 152–3.

149–51. *Then . . . account:* These lines are given by Morris to Penthea but the change is unnecessary. It is a veiled warning from Bassanes.

152–3. *sickness . . . exercise:* The stoic thought lies close to the centre of Ford's philosophy of life as it is expounded in the plays.

ACT THREE

Scene One

Tecnicus' expounding of his concept of honour forms a moral centre to the play by which actions and motives of the characters can be judged. Orgilus' claim at lines 27–30 brings two sorts of honour into opposition (though the audience is more aware of this than Tecnicus). Penthea's 'honour' of the previous scene, Ithocles' notion of honour as it emerges in IV, i, and perhaps Bassanes' injured honour of III, ii, contribute to a pervasive examination of the subject.

10–12. *Our . . . them:* Cf. I, iii, 2–6.

41. *lucre of:* Usually emended to 'lucre or' which seriously weakens a speech about the lack of moral basis for private revenge.

45. *Thus as:* I take this to mean 'And therefore' ('as' being almost redundant) and end the sentence at 'truth' (line 48) whereas other editions end the sentence at 'meanings' (line 51). Q. has a colon after 'truth'.

46–8. *for . . . truth:* This is a fine definition of the Elizabethan notion of 'opinion'.

60–70: *Here . . . Delphos:* It is no coincidence that after Tecnicus' reflection on the power of the gods – an awareness in the play which frames the private actions and emotions of the characters – the prophecy from Delphos is brought in. The play contains a classical notion of a religious universe, and the oracle carries inevitable associations of the world of Oedipus. Delphos is a corruption of Delphi, the place of Apollo's oracle.

Scene Two

An important stylistic feature of the play is its songs, of which there are four, two in this act and one each in acts IV and V. Each concerns love, and the last two connect love and death. They contribute to theme and mood, and to the stylization which the characters themselves, as well as Ford, are concerned to impose on life. At least two of them are beautifully composed. The romantic and plangent note of the song here contrasts violently with the obscene imaginings of Bassanes.

Scene Three

The early part of the scene completes the moral recovery of Ithocles, by repentance and expiation, already well begun in II, ii. In the second part of the scene, Bassanes reaches a nadir in his diseased fancies brought on by jealousy. From this point on, he too must make a moral – and psychological – recovery, learning the lesson of 'manly wisdom' which Ithocles himself has in part learned. Ford's depiction of jealousy in this scene, and previously in the play, owes much to Burton's *Anatomy of Melancholy*, though Bassanes' bestial imagery is perhaps a reflection of Othello's.

9–10. *the last . . . being:* She refers to Thrasus' agreement to the marriage of Penthea and Orgilus (see I, i, 23–8).

22–3. The handmaid . . . streams: I have adopted without enthusiasm Gifford's emendation of Q.'s 'The handmaid to the wages,/
The vntroubled of Country toyle, drinkes streames'.

39. act: Q. reads 'art' which Anderson glosses as 'practice?'

43. Wilt . . . now: Penthea's desire for death is real, as her
subsequent actions show, and not just a piece of rhetoric. She needs
to die to safeguard her family, as well as her own, honour.

58. Stygian banks: Banks of the Styx, the river of forgetfulness
in Hades, over which the shades of the departed were ferried by
Charon.

63. 'Tis: Dyce's reading. Q. has 'as'.

67. All . . . forg'd: 'All your new attitudes (of repentance and
contrition) are mere pretence.'

98–9. to . . . sun: Allusions to Ixion, who attempted to seduce
Juno, was tricked into embracing a cloud and thereby begot the
race of Centaurs; and to Phaeton, who drove his father Phoebus's
chariot of the sun one day, lost control of it and was destroyed in
the attempt. Each allusion foretells Ithocles' imminent fall as the
overreacher. (See note to II, ii.)

117–18. franks . . . swine-security: Gifford points out the allusion
to 'franks' or small enclosures in which boars were fattened.

129 ff. Bassanes' change of mood is explained by Burton who
says the jealous man will 'swear and belie, slander any man, curse,
threaten, brawl, scold, fight; and sometimes again flatter and speak
fair, ask forgiveness, kiss and coll, condemn his rashness and folly,
vow, protest, and swear he will never do so again . . .'

135. Pandora's box: Pandora, the first woman who ever lived,
was furnished by Zeus with a box to be given to the man she
married. It contained all the evils and illness which have since
afflicted the human race. The relevance of Penthea's allusion is
increased by the fact that Pandora married the wrong man.

144. Juno's forehead: Juno was the goddess representative of
women, especially of wives, and the protectress of marriage.

174. To . . . jealousy: The line is obscure and may be corrupt.

Scene Four

Courtly compliment and wooing replace the intensity and violence of previous scenes. But with the welcoming of Orgilus back to court, the threat to decorum and stability lies just beneath the surface.

10–12. *since . . . gladly:* The significance of these lines, in a play containing the disastrous results of an enforced marriage, is obvious. Cf. Amelus at IV, ii, 205–9.

75. *Thine . . . Ithocles:* Calantha's choice of Ithocles matches Prophilus' taking out of Euphranea in I, ii.

Scene Five

Tecnicus' fears of III, i are echoed now by Crotolon, but Orgilus allays his anxieties and supports the intended revelry in order to strike, as the revenger traditionally chose to, at the height of rejoicing. Lines 84–8 make it appear that Ford may originally have intended to use the 'play within a play', a convention of the revenge formula, in more elaborate form than he finally did. (Cf. V, ii, 2–5.) Orgilus' song, lines 70–81, provides the play's most concentrated affirmation of creative love.

Scene Six

The climax of the third act brings the two heroines alone together for the first and only time in the play. Penthea's frank ingenuousness is counterpointed by Calantha's silences and reticence. Penthea's testament is both an artistic way of marshalling her thoughts and a piece of real earnest, as the death-wish approaches reality. Deeply felt emotion is latent but unexpressed in a scene which is a perfect demonstration of the aristocratic code by which Ford's characters live.

13. In one sense, Calantha's charge is just; Penthea is perhaps morbid. But the weight of lived experience behind Penthea's reply, a beautifully modulated speech of abstractions, gives once more a sense of shifting perspectives. Calantha, too, is to learn at first-hand the truth of Penthea's position.

35. *and:* Morris's reading. Q. has 'I'.

60–1. *'Tis ... untouch'd:* N.B. Penthea's distinction between honour, her personal estimation of herself, and fame, her valuation in the eyes of others. Only to herself is she a 'spotted whore', though this is contradicted at IV, ii, 147–8.

79–81. *Impute ... it:* Penthea herself explains why Ithocles' 'ambition' has become an irrelevance in a play about love, honour and revenge. See note to II, ii.

ACT FOUR

Scene One

The related themes of self-control and decorous behaviour dominate the scene. Armostes the appeaser's advice to Ithocles of patience and his warning against over-ambition parallel earlier dialogues between Orgilus and Tecnicus and Orgilus and Crotolon. The love-affair of Ithocles and Calantha advances merely by hints and allusions. Tecnicus' fatal prophecies seem to provide an answer to the growing complications.

69–71. *Ixion ... centaurs:* See note to III, iii, 98–9.

98. *mushrooms, cedars:* At I, iii, 130, Orgilus uses mushroom to connote lowliness; the cedar was a common emblem for the high and mighty.

102–4. *Painted ... lion:* The implication is that Nearchus, a thing of youth and inexperience, rests behind his royal connexions in harassing Ithocles, the muzzled lion. The allusions are not entirely clear; perhaps the belief that lions were afraid of royalty is involved.

105–16. Armostes and Orgilus work against each other, the one to dampen, the other to encourage Ithocles' 'unruly passions'. Orgilus, set on revenge, wants Ithocles to prove his own worst enemy.

120–1. *The . . . deadly:* various emendations and interpretations have been suggested because of the apparently meaningless repetition of 'mortal' and 'deadly'. But they were not synonymous, 'mortal' meaning 'serious' rather than 'deadly'. Compare Thamasta's couplet in *The Lover's Melancholy:* 'Wounds may be mortal, which are wounds indeed; But no wound's deadly till our honours bleed.'

127–30. *Tell . . . Delphos:* Like the Friar in *'Tis Pity She's a Whore* (and possibly Frion in Perkin Warbeck), the hero's moral counsellor deserts him as things draw towards an inevitably tragic climax.

138. *Let . . . confer:* Craft and courtesy come together in Orgilus' hypocritical treatment of Ithocles.

141. *Oedipus:* The Greek tragic hero who also failed to pay proper attention to prophecy from Apollo's priests. In this scene, by implication, Tecnicus becomes associated with the seer, Tiresias.

145–7. *Leave . . . me:* A classic statement of the self-sufficiency of the tragic hero riding for a fall. It is no coincidence that Ithocles' lofty dismissal of the 'powers above' is followed by his personal hosannah: 'Divine Calantha!' There is a muted parallel here with Giovanni of *'Tis Pity She's a Whore* who also makes his love his religion.

Scene Two

The three movements of the scene, Bassanes' attempted self-cure, Ithocles' summons to his love, covertly aided by Nearchus, and, sandwiched between, Penthea's madness and impending death create the sense of the frustration of human wishes which characterizes the moral universe of *The Broken Heart*. Bassanes' improvement is too late to save Penthea, and Penthea's madness tutors

Orgilus in a revenge which will frustrate the love-relationship of Ithocles and Calantha. In this way the structure without a central protagonist becomes an important part of the play's meaning.

14, 15. *honeycomb of honesty, The garland of goodwill: A Garland of Goodwill* (1576 and 1629) was a popular collection of ballads; the 'honeycomb of honesty' may have been something similar.

24, 5. *quintessence, elixir:* 'Quintessence' is the fifth essence of medieval philosophy, thought to be the substance of which the heavenly bodies were composed; elixir, in alchemy, was supposed to change base metals into gold, or was a drug which conferred immortality.

58 ff. The presentation of the mad Penthea owes something to Ophelia in *Hamlet*, but the differences are as important as the similarities. It is likely that Cornelia in *The White Devil* is also an influence. Penthea's language forgoes Ford's characteristic use of abstractions and elaborate syntax, in order to produce the childlike directness with which Penthea confronts her agony.

67. *Impostor:* Morris's reading. Q. gives '*impostors*'.

69. *sirens:* The sirens were fabulous mermaids, two or three, who lured men to destruction by their song. Their aptness for this context seems small, but in some traditions they had a good character and supplied the music of the spheres (as in Milton's 'At a Solemn Music').

81. *swan:* Q's reading, emended by Weber (1811) to 'sun', a correction followed by all subsequent editors. I prefer the quarto reading because a contrast is made between the swan and the 'light of nature' of the next line which is the sun, symbolically representing Penthea. The swan may have been suggested to Ford by his reference to the death-song of the sirens; it connotes a faultless whiteness (a black swan is proverbial for something that does not exist) and it is sacred to Apollo and Venus (fitting the classical paganism of the play).

119–21. *Remember ... yours:* Usually taken as a reference to II, iii. Penthea's comments here and at lines 74–5 ('I've slept With mine eyes open a great while') suggest that her realization that she must commit suicide came late but decisively, and in the garden scene itself.

129–31. *every ... ears:* The amethyst was thought to prevent drunkenness. Penthea's suggestion seems to turn Orgilus into the type of the married bachelor, caught for ever between marriage and consummation. Compare her reference to 'virgin-wives' and 'married maids' at lines 52 and 56 in III, vi.

177. *th'augury:* Q. Sometimes emended to 'angry'.

200. *lord ascendant:* An astrological term. The 'ascendant' is the point of the ecliptic which at any moment is just rising above the eastern horizon. Here, the reference is to Ithocles' influence over Calantha's love.

205–9. *for ... Orgilus:* Amelus' lines underscore the play's comment on enforced marriage.

Scene Three

Ithocles reaches the height of his fortune just as Amyclas' fate is presaged and the sad song announcing Penthea's death is heard. Again, the effect is to stress the futility of human aspirations. Ford's lack of care with regard to conventional plotting is shown here in the way in which the story makes several awkward lurches forward.

77–87. This episode is usually taken as a betrothal ceremony and line 88 is annotated by Morris: 'There has obviously been a previous (offstage) avowal of love and agreement to marry between Calantha and Ithocles.' But if it is a betrothal, this makes nonsense of Ithocles' secret disclosure to Orgilus, at lines 121–3, that the princess is contracted to him. One way out is to regard the earlier business not as a contracting, but as an acceptance of Ithocles as a courtly suitor. Hereafter, in public, Calantha refers to Ithocles as her servant, and no marriage date is suggested. It might be expected that a double marriage would ensue (the other couple Euphranea and Prophilus) if this were a betrothal. Cf. the formal acceptance by Thamasta of Menaphon as a suitor in *The Lover's*

Melancholy, I, iii ('Henceforth I'll call you servant'). See note to
v, iii, 58, 61.

127–39. Apart from the theatrical effectiveness of the dramatic
irony in this exchange, the dialogue also serves to outline a possible
future which fate will not allow. It is a technique closer to that of
the novel to provide various alternatives for the way in which
events could develop.

Scene Four

A scene contrived carefully both by Ford and by Orgilus, it
combines melodrama, excess and civilized values in a way typical
of the playwright's art. The total effect of the scene is not sensational or theatrical in the bad sense but sad and meaningful.
Friendship and selfless admiration contribute to a complex effect in
which, typically, emotions are understated and motives only
hinted at.

S.D. *an engine:* A device for trapping the arms of the person
who sits in the chair.

4. *Phaeton:* See note to III, iii, 98–9. The image of the man who
overreaches himself introduces an attack on Ithocles' ambitions,
lines 30–4, which seems unjustified. However, 'ambition' in the
seventeenth century sense of 'keen desires for a pleasurable life'
is entirely in key with the central themes of the play (cf. lines 67–70).

ACT FIVE

Scene One

Bassanes, here and in the rest of the play, uneasily shifts between
a figure of fun and a character representing the moral regeneration
necessary to make sense of the sort of life that *The Broken Heart*
presents. It is perhaps an aspect of Ford's realism that the later
Bassanes never escapes wholly from his earlier, temperamental
failings (his stoicism is not entirely a true resistance of temptation
but in part an indulgent cultivation of emotional asceticism).

5. *'Tis ... herbs:* Apollo was known as the Healer, and first taught men the art of healing.

12–15. *The ... owls:* All well-known omens of ill luck, though 'doublers' is an obscure term (sharp turns of a hare crossing one's path?) and Morris emends to 'doubles'.

43. *The virgin-bays:* Bay or laurel leaves were supposed to afford protection against lightning; cf. in Holland's translation of Pliny: 'Of those things which grow-out of the earth, Lightuening blasteth not the laurel tree.'

53. *Actaeon:* Q. reads '*Action*', rendered as 'action' by all editors. In the Renaissance, Actaeon was the type of the cuckold, on account of the stag's horns (given him by Diana, enraged because he saw her naked). It seems that Orgilus regards himself as having been cuckolded by Bassanes through the agency of Ithocles. His revenge against the latter represents his 'glory'. Q. is carefully punctuated, and the capital and italics of '*Action*' suggest a proper noun, one which parallels 'Jove' of line 50. Ford elsewhere refers to Actaeon and cuckoldry in *Love's Sacrifice*, II, iii.

Scene Two

The dance episode has created more controversy in Ford criticism than any other aspect. William Archer, *The Old Drama and the New*, 1923, can be allowed to represent one point of view: 'The whole thing is a piece of funereal affection. No one is helped by it: no one is served: no decency is maintained. On the contrary, decency is outraged when a daughter goes on dancing by the bier, so to speak, of her father. The imagination which conceived the scene is warped by that bias towards the unnatural which led the author to found another play on the passion of a brother for a sister.'

24–7. *And ... bluntly:* This is a fine statement of the renaissance belief in 'ceremony'. The actions of the play – murders, deaths, testaments, funerals, betrothals and betrothal-breakings – are dominated by a sense of ceremony.

ACT FIVE, SCENE THREE

72–3. *Could ... slight:* Briefly Euphranea joins Calantha (and Bassanes) as an example of the courageous stoic.

93–4. In *Macbeth*, IV, iii, Macduff, whose family has been murdered, is enjoined to 'Dispute [= resist] it like a man.' His answer is: 'I shall do so;/But I must also feel it as a man.' In this scene we see Calantha's resistance; in the next, her capacity for feeling.

98. *To ... death:* Ford may have chosen this because it was the form of death of the famous stoic and Latin tragedian, Seneca.

103. I.e. 'But I must beg for some help.'

135. *pair-royal:* In a card-game, three cards of the same denomination; with pun on the rank of those already dead.

149–54. *So ... thee:* The indebtedness, in poetic style, imagery and stoic courage, of Orgilus' last moments to Flamineo's in *The White Devil* has often been noticed.

Scene Three

Largely emblematic, the final scene summarizes the themes of the play by presenting Calantha as the epitome of the virtues of courage and restraint which the men have had to learn; and by making her the final victim of life's obstructions to human fulfilment. Again, ceremony snatches back part of the victory achieved by a bleak fatality.

27–33. *sad ... hearses:* Bassanes provides, as does Horatio at the end of *Hamlet*, a useful summary of the contents of the play. Note the domesticity – family and friend relationships – that dominates his list. It is a play of private emotions rather than of public events.

53. *This is a testament:* The parallel with Penthea's more private moment in III, VI, 36 ff. is obvious and intended.

58, 61. *neglected husband:* The final parallel between Calantha and Penthea now becomes evident. Just as Orgilus is the unacknowledged husband of Penthea, so Ithocles is the unacknowledged husband of Calantha. From calling him 'servant', Calantha, on a day which is her coronation, marriage and funeral, can now call

T.P.F. – 18   393

him 'my contracted lord' (line 63); and so she remarries him in a public ceremony and joins him in death.

81 ff. *A Song:* Something of the content and rhythm, and certainly one of the rhymes ('must/dust') recall the dirge for Imogen in IV, ii of *Cymbeline*.

84. *Is untroubled:* Q. reads 'Is not untroubled'; Gifford substituted 'or' for 'not'; Anderson retains Q. and quotes Sherman: 'If one properly emphasizes *outward* the sense of the quarto is sufficiently clear, in spite of the slight obscurity of the double negatives: glories . . . can please only the *outward* senses when the mind is troubled or not refined by peace.' But Calantha's song expresses some of the sense of Orgilus' speech at II, iii, 34–9, and it has been a theme of the play that only spiritual contentment can make possible a creative enjoyment of pleasure (Bassanes' whole problem). Gifford may be right, but I expect Ford wrote 'not', cancelled it, and then wrote 'untroubled'.

PERKIN WARBECK

SOURCES AND INFLUENCES

There is a character named 'Warbeck' in *The Witch of Edmonton*, 1621, written in collaboration by Dekker and Ford. Attempts have been made to see Dekker's hand in *Perkin Warbeck* in order to explain a play which seems so far outside Ford's customary interests and achievements. But all the external evidence supports Ford's unaided authorship, and the attempted revival of a form long obsolete, the chronical history-play, satisfactorily accounts for the differences between this and his other work.

It has been said that the history of the English chronicle play ends with *Perkin Warbeck*. In writing his play Ford turned to Shakespeare, basing his dramatic opposition of Perkin and Henry on Shakespeare's opposition of Richard and Bolingbroke in *Richard II*. Ford's play can be seen as continuing Shakespeare's historical sequence, taking up the story after the defeat of Yorkist Richard by Richmond (in *Richard III*), and showing Richmond as the experienced and successful Henry VII. However, only a circumscribed period of Henry's reign is presented, and if Ford's play continues to fulfil the functions of the Elizabethan chronicle – nationalistic glorification, the analysis of the past to provide a commentary on the present, the demonstration of cause and effect in the political world, the study of statesmanship, and so on – nevertheless, an historically peripheral character, Warbeck, occupies Ford's central interest and is the focus of the play, and *Perkin Warbeck* can only in part be seen as a traditional chronicle history.

Ford's source material comes from two historical accounts, Thomas Gainsford's *True and Wonderful History of Perkin Warbeck*,

1618, and Bacon's *History of the Reign of King Henry VII*, 1622.
Ford used them closely and carefully, mixing details from each,
but occasionally altering facts to create a viable dramatic structure
and to pursue interests of his own. Resemblances and differences
are pointed out piecemeal in the Commentary, and I have included
selected passages parallel to Ford to demonstrate indebtednesses
and to aid understanding and criticism of the text.

THE HISTORICAL SITUATION

Richard III's defeat and death at Bosworth virtually ended the
protracted Wars of the Roses, the struggle between the houses of
York and Lancaster. Henry Tudor was the Lancastrian claimant,
and after his coronation as Henry VII in 1485 he married Elizabeth
of York, the eldest daughter of Edward IV, thus uniting the two
houses. But Henry's own claims to the throne were not particularly
strong. He was the grandson of Catherine of Valois (mother of
Henry VI) and a Welsh clerk of the wardrobe, Owen Tudor,
whose son, Edmund (Henry's father) had married Margaret
Beaufort. But the Beaufort line, though it led back ultimately to
Edward III, had its own stage of dubiety in John of Gaunt's union
with a mistress, subsequently legitimized. And so Henry was
vulnerable to attempts to produce real or counterfeit Yorkist
pretenders to the throne, a throne which he held onto with wit
and resourcefulness. In 1486 there was the rising of Lord Lovell;
next year the imposture of Lambert Simnel as the Earl of Warwick,
the son of Clarence (who was in fact in the Tower); and from 1491
to 1497 the gallant adventures of Perkin Warbeck, who passed
himself off as the younger of the two sons of Edward IV, the
princes in the Tower, believed to have been murdered by their
uncle, Richard III.

CHIEF EVENTS OF PERKIN WARBECK'S LIFE

Perkin Warbeck was born in Flanders and his parents were John
Osbeck, controller of the town, and Catherine de Faro. In 1491 he
turned up in Cork, Ireland, and was accepted as Richard, Duke of

York. Next year he was received at the French court of Charles VIII but was then forced to move (by a treaty between Henry and Charles) to Flanders, where the Yorkist Margaret of Burgundy, widow of Duke Charles the Bold, welcomed him as a nephew. (She may originally have prepared him for his role as pretender.) In 1493 he was welcomed in Vienna by the Emperor Maximilian I and recognized as king of England. Meanwhile, Henry's agents persuaded Yorkist plotters Clifford and Barley to defect, and Clifford, returning to England, gave information implicating the lord chamberlain, Sir William Stanley. Stanley was executed in 1495. In the same year Warbeck, backed by Maximilian, made an unsuccessful landing in Kent, got a lukewarm reception in Ireland, and finally received a cordial welcome in Scotland from the Scottish king, James IV. There he married the king's relative, Lady Katherine Gordon. An unsuccessful incursion by James into England was followed by a Cornish uprising, the people rebelling against extra taxes levied by the English Parliament to cope with the danger from the North. Henry's forces routed the rebels at Blackheath. Hialas, an envoy from Spain, worked for a peace treaty between Henry and James, as a result of which Warbeck was obliged to leave Scotland. He went to Ireland, 1497, and the same year landed in Cornwall, led an unsuccessful rebellion, took sanctuary at Beaulieu, and finally surrendered to the king's forces. He was imprisoned, but escaping in 1499, was recaptured, put in the stocks, and forced to make a public confession. Later, in the Tower, he plotted with the Earl of Warwick, and both were executed. Lady Katherine, received at the king's court on her husband's imprisonment in 1497, spent the rest of her life there and was married three more times.

DEDICATORY EPISTLE

William Cavendish: 1592–1676; first Earl of Newcastle; poet and patron of, among others, Jonson, Shirley and d'Avenant; royalist leader in the Civil War, went into exile after Marston Moor (1644); created Duke of Newcastle in 1665.

1–2. *a late . . . pen:* This is usually taken to be a reference to Bacon, who died in 1626 and whose Henry VII is a principal source of the play.

[After the Dedicatory Epistle in Q. there are five commendatory verses of no intrinsic merit or interest. One is by George Donne, a son of John Donne; another by John Ford, the author's cousin.]

THE PERSONS PRESENTED

I have followed Q. in dividing the list into English characters, Scottish characters, Warbeck's faction, and Women. For the most part I have followed Ure's name-spellings.

PROLOGUE

2. *out of fashion:* Ure notes that after *Henry VIII* (1613), less than a dozen English history plays are recorded.

ACT ONE

Scene One

Public poetry, proper to the court occasion, allows for a detailed historical exposition without a sense of strain. Henry, characteristically, takes opportunity to check up on the enthusiasm of his nobles' allegiance. Meanwhile, the hero of the play is introduced in a highly-slanted fashion: he is a cub, a gewgaw, smoke of straw, whelp, one 'fit to be a swabber to the Flemish'; his 'aunt' and supporter is devilish, a monster and a beldam. Ford deliberately invites us not to take Warbeck seriously at the start of the play.

16–21. *For . . . ambition:* Gainsford speaks of the usurpations, upheavals, wars, etc. 'which for 90 years filled the wrinkles of the face of our commonwealth of England with the blood and sweat of ten kings and princes of the race royal; 60 dukes and earls; 1000 lords and knights; and 150,000 soldiers and people'.

23. *rain'd:* Dyce. Q. reads 'raign'd', Anderson and others read 'reign'd'.

34. *boar's sty:* An allusion to Richard's coat of arms.

42-3. *Margaret ... division:* Gainsford, referring to Simnel's plot: 'In the meanwhile, the fire-brand and fuel of this contention, Lady Margaret, Duchess of Burgundy, had blown the coals to such a heat ...'

47. *Gloucester:* I.e. the later Richard III.

52-62: *In ... malice:* Bacon reports Sir William Warham's address to Philip of Burgundy: 'It is the strangest thing in the world, that the Lady Margaret ... should now when she is old, at the time when other women give over child-bearing, bring forth two such monsters; being not the births of nine or ten months, but of many years. And whereas other natural mothers bring forth children weak and not able to help themselves, she bringeth forth tall striplings, able soon after their coming into the world to bid battle to mighty kings.'

57. *twins:* Lambert Simnel and Perkin Warbeck.

66-8. *strange ... base-born:* Warbeck will later make the identical point (see v, iii, 56-70).

91-4: These are supporters of Lambert Simnel's invasion from Ireland which was defeated at Stoke near Newark in 1487. The Earl of Kildare was Henry's lord deputy in Ireland; the Earl of Lincoln was a cousin of Richard III; Swart was a German leader of mercenaries, described by Gainsford as 'a martial man by profession, bold, expert, and daring'.

107-8. *Geraldines, Butlers:* Two great Anglo-Norman families in Ireland.

117-18. *the bastard ... rebels:* These joined Perkin in Paris.

123. *the archduke:* Emperor Maximilian I of Hapsburg, archduke of Austria, who backed Warbeck's venture in Kent.

123-4. *She ... England:* Bacon says that Margaret gave him 'the delicate title of the White Rose of England', the white rose being the badge of the Yorkists.

135-6. *It ... th'Tower:* Bacon explains Henry's action on hearing of Clifford's return: 'And the place of the Tower was chosen to that end, that if Clifford should accuse any of the great ones, they might without suspicion, or noise, or sending abroad of warrants, be presently attached [= captured]; the court and prison being within the cincture of one court.'

Scene Two

Dalyell is entirely the invention of Ford and Huntly is almost so (he is mentioned as Katherine's father in the sources but not characterized). Katherine herself – as Ford develops her – is only contained in the slightest hints in the sources. And so in this part of the play, and Warbeck's interaction with it, Ford creates some of his most characteristic effects, and pursues favourite themes of obstructed love and noble stoicism.

16. *piece of royalty:* Katherine was a kinswoman of James IV, Huntly having married the daughter of James I of Scotland.

30. *Adam Mure:* He was a knight of Robert the Bruce, whose daughter Elizabeth was the first wife of the man who became Robert II. The son of Elizabeth and Robert was crowned Robert III, the father of James I of Scotland. So Elizabeth 'begot the race of Jameses'.

101–2. *the . . . life:* Ironically, this is a lesson Katherine learns very well. See IV, iii, 101–3.

148–57. *If . . . issue:* Katherine accepts Dalyell as a servant in the platonic sense implied by courtly love. In the circumstances, her choice of marriage and procreation metaphors seems decidedly tactless.

Scene Three

12–14. The imputation of witchcraft to Margaret occurs early in Bacon: 'At this time the king began to again be haunted with spirits, by the magic and curious arts of the Lady Margaret; who raised up the ghost of Richard, Duke of York, second son to King Edward IV, to walk and vex the king.' This also probably lies behind I, i, 6.

35, 38, 40. *meteor, fiery blaze, comet:* Bacon: 'She [Margaret] began to cast with herself from what coast this blazing-star should first appear, and at what time. It must [be] upon the horizon of Ireland; for there had the like meteor had strong influence before.'

43–6. *flourishing . . . outlaws:* A reference to Warbeck's attempted rising at Deal in Kent, launched from Flanders and – historically – not yet taken place (Clifford's interview was in January, 1495; the Deal venture in July).

49. *Stephen Frion:* Henry's French secretary in 1485, he went over to the service of Charles VIII in 1489 and Charles allowed him to join Warbeck.

53. *French . . . actions:* Cf. 'French dissimulation' of I, i, 112.

60. *Skelton:* Gainsford's and Q. spelling, is 'Sketon'; 'Skelton' is historically correct. Ford brings these 'counsellors' into the story earlier than do the historical accounts, in the interests, of course, of dramatic compactness.

73–4. O . . . *one:* Cf. Soranzo's talk of the justice of breaking the unlawful oath in *'Tis Pity She's a Whore,* II, ii, 87–9.

87–8. *Urswick . . . it:* The sources stress that Henry was deeply moved to find Stanley among the conspirators, but the business with the light has a curiously calculated air. The control of one's emotions is a highly regarded quality in Ford's scale of values; later (IV, ii, 20–2), Warbeck is to be accused of betraying his lack of authentic nobility by a passionate outburst. Cf. below, lines 113, 120.

101–19. *Yet . . . own:* Bacon: 'The king seemed to be much amazed at the naming of this lord, as if he had heard the name of some strange and fearful prodigy. To hear a man that had done him service of so high a nature as to save his life and set the crown upon his head; a man that enjoyed by his favour and advancement so great a fortune both in honour and riches; a man that was tied unto him in so near a band of alliance, his brother having married the king's mother; and lastly, a man to whom he had committed the trust of his person, in making him his chamberlain . . . Clifford was required to say over again and again the particulars of his accusation.' Henry had been very generous to Stanley: 'Yet nevertheless, blown up with the conceit of his merit, he did not think he had received good measure from the king, at least, not pressing-down and running over, as he expected.' He demanded overmuch, so that 'the king's wit began now to suggest to his passion, that Stanley at Bosworth Field, though he came in time enough to save his life, yet he stayed long enough to endanger it.'

129–34. *Ten . . are:* Ford has backdated this episode (which took place in the summer of 1497) to improve dramatic fluency. The blacksmith and the lawyer were Michael Joseph and Thomas Flammock. Audley joined the Cornish at Wells and led them to Blackheath.

ACT TWO

Scene One

The opening exchange gives a subtly different reaction to Warbeck from the official one of the main part of the scene. The end economically suggests character-relationships which cut across the ambiguities of Warbeck's position. The simple and noble poetry with which Ford endows the hero on his first entrance strikes the keynote of his appearances in the rest of the play – an apparent ingenuousness and distinction which flies in the face of the truth of his identity as presented in Act I.

24–8. *So . . . own:* Richard I was helped by Philip II of France; Robert I by Edward I of England.

After 39 S.D. *DALYELL . . . music:* This is the sort of elaborate ceremony so much favoured by Ford, though here, of course, having a measure of dramatic irony. James's court appears to be a more decorous place than Henry's, the contrast resembling that made by Shakespeare between the English forces and the French before the battle of Agincourt in *Henry V* – between efficiency versus flamboyance.

103–4. James's acceptance of Warbeck depends on the pretender's eloquence. Language and polite style play an important part in the play and are the key to Katherine's heart.

ACT TWO, SCENE TWO

Scene Two

Henry appears at his most capable in this scene, putting down conspirators and organizing the defence of the realm. The rigour of the sentence against Stanley is made to appear none of the king's work and he maintains an image of being 'composed of gentleness'. Stanley approaches death with the stoicism of a Ford hero.

24. *Vere's:* Vere is Oxford's family name.

33. *him:* Weber's emendation (noted by Ure) of Q.'s ''em'.

51. *But .. himself:* 'Every man must first of all protect his own interests.'

83–91. *Come . . . base:* The incident owes nothing to the sources and it has been suggested that Ford is preserving a traditional story, perhaps unconnected with Stanley's history.

95–6. *Give . . . irrecoverable:* Cf. *'Tis Pity She's a Whore*, I, ii, 59.

143–5. The forces are carefully deployed so that Henry, unlike James, leads from the rear.

Scene Three

The scene advances the plot by presenting the betrothal of Warbeck and Katherine but nowhere is Ford's subtle indirectness more in evidence. Warbeck and his bride-to-be are on stage for only a little over thirty lines of which Warbeck speaks six and a half. The rest of the scene is taken up with reactions to him and to the betrothal – mostly unfavourable – and with the presentation of Warbeck's motley followers. Again, the insults cluster before he appears: dukeling mushroom, Phaeton, straggler; but it would make both James and Katherine appear merely foolish if James's description at lines 73–6 were not given credibility in the theatrical presentation of Warbeck. The intensity of Huntly's disgust and grief is finely achieved.

16. *Phaeton:* See note to *The Broken Heart*, III, iii, 98–9.

21 ff.: James's handling of his counsellors and nobles contrasts sharply with that of Henry's. At the English court, Henry tutors

his nobles in telling him what he wishes to hear; James asserts his
royal authority in an almost despotic way (see lines 48–52).

42. *Instinct of sovereignty:* Either 'The promptings which come
to me because of my sovereignty' or 'My instincts about Warbeck's
genuine royal blood.'

54–7. *then . . . builded:* Ure explains: 'If Katherine were to marry
a yeoman, her dowry from the king could be her bridegroom's
ennoblement prior to the marriage, i.e., the opposite of marrying
someone (Warbeck) who claims to be noble before marriage but
turns out afterwards not to be.'

59–62. *That . . . provision:* James admits having persuaded
Katherine to the marriage with Warbeck ('kingly York') but
refers to her agreement to whatever he wishes as his justifi-
cation.

79, 81. *monarchy, sovereign:* Warbeck's metaphor of the sovereignty of lover is used meaningfully throughout the rest of the
play to unite the public and private worlds of his ambition, and
to give to his life an integrity which, again, the facts of the case
belie. Cf. III, ii, 168–9.

93. *Alexander:* Actually 'George'; there is a mistake in the
sources.

109–182: Late in his account, Gainsford says that Warbeck
'had such poor counsellors, as a man would smile at for pity,
rather than laugh at for scorn'. Elaborating on his sources, Ford
makes of Warbeck's followers a comic subplot, mimicking the
'appropriate' language of the various trades in the manner of
Shakespeare's stage Welsh, Irish and Scottish in *Henry V*. (Heron
is a mercer, Skelton a tailor, Astley a scrivener.) It has been shown
that John a-Water's idiom actually comes from Gainsford's
description of John de la Pole in the part of Gainsford's history
telling of Lambert Simnel. The effect once more is to make a case
against Warbeck when he is not on stage.

148–9. *lousy hole:* The part of the Counter prison where the
poorer prisoners were confined.

186. *Beyond . . . sufferance:* 'Beyond the suffering dealt out
equally to all mortals.'

ACT THREE

Scene One

Henry, with a nice balance of severity, mercy and reward for loyalty, shows his impeccable statesmanship. But the scene as a whole, competently achieved as it is, lacks anything which obviously engaged Ford's particular interest or attention.

3. *sons o'th'earth:* Reference to the Giants, the children of Gē (frequently confused with the Titans), who conspired to dethrone Zeus and were defeated and imprisoned in the earth.

5. *De la Pole:* Earl of Suffolk and brother of the traitor mentioned at I, i, 91.

33. *charm:* Henry's charm, unlike Warbeck's, is one of political manoeuvre rather than personal magnetism.

38–41. *this . . . night:* Bacon reports that Saturday was accounted a lucky day for Henry because on a Saturday he entered London in 1485 and a Saturday had been the day of the Battle of Bosworth (though this was not actually so).

62. *full . . . least:* Bacon: 'On the king's part there died about three hundred; most of them shot with arrows, which were reported to be of the length of a tailor's yard, so strong and mighty a bow the Cornishmen were said to draw.' But Ford's actual phrase comes from Gainsford ('arrows a full yard long'), as does his number of loyal dead (four hundred, at line 75).

Scene Two

In a splendid scene of mixed effects, Ford presents the tortured anguish of Huntly (a father whose love for his daughter causes a pain akin to that of Ford's other frustrated lovers), the courtly poetry as James prepares for a venture in an heroic spirit which the venture itself will make a mock of, and the dignified reticence of Warbeck and Katherine's love-talk in their first dialogue alone on stage.

11. *King Oberon and Queen Mab:* The two fairies appear to be associated in literature for the first time as king and queen in Drayton's *Nymphidia* of 1627.

29-31. *I . . . destiny:* Dalyell tutors Huntly in stoicism. Huntly, in the lesson he must learn about his excess passion, is a similar figure to Bassanes in *The Broken Heart*, and even jealousy may be a failing common to the two middle-aged men (Cf. lines 39-40).

33. *ap'd:* Q. reads 'ap't', all modern editions 'apt', glossed by Gifford as 'tough'. Huntly's extravagant statements are not meant to fool Dalyell.

36. *quartan fever:* Fever so called because the fit associated with it was observed to happen every fourth day.

75. *to posterity:* Either 'reaching as far as posterity' or 'for posterity to remember'.

78. *in consort:* Either 'in harmony with yourself' (i.e. all his passions balanced) or 'in harmony with me' (in his stoical patience).

S.D. after 111: This is presumably the entertainment referred to at the end of II, iii.

166. *In others' pity:* ? 'In others' compassionate estimation.'

166-7. *yet . . . wife:* This, the most significant feature which Ford develops in his characterization of Katherine, owes almost nothing to his sources.

Scene Three

The scene where everything is not revealed but much hinted at is always of special liking to Ford; and so the world of political agents and secret bargaining catches Ford's interest more readily than the world of court rhetoric and state proclamations. Ford in fact created this episode; in the sources, Hialas and Henry do not meet.

10-11. *his .. Moors:* A reference to the defeat of the Moors at Granada in 1492 which marked the end of Moorish power in Spain.

34-5. *Be . . . teacher:* Ure associates the moment with the handing over of the money referred to at lines 44-6, but Henry appears to be gently reproving Hialas for telling him something he already knows about, the need for secrecy. It appears to be a little moment of vanity, and as such is a small but telling addition to the characterization of Henry.

46–7. *What . . . wisdom:* It is not clear when the muttering takes place – as Hialas exits with Urswick (awkward theatrically) or before the scene opens.

53–8. *'A . . . creation:* Warwick, nephew of Edward IV and a prisoner in the Tower, was subsequently beheaded (see v, iii). Arthur married Catherine of Aragon in 1501 but died shortly after. Catherine then married Arthur's brother, later Henry VIII.

65–7. *Let . . . Arthur:* Henry is suggesting that his own, or perhaps Arthur's, claims are better than Warwick's because Warwick is only the nephew of Edward IV, whereas Elizabeth, Arthur's mother and Henry's wife, is Edward's daughter.

Scene Four

Ford, here, runs together two historical events, the raid into England of September 1496 at which Warwick was present, and the seige of Norham, July 1497, at which he was not. Surrey's advance and spoliation in Scotland belongs to the second episode. The character-interest in the scene lies in James's growing disaffection with Warbeck and the imputation of effeminacy to the latter.

33. *viper . . . entrails:* See note to *The Broken Heart*, II, ii, 1–2.

47–8. *The . . . meditations:* This is the first hint that James comes to realize that he has backed the wrong horse.

50. *Well:* I take this as a sharp – and discourteous – reply to Warbeck. Q. follows it with a dash, signalling a change of address. Other editors make it part of James's query to Durham.

56–82: Ford follows Gainsford more closely than Bacon here, though Bacon's James is 'half in sport', Gainsford's James is 'half angry, and more than half mistrusting [Warbeck's] dissembling, yea fully resolved on his weakness and pusillanimity'. In the context of Ford's play the moment is complex. James is beginning to appear callow and heartless; Henry has already appeared 'politic' and calculating; curiously, Warbeck appears to possess a finer nature than either.

83. *An . . . man:* James's crude irony marks the lowest point the king reaches in his public relationship with Warbeck. When we see the two together in IV, iii the mask of courtesy and ceremony is again in place, even as James dismisses the pretender from his court.

ACT FOUR

Scene One

5–9. *Cundrestrine . . . Ayton Castle:* Four border castles near Berwick. The sources stress the strength of Ayton, where the scene takes place.

22–35. *Thus . . . James:* The incident comes from Gainsford, not Bacon, and characteristically Ford throws an air of ambiguity over it. Viewed in III, iv, James's challenge looks like a mixture of gallantry and humanity; in this scene a mixture of foolhardiness and shadow-boxing (Durham's 'gay flourishes', line 60, is from Gainsford's 'mere flourishes').

50–1. *with . . . vainglory:* The sense of 'unbrib'd' is obscure, but Surrey is courteously introducing the idea that he may be victorious and asks for pardon for his temerity. 'Unbridl'd' would fit the context.

Scene Two

The barely-contained quarrel between Frion and Warbeck stresses the precariousness of the pretender's position, prepares for Frion's eventual desertion, and adds a touch of humanity to the figure of Warbeck himself. From this point, he can only grow in courage and self-assurance as his fortunes dwindle. Ford creates the scene out of nothing in the sources.

33–4. *Gold . . . temptation:* Warbeck appears to insinuate that Frion will desert for money.

52. *advise . . . affairs:* Warbeck's request to Frion to consult with

his counsellors is a contrast to James's high-handed decision-taking and a burlesque of the 'democracy' evident in the English court.

58–9. *Cornish choughs:* The Cornish chough is a species of red-legged crow native to Cornwall; but Astley may be referring simply to choughs or jackdaws, famous for their chattering, which in this instance come from Cornwall.

88–9. *that . . . busy:* A-Water's expression is inverted. He means: 'Being wise and conscientious is being a nuisance to others.'

Scene Three

The scene marks James's growth in political sagacity and opens up a hypocritical gap between pious, diplomatic language and real motives. In this world of shifting appearances, Warbeck's constancy to an ideal, however false the ideal itself, shows the more strongly. The gentle domestic exchange with which the scene ends shows Ford's restrained power and sensitive delicacy at its best in portraying husband/wife, father/daughter and friend/friend relationships. The new regard of Dalyell for Warbeck is a notable instance of Warbeck's gathering tributes as he loses the game.

136–7. *Wise . . . it:* Warbeck appears to be saying that wise men will consort with adversity with a specious show of flattery but must eventually look after themselves and not dedicate themselves to adversity's service. The Fordian hero, like Warbeck, does dedicate himself to adversity, thus seeking a higher wisdom. Ford develops the idea of Frion's desertion from a hint in Bacon that at a council at the time of the invasion 'secretary Frion was gone'.

Scene Four

Henry appears at the height of his powers, and his confidence and skilful management make Warbeck's venture appear what it is, a last desperate throw. At lines 46–63 is Henry's defence of his statesmanship and a lament for the ill rewards he receives for his pains. If the play is in part a study in kingship, thematically this scene summarizes the practical lessons to be learnt. Shakespeare's *Henry IV* lies not far from the surface in all this.

51–4. *our ... disturbance:* Henry refers to the cost of his intelligence service.

66–8. *Wise ... act:* It is difficult to gauge how far this is meant to sound superstitious or sycophantic, and how far Ford joins in the general praise of Henry's powers. Bacon's account early on tempers praise with a little asperity: 'The king by this time was grown to such a height of reputation for cunning and policy, that every accident and event that went well, was laid and imputed to his foresight, as if he had set it before.'

69. *Frion ... caught:* There is no basis for this in the sources, but it neatly ties up a loose end.

71. *Morton:* Famous in history as the inventor of 'Morton's fork', he was archbishop of Canterbury, 1486–1500, and chancellor of the exchequer from 1487. His 'translation' might be to Heaven or to the papacy. In fact, Fox became bishop of Winchester in 1501.

79–86. Henry moves his troops in the right direction before he knows of Warbeck's invasion – an example of his 'providence'; but perhaps Ford is suggesting that the post brought the news via Henry's intelligence service.

Scene Five

It has been shown that the scene in part depends on *Richard II*, III, ii, the scene in which Richard lands on the Welsh coast. The hollow note behind some of Warbeck's rhetoric may reflect his false hopes or Ford's lack of skill in this sort of language.

14–16. *but ... gentleman:* Most editors put a comma after 'affliction', but Katherine expresses the stoic idea of gaining comforts from affliction by bearing it without complaint. Ure takes 'learn ... to' to mean 'teach', but this seems to fit neither context nor character. Katherine is saying that she is learning the stoic lesson from Dalyell ('this truly noble gentleman') and Jane, both of whom have voluntarily accepted positions of danger and affliction. They modestly disclaim, lines 19–23, any such merit.

26. *The lion:* As the king of beasts, the lion commonly denoted royalty.

41–2. *Sigillatum ... est:* 'Sealed and dated on 10 September in the first year of the king's reign, etc.; confirmed.' Astley is still being a scrivener.

57–9. *How ... greatness:* 'Royal birth silences people bribed by retainers ("trains") to support political authority like Henry's ("greatness").'

ACT FIVE

Scene One

Characteristic of Ford's art, the news of Warbeck's utter failure is received by the audience as it overhears its reception by Katherine. Notice how at the crucial moment in the historical sequence the play focuses on an utterly personal and private aspect of it. In this scene and the last of the play, Katherine develops into a typical Ford heroine, stoical, dignified, and entirely faithful to her husband. 'A weak woman's constancy in suffering' is a theme which fascinated Ford. The end of the scene counterpoints the public rhetoric of formal discourse.

65–8. Ford more or less makes up this detail in extenuation of Warbeck's (otherwise) dishonourable flight. It is a crucial pointer to Ford's intentions at this stage, and Katherine's hint of accusation at lines 61–4 is clearly aimed at stopping the audience arriving at the same conclusion on its own.

Scene Two

In this scene and the last is contained Ford's most daring departure from his source – not having Warbeck at some point confess to being a counterfeit. To make the point as dramatically effective

COMMENTARY AND NOTES

as possible, Ford contrives the two confrontations, in this scene
and the next, between Warbeck and Henry and Warbeck and
Simnel. (Bacon denies that Warbeck and Henry ever met though
Gainsford reports such a meeting; no source suggests a meeting
between Warbeck and Simnel.) In the two scenes, the construction
is particularly admirable. In the first, various events are deftly
slotted in – a footnote on the political education of James, Henry's
dealing with the subplot counsellors, and Katherine's charged
reception at court, very properly allowing Warbeck to dominate
the next and last scene.

18–19. *The . . . betimes:* James was about twenty-three. This is
praise indeed from Henry whose 'wisdom' is a political prag-
matism. Early in the play, James seems to represent elegance and
youthful gallantry, two qualities notably absent from the English
court. But James's idealism in supporting Warbeck turns out to
be superficial.

40–1. *From . . . Beaulieu:* A sanctuary was a church or other
sacred place in which a fugitive from justice was immune from
arrest. Beaulieu, in Hampshire, was a Cistercian monastery,
destroyed at the Reformation.

43–8. *I . . . well:* This is a distortion of the sources which show
that Henry promised Warbeck life and pardon if he gave himself
up.

59–61. *when . . . court:* This is a reference to Henry's retirement
(when Duke of Richmond) to the court of the Duke of Brittany
in 1483 after his unsuccessful attempt to support the Duke of
Buckingham's rising against Richard III. But in fact, he had lived
in asylum in Brittany from 1471.

76–9. *so . . . truth:* This is often accepted as an explanation of
Warbeck as Ford envisages him, and so the play becomes a
psychological study of a Walter Mitty figure. Bacon explains it
thus: 'Nay, himself, with long and continual counterfeiting, and
with oft telling a lie, was turned by habit almost into the thing
he seemed to be, and from a liar to a believer.'

80–7. *Truth . . . greatness:* This is an astonishing moment as truth and counterfeit appear to reverse roles. It is the sort of moment of ambiguity for which Ford is famous.

140–74. *Oxford ... blessing*: Henry's reception of Katherine seems to depend on Gainsford: 'Some say he [the king] fantasied her person himself, and kept her near him as his choicest delight.'

Scene Three

The ambiguity of Warbeck, whereby the audience's response to the central hero is kept constantly fluid, is finally shelved in this last scene, and Ford resolves the enigma by showing two sorts of truth, the truth which belongs to facts and birthrights (of heraldry and the popular press – lines 24–8); and the truth of a man's integrity, at its crudest, a man's belief in himself. With regard to the latter, Warbeck's disgust with Simnel, lines 54–65, and his total lack of fear of death are part of the same awareness. Warbeck's choice of death is not morbid; it is the logical answer, given the premises of the argument as he sees them. Notice how the usual undercutting of his position at lines 104–11 becomes curiously shrill and ineffective, as it always was likely to when comment and object of comment were brought face to face. The hint for Katherine's development into the type of the constant wife comes from Bacon: 'In all fortunes she entirely loved [her husband], adding the virtues of a wife to the virtues of her sex.' But Ford departs from his sources in an entirely characteristic way – carrying Katherine's constancy beyond the death of her husband (lines 150–2). Utterly typical, too, is the solemn oath-taking of this last act of the domestic drama of the play. The part reconciliation between Huntly and Warbeck is one of the most attractive moments in the whole of Ford's work. The end is a well-contrived climax, with Warbeck finally king over death, and with Henry, king by superior statesmanship (he enters with Durham and Hialas) rather than divine right, uttering the conventional moralization on what has happened.

4. *malefactor:* Ure. All other editions read 'malefactors'.

14–18. *Twice . . . attempt:* It was the second of Warbeck's attempted escapes from custody, from the Tower in November 1499, which involved Warwick and brought about the execution of both men.

80–1. *If . . . soul:* Urswick regards Warbeck's refusal to confess and so avoid execution as a culpable suicide and therefore one which endangers his soul.

85–7. *Some . . . penance:* I am not sure of the stage-action at this moment, but Katherine's intention clearly is to join her husband in the stocks.

99–100. Warbeck suggests that Katherine is being unkind to her high status, kinship to the king of Scotland, in being constant to the humility to which his own relationship degrades her.

105–10. *Thus . . . night:* It has been noted that Urswick's details of demonology come from R. Scot's *Discovery of Witchcraft*, 1584. The speech raises in direct form the problem of Warbeck's guilt or delusion (or both), looked at from within the play. By this account, Warbeck is a madman, or someone possessed by the devil. See next note.

158. *madam:* Q.'s reading. Gifford attractively, though I think unnecessarily, emended it to 'madman'. Presumably, Surrey turns in quick succession to each of the principal actors of the moment: Warbeck, Katherine, Huntly.

162. *Thy:* Q. reads 'The'.

MORE ABOUT PENGUINS

Penguinews, which appears every month, contains details of all the new books issued by Penguins as they are published. From time to time it is supplemented by *Penguins in Print*, which is a complete list of all books published by Penguins which are in print. (There are well over three thousand of these.)

A specimen copy of *Penguinews* will be sent to you free on request, and you can become a subscriber for the price of the postage. For a year's issues (including the complete lists) please send 4s. if you live in the United Kingdom, or 8s. if you live elsewhere. Just write to Dept EP, Penguin Books Ltd, Harmondsworth, Middlesex, enclosing a cheque or postal order and your name will be added to the mailing list.

Recent additions to the Penguin English Library are listed overleaf.

Note: *Penguinews* and *Penguins in Print* are not available in the U.S.A. or Canada

THE PENGUIN ENGLISH LIBRARY

Edited with an introduction by John Sutherland, Lecturer in English at
the University of Edinburgh, and Michael Greenfield, Lecturer in
English at the University of Singapore.

THE SCARLET LETTER AND OTHER TALES *by Nathaniel Hawthorne*
Edited by Thomas E. Connolly, Professor of English at the State
University of New York at Buffalo